D0829158

"You're going to have to do something about 'em, you know. They ain't natural."

"Who?" Khorii asked.

The old woman leaned forward. "Haants. You know, ghosts, girl, spooks. Boo!" Khorii recoiled briefly, and the old woman cackled. "I'm talking about spirits of the ones who died during the plague. Things that look like them are flittin' around everyplace like fruit flies at a picnic. But it's only their looks that are like our dead." She whispered again, stabbing a bony, wrinkled finger at Khorii for emphasis with each syllable. "Only these ones got no spirit that's any kin to the last occupants of the forms they're takin'. I am here to tell you that, however much that bunch may look like our sons and daughters, nieces and nephews, they are up to no good." The old lady rapped the edge of the table with her cane. "Like I said, they ain't natural ghosts."

"I don't know a great deal about human folk-lore," Khorii said, "but my understanding is that ghosts are not natural in the first place."

The old woman glared at her, clearly offended. "Not too long ago I'd have said unicorn people weren't natural either, but here you are," she said.

Yes, I am, Khorii thought. *But are you?*

THE WORLD OF ACORNA

Second Wave: Acorn'a Children by Anne McCaffrey and Elizabeth Ann Scarborough

First Warning: Acorna's Children by Anne McCaffrey and Elizabeth Ann Scarborough

Acorna's Triumph by Anne McCaffrey and Elizabeth Ann Scarborough

Acorna's Rebels by Anne McCaffrey and Elizabeth Ann Scarborough

Acorna's Search by Anne McCaffrey and Elizabeth Ann Scarborough

Acorna's World by Anne McCaffrey and Elizabeth Ann Scarborough

Acorna's People by Anne McCaffrey and Elizabeth Ann Scarborough

Acorna's Quest by Anne McCaffrey and Margaret Ball

Acorna by Anne McCaffrey and Margaret Ball

Coming Soon
Third Watch: Acorna's Children

See also

Anne McCaffrey's The Unicorn Girl
An illustrated novel featuring stories by Micky Zucker Reichert, Jody Lynn Nye, and Roman A. Ranieri

ATTENTION: ORGANIZATIONS AND CORPORATIONS
Most Eos paperbacks are available at special quantity discounts for bulk purchases for sales promotions, premiums, or fundraising. For information, please call or write:

Special Markets Department, HarperCollins Publishers, 10 East 53rd Street, New York, N.Y. 10022–5299.
Telephone: (212) 207–7528. Fax: (212) 207–7222.

ANNE MCCAFFREY
and ELIZABETH ANN SCARBOROUGH

ACORNA'S CHILDREN
SECOND WAVE

An Imprint of HarperCollinsPublishers

This book is a work of fiction. The characters, incidents, and dialogue are drawn from the author's imagination and are not to be construed as real. Any resemblance to actual events or persons, living or dead, is entirely coincidental.

EOS
An Imprint of HarperCollins*Publishers*
10 East 53rd Street
New York, New York 10022-5299

Copyright © 2006 by Anne McCaffrey and Elizabeth Ann Scarborough
Excerpt from *Third Watch: Acorna's Children* copyright © 2007 by Anne McCaffrey and Elizabeth Ann Scarborough
ISBN: 978-0-06-052542-2
ISBN-10: 0-06-052542-8
www.eosbooks.com

All rights reserved. No part of this book may be used or reproduced in any manner whatsoever without written permission, except in the case of brief quotations embodied in critical articles and reviews. For information address Eos, an Imprint of HarperCollins Publishers.

First Eos paperback printing: July 2007
First Eos hardcover printing: August 2006

HarperCollins® and Eos® are registered trademarks of HarperCollins Publishers.

Printed in the U.S.A.

10 9 8 7 6 5 4 3 2 1

If you purchased this book without a cover, you should be aware that this book is stolen property. It was reported as "unsold and destroyed" to the publisher, and neither the author nor the publisher has received any payment for this "stripped book."

*This book is dedicated to the owners,
Julie and David McCulloch, and staff of the
Elevated Ice Cream Company and Candy Shop of
Port Townsend, Washington,
where much of this book was written.
Our characters seem to really enjoy joining us and the laptop
in the plush booths with the red tabletops and telling us
about their adventures while we drink green tea
and eat Guittard dark chocolate ribbons.*

Acknowledgments

We would like to thank Denise Little of Tekno Books for doing the initial editing on this book and most of the others in this series. We would also like to thank Diana Gill, our editor at HarperCollins, for her many excellent suggestions and input into this series. Both editors have been wonderful about discussing ideas with us. We would also like to thank Margaret Ball, who, with Anne, created many of the original characters, including the young Acorna in the first two books in this series, *Acorna* and *Acorna's Quest*.

ACORNA'S CHILDREN

SECOND WAVE

chapter 1

The scream awakened Khorii from a deep and well-earned sleep. Swinging her feet out of bed, she stood for a moment, disoriented, trying to determine the source. Had she dreamed it? But, no, there it was again. Childish, high-pitched, feminine, and—invasive. It was in Khorii's mind as well as in her ears.

Sesseli!

She ran for the door to her room and tripped over the cat.

"Khiindi Kaat, please *move,*" she said to the smallish, fluffy, gray-striped cat who gave her an offended look. After all, *she* had assaulted *him* just when he was setting about on his errand of mercy to see what was making his friend Sesseli scream like that. If only these stupid bipeds didn't find it necessary to put doors in one's way.

Khorii lifted him with her hoof and moved him to one side so she could open the door.

Finally! Khiindi thought.

He sprinted out ahead of her down the hall to the dormitory room occupied by their young friend, the charming six-going-on-seven-year-old Sesseli, an orphan from Maganos Moonbase.

Khorii yanked open Sesseli's door and ran in, expecting to find the child injured at the very least. Possibly worse. Instead, Sesseli was standing at her rain-streaked window, which overlooked the former town square of the mostly deserted city of Corazon. Khorii thought at first that perhaps a thunderclap or a particularly close bolt of lightning had frightened the child. But in that case, wouldn't she be backing away from the window instead of crowding close to it? Besides, the soundproofing in the dormitory was excellent, and Khorii herself hadn't heard any thunder. The monsoon outside sounded like nothing more than the patter of rain on her own window.

"What is it, Sess?" she asked, using thought-talk so as not to startle the child further. Khorii was an expert at thought-talk—all adult members of the Linyaari were. Khorii's whole home planet routinely communicated that way. Sesseli, though human rather than Linyaari, was herself a telepath with telekinetic abilities. Like Khorii and Khiindi, she was a member of the very young crew of the *Mana,* a supply ship whose crew and former owners had all died in the recent space plague with the exception of Jaya, the captain-in-training.

The captain now in charge, former astronavigation instructor Asha Bates, was right behind Khorii, entering the room so fast she stepped on Khiindi's tail. With a yowl that made Sesseli jump, Khiindi hopped on the bed, out of the way of clumsy feet, and from there was scooped up by Sesseli, who buried her face in his fur.

"It moved," the child said. "It moved all by itself. I didn't make it, honest."

"What moved, sweetie?" Captain Bates asked, stepping around Khorii to join Sesseli at the window.

"That. The marker," she said, pointing. The former city square had become the final resting place for masses of the plague victims, each huge grave marked by a plascrete stone with the pictures of each dead face—or if the face was too far gone to be identifiable, some other identifying object—a ring, a watch, an amulet or scrap of clothing. The names of those who could be identified before burial were also attached. For fear of the horrible disease that had swept the galaxy, these dead could never be given more individual burials, but at least any surviving descendants who showed up later would be able to learn the fate of their relatives or friends. It was the best the children and mostly elderly adults remaining in Corazon, as in other stricken areas, could do for the less fortunate.

"It is probably just the rain, Sesseli," Khorii said, trying to reassure her. "It got muddy enough around the marker to loosen its moorings and it slipped."

"Or could it have been looters?" Captain Bates asked. "Maybe they were messing around there and destabilized the stone, so it shifted as the ground settled or something. That could have been what you saw, pet."

"Unless there's another telekinetic around here we don't know about," Hap Hellstrom said from behind Khorii. Like the others, Hap was part of the *Mana*'s crew. All of them except Jaya had boarded the stranded supply ship while it orbited Maganos Moonbase, forbidden by the school's administrators from landing. The school on the moonbase and all the students and teachers as well as the moonbase's managers, Khorii's human grandfathers, Calum Baird and Declan Giloglie, and their wives, were fine. The rescue party from Khorii's home planet, Vhiliinyar, had, with her help, scoured the moonbase and its nearest world, Kezdet, eradicating all traces of the plague, which had not yet become entrenched there.

Paloduro, the planet of which Corazon was the chief city, was where the plague had seemed to originate. It had been cleansed by Khorii's parents before they became so exhausted they contracted a mutant form of the illness, which made them carriers. They had returned to Vhiliinyar with their human friend Captain Becker, his feline first mate, Roadkill, suspected sire of Khiindi, and his android first mate Maak, creator-father of Khorii's android friend, tutor, protector, adopted brother, and often her main source of annoyance, Elviiz.

Elviiz, who had appeared in the doorway beside Hap at the same time as Jaya, said, "I will go there now and determine the validity of Captain Bates's hypothesis." He didn't always talk like that but just after he recharged, he always seemed to express himself in that annoyingly I-can-store-and-process-gigabillions-more-bits-of-information-gigabillions-of-times-faster-than-any-of-you-mere-human-gits way.

But in this case he was making himself useful, so Khorii didn't mind. She sat on the bed and pulled Sesseli and Khiindi into her lap, then she laid her horn against Sesseli's fluffy blond head. The short golden spiraling horn in the middle of her forehead allowed Khorii and other Linyaari to heal trauma, pain, injury, and illness to a degree that seemed miraculous to most humans.

"It wasn't just a bad dream, Khorii," the little girl told her privately. *"I woke up and went to pee and stopped to look out the window on my way back to bed. I saw it move, plain as day."*

The wind and rain made the night and the city streets and buildings dark. But although most of the city's bright lights had died with its people, the survivors kept the central graveyard well lit so that no one would venture there by mistake. As Captain Bates had mentioned, the ground was still settling from the excavation of the mass graves and it would be far too dangerous for a living person to fall into a sinkhole and land among the dead. Though Khorii's parents and later others of the Linyaari rescue team had cleansed the dead of contamination, one never knew and, besides, the experience would be enough to give one of the child survivors of the recent tragedy nightmares for a lifetime, given what they had already endured.

Through the window, Khorii saw Elviiz. His silvery white mane, normally thick and fluffy on top and extending down the sides of his face, was instantly drenched flat the moment he stepped into the street. He walked as if there were no rain at all, and indeed his shipsuit was impervious to moisture, and his extra weight and strength let him walk easily, even against the strong wind. He stopped on the sidewalk surrounding the cemetery. Although the graves were recent, vegetation grew quickly because of the hot and humid climate of Corazon, and the graves were already covered by grasses and tropical wildflowers, even low bushes and ivy in places. Except for the marker stones, it looked very lush and inviting to someone who, like Khorii, was a grazer, but she would starve before she'd ever eat any of *those* plants.

Elviiz did not proceed into the graveyard itself, but stood on the edge and scanned the glistening vegetation and muddy ground. He had optical sensors that could determine things like soil density and depth, and because he was not entirely flesh and blood, he was much heavier than a normal boy his size. If there were sinkholes, he'd be likely to fall in one, and he was smart enough to know that.

After a few minutes he crossed the street again and returned to the dormitory.

Elviiz, Khiindi, and Khorii had been staying in the dormitory of the University Paloduro for the past three nights while she took her mandatory rest from her plague-hunting duties. As the only Linyaari with the ability actually to *see* the disease organisms, her presence was critical to the plague eradication effort. But she, like all Linyaari, was required to rest after every major operation so that she did not end up as a carrier, as her parents had. So although her horn was still perfectly opaque, and after the first night she hadn't even felt very tired, she more than any of the others understood the necessity for the rest period.

She had returned to Corazon because it was the last place she'd seen her family and because all of her new friends were there. With so few uncontaminated resources and places available to the survivors, a brilliant young man named Jalonzo, his grandmother Abuelita, and some of his game-playing friends had taken up residence in the university's dormitory. Jalonzo, Hap, and Jaya had been working on a vaccine for the plague, something that would be available when the Linyaari all returned home. In fact, they had been very excited yesterday by one formula they had concocted and had talked of nothing else all afternoon. They were the ones who had suggested moving into the dormitory because it was convenient to the well-equipped university research laboratory Khorii had meticulously cleansed for them.

By the time Elviiz returned to Sesseli's room, he was perfectly dry again and accompanied by Jalonzo, who was asking him a number of technical questions about his observations. A few minutes later, Abuelita showed up. "Since everyone is already awake, we may as well take this meeting to the common room. I'll make cocoa, and perhaps that will help you all return to sleep."

They walked together to the common room, Captain Bates holding Sesseli's hand. Khiindi leaped onto Khorii's shoulders as she caught up with Elviiz and Jalonzo. "What caused the shifting?" she asked. "Did you find out?"

"Naturally, I discovered the cause of the displacement of the monuments—Sesseli only saw one, but several have moved from their original positions as my sensors could detect from the moisture and compactness of the soil beneath the stones as well as some breakage of surrounding vegetation. I have compiled a list of the plants involved and their specific areas of injury if that would be of use?"

"Not right now, Elviiz. You were going to tell us what made the stones move?"

"It was as I suspected. The ground has shifted and subsided with the increased soil density from the rain. In fact, quite substantial sinkholes have developed over the affected graves. In one case, the stone actually fell into the grave. I did not attempt to retrieve it because of the possibility of contaminating myself."

"Good thinking," Jalonzo said. But of course, good thinking was the only kind that Elviiz did.

The common room was meant to stimulate minds and bodies and at the same time provide a comfortable area to study amid the din created by other students playing games, eating, and talking. Tables and chairs brightly painted with flowers and birds sat in the middle of a green area rug with borders of lime and aqua. Twisted sculptures of glass provided light for the space, supplemented with smaller lights in each of the padded booths lining two walls. Their upholstery matched the rug. The walls were a golden orange with arched holes sculpted into them—nichos, they were called. These contained trophies, portraits, and other artwork made by students mostly now among the dead. Masks both grotesque and comic were numerous, as were brilliantly floral-embellished animal figures and alien-looking monsters. A Ping-Pong table, for a game Captain Joh Becker described as being more ancient than the ruins of Terra, stood there with its ridiculous little net strung across the center and its balls and paddles carelessly tossed onto the surface, waiting for the next players. A snooker table balanced the Ping-Pong one on the opposite side of the long, shuttered cantina window, which was used to provide students with casual meals and snacks. The shutters were painted bright blue and decorated with intricate street scenes of Corazon at carnivale, the festive weekslong celebration that had ended when the plague arrived to strike down the revelers.

Khorii and her friends chose a table nearest the cafeteria, where Abuelita was preparing her specialty, a delicious hot cinnamon-and-pepper-laced chocolate beverage. Jalonzo did not sit, but went to the kitchen and returned with a tray of the frothy drinks. Abuelita followed him, wiping her hands on a bib apron to keep her bed gown tidy. Because decontamination cost the Linyaari dearly in terms of their strength and energy, survivors kept their possessions and wardrobes to a minimum. When Jalonzo and the others developed another effective cleansing process, there would be time enough to reclaim less critical items from all their abandoned homes, offices, and businesses.

The Linyaari, for whom clothing was optional, took the word of the survivors about what was essential and what was not for each of them. In Abuelita's case, clearly a bed gown and apron were necessary.

When Elviiz had shared his findings with everyone while they sipped their chocolate, Abuelita ran a hand over Sesseli's blond curls as if to smooth them, which wasn't actually possible. Nothing short of genetic modification would smooth those curls out. "You see, *chica,* it was nothing to fear. Merely a natural thing."

Sesseli shook her head. "I don't think so."

"I assure you, Sesseli . . ." Elviiz began, but the little girl kept shaking her head.

"It shifted, but something made it shift."

"Are we talking vampires here? Walking dead maybe?" Jalonzo asked matter-of-factly.

"Jalonzo, don't scare the *niña,*" Abuelita said. "Such things are common in those games you play, but they are not real things. You are a brilliant student of the sciences, and you know such creatures are impossible and imaginary."

Jalonzo shrugged. "Perhaps, Abuelita, but such stories often have some basis in fact or actual events. Misinterpreted or misreported, no doubt, but not imaginary. We have had so

many deaths, and the burials were so hasty, the bodies unexamined for fear of contamination." He leaned forward, widening his eyes and saying in a deep, quavery voice, "What if
some who were buried were not dead, and dug their way up
from the graves, clawing their fingers to the bone, maddened
by what they experienced and their effort to survive, perhaps
deranged from lack of oxygen while entombed with the
dead?"

"Stop it, Jalonzo," Khorii said. "It's not true that the dead
were unexamined. As you very well know, my parents and I
and other Linyaari decontaminated each corpse before it was
buried, and as you also know, that involved close personal
contact on our parts. And we *know* death from life."

Abuelita said quickly, "He meant no disrespect, of course,
Khorii. We are eternally grateful for what you and your people, particularly your parents, have done for us, and I weep
for the sacrifices they made to save us. With the resilience of
youth my grandson has already forgotten that he laid to rest
friends among the dead, and tries with his stories to create
the false drama and fear that the young so inexplicably
enjoy."

"He gave *me* goose bumps," Hap said appreciatively.

"Now I suggest that we return to our beds. *Niña,* if you
wish, you may sleep with me tonight. We should switch your
room to one overlooking the interior courtyard instead of the
square." The interior courtyard was paved for sporting activities, so no bodies had been interred there.

Sesseli shook her head. "No, but can I borrow Khiindi,
Khorii?"

"I doubt he'll object," Khorii replied, looking for her life-
long feline companion. He was on no one's lap, nor was he
licking the dregs of chocolate from anyone's cup. She called
him, and he did not come, but that was no cause for alarm.
Khiindi was an entity unto himself and chose where he
wanted to be. If her request did not interfere unduly with his

own agenda, he would come. Otherwise, she had to wait until he finished what he was doing.

He had been a birthing present to her from the regent of Makahomia, Nadhari Kando, aunt of the future high priestess Miw-Sher and former security chief for Khorii's human Great-uncle Hafiz Harakamian, patriarch of the mighty House Harakamian empire. On a visit to Makahomia with Captain Becker, Nadhari had renewed her family alliances and Roadkill had formed alliances of his own with some of the beautiful and revered Makahomian Temple Cats. Khiindi was believed to be an offspring of one such union.

When Khiindi failed to reveal himself, Khorii rose to look for him. She finally found him crouched, tail bushed and fur on end, under the snooker table. He was glaring up at one of the nicho-framed grotesque masks, and growling menacingly.

In Khiindi's opinion, something was terribly wrong.

chapter 2

Hhorii reached under the table and retrieved Khiindi, something that was not always the safest thing to do at times like this. But, instead of scratching her or wriggling loose, now he tried to burrow his nose under her arm. He was quivering with fear, the poor little cat. The mask had frightened him. Khorii stroked him and studied the mask from a distance. Keeping her distance was prudent, since when she tried to get closer, Khiindi's claws dug into her.

The piece was made of some sort of clay. Like most of the other artwork she had seen in the city, it was painted in bright shades—red, ochre, and chartreuse with its googly eyes outlined in black and the red-tipped teeth a ferocious white. She was only starting to understand the human idea of art and aesthetics, and knew that it didn't all have to be pretty. But why would anybody want to live with such a thing as the mask?

Clearly, Khiindi shared her taste in art in this case. The cat hissed again, then buried his face in Khorii's mane.

Khorii took the hint and moved away from the ugly, though vibrant, piece of art.

Returning to the table, she told Sesseli, "I think Khiindi will be as glad to have you as you will be to have him, but who will keep me safe? May I stay with you, too?" She wasn't sure why she made the offer. Maybe it was just something about the atmosphere, by which she did not mean the mixture of elements comprising the air. Many Standard months had passed since this planet was cleared of plague. The dead had been laid to rest, and the living had tried to resume some semblance of their previous lives. But tonight, the air felt heavy with a sense of foreboding and almost weighted down with fear.

Which was strange, because she had never been uneasy like this before, even when the plague had been active everywhere on the planet. There was sadness in the collective thought-forms of the living inhabitants, of course, and anxiety about the future, but certainly not fear, not since they'd stopped the plague and cleansed reasonable living space for the survivors. The city had been remarkably calm, considering what had happened here. The need for the survivors to escape contamination had kept looting under control, especially after some initial incidents when looters had dropped dead with their booty still in their arms. Even the thieves were keeping out of trouble after a few events like that.

Until the arrival of the Linyaari, the living had not known who was safe and who was not, and so had not formed the mobs or roving bands of thugs Khorii had seen on vids filmed after other disasters. Even after the Linyaari arrived, much of the planet was still quite dangerous, so people stayed in areas they absolutely knew were safe.

There were so few people remaining that there were uses for everyone, and most people could find some purpose they could fill better than someone else, even though almost all of the survivors were either under the age of fourteen or much older by human standards, in their late fifties and up.

Because of Khorii, the *Mana*'s crew was more diverse in age. She had been able to spare them from contracting the plague, or had been able to heal them if they caught it.

So although this was a sad place, it was one where hope as well as worry about the future now flourished. The amorphous fear scenting the air was something new to Khorii, and hard experience had taught her not to disregard her perceptions.

But she didn't see what she could do about it now except to accompany a scared little girl to bed.

Sesseli was glad for the offer of Khorii's presence. In the end, she, Khorii, and Khiindi all returned to Khorii's room rather than Sesseli's because the room was bigger, and Khiindi's food dishes and box were there.

Before they parted, Jalonzo said, "I am sorry, little one, for my silly story. I did not mean to frighten you. In the past such tales have been entertaining to me and my friends. But I believe you when you say that you saw something out of the ordinary. So, if you stay with Khorii tonight, I myself will sleep in your room in order to be alert for any other strange occurrences in the cemetery."

Elviiz said, "And I will be outside the door of Khorii's room, to make sure no harm comes to you."

Sesseli managed a small smile of thanks.

And all of them went their separate ways to bed.

Khorii and Sesseli should have fit easily into the single bed in Khorii's room, since Sesseli was small and Khorii slightly built. The real problem with making enough room was that Khiindi immediately plopped down between them and somehow nudged each girl so expertly that they were lying with part of their spines hanging over the edge of the bed while Khiindi stretched his full horizontal length in the middle. His front paws and snout touched Sesseli's middle, but he resisted any attempt on her part to draw him closer. His tail and his back paws touched Khorii's waist. He snored and drooled and purred when touched, but his claws kneaded in and out, pretending bliss but actually guarding his territory. Khorii felt herself slipping over the side of the bed one time too many and finally picked up the bed-hogging cat and tossed him off the bed. Then, very quickly, she turned over so that her backside was to the middle of the bed, covering most of the warm spot Khiindi had created for himself. Had she not done so, she knew from long experience that he would jump back up and resume his position in the middle before she could lay her head down again.

Khiindi settled for mewing indignantly and leaping over her to land on Sesseli. The child, already fast asleep, squeaked with surprise, then draped her arm across the furry fraud and cuddled him close. It was very warm with the two girls and the even warmer cat so close together. Corazon was a very warm place already. There were fans, of course, and there had been central cooling at one time but it had broken down during the plague, and nobody still living knew how to fix it.

If Uncle Joh hadn't had to leave, he could have fixed it, Khorii knew. He could fix anything. Hap Hellstrom was good at fixing things, too, but after looking at the system, he decided it would take some research to do the job right, and he preferred to spend his time discussing vaccines and plague-cleansing techniques with Jalonzo. So the dorm was a bit too warm for true comfort.

However, now that the rainy season was upon them, it was a little cooler, though still steamy and clammy.

Khorii slept for three blissful hours before she was awakened by a rhythmic tapping on the door. It was Elviiz. He always used the "shave and a haircut" tap handed down to him from his father, Maak, who had learned it from Uncle Joh and treasured it as a little-known ephemeral item of human communication undocumented in computer files or any other he had accessed. Sometimes Khorii marveled at how easily Maak was impressed, but it was kind of sweet, really, when it wasn't irritating.

She reluctantly rose again, sure that Khiindi would reclaim the middle of the bed in her absence, and cracked the door open, whispering, "What?"

"Are you well?" he asked. "No further disturbances?"

"Not until now, no," she said pointedly.

"Then I will inquire after Jalonzo and ascertain whether he is still in Sesseli's room, or whether, perhaps unable to sleep, he has decided to resume his work in the laboratory."

"Elviiz, it's the middle of the night," she said. Night, of course, meant nothing on shipboard for Khorii, or indeed ever for Elviiz, but dirtside for most people the nighttime hours were strictly reserved for sleeping. "Why would he do that?"

"I do not know that he has," Elviiz said, "but my auditory sensors have detected unusual sounds from that vicinity."

She should have known that Elviiz would not have awakened her for frivolous reasons. Androids had to really work at frivolity, and it seemed to take more maturity than Elviiz had for them to be even mildly frivolous. Certainly, Elviiz had tried his share of humorous comments, but most had fallen flat. The android more often tended to be alarmingly sincere. He didn't play pranks. He didn't intentionally make trouble. And his sophisticated sensors caused him to react to stimuli that would have gone unnoticed by most people—including her.

"I'll go with you," she said. "If someone who has the plague has invaded the laboratory looking for a cure, I'll need to heal them and decontaminate the area before it is safe for Jalonzo to continue his work."

She turned and bumped into little Sesseli, who had crept up behind her to listen. "I'm going, too," she said.

Elviiz frowned at Khorii. "You are resting while you are here. It is against the rules for you to heal anyone or decontaminate anything until you are fully recharged."

"I'm not an android or a robot," she said reasonably. When Elviiz looked offended at the comparison, she added in a more conciliatory tone, "Though androids and robots are wonderful, of course. Elviiz, you don't need to worry. I'm much younger and stronger than my parents. My horn is perfectly opaque, and I'm fine. It's not like I'm going to do any mass healing. Probably nothing at all. But I can't just let someone die right under my nose, can I? And none of us can afford for your research and Jalonzo's to stop because you can't use the lab."

"Very well, do as you wish. But I will go first to ensure that it is safe for the merely organic." Khorii knew that was in answer to her android crack, and she supposed she deserved it. She sighed.

Elviiz stomped off down the hall. She stuck her head all the way out the door, and said in a loud whisper, wishing as she sometimes did that she could thought-talk with Elviiz, "I'll just check and see if Sesseli . . ."

She turned and bumped into the child, who had crept up behind her to listen. "I'm going, too," Sesseli said.

On the bed, Khiindi yawned and stretched and sat up, his ears at an angle that showed he was not pleased with the disturbance. He began washing his paw.

Then, as she and Sesseli left the room, he hopped down from the bed and sprinted through the door ahead of them, down the corridor after Elviiz, who had started without them.

"Everything these days is a parade!" Khorii grumbled. It was good to have friends and relatives around but she got a bit weary of being constantly surrounded by them. When she accompanied the Linyaari rescue crews, there were always several people with her, so that she could tell them where the plague was and almost as importantly, because they needed to conserve their healing strength, where it was not. When an area was contaminated or a person was sick with the disease, she saw swarms of tiny blue lights or dots that nobody else perceived. Many Linyaari had a particular psychic talent aside from the normal communication skills they all acquired sometime around puberty. Khorii's mother, Khornya to her own people and Acorna to her human friends and adopted family, had even as a child been able to tell the mineral content of an asteroid just by looking at it. As she grew older, Mother had begun to be able to sense what was contained in certain spaces. All Khorii got were these stupid plague dots. It was an important talent, she knew, and at first she was grateful to have been given such a useful gift and to be special because of it. Now she wished she could share the dubious honor.

It had been six whole Standard months after the plague began and three months since she had seen the plague around her parents that confirmed their suspicions that they were carriers. She was tired of being *quite* so special. If only a few other Linyaari—even one—had the same talent, she could rest without worrying about people dying in the meantime and could have some time to herself once in a while.

Up the hall, Elviiz stopped to knock on Jalonzo's door. The tall boy, heavy but quite strong, came out to talk. He ran a hand through his long black hair, making it stand out at all angles. By the time Elviiz explained his presence, Jalonzo was out the door, barefoot and dressed in shorts and a light knit shirt.

Elviiz easily caught up with him, and the two disappeared around the corner to cross the shaded glass skyway that led to the science building. Khiindi bounced behind them until just before they turned, when he leaped onto Elviiz's shoulder. The cat's tail rounded the corner last of all.

Khorii hurried to catch up, and Sesseli tried to keep pace. Khorii turned, and said, "You can come. We may need your talent. But stay out of the lab and out of the way until I tell you it is safe."

The little girl protested, "But I wouldn't get the plague, Khorii. I'm too little. Jaya says only grown-ups who aren't old people get the plague. It's tied to hormonal development, you know," she added sagely, without stumbling over the larger words. Sesseli was so cute and small it caught one off guard that she was also, for a human child, extremely precocious, which was the word humans used for someone whose intelligence and language skills were more advanced than most younglings in their age group.

"I do know, Sesseli, but plague is not the only dangerous possibility. There could be bad men like Marl Fidd."

"It couldn't be him, could it?" Sesseli asked, so alarmed that Khorii was sorry she'd mentioned the name of the bullyboy who had come uninvited aboard the *Mana* with Captain Bates and had proceeded to blackmail, threaten, and assault the rest of the crew mentally or physically until Khorii finally got the better of him. "You killed him, didn't you, Khorii?"

Khorii stopped and squatted beside the little girl, turning her so that they faced each other. "*Killed* him? Whatever would make you think a thing like that, youngling? You know my people do not believe in killing or harming others. Of course I didn't kill him. Did you pick up some wish of mine that he was dead? Because I did wish it sometimes, when he hurt you or the others. But I didn't kill him. I didn't have to, though I wouldn't be surprised to learn he has died since I left him."

Tears welled up in the large blue eyes and ran down the soft pink baby cheeks. "I'm sorry, Khorii. I know you're not mean. And you didn't ever say you killed him, but when you didn't say what happened, I hoped you had. He's mean, no, he's worse than mean, he's des-pic-able."

"Maybe so," Khorii said. "But he's not dead. At least not by my hand." She stood again, taking Sesseli's hand, and they turned the corner and stepped onto the sky bridge. Hail joined the rain in an attack on the geometrically patterned art of the colored glass forming the corridor. Khorii hoped the glass was as strong as it ought to be or the fist-sized balls might break it. Who would replace it then? Some elder experienced in the construction industry? How would the other kids know how to do *anything* they needed to do to survive without their parents or even business owners to teach them or do it for them? She really must speak to Abuelita about organizing the remaining elders to start teaching the youngsters their skills. While it was sad that the older kids most capable of working would lose the rest of their childhoods, the loss of their parents had accomplished that. Becoming more self-sufficient might let them stay on their homeworld at least instead of someplace like the school on Maganos Moonbase, or one of the horrible children's camps still flourishing where her mother's influence had yet to penetrate.

Thunder boomed, rattling the windows in their panes, followed closely by a dazzling crack of forked lightning that briefly illuminated the campus and courtyard. Odd. The sheets of rain and hail almost seemed to assume amorphous shapes, silver-blue veils of mist drifting across the paved courtyard, rolling across the splashes and hailstones rebounding from the hard surface. The strobe of lightning was gone in an instant, and the outside was plunged into darkness again. Inside the tunnel, lights flickered in their overhead grids. Something white and silvery blew across the corridor from one side to the other ahead of them. Another silvery shadow capered ahead of them.

Sesseli let out another squeak, and Khorii squeezed her hand, saying in thought-talk, because anything above a whisper seemed too perilous here, *"Condensation, probably. Little localized clouds, carried by drafts."*

Sesseli crowded close to Khorii's thigh as the two walked across the bridge, cautiously and slowly at first, as if expecting at any moment that the glass would implode or the bridge would fall. Halfway across, Khorii quickened her pace until she was almost dragging Sesseli with her in her haste to cross. Finally, by unspoken agreement, she hoisted the little girl into her arms, set her on her hip, and galloped the rest of the way to the laboratory, her hard hooflike feet thudding against the thin carpeting.

Khiindi sat yowling indignantly outside the closed laboratory door.

Sesseli lifted him and rubbed her face into the soft fur of his side. He mewed in a pitiful tone. Wasn't it terrible the way these people treated harmless cats and little girls?

Khorii opened the laboratory door. With the soundproofing in the building, Elviiz would be the only one who could hear noises beyond that door.

He was there, as was Jalonzo, staring at the floor.

Beyond them, the door to a cooling container hung open. At their feet, shards of broken curved objects, liquids spilling from them.

"The formula," Jalonzo told her, not looking up. "Someone tried to destroy it."

"Tried to?"

"I have my handwritten notes," he said, shrugging. "I can make it again if I can find more of the right ingredients."

"I also have Jalonzo's notes," Elviiz said. "I uploaded them as soon as we returned from our mission, Khorii."

"It's a good thing we came back when we did," Khorii said. It helped her feel a little less guilty about not being out with the rescue teams, knowing that because of their return Elviiz was in time to back up research that might find a permanent cure for the scourge of the known universe.

Hap Hellstrom came in, trailed by Sesseli, still holding Khiindi. "What happened here?" the tall lanky boy with the pale hair asked.

Jalonzo told him, ending with, "No harm done, really."

"Not this time," Hap said darkly, "but who would do

something like this? A cure for the plague will benefit every-body."

"I can't imagine who would be so destructive," Khorii agreed.

Sesseli stuck out her lower lip, and said, "I can."

Khorii knew who she had in mind. "No, Sesseli, I don't think Marl can leave Dinero Grande, especially with no cure for the plague. That house where I left him was full of it except for the areas I cleared. I feel kind of badly about it, really."

"He'd have done the same to you," Hap said bluntly. "To all of us. He was going to blow us up, remember?"

"I know. Still, I wonder if we should not return with help and put him under more conventional restraints somewhere safer."

"It won't *be* safe once Marl's there," Hap said.

"This guy must have been a real winner," Jalonzo commented. Khorii had dealt with Marl before the *Mana* landed in Corazon.

"You don't want to know," Hap said. "This is just the kind of trick he'd pull."

"But how would he know about it?" Jalonzo asked. "Or even get in? I lock up when we're not here, and the door was still locked when Elviiz and I arrived."

"The guy's a born crook. He'd know how to do that if anybody would," Hap insisted. "He'd do something like that just to mess with our minds."

"Maybe," Khorii said. "But I think you give him too much credit. This gives us even more reason to return and check on his whereabouts. If he is not still in the house on Dinero Grande, then we can worry about Marl. If he is, then we must secure him somewhere away from the disease. It is *ka*-Linyaari—against our ways—to kill, but it is also frowned upon to leave anyone, even an enemy, to die when we could save him. And then we can worry about our real danger."

"What? The plague?"

"No, finding who or what did this," she said, indicating the damage. "And how they gained access."

chapter 3

You need more rest, Khorii," Jaya said. "You've been working much too hard if you think I am ever going to let that thug back on my ship."

"We need him where we can keep an eye on him," Khorii replied. "And this time we can take restraints from the police station. Jalonzo wants to go, too, along with a couple of his larger gaming friends. Marl will have an entire jail to himself here."

Captain Bates hadn't said anything as Khorii outlined her plan to Jaya. Khorii, Jaya, Captain Bates, and Sesseli sat around one of the round tables in the common room while Abuelita clinked dishes in the kitchen. Each of them had a fragrant and steaming cup of chocolate in front of her, and Jaya, Captain Bates, and Sesseli each had a cinnamon pastry. The scent from the large batch Abuelita had baked earlier still filled the common room. She made dozens of batches at a time actually, something easily accomplished in the cafeteria's industrial kitchen. Later, people would come and pick up the rolls and other foods Abuelita prepared and take them around to places where survivors gathered. At midmorning, additional people, mostly women and girls but some of the boys and a couple of men as well, arrived to assist Abuelita in cooking food that would sustain anyone who came to the cafeteria from midday until darkness fell. Some of this cooking would also be distributed among those who could not easily walk. There were other kitchens in the area, in former restaurants, schools, and churches. Soon the people helping Abuelita would leave to staff those feeding stations, but for now, with everyone still so frightened and grieving, it was comforting to come to one place to find a meal and so many other survivors. The Linyaari rescue teams had suggested this sort of arrangement be adopted on other worlds, in other cities and towns.

Khorii used the roof garden for her own grazing, sure that no one had died or was buried there. It was small but easy to maintain, with its own water supply and plenty of sunshine. Well, part of the day. The funny thing about the rainy season was that usually the sky was sunny and warm during the early part of the day, but in midafternoon the rain began and by evening at the latest, the rains turned to violent storms.

"I think Khorii has a good point," Captain Bates said. Her wavy brown hair was pulled back at the nape of her neck, around which she wore a stunning beaded necklace with long, sparkling fringes that matched her earrings. It was a startling transformation since none of them had ever seen their astrophysics and astral navigation teacher in anything but utilitarian clothing before. But it turned out that for most of her life before she was a teacher, Captain Bates had been making beautiful things when she finished the prodigious amount of work she seemed to accomplish each day. "I don't need much sleep," she told them. "So I need something quiet to do."

Before the last Linyaari rescue ship took Khorii on her mission, the captain had come to her with a sheepish expression on her face. "This is very selfish of me, I know, but I need you to cleanse a place for me. It's not very large, but it's something I need, and I think it can be used to help some of the survivors as well."

Khorii had felt very low at that time, since her parents and Captain Becker had gone into self-imposed exile among the Ancestors on Vhiliinyar. Asha Bates had led her to a small shop on the fringes of the city, between the downtown district and the factories, warehouses, and residential facilities where Jalonzo and Abuelita had lived prior to the plague.

"I was helping the team with search and rescue in the areas your parents couldn't cover, Khorii, driving a supply shuttle with fresh untainted grasses and water for them if they needed it. While they were working in an apartment building, I noticed a shop next door. I only read a little Spandard, but the hanks of beads in the window told me what was sold there. I was embarrassed to ask the team to cleanse the shop for me when they had so much to do to help others. But, well, making things is therapeutic. When I was a kid, my mother and I got parked on the terraformed moon the colonists call the Bosque Redondo. Most of the settlers were Dine and Lakota people, tribal people who were resettled there from Old Terra. Their original homelands were among the first to be rendered uninhabitable, long before the rest of the planet. Anyway, they named the moon after a historic prison camp where the Dine had once been forced to live far from their homeland. But it wasn't intended to be a prison, and people could bring with them whatever they liked. High-tech stuff was useless to most of them since the power supplies were limited there, so they brought the low-tech traditional things their ancestors had used. This time, though, they were able to bring the means to create and manufacture the materials they needed to make beads and fabrics as well. It turned out to be one of the best places I ever lived. If I had been the crying type, I'd have cried when we left there. My mother was busy fascinating the local men and cheating them at cards and dice; but the women felt sorry for me and taught me to bead and weave, sew blankets and quilts. I wanted to teach classes to the kids at Maganos, but Phador thought beading was beneath the dignity of an astrophysics instructor."

Cleansing the shop hadn't actually required much effort since Khorii had found ways to decontaminate large numbers of things and heal large numbers of people using water to conduct the power of her horn. As it turned out, most of the shop wasn't contaminated anyway. Khorii saw the blue dots she identified with plague hovering around only certain displays in the store. Sesseli, young enough to be immune to the hormone-related disease, happily hauled plasgrass baskets full of glittering crystals, glowing pearls, and shiny seed beads as well as trays of intricate creations Captain Bates said were made with the use of a torch. Each basket was then immersed in the old-fashioned bathtub of the shop's lavatory. Like many shops in many places, it had once been a home, and the new owners left the sanitary facilities as they were. Khorii dipped her horn in the water, purifying it, and the cleansing was transferred to the basketsful of beads as well. The shop's books, videos, computer, and some bead looms were the only items that needed individual attention.

The next morning, Captain Bates had presented Khorii with a beautiful blue-and-silver bracelet beaded with the pattern of the constellations visible in the night sky of Vhiliinyar. "I got the rescue team to pull up the configuration on their computer," the captain told her. "This way you will be able to look at the same stars as your folks."

Khorii did not wear it all the time because she did not wish to dirty it while she was working. She kept it in her travel pack and sometimes before she went to sleep pulled it out to admire it, pretending for a moment that the silver beads were the stars of Vhiliinyar and that they would beam her love and longing to her family.

Jaya looked balky for a moment, but she trusted Captain Bates and Khorii, so she finally said, "Okay. I guess we'd better collect Marl and get it over with so Khorii will have a chance to rest up before she has to rejoin the rescue teams again. But I want him locked up tight and guarded all the time."

"My thoughts exactly," Captain Bates agreed.

Dinero Grande was a short commuter hop from Corazon, and the *Mana* was fueled and ready to go with all hands on board by midafternoon.

Captain Bates and Jaya landed in the private space dock of La Villa de Estrella, house of stars, the mansion Marl Fidd had marked as his own share of the booty. He had forced Khorii to go with him so that she could cleanse the house and anything else he wanted, but she had outsmarted him, then outrun him, leaving him shaking his fist at Captain Bates's shuttle as it left him behind. Had he not been so awful, she'd have felt bad that she had not thought to rescue him before now, but somehow even suggesting to the Linyaari teams that there might be any-one in this area had totally slipped her mind, what with all of the other people she had to help.

She had cleared the kitchen for him, so if he was smart, and he was, he would plant himself in there and wait for help. He would have enough to eat and drink and could sleep on the floor, but unless he got desperate enough to risk infec-tion from the bodies littering other rooms of the villa, he was trapped with no shelter except one that offered a full fridge and a nice wine cellar.

His lodgings on Corazon would be a big comedown.

The recapture was uneventful. Once within Dinero Grande's orbit, the *Mana* dispatched the roomiest of the three shuttles aboard, Elviiz at the helm.

With Khorii leading the way, they left the shuttle and entered the opulent mansion, where she, Elviiz, Hap, Jalonzo, and his burly gaming buddies made their way through the grand entryway and connecting halls to the kitchen.

Khorii blinked incredulously. There were no longer any of the blue plague dots sparkling in the air. She hoped Marl hadn't figured it out that apparently she had either cleared the place better than she had believed or that it had somehow dissipated. But if the plague had vanished, it was the only contaminant in the air that had. The place was rotten with the stench of decay from the decomposing bodies in other rooms.

To her relief, they found Marl in a drunken stupor on the kitchen floor. He was a far cry from the vain and elegant young tough she had deserted by hopping into the shuttle.

He'd grown fat from having nothing to do but eat the rich food stored in the kitchen and drink the wine she'd glimpsed in storage racks along the walls. His dark hair, formerly close-cut, was long and matted. He stank. There was much to drink in the kitchen but since he could not reach the villa's generator from the kitchen or any of the places he had seen Khorii clear, he had not been able to reactivate the water pump.

One corner of the room he had used as a toilet and in other areas he had vomited. Many times.

Surprising the others, who regarded the sleeping thug with distaste, Jalonzo ignored the stench and knelt beside him, tapping him on the shoulder. "Hey, *amigo,* wake up." When Marl grumbled, sputtered, and drooled but otherwise made no response, Jalonzo, who had organized care for plague victims in an auditorium full of his gaming friends and become used to the foulness of human illness, maneuvered Marl so that he could lift his shoulders, then nodded for the others to help him. Together, they hauled him out to the waiting shuttle.

Khorii struggled with her conscience. She was supposed to rest so she could help with the search and rescue missions but really, she still felt fine, with lots of energy again and no signs of depletion of her horn's power. The plague seemed to be absent from the areas she'd previously cleared, so she thought it would be no trick to decontaminate the rest of it. The mansion could serve as a center for rebuilding the area once survivors migrated this far. She didn't want them to blunder back into the plague. Besides, she was curious to see if the plague still lingered in the other rooms. If it was gone there, too, and she could determine why, the contamination throughout the galaxy might be far less prolonged than they had dared hope.

Her shipmates were dead set against her returning to the mansion.

"You know the rules, Khorii," Elviiz told her. "Every bit of cleansing work you do when you should be resting may mean one less sick person you can heal."

"But I hardly heal anyone on those missions, Elviiz!" she protested. "The teams are so afraid I'll get so tired that I won't be able see the plague anymore that they won't let me do anything else. You can tell by looking at my horn that I'm fine. I really am. If survivors blunder into an area as contaminated as this one, they could start the plague all over again. And you know how it mutates."

She won, as she knew she would. Who was the one with the horn among them, after all? Who was the one who could see the plague? She was.

Besides, she didn't think she would be taxing her horn at all going back in there. If the plague was gone, she'd have spent none of her horn's energy except maybe to make the place smell better.

She didn't win when she tried to persuade Elviiz to stay with the shuttle. He insisted that he come with her while the others returned to the *Mana* and secured Marl Fidd. Then the

shuttle could return for Khorii and him. Khorii had to agree
that this was a good plan. Although she hated to tell him *everything* since he already knew so much more than she did,
his data-collecting capabilities would doubtlessly be helpful
in trying to determine the various conditions in the atmosphere, aside from her horn's power, that might have caused
the plague to dissipate.

They began a systematic search of the mansion. She had
previously glimpsed bodies in some of three rooms, but although the stench from them remained, the plague was not
in those rooms either. And except for the skeletons and a
few scraps of flesh and clothing, plus quite a lot of very fat
insects, little remained of the corpses. Khorii was glad of
that.

Meanwhile, having collected the data and samples she
requested, Elviiz decontaminated the kitchen. The android
activated the water pump without the aid of the larger generator and pulled what seemed like a vein from his leg,
pulling and pulling until it reached the required length, attached it to the faucet of the lake-sized sinks, and sprayed
down the floor. It was made of a solid sheet of granite ag-
gregate and sloped into a drain in the floor opposite the
sinks, something Elviiz had noticed immediately that
seemed to have escaped Marl's attention during all of the
many months he had remained in the room. Once the liquid
waste was disposed of, Elviiz used his laser on a low setting to turn the solid waste to dust, which he also washed
down the drain.

Which brought up an interesting question.

"Khorii?" His inquiry took her by surprise. She had
stopped her serious work to decontaminate a closet containing gowns in a rainbow of fabrics. Many of their components were embellished with embroidery, beadwork, crystals,

sequins, even real gemstones, and trimmed with ribbons, fur, fringe, lace, and strips of other embroideries. Khorii had apparently done a very thorough job of decontaminating the contents of a jewel chest, too, as many glittering and sparkling items of personal adornment lay spread and heaped upon a mirrored dressing table.

She looked up, her eyes shining in a way he had never seen any male's shine. Their silvery color reflected the hues of the gowns and the sparkle of the trims and jewels. "The people these belonged to are dead, Elviiz. Do you think it would be wrong to take some of these beaded trims back to Captain Bates for her work? Not the valuable gems of course, just the beads and less precious things. Actually, perhaps it would be wise to collect the portable valuables and label them as coming from this place, then store them somewhere safe in the event that there are heirs wishing to claim them."

Elviiz said, "That is a job for policemen, Khorii, not for healers. What about the septic systems?"

"What about them?" she asked, and then her face showed comprehension. "Oh."

"Yes, I was disposing of Marl's waste when it occurred to me that some infected material may have invaded the septic system and quite probably nearby waterways. Instead of cataloging the material possessions of the deceased, perhaps since you have decided to decontaminate this place, it would be good to include the septic areas and the waterways and water table serving this home and others in the area."

He was no longer concerned that she would deplete her horn's power. Although the horn's cleansing powers required no conscious effort on the part of the Linyaari possessing it, Elviiz knew the postures Khorii assumed when she was deliberately performing the task, the facial expressions she assumed. So far, this house had not required her horn's powers at all.

Elviiz tapped his chest com unit and informed the *Mana* that he and Khorii would be delayed somewhat longer.

Upon awakening in his new quarters aboard the *Mana,* Marl Fidd spewed obscenities along with the contents of his stomach at his captors. They had him penned inside a huge cargo net, bolted to the deck and the bulkhead as it was for heavier loads. The mesh was too fine to climb and it rose twelve meters or so where it was attached to the ceiling. They'd kenneled him good, they had. Marl expressed his opinion with another selection from the extensive linguistic cesspit portion of his vocabulary.

The huge kid with the long black hair who was standing guard outside the net widened his eyes and shrugged. "*No hablo* Standard, *amigo,*" he said apologetically.

Marl wound down after that, not wishing to waste his energy and his gift for shockingly creative verbal expression on this stupid git. Instead, he looked around, getting his bearings. They'd strung up cargo nets to isolate him, but he was in the larger cargo hold aboard the supply ship. It was empty. None of the drugs he'd made the others load from the docks of Rio Boca remained, nor the supplies that had been aboard when he first boarded. All that remained of the cargo were the boxes that formed the walls of the makeshift graveyard the Hellstrom kid and the android had created for the *Mana*'s original crew. Hellstrom wanted to impress the girl, of course, but it wasn't like she was going to give him anything for it. Lot of bother for nothing, in Marl's opinion. Why not just space 'em? That's what he'd have done.

He pantomimed being thirsty, needing a drink, and the big kid pointed at a bottle of water inside the makeshift jail.

Marl noted that the kid was not about to come right up to the net and seemed to be trying to hold his breath. That was understandable. To his surprise, Marl found he had been doing the same thing ever since he came to. He definitely was not looking or smelling his best, but that was Khorii's fault. Going off like that without making sure he had water or power. Bloody inconsiderate alien cow.

Or mare or nanny goat, judging from her more exotic attributes. Those didn't interest him at the moment, though he was sure she was nearby.

He pantomimed bathing to the kid next. The obliging oaf said something in his local gibberish over the com and got an answer in the same language. A short time later another big kid showed up with a bundle of clothes and some soap. Behind him was another carrying a huge hose. The first kid slipped the soap through the mesh with a flip so it landed where Marl could reach it. Then, without waiting for him to undress, the guard hosed him down with such a powerful blast it knocked him on his ass.

Marl swore again, and the kid aimed the blast at his head, nearly drowning him. Inhumane treatment of a prisoner that was. Definitely have to report the kid, though that was a laugh. Nobody to report anybody to left anymore. That was what Khorii and her gang didn't get. They were on their own now. They made the rules. One of these days *he* would make the rules; and then this giant jerk had better watch out. Marl Fidd never had been one for reporting people so much as repaying them, with interest, for any injury, insult, or other failure to recognize that he was definitely a power to reckon with.

The kid didn't get it for sure. He calmly waited until Marl undressed and soaped up, then hosed him again with definite glee.

The water shut off, and Marl stood there shivering as the puddle drained away into the deck's recycling system. While his buddy watched, the big kid unbolted the edge of the net and pulled it aside far enough for him to give the bundle to Marl.

Once Marl's hands were full, the kid immediately left

again and rebolted the net. This made a dandy brig, okay. Have to remember this arrangement when he took over the ship next time. Good holding pen for extra crew members he might need later.

The bundle was wrapped in a towel, which Marl used with one hand while keeping the clothing dry under his other arm. They could have at least put a bunk in here.

He opened the clothing bundle and another bottle of water and three nutrient bars fell to the deck. After the rich food he'd prepared for himself on the mansion's gas range, this was a bit of a comedown. However, his head ached, and his stomach still roiled from the wine of the night before. He'd gone through the best years in the kitchen's supply within the first couple of months. He had been down to the cooking sherry and was appalled that the mansion's chef had been gypping his employers by using such inferior swill.

The clothes were not a bad fit, standard shipboard gear for most crewmen, and as soon as Marl was dressed again he fastidiously dried off a patch of deck close to the bulkhead and sat down to pull on the soft slippers thoughtfully included in his care package. Must be the doing of one of the females, he thought. Women fancied him, though ones like Jaya and Bates pretended to be disinterested or even repulsed. Just being coy, he reckoned. Sooner or later, one way or another, they'd all come around.

The big kid and his buddy sat down—*they* had cartons to sit on and one between them on which they began playing cards. He went over to the net to kibitz, for want of anything better to do, but all their remarks were in Spandard, and they ignored his.

He was so bloody bored with being *bored*.

Wandering back to the water bottle and nutrient bars, he sat down and ate and drank the lot, despite his uneasy gut. He barely finished the last one before he was out like a light.

He wasn't sure when he awakened that he actually was awake. Someone had put cuffs and leg irons on him and shackled them to the bulkhead. The second big kid was outside the net, his crate pushed up against the wall, his head drooping against his chest, fast asleep. No sign of the first kid.

The overhead lights were dimmed to conserve energy. The ship's engines still hummed in the background, so they had not landed. Marl wondered where the frag they were taking him anyway. Back to Kezdet?

He hadn't had any news the whole time he'd been in the mansion, hadn't dared go out to try to learn anything else lest he get the plague. Once he began drinking himself to sleep, he'd often wondered just how well Khorii had cleaned the kitchen of plague anyway. He'd enjoyed some spectacular hangovers that made him think he was definitely about to die. But he had continued to live, and he wanted it that way. So he'd stayed put. What had happened in the meantime? If kids were standing guard over him, apparently the Federation cops were still out of commission.

This was no Federation brig either. Even if he hadn't recognized the subtler features of the *Mana*'s cargo hold, the onboard boneyard was a—ha-ha—dead giveaway.

When he sneered in its general direction, which was when he saw the movement over there. Just movement, like air currents shifting which, naturally, they didn't much on shipboard other than what came out of the ducts, and that wasn't exactly active.

He kept watching. Maybe some of the water from the hose had dripped onto the mesh and was dripping down—maybe that's what he saw. Maybe he needed his eyes checked.

But no, the floor around him was now totally dry, so the netting would be, too. It was plas-encased titanium, so it would have shed the water long ago.

He watched intently. He wanted to stand and go over to the net and peer through it to get a better look, but his legs had fallen asleep and, shackled as he was, he was on a rather short leash. Why did he bother about it anyway? Probably just one of the bloody cats using Jaya's parents' graves for a sandbox.

"Ssst," he said, trying to wake his guard and for some stupid reason trying not to make much noise about it. Face it, he was desperate for entertainment.

The boy didn't stir. Marl thought maybe his food or drink had contained a sedative so they could come in and chain him without any bother; but the way the guard was snoring, you'd have thought he was sedated, too.

A bunch of times, Marl had thought the mansion kitchen was a nightmare, and he'd wake up back on Maganos, but then sometimes he'd thought Maganos was a nightmare, too, and his life before that and before that. So this new nightmare wasn't exactly startling. It was unusual though. Marl fancied himself well-grounded in reality, however nightmarish, and he didn't usually see things that didn't actually seem to be there.

Another movement caught his eye as the cargo bay hatch slid open and there was a soft plop followed by small muffled footsteps across the bay.

Marl saw the cat at the same time the cat saw him. The wretched thing was hard to see in profile, a gray-stippled cat against a gray shadow-stippled background. But when the cat turned its face toward him, its big gold eyes glittered with red in the dark.

Marl didn't know why he hated this particular cat so much except that Khorii seemed to love it and it had a better life than he did overall. It didn't deserve that. Whereas Khorii and other imbeciles saw small furry beasts as alternatively shaped stuffed pandas, to pet and cuddle and play with, Marl had always been interested in how tough they were to catch, how loud they screamed, how fast they stopped when he took them apart. They were things to him.

Objects. Practice.

But this one was different. Why?

"Because you're somewhat like me. However, you are mistaken to think of me as prey. Beneath this cute and fluffy exterior hides a true force to be reckoned with. Pull my tail again at your own peril. My wrath is mighty."

Who *said* that? He looked around for Khorii or Sesseli, the little psychic freak. But there were only the boy and the cat, who turned away from him, tail high, and trotted toward the graveyard.

He was in very bad shape indeed from his long residence in the kitchen. Cats did not talk and they especially did not talk inside his head. Besides which, this particular moggy was terrified of him. If he so much as said "Boo!" it would run away.

While he was thinking about it, the cat stopped. It looked up at the graveyard, jumped a couple of meters into the air, and landed halfway back to the hatch, whereupon it kept scooting until it was out of the bay, the door still open, its little paddy paws thundering down the corridor like a herd of pachyderms.

Marl hadn't realized he'd yelped when the cat jumped but he must have, because his guard woke up.

"Huh?" The boy shook his head to clear it and looked at Marl. *"¿Qué pasa?"*

"There's something moving about over in the graveyard," Marl told him, certain now that there was since the cat had seen it, too. He pointed, in case the kid really didn't understand Standard.

The kid lumbered to his feet and plodded toward the mound of dirt.

He stood on tiptoes outside the crate wall, looked from

one side to the other, then plodded back toward the cargo net, shaking his head and shrugging.

Although neither the kid nor Marl closed their eyes after that, he didn't see the movement again. On the bright side, he didn't see the cat either.

chapter 4

I told you the trip would tire you," Elviiz scolded. "My optical sensors detect a definite translucency in your horn."

"My horn and I were fine until you decided I needed to purify the entire water supply of Dinero Grande," Khorii replied. "And the sewers besides. Yuck."

"Had you not insisted on relocating Marl Fidd, you would be fine. I did not intend for you to perform all of the purification yourself, only to ascertain the need for it."

"There was no sense in leaving it to infect someone else," she told him. "Now, if you'll stop nagging, I'm going to take a nap."

It had taken hours to find the waterways and sewer system and purify each separate component. Then they had to wait for the shuttle to pick them up. Khorii had yawned all the way to the *Mana* and, once aboard, had grazed her fill in the 'ponics garden before returning to the bridge. She kept nodding off there, too. Elviiz had busied himself double-checking the security arrangements for Fidd while Hap happily occupied himself in the engine room. She didn't get any real sleep aboard ship, however, because Khiindi jumped onto her lap the moment she sat and yowled at her. When she tried to ignore him, he used claws. He was very upset about something, but, then, Khiindi could be excitable. Perhaps he was protesting Marl Fidd's presence on board again.

The trip back to Corazon, once begun, was not a long one, so she stroked and comforted her furry friend for the duration, though her attentions only diminished his anxiety enough that instead of yowling at her and clawing, he spoke to her in raucous meows, flipping his tail and flattening his ears when she tried to pet his head.

She let Jalonzo and his friends deal with Fidd. Hap helped, but then returned to the *Mana*. He and Jaya wanted to repair and refurbish it for longer journeys it would be making soon with decontaminated supplies it would carry to the plague survivors on other worlds.

The rain was falling again, though full darkness had not yet descended and the wind was merely brisk, the lightning flashes distant. The hailstones of the previous night had melted into puddles.

Khorii stopped by Sesseli's room to tell the child she had returned, but the little girl was not there. Probably she was in the common room helping Abuelita with the baking.

Khiindi rode her shoulders all the way to her room, but when she tried to shut the door he became agitated again, so she propped it open before throwing herself onto her bed. In a few moments she was back on Vhiliinyar with her family.

Everyone *was there, grazing and racing with the ancestors, Mother, Father, her, Ariinye, Elviiz, Maak, Uncle Joh, Khiindi, and RK. Their meadow was the one near the entrance to the time caves, surrounded by the mountains on three sides with the lake on the fourth. All around the tops of the mountains stood their friends and relatives including both sets of Linyaari grandparents, Father-Sister Maati, her mate Thariinye, Great-aunt Neeva, Khaari, and Melireenya* *of the* Balakiire, *Mother's old ship. Maarni and Yiitir, the resident experts on Linyaari folklore and history were there and even Uncle Hafiz and Aunt Karina, who looked oddly Linyaari from this distance.*

In the lake, their distant relatives, the alarming-looking sii-*Linyaari dived and played with some of the poopuus, the sea-dwelling humanoids Khorii had befriended on Maganos Moonbase. They were visiting especially for the occasion and to meet the* sii-*Linyaari, about whom Khorii had told them so much.*

But what was *the occasion exactly? It was a party, that much was evident. She felt as if she'd just arrived, but she wasn't sure how she knew that. "Are we having a festival?" she asked her mother.*

"No, yaazi, *we are celebrating the homecoming. Now that the plague has been conquered and our people have re-turned, we have plenty of cause to celebrate, don't we?"*

"And best of all, you're here," Ariinye said, taking Khorii's hands. It was like looking into a lake and seeing her own reflection. Ariinye's hair was even styled and streaked like Khorii's, though hers bore an aqua streak instead of fuchsia. "I missed you, sister. Let's race."

Their hooves pounded across the meadow making an alarming racket, much louder than they should have sounded in the tall, luscious grass. Then something soft touched her lips. She opened her eyes to see Khiindi looking down at her. Someone was pounding on the door of her room.

"Khorii, the *Balakiire* has just landed," Elviiz said. "It would be courteous for you to greet them."

She rose, dumping Khiindi off onto the bed. It was a dream. Of course it was a dream, she thought, sad for a moment, and missing her family. She should have known it was a dream. She didn't even *have* a sister, much less a twin. She was a bit like the *Condor,* with Elviiz as her android brother and Khiindi as her feline brother. It would be great to have a sister. A tear surprised her, and she wiped it away. She was still tired. That was why she felt teary over a silly dream. She should have listened to Elviiz and let Marl stew in his own filth for a while longer. He hadn't seemed to mind particularly or been the worse for wear except to be dirtier and chubbier. Now that the *Balakiire* was here to take her on a mission to save sick people, she wasn't ready.

"Do not hurry on our account, Khorii." Aunt Neeva's thought touched Khorii's mind like a balm. It was so *good* to feel her there again. *"Elviiz explained the situation to us, and you did well. You must rest before we set out again, but we can spare the time. The quarantine successfully contained the plague in many areas, and in those that were stricken, it seems to have run its course. No new outbreaks have been reported. We will need you to do a sweep with us soon to affirm that, but unless we hear differently from one of the other ships, our healing missions may be over. We may need fresh teams to help rebuild and restructure the societies on the stricken worlds, perhaps even improve that aspect of them, but many of us can go home."*

Khorii brightened, clapping her hands excitedly at the news. *"I knew that! It was in my dream. I must have been picking it up from your thoughts as you landed. There was a wonderful party at home with my parents and everyone. I even dreamed I had a twin sister!"*

"That would be startling news to your parents," Aunt Neeva said with a smile in her thought. One without visible teeth, of course. Showing teeth, Khorii would have to remember when she went home, was considered hostile among the Linyaari. To show teeth meant "I'm thinking of biting you."

"I had a good rest," Khorii said. *"I should be ready to go with you soon."*

She pulled on her shipsuit and slipped on the starscape bracelet Captain Bates had made for her so she could show it to Aunt Neeva and the others. Elviiz was waiting for her outside, but she found that hearing Aunt Neeva's news had a restorative effect that, coupled with her sleep and the wonderful dream, made her feel downright frisky. She passed Elviiz and trotted down the hall so full of energy that a straight run was too tame for her, so she had to do pirouettes and leap up and try to touch the ceiling from time to time just for the joy of it. The dream wasn't just a wish! It was going to come true very soon. She wondered if the poopuus *could* come for a holiday. Maybe what was left of their families on their old world could come, too. Their planet was dying. Other species had never been allowed on Vhiliinyar, but that was changing a little, now that her people had seen how good people like Uncle Hafiz and Captain Becker were. And so many Linyaari had come to the rescue of the plague-ridden planets—some of the most conservative of her people, who ordinarily would never leave their homeworld, had come to help. In the process they would no doubt have become less wary of other races, even the humanoid ones populating most of this galaxy.

She raced down toward the common room, but even before she reached it her mood changed abruptly. An overwhelming wave of fresh grief flooded through her. Entering, she saw the noon meal in progress and the room filled with youngsters and elders, many of whose faces were so mournful the emotions overflowed into tears. The younger children howled and shrilled demands for their mothers, fathers, or other loved ones, long since dead and buried.

Khorii sighed. Abuelita and her helpers, also sniffling, carried plates of cinnamony churros from table to table, calming a slender path through the cacophony. Khorii met Jalonzo's grandmother in the middle of the room, when her plate was empty. "What brought this on?" she asked, having no wish to try probing all of these chaotic minds.

"Last night three of the *niños* saw their mothers, two saw

their fathers and Concepcion Mendez saw her daughter, Anunciata, who left behind three children. Two died but the other, little Elena, saw her mother, too. Anunciata and all of the others have been dead since before you arrived, Khorii, and are buried in the square with the others."

"Why would they all dream the same thing in the same night?" Khorii asked, looking around.

"They swear, Concepcion as well as the children, that it was no dream that woke them, but truly their lost ones. No sooner had each of them awakened than the dead relative left them. Concepcion, who was a schoolmate of mine and, I tell you, lacks all imagination, was so convinced she saw her daughter that she grabbed her cane and pursued the girl, convinced a miracle had occurred.

"But the girl did not look back and did not wait and disappeared down the street."

"Did any of the children try to follow their parents?"

Abuelita nodded. "But none turned back for them or spoke a word. If they were ghosts, it was cruel to return and remind people of what they've lost, especially the little ones. The young forget and get on with life quickly if allowed. But deep down, they still grieve and are confused, and these wraiths or dreams or whatever they were resurrected that."

It was a good thing Khorii was telepathic because if she had not been, she would have missed much of what Abuelita said. In some areas the wails gave way to sniffles, but other sections of the room were as loud as ever.

"Is that why they were *all* crying?" Khorii asked. "Why? When only six people saw the dead?"

"You are too young to know about children, and perhaps children of your people do not behave the same way, but generally when one starts crying, all of the others follow suit. Me, I am near tears myself."

Khiindi, who might have comforted the children, instead

circled Khorii, meowing anxiously up at her, as if demanding to know what she intended to do about this.

Elviiz stood in the doorway from the dormitories looking puzzled. And then, to Khorii's intense relief, four tall white figures with silvery manes and shining horns like her own entered from the street.

Neeva, Melireenya, Khaari, and a young male Khorii had seen before but did not know well, took in the scene. Almost at once, the remaining howls and wails descended into sobs, sniffles, and in a matter of seconds, to smiles and chatter once more.

"How did you do that?" Khorii asked Neeva.

"You still have much to learn about using your telepathic powers," Neeva replied.

"And it helps that there are now five of us," the young male added, as Khorii began to feel that she should have less time quizzing Abuelita and more time comforting the children.

Even Khiindi had found a lap to purr on.

"I have to learn to do that," Khorii told the other Linyaari. *"It would have been useful so often before."*

"It's as well that you did not," Neeva said. *"We need you to come back out with us and confirm that the plague has died out in some areas of its own accord. Once we know for sure, we can make plans for restoration and for our own return home."*

"These yaazis *think they saw their dead parents?"* the Linyaari boy asked. *"Don't they know that spirits do not return to the same bodies and lead the same lives, but are reborn as foals to begin again?"*

"All cultures do not believe as we do, Mikaaye," Melireenya said, then Khorii remembered who he was. This was Melireenya's son. He had been on narhii-Vhiliinyar with his father, helping shape a new and less exclusive Linyaari society.

Khorii joined them at one of the tables near the door. Now that the children were done crying, they were curious about the newcomers. By now they knew Khorii, but they had not seen so many Linyaari all together. And the calming influence the newcomers had sent to soothe them let the children know they were not only approachable, but in control. Several came up to the table with practiced grimaces, showing off scratches or scrapes and asking for healing. One enterprising little girl ran out to the grassy strip between the building and the sidewalk and picked a handful of grass she offered to Neeva, who accepted it graciously but did not actually eat any.

"Odd things have been happening here," Khorii told the other Linyaari. *"I don't think I should leave here. They need me."*

"We all need you, yaazi,*"* Melireenya said.

Sesseli burst through the dormitory door and ran to Khorii. "You're not going to leave *now,* are you? I don't want you to go!"

"Shush, Sess, you'll make all the babies cry again," Khorii said, hugging her. "I'll be back, but my relatives think the plague may be ending, and they need me to make sure. You know I'm the only one who can do that."

"Yes, but who will take care of all the little children if they get hurt or sick again?" Sesseli asked. She didn't mention that, with Khorii and Khiindi gone, she would feel lost, too.

"Abuelita will need you to help her, and Captain Bates might need help teaching the children about the beads and sewing."

"And I will need you to teach me everybody's name and where everything is," Mikaaye said. "Because you are right, of course. Someone must stay and look after the injuries and illnesses among your people. I cannot see the plague as

Khorii can, but I can do all of the other things, so I will stay to help you. I am Mikaaye."

Sesseli composed her face and stuck out her small, soft hand. "I am Sesseli, Mikaaye. Do you have a kitty?"

chapter 5

Paloduro and its sibling planets, Rio Boca and Dinero Grande, had been stricken with the plague before it spread via Federation and private vessels to other worlds. "We'll start our sweep with the last incidences of infection," Neeva said. "If it remains virulent there, then we'll decide what to do next."

To save the energy of their horns for healing, the Linyaari rescue teams conducted all routine conversation verbally, saving their energy-demanding thought-talk for more urgent matters or for far-distant communication that could not be conducted by any other means.

"Good plan," Khorii agreed. Nobody treated her like a youngling on these missions. She had a say in what happened, and her abilities were respected. She was a full-fledged team member.

"So. Kezdet and its moons."

"Do you know if Maganos Moonbase ever pulled in the supplies we off-loaded for them?" Khorii asked. "Even though we *told* them I'd decontaminated everything, the man running the school for my grandfathers said they couldn't risk it. He was willing to let Jaya die up there despite having supplies they needed."

"He was clearly new to our ways," Neeva said with a wry smile. "But yes, the supplies were collected unofficially by several of the more enterprising students. I understand the administrator attempted to expel them for their efforts, but your grandfathers and Uncle Hafiz overruled that. I understand the administrator in question is still on Maganos but will be seeking other employment once quarantine is lifted."

"Good," Khorii said.

"Yes," Elviiz said. "It seemed strange to me that the head of the school possessed an intellect well below that of the majority of the students."

"We need to check the water supplies and sewers, too," Khorii said. "Elviiz thought of it when we were on Dinero Grande. If they are contaminated with the plague, the people and creatures who depend on them may contract the disease that way or become reinfected."

"Yes, dear, but even without the benefit of Elviiz's advice, our decontamination teams have been doing that. However, it is a good idea if you check them for latent evidence as well."

"Aunt Neeva," Elviiz said, "have your teams performed this task in rural and outlying areas as well as the population centers? The waterways of Dinero Grande near the mansions were contaminated by the private wells in the area. The cleansing processes used for waste disposal were inadequate to eradicate the plague organisms also."

"We'll double-check with the teams about that, Elviiz, but I think they covered it."

The trip from Paloduro to Kezdet was quite different from the one Khorii had made in the opposite direction aboard the *Mana*. The *Balakiire* saw no derelicts; nor did they receive any distress calls. On the other hand, the official Federation vessels that once patrolled the spaceways were notably absent along their route.

The *Balakiire* received frequent hails from other Linyaari vessels—more than Khorii had realized her people possessed. All teams were reporting that the plague seemed contained at last and that the last new outbreak had occurred over a Standard week ago. Elviiz voiced his concerns about the rural water and sewage systems to the teams, and if they had not already addressed the issue, they promised to do so at once.

"It's odd how it's just gone away, isn't it?" Khorii asked.

Neeva shrugged. "Perhaps the causative organism has a limited life span and, without a live host, dies."

"I guess that must be it," Khorii agreed, but she remained worried about it. After all of the death and suffering, it seemed strange that the disease had suddenly and inexplicably ceased.

When Khorii's mother, Acorna, first came to Kezdet, no one had ever seen a being like her before. Now, when the *Balakiire* docked at the planet's main port, five other brightly decorated egg-shaped vessels nestled in newly retooled berths beside her. The white-skinned, silver-maned Linyaari rescuers were as prominent in the city and on the planet at large as once the Federation forces had been. The healthy young adults among the galaxy's peacekeepers had been among the first to succumb to the plague, crippling communications and relief efforts and impeding the implementation and enforcement of the quarantine.

"We'll take a flitter to the Nanobug Market," Neeva told her. She had to use thought-talk because she could not pronounce some of the names. Linyaari, who had grown up speaking only their own tongue, had a terrible time pronouncing Standard words. Khorii had been indoctrinated into Standard from babyhood by Elviiz, so other than a slight lilt to her speech, she sounded much like other Standard speakers from Kezdet. That was where Maak and Uncle Joh came from, and they had the accent of that world.

A paved flat area at the front of the space terminal was full of flitters of every description. Melireenya selected a roomy one to accommodate the entire team, number 365. "We organized teams of the older survivors to bring decontaminated abandoned flitters here. The numbers correspond to a computer record stating where each was found and, if the vehicle had contained one, a holoprint of the victim's face and where each was interred. Later, perhaps, the survivors of the owners may wish to reclaim some of the vehicles, but now most of them are too young to fly."

"You kept very good records."

"Liriili was in charge of that. Yours is not the only special talent that has come to the fore with this crisis. She also discovered, especially among the remaining human elders, assistants nearly as—there is a Standard phrase Captain Becker employs?"

"Nitpicking?" Khorii suggested.

"That's the one."

Liriili was the former administrator of narhii-Vhiliinyar, much disliked, or at least less beloved than most, for her fault finding and superior attitude. It wasn't entirely her fault. She was empathy-impaired. But Aunt Maati, who had been Liriili's page as a youngling, could barely stand her, even though Liriili had been rebuked and chastised by the Council and was somewhat easier to get along with than she had been. Meticulous recordkeeping was just what Liriili would do well, along with supervising others as detail-oriented as she was, especially if they also shared her lack of empathy, which would make cataloging the dead a bit easier, Khorii supposed.

Uncle Joh had spoken of the Nanobug Market of Kezdet with great enthusiasm. Before undertaking his many lucrative private contracts with House Harakamian, the salvage and recycling tycoon, as the *Condor*'s captain liked to think of himself, had ended each voyage by setting up a kiosk at the market to display and advertise his scavenged merchandise. He had described in detail the many types of food available, of which to Khorii only the floral arrangements sounded appetizing. Toys, exotic clothing, gemstones from many worlds, animals and plants of all descriptions, household items appropriate to many colonies from the most primitive to the most technical, and billions of other useful or interesting objects.

And those, Uncle Joh would say, were just the legal ones! In the old days, the market had contained a slave market as well, where child slaves and adults who had grown up as slaves were bought and sold. Also, he said that females and some males, many of them slaves, who would mate indiscriminately for a price could be hired there.

You could also buy stolen goods, black-market pharmaceuticals, forged documents and currency, and pieces of Federation uniforms for the illegal impersonation of law enforcement personnel.

Dancers, jugglers, acrobats, fire eaters, magicians, people who could create a custom hologram on the spot, strolling interpreters to help with any possible language barriers and others to write letters of business or to prospective mates for a price. Some would even compose and read literary creations amid the bustling crowds.

Uncle Joh had promised to take Khorii and Elviiz with him during their visit to Maganos Moonbase, which was close to Kezdet. Khorii had been greatly looking forward to it.

What a disappointment!

The flitter approached vast fields of what could have been Linyaari pavilions, tentlike structures but in many sizes, shapes, and colors. Most were shuttered, many were ripped or partly disassembled. Weeds grew waist high among them, all but obscuring the paths of loose gravel connecting them. The Linyaari presence had long ago dissipated any lingering odors.

Hillocks here and there, Neeva told her, were where beasts stricken by the disease had been buried where they fell. Walking through the maze of weeds, rickety tables, splintered poles, and ripped tents, Khorii felt a great sadness but saw none of the blue plague dots dancing before her eyes.

"I believe it would be safe to graze here," she said tentatively.

"That would be a great help for our people still working here," Khaari said. "We could hardly decontaminate every specimen of plant life growing here, and there are so few fertile areas on this world."

The live part of the market now was a place where survivors who had been separated from loved ones at the time the plague struck came seeking word of them. A huge tent contained wall after wall of photographs of the known dead on one side, and those being sought by survivors on the other. Children circulated among the crowd of other children and elders with handheld units linking to a central computer bank. It contained data collected by Liriili's people cataloging the dead by photograph, location, and identifying information or possessions with them when the bodies were collected. In most cases, it also had information as to where the bodies were buried.

"The children helping the others are very brave," Khorii remarked.

"Yes they are. Many seem to find some solace for their own pain in helping others, even if the information they provide is not always what the seeker wished."

"I see no evidence of plague here," Khorii said at last, and they left the tent, exiting into another part of the market. In this section, trade had resumed as briskly if not as merrily as Uncle Joh had described.

Neeva smiled at her, reading her interest. "Perhaps you would like to search this area alone, Khorii, while we return to the tent and help comfort the grief-stricken."

Khorii agreed to this readily, if not as enthusiastically as she might have done in a preplague market.

If the vendors were fewer, the goods were still quite numerous, and she wondered how much had been looted from decontaminated houses. Or perhaps not decontaminated, once some individuals had realized that they were immune to the disease. She must examine the merchandise closely.

Many of the vendors were quite old, and she could tell that some were doing exactly the same thing they had done before the plague.

"Hey, girlie! Have I got a deal for you! Bring that cute little horn of yours over here and be the first kid of your species to have one of these very special, rare, and wonderful items just in from Newcastle Colony."

"What items?" she asked. "How did they get here?"

The old man tapped a large wart on the side of his red-veined nose, "Ah, that's for me to know and you to find out. Come closer, that's it, I won't bite," he said, though he was showing lots of rotting and blackened teeth. "You're gonna love these."

He beckoned her nearer and nearer, to come around the table behind which he stood amid a jumble of furniture, mechanical parts, the fixtures with which humanoids cluttered their homes.

When she did as he requested, he opened the tent flap and pulled out a large heavy case, opening it at her feet. Brilliant fabric in more colors and textures than she had ever seen spilled from the case, along with spools of thread, ribbons, and glittering trims.

The man lowered his voice. "Half my tent is full of this stuff. One of my suppliers docked just as the plague hit and died almost as soon as he stepped foot on Kezdet. The merchandise was abandoned, and I had to go to considerable pains and expense to liberate what is rightfully mine. That old nag your people have in charge of the meat wagons wouldn't let anyone near the docking bays for a long time. No offense," he said quickly, holding up a palm in a peace-making gesture. "Only thing is, see, I want to protect my customers, so if you'd be a good girl and touch your horn to this stuff to make sure it's safe, I'll give you the bolt of your choice and a ribbon for your pretty curls besides."

Hmmm. What would Uncle Joh do? Or Uncle Hafiz? No dots danced from the case, but she could read the man. If she told him all of this was safe, he'd be digging into all sorts of places that might not be to loot things that were not his at all. And the fabric was very beautiful. She was sure that Captain Bates, Jaya, and Sesseli and probably many others would enjoy new garments made from these materials.

She looked around. Elviiz was several tents away, collecting data. Khiindi was chasing something that scuttled into a closed tent.

"My counteroffer is this," Khorii said, hoping she sounded businesslike. "I will decontaminate your goods, but in return you will give me the case of my choice and will also donate half of the recovered merchandise to help clothe and shelter the survivors."

"That's robbery!"

"Sir, I am disobeying my elders to diminish my horn's power for such frivolous purposes. Every increment of my strength expended on this may mean one less life I can save or injury I can heal. However, this is very attractive merchandise, and I can see that you have braved much to recover it. I can justify cleansing it for you only if you share some of it to clothe or shelter those in need. With the rest, you are free to profit as you will."

"Whew! You drive a hard bargain for a sweet young thing, but you have me over a barrel, so okay."

None of the cases showed signs of the plague, but Khorii went through the motions of decontaminating the lovely stuff nonetheless, all the time clearing her mind of the grief and pain around her by focusing on the sheen of the silks and satins, the beauty of the patterns, the shine of the sequins, beads, and metallic threads, the flutter of ribbons. She imagined the garments that could be made for her friends and herself from each of her favorites and finally settled on the first case he had shown her. She planned to suggest that he donate the containers filled with the most durable and utilitarian fabrics to complete his bargain.

But when she indicated her choice he shook his head, "Not that one. Have you got any idea what that stuff cost me?"

"Nothing at all according to what you told me."

"But that one has the best stuff in it."

"That means I have good taste, doesn't it?" In a way, she was glad the man was trying to back out of the bargain because it made her feel better about not really needing to cleanse his stock. She had inspected it, however, which was what she was doing everywhere, and what she wanted was not for her personally. It would do this man good to contribute something to someone else's welfare.

"Oh, have it your way. Take the damn thing," he said.

She reached down to fasten the case and he grabbed her, holding her bent over and covering her mouth with his hand. "Now then," he said in a low voice, "I got a better idea. You and me could make good partners. There's worlds of ownerless stuff out there, just waiting for someone to give it a home, except it's a little buggy. You take care of that for me, I'll take care of you. Be like your own daddy."

This is getting monotonous, Khorii thought. *First Marl, now this old crook. At least Uncle Joh doesn't force anyone to clean his salvage for him.* "Auntie Neeeva?"

But a tail brushed under her nose as Khiindi ran behind her.

"Yeow!" That was the scavenger, not Khiindi. The man released his grip on her so quickly she fell forward into the case of fabrics. Khiindi suddenly dropped to the ground, while the man moaned something incoherent and clutched his male reproductive organs through the cloth of his loose trousers.

Khorii momentarily pondered what to do. It might be misunderstood if she attempted to heal him. Human beings tended to be a bit shy about their reproductive organs, from what she had gathered.

But when she turned to look at the man, there was Elviiz, holding her assailant up in the air by the collar of his tunic. "If you become Khorii's father, sir, you must adopt me as well. I am her brother."

"And I," said Neeva, flanked by Melireenya and Khaari, "am her mother's mother-sister. You are kind to offer to care for this youngling, but she is not available for you to salvage. She has perfectly good parents, two sets of grandparents, and several collateral kinsmen as well. Put the gentleman down, Elviiz."

Elviiz dropped him, and the man took off, yelling, "Take the lot! I don't care. Just leave me alone!"

"How generous," Khorii said. "He had promised to give only half of his stock of fabric to clothe the survivors. He must be so sorry he became greedy and attacked me that he wishes to atone by donating all of it."

"From now on perhaps it would be best if you stayed with us after all," Neeva said.

"I was fine. Khiindi and Elviiz wouldn't have let anything happen to me," Khorii protested.

"It is not your safety that concerns us. How would we explain the damage Khiindi and Elviiz might inflict if someone else attempted to detain you? We do not want others to misunderstand our race or our purpose here. We are helping, not invading and conquering . . . anybody. Our people simply don't do that sort of thing," Neeva said severely.

Elviiz hung his head. Like his father, Maak, he wanted to

be considered a true Linyaari, just like fully organic members of the family. He would never have brought shame on them deliberately or caused bad relations with humans.

Khorii said, "Of course not. That's why Uncle Maak made Elviiz as he did. And Khiindi, as you know, is of Makahomian Temple Cat stock, and they are bred to protect their people."

"Yes, dear, but look at Elviiz. He has a Linyaari heart. He dislikes being put in the position of having to use force because you have placed yourself in a dangerous situation. No doubt Khiindi would prefer to limit his exertions to smaller vermin as well."

Khiindi looked up from cleaning the claws of his back feet and uttered a loud, "Prrrt?"

"It was not good of you to trick that man," Neeva continued. "It lowered you to his level."

Khorii hung her head. Neeva was right.

"However, the fabric will be very useful, and we all heard him give it to us for the survivors." She touched Khorii's horn softly with her own, the Linyaari version of a kiss. "And you are absolutely correct, *yaazi*. The goods in this case will particularly please your friends."

chapter 6

Hey, gang, come aboard! You got to hear this. Hafiz is on the horn with some great news," Captain Jonas P. Becker called from the descending robolift of the *Condor,* flagship of Becker and Son Interplanetary Recycling and Salvage, Ltd.

Acorna and Aari stood up from grazing in the lush meadow the Ancestors had allocated for their personal use and trotted over to the robolift. RK, Becker's feline first mate, leaped from the captain's shoulder to Acorna's.

"Beam us up, Maak," Becker said into the com he'd just installed on the robolift.

"How do I do that, Captain?" the android asked in a mystified tone.

"You can't, buddy. I just always wanted to say that. You don't really have to do anything. I'll push the button like I always do." Acorna and Aari smiled at each other. The captain was so pleased with something that his mustache was absolutely fluffy with joy. He was also carefully shielding his thoughts so they could enjoy the surprise element of the news he wished them to hear for themselves.

They ascended to the cargo deck, then up to the bridge. The robolift previously had gone only to the cargo deck.

"This is a wonderful surprise, Joh," Aari told him. "Making the lift go all the way to the bridge is both logical and practical."

"Yeah, well, I thought of it when I was getting my strength back after the plague. The stairs were just too much, you know? But this is nothing!" He snorted and waved one sausage-fingered hand dismissively at the lift. "Come on, can't keep His Hafizness waiting. He made me promise not to tell you so he could."

Becker capered ahead of them and then, with a low bow, as if presenting royalty, indicated Hafiz Harakamian's impatient countenance on the com screen.

"Acorna, most felicitous of female foster offspring! And Aari, supremely salubrious son-in-law. Greetings!" Hafiz nodded, a deep blue catseye chrysoberyl winking at them from the center of the peacock-feather fan adorning his turquoise turban. "Sit down, my dears, make yourselves company. Jonas, are you a barbarian? Serve your guests cakes—er—seed cakes, of course, and a sparkling libation. The tidings I bear require celebration, think you not?"

Hafiz himself was seated, and behind him a flowing curtain of amethyst and violet draperies indicated that his beloved Karina was hovering in the background. This impression was confirmed when her purple-catseye-encrusted hands caressed the teal-and-gold brocade shoulders of her husband's robes.

Aari and Acorna sat. Roadkill walked from Acorna's shoulders to the back of the command chair and draped himself across it, his bushy tail tickling her cheek.

Acorna knew the form Hafiz preferred, especially when he wanted to spin out a story, as he seemed to wish to do now. "How have you been, Uncle Hafiz? I trust you and Karina are well and that your enterprises flourish?"

"How kind of you to inquire, my child. I am well as is my beloved. As for my enterprises, as you know they faltered somewhat while the disastrous disease threatened to eradicate life in our home sector. Your father, Rafik, tells me that our losses are so great he has been unable to calculate them accurately as yet. So many of our employees in so many of our enterprises have succumbed that data has been difficult to gather."

"But Rafik is well?"

"He is. As are your other fathers and their families. Your people retrieved and cleansed many of our vessels and other properties, so House Harakamian is in better order than the businesses of its—for the most part late—competitors."

"We were all happy to have the occasion to repay your fathomless kindness to us and our worlds, Uncle Hafiz," Aari replied. "Have you had any news of Khorii?"

Aari was much less accustomed to the circumlocutory manners that were Hafiz's habit. As Joh Becker put it, Aari liked to "cut to the chase."

"Ahhhh." Hafiz smiled deep into his beard and mustache, leaned back in his chair and laced his fat, ring-encrusted fingers across his royal blue sash. Had RK favored a palette of blues instead of his brindled gray coat, he would have looked much the same after hiding a particularly well-aged deceased rodent amid her bedclothes. "That I have, my children, that I have. I received a most encouraging relay mere moments ago from the *Balakiire*. Khorii is with them now, and thus far, are you ready?"

"They're ready already, Hafiz!" Becker told him. "Enough's enough. Tell them before they read my mind."

"Thus far Khorii has confirmed their impression that the plague has run its course. There have been no new outbreaks, and all previously contaminated areas are, according to the talented pearl of your family oyster, now clear of the disease."

"Then she—everyone else, too, of course—will be coming home soon?" Acorna asked. Her hands trembled in her lap. She reached up with her left and stroked RK's tail.

"As soon as possible," Hafiz said, nodding. "But you understand, beloveds, that it may *not* be possible for her to return very soon. She alone can confirm that all traces of the illness have vanished, and the area of infection was, as you know, quite extensive."

Becker chewed his mustache, as if trying to decide something, then said, "Hafiz, tell Khorii if she wants a good litmus test for the course of the disease to check the *White Star,*" he said. "I'd appreciate if you passed it on just that way and went through as few relays as possible—better yet, send it to the *Mana.* I don't exactly want the whole Linyaari fleet trying to read my mind on this one."

Hafiz raised an eyebrow.

"Don't ask," Becker said, and Hafiz nodded. The two men of business respected each other's mysterious silences, at least superficially. That didn't mean they might not do some sneaking around later trying to find out what the other one was up to, but they kept it polite for the sake of their mutual friends. "But if she checks the *White Star* and it's clear and there are still no new outbreaks, it should be safe for her to return home."

"As you have said, so shall it be done," Hafiz replied formally.

"Is that all?" Aari asked, sounding a bit disappointed. Acorna knew he would have preferred to hear that their daughter was currently waiting for someone to collect her from the Moon of Opportunity and bring her back to Vhiliinyar.

"It is," Hafiz said. "And now, I must forsake your company, which is like unto a waterfall in the desert of my despair, and return to—yes, dear?" He looked up, nodded, and patted the feminine hand on his shoulder. "Karina has something she wishes to impart to you as well. Farewell for now."

"Farewell, Uncle Hafiz," they said, and Acorna added, "A thousand thanks."

Karina Harakamian settled her drifts of draperies into the chair like a purple flower shedding its petals. She beamed triumphantly at them through the com screen, her eyes twinkling like her many jewels. "No disrespect to my hubby, kids, but I've had a vision that portends even better news than his!"

Karina must be excited indeed, Khorii thought, because she had momentarily forgotten the funereal tones she ordinarily employed to announce her "visions."

Generally, Karina also chose to have her visions in the presence of those who would be most impressed by them. Contacting them after the fact was not her style. "When did you have this vision?" Acorna asked her, putting more eagerness into her voice than she actually felt. Often Karina's visions of the "future" simply restated the present. Occasionally she had a true flash of insight, but during those times, in Acorna's experience, her presentation was quite dramatic, if accidental, usually coming within the framework of one of her questionable trances.

"Just now!" she said. "While Haffy was speaking to you. It was quite clear though disappointingly brief and, forgive me, dears, but this is the way my gift works, a bit cryptic."

As if they were not all well aware of that!

"What was your vision?" Aari asked.

"Simply this, and do remember I am but the messenger. Hafiz and Neeva are being overly optimistic. Khorii will not return to you before twelve months and a day have passed, but your daughter is close at hand, and you will be reunited within the week."

"Standard measurement?" Acorna asked, as it differed from the Linyaari concept of time.

Karina cupped her right eye with her thumb and index

finger, consulting her inner timekeeper, then nodded. "Standard, yes."

They thanked her, and the com screen went blank.

"What in the multiverse did she mean by that?" Joh Becker asked them.

She was such a freak that she didn't even have a proper name, like all of the others. The Friends called her The Mutation and sometimes addressed her as Mu. The Others called her Narhii, which in their language meant "New."

But she was not new any longer. She had existed for six full rotations of the Star and was tall, awkward, and changing. As a baby and a toddler, she had longed to be held, but the Friends were far too busy and the Others didn't have arms, though they lay beside her and nuzzled her with their soft noses when she brought her troubles to them, and sometimes touched her horn with one of theirs, which comforted her instantly, though it was not what she instinctively craved.

She shared many characteristics with the Others, physiologically, but she was a biped, like the Friends. Most of the time most of them were bipeds anyway. They changed shapes when it suited them. Even their dwellings changed shapes depending on who was utilizing them and for what purpose.

She preferred the flower-strewn fields where the Others lived, though they sheltered in caves during bad weather, eating dried grasses and grains provided by the Friends and reminiscing about what their ancestors told them about life on their planet of origin.

The Friends had good stories, too, and they didn't mind if she listened, but they had no interest in educating her. Their involvement with her was mostly scientific. They studied her. A portion of every day of her life had been spent in the laboratory, having her bodily fluids collected and analyzed, being stuck with needles to take her blood, being scanned by computers, tested, and documented.

Worst of all, they invaded her mind. They not only seemed able to tell what she was thinking, but they made her think about specific topics, and when she replied, verbally or just by thinking, they probed and probed for more details. When she was little, she had tried very hard to answer their questions in such a way as to please them; but they never seemed pleased by anything and, indeed, always seemed impatient.

During the last two seasons, their attitude toward her changed from one of boredom to anticipation. They had begun to expect something from her. The nature of their questions changed. Had she experienced unusual bleeding from her reproductive orifice or a feeling of heaviness in her lower abdomen? Any warmth or unusual urges?

She had no idea what they considered unusual, but the questions made her uncomfortable anyway. Did they think she was ill? Would they care? She had never been ill, but the Others spoke about it among themselves, and how a touch from one of their horns could remedy even the worst illness, which seemed to be a bodily malfunction. Her body, misshapen as it was compared to everybody else's, had always functioned well enough to suit her, if not the Friends. They were not deliberately unkind, and if she expressed a need for something tangible, they supplied it in a disinterested way, but the new gleam in their eyes was not appreciation or fondness, and their probing and questions were even more relentless than they had been before.

Finally, she was sitting at the table with Akasa, the female who was most often her questioner. Akasa had not been satisfied with her answers. "You are reaching what should be puberty for your kin—for you," she said aloud. "Do you feel no changes, no urges, no different wishes toward other beings, especially males?"

Odus, the male interrogator, entered the room. He would

have been watching from behind the wall panel, opaque from within the room, transparent from the observation area beyond. At times there had been a large invisible audience present at her sessions with Odus or Akasa, she knew because she saw them leave their chamber when she was allowed to leave.

"We are approaching her the wrong way, Akasa," he said. He had taken the form of a tall male biped, with blue eyes and golden curls and an erect posture. In this form he was often at his most dismissive, more interested in appearing wise and clever to those beyond the panel than in her responses. In his most customary alter-form as a golden-maned, four-legged large feline he was somewhat more likable, though his roar was fearsome.

"And what would the right way be?" Akasa asked.

"How can we expect her to attain the proper state without the proper stimulation." He shed his robes easily, as the Friends often did when transforming, and changed swiftly, his muscular torso remaining golden and much the same but his face elongated, he sprouted a small beard, and his hair curled down his spine and up his calves. His soft five-toed feet solidified into a solid unit, then split until they were two-toed hard feet like her own. His five fingers fused to three. His male reproductive organs had grown, and his phallus had assumed an alarmingly erect posture.

"There now, Mu, I am a male like you. How does that make you feel?" he asked aloud while searching her mind for any deeper or hidden responses.

She looked at Akasa, whose expression was both curious and disapproving.

"It makes me feel that I would like to leave now and go out to graze with the Others," she replied honestly. To her relief, they acquiesced, and Odus, unable to maintain a tertiary transformation for any length of time, reverted to his lion form.

The openness of the fields, the scent of the flowers, the breeze ruffling her mane, helped calm the queasiness that she felt beholding the Friend she had known from infanthood in that mocking guise.

"Poor Narhii!" said Nrihiiye, the senior dam among the Others who was her special friend. Although the Friends always wanted her to answer their questions in detail, the Others, particularly Nrihiiiye, always knew how she felt. Like the Friends, they heard her thoughts, but unlike them, the Others listened to her without probing and did not expect her constantly to define and explain what was inside of her that even she did not understand.

"No wonder you are upset," her mate, Hruffli, said, nuzzling her. "I could just kick Odus and Akasa so hard they landed on the Star itself! They have no sense. I don't know why they act like other creatures have no will of their own. They're telepaths. They should know better."

"It's not just carelessness, it's selfishness," Nrihiiye disagreed. "They are so eager to use Narhii as breeding stock that they have frightened and repulsed her. Don't they know there's more to mating urges than form? I suppose not. They're rather indiscriminate in their unions."

Hruffli stamped his foot angrily. "This is bad. Unnatural. Not to be tolerated. This filly belongs with her own people. Among them she will find a suitable mate when the time and place are right."

"I don't *have* any people!" Narhii wailed.

"Yes, you do," Hruffli said.

"I do?" she asked, surprise and—yes—relief—flooding through her. "I'm not just a mutation? A solitary aberration?"

"Whoa there, sweetweed," Nrihiiye cautioned her mate, "we promised the Friends not to disclose any of that."

Narhii's relief and pleasure receded as the betrayal stung her. She had people and Nrihiiye knew and hadn't told her because of some stupid promise to the Friends?

"We *couldn't*," Nrihiiye said. "We owe our lives and the continuation of our race to the Friends. And though their means may be questionable, their motives are not so bad. They know they created your race in the future, but they haven't figured out how they did it."

"Stinks worse than hound-shite to me," Hruffli said. "Thornin' simpleminded of such lofty bipeds to try to create a race by bringing a member of it back here to seed it. And anybody would know that if you have the filly, you need the colt as well."

"Yes, Hruffli, but you know how they are. They tell us they'll do the science and we can do the healing and purifying and keep our chin whiskers out of their business. If you ask me, it's all that gallivanting around they do from one time to the next as well as one world to the next. That lot never know where or when they are, much less who they are. No wonder they have to keep asking Narhii who she is."

"Look at her!" Hruffli said. "She's more like us than them. She is our business, and I'll not have them frightening her away from stallions forever by having one of those— those—they're not *my* friends—interfering with her. I don't care if they take us back to Terra to be run to ground by the horn hunters. No matter how it works or when it happens, Narhii is our grandchild."

"We can't. There is nowhere for her to go, Hruffli. That's always been the problem."

"There thornin' well is. She can use that contraption they used to fetch the ones who got away."

"But it's broken in the future. I heard Grimalkin say so. She might be lost in time, and then where would she be?"

"Not here for them to warp her natural inclinations, that's where," Hruffli said. "You know Grimalkin. That slyboots would say anything to cover his own tail, and he stole her, or she wouldn't be standing here. Those others like her seemed respectable. She can use the contraption to find them, and they'll look after her."

"Got it all figured out, eh, Hruffli?" Neicaair, another stallion, spoke up.

"I reckon," Hruffli said, his chin whiskers jutting and his eyes narrowed. His left front hoof scraped the ground three times, defiantly.

Neicaair backed down a fraction. "Say they're right though and she's the key to re-creating her race. The Friends *know* about those things. Lot more than you do or any of us. If she is and we put her in the contraption and she goes off looking for her people, there won't *be* any, will there, because she didn't finish the job they brought her here to do."

Neicaair's mate Morniika flopped onto her side, her hooves kicking back and forth. "Stop! You're making me dizzy, Neicaair, and the rest of you, too. It isn't up to us to decide. If the Friends think Narhii is old enough to begin thinking about mating, then she is old enough to decide what she wants to do."

"Of course, wildflower, you're absolutely right," Neicaair replied. Narhii thought he seemed eager for the escape route she offered. "And if the girl chooses to leave, who are we to stop her? So, Narhii, what will it be? Stay here and be goaded into mating with one of those old plugs who've been studying you like you were scat on their hooves your whole life or risk annihilating your race and maybe getting lost in time and space looking for those other bipeds who look like you?"

If they hadn't known all along that she didn't belong here, that she was not the only one of her kind, that in fact she had probably been stolen from the future, if they hadn't *told* her, she wouldn't have been able to go. The Others were as close to family as she'd ever known, the only warmth or affection or play in her life. But they had known, and they also knew how freakish she felt and how much she longed to belong and until now none of them had told her. They'd kept it a secret even though it was *her* secret, her truth, and one she deserved to know.

"The machine," she said. "I won't get lost, and somehow or other they'll start my race without me and my people will be waiting, my dam and my sire. They've probably worried about me and wondered where I was my whole life."

chapter 7

Seeing her human grandfathers made Khorii more homesick for her family than ever. She had hoped that they could talk to her parents directly on the com relay, but by the time they got through, they could only leave the hopeful message with Uncle Hafiz before they had to leave again. Soon, Neeva promised, they should be able to declare the Federation-controlled quadrant free of infection and return home.

If wishing alone could have driven off the plague, it wouldn't have stood a chance, but the Linyaari were scientifically if not technologically inclined. Proper sampling and testing must take place, even though Khorii was the only one able to do it.

They sent the message from LaBoue, where Khorii inspected House Harakamian's private enclave and pronounced it clear. As it should have been, since a Linyaari rescue team had already combed it. Following Khorii's example, they had rounded up the personnel, had them climb into a pool, and purified the pool's water and the people at the same time. Then the same water had been used by the staff to clean everything in sight. The gardens there flourished as never before.

It was good to see Grandsire Rafik and his brood, all of them happily plague-free. They had gone en masse to the birthing hospice (not an actual hospital, as Khorii had believed) on Kezdet, where Khorii's new auntie was born. Mother's human fathers had been partners and crewmates in an asteroid mining business before Grandsire Rafik became the head of House Harakamian when Uncle Hafiz retired. Now the other two grandsires, Calum Baird and Declan "Gill" Giloglie and their families were not only employees of but shareholders and board members of House Harakamian, as well as being the directors of Maganos Moonbase, which was the *Balakiire*'s next stop.

Khorii made the appropriate noises over the new pink, but hornless, little one with its wispy red ringlets and answered questions about her work and her new friends.

As soon as it was permissible, she and Khiindi escaped the adult conversation and headed for the pool occupied by the students from the water world of LoiLoiKua, nicknamed the poopuus or pool pupils by the other students. Khorii had visited their world and saved as many of their relatives as possible. She was intensely grateful that the "far talk," a long-distance psychic derivation of the language of long-extinct whales, had already carried the bad news to the students who were now orphaned or who had lost family members.

The poopuus swam up to meet them, and three fish flopped onto the deck, gifts for Khiindi, who had become their particular friend.

The poopuus seldom made friends with bipeds, much less quadrupeds. Their people had mutated long ago from being island-dwelling bipeds to ocean-dwelling mammals whose legs had fused into tails and whose feet had webbed into serviceable flippers.

Khiindi, of course, simply wanted to be where the fish were. Khorii loved her cat but knew him for the consummate opportunist he was.

They didn't question her or even talk to her very much, but let her swim with them and, when she was relaxed enough, play. When she was underwater, she heard their voices as a kind of song. Being able to swim without having to purify anything or anyone in particular was so soothing.

The visit was all too brief, however. Khorii and the crew of the *Balakiire* had to resume their mission. As she dried off and bid farewell to the poopuus, Khorii consoled herself that the sooner they left, the sooner they'd be done and she could go home again.

The relay from home arrived after they returned to the ship.

"What is this *White Star*?" Neeva asked.

Khorii rolled her eyes. Trust Uncle Joh to think of his salvage even when the most serious work was under way. "It's nothing. A derelict ship we found, full of plague victims. But everyone was already long gone before we found it. It will certainly keep."

Neeva accepted her assessment. They made numerous inspections of other worlds, moons, and occupied asteroids. Occasionally there was a small pocket of plague that had cropped up recently, but nothing like the original outbreak. People had learned that children and elders were fairly immune, and were better able to contain the disease when a case or two occurred. Of all of the populations the *Balakiire* visited, only three had fresh outbreaks, and among these, there were only two fatalities before the Linyaari arrived to completely eradicate the menace.

LoiLoiKua, Khorii was pleased to learn, was also free of plague, as it should be. This was where Khorii, in trying to save the kinfolk of her friends on Maganos, had ended by purifying the ocean that covered most of LoiLoiKua and everyone in it.

That was how she first discovered that people could be

cured of the plague by contact with water she (or, later, other Linyaari) purified.

The *wii-Balakiire* set down on one of the islands along the central ridge separating the ocean into two sectors. Elviiz piloted the shuttle and stayed with it while Khiindi hopped out to patrol the shore for any stray fish that might have lost their way and beached themselves. Khorii dived into the water. She was surprised when no one came to meet her and swam out some distance before several of the people she'd met on her first trip popped up in front of her.

"Greetings, Korikori!" they chorused.

"Greetings from your children," she told them.

"Is that what brought you here?" asked Nanahomea, grandmother of Likilekakua, one of Khorii's poopuu friends, and matriarch of a clan of the LoiLoiKuans. *"We did not dream you would return to us, much less so quickly. We are happy to see you."*

"I'm happy to see you, too," she said. *"Actually, I'm on a special mission with others like me to learn if the plague is still active. Has anyone else become ill since I was here before?"*

"No. Our ocean, our shores, and our people were all healed when last you swam among us. So at least we have no new illness."

Her thought politely concealed another, a worry or a fear that she was not stating. Khorii knew. Thought-talk, especially between people who did not know each other well, was a lot like the ocean. There were the surface thoughts, placid ripples or roaring waves, and those were what were expressed. Linyaari courtesy dictated that one did not delve below the thoughts most openly expressed. Of course, what was expressed openly revealed some of what lay underneath, in most people. And sometimes, without meaning to, the speaker dredged up material from the deep that flashed to the surface before sinking again.

"No plague but something else, other than your grief, that troubles you?" Khorii asked.

"No, nothing that has caused any actual trouble, but things have happened, things have been seen, which should not be possible."

A thought image came to Khorii of something huge and menacing lurking in the depths, sheltering in the reef where it could not be seen except for the snap of a massive barbed tail, a double bank of boulder-sized teeth.

"New life-forms?" Khorii asked, and because Jalonzo had tried to explain his fantasy game to her so such things were on her mind, *"Monsters?"*

"Things which have never existed here before," Nanahomea said cautiously. *"No one has seen a whole one. The parts that have been seen resemble slightly the creatures who died in the early stages of the plague, after Raealacaldae poisoned the water. But these creatures are not the only disturbing matters."*

"What else?"

"I have seen lights inside Raealacaldae's dwelling, and it makes noises."

"What kind of noises?" Khorii asked.

"It sounds as if dry things are moving in there," Nanahomea said after thinking it over. *"Dry things are leaping from their moorings and diving onto dry ground. The noises they make sound as if they are breaking into parts. Small explosions have also been heard, and scrapings, clankings, noises that only Raealacaldae made when he lived on the land here. We seldom make them because we live in the sea, where all falling things are buoyed by water."*

"I will look inside the sand castle for you and see if I can determine what's making the noises," Khorii said.

She swam back to shore and stood on the beach. The flowers that had covered both the beach and the bodies of the

dead were long gone, blown away by winds or rotted until
they became part of the soil, as the bodies must have. Here
and there Khorii saw holes in the sand, sinkholes, similar to
the ones in the square in Corazon. Did they have a rainy season here, too? She would have to ask Nanahomea.

Seeing the door to the sand castle standing ajar, she
thought that the wind had been blowing through the castle,
sweeping through the former Federation administrator's
possessions as it had swept away the flowers.

Of course, that would not explain lights, but perhaps they
were timed to come on automatically at certain times of the
day or night, to coincide with the routines Raealacaldae had
performed.

She had not entered the sand castle on her former trip.
Her business was with the living, but if the material objects
left behind by the dead were causing the ocean dwellers'
concern, she didn't mind helping out.

"Hello?" she called, and immediately winced at her own
rationality. There was no one here to answer, or even hear
her greeting. She stepped inside and looked around. The little steepled windows made long blades of light on the floor,
sparkling off shards of glass. The shadows were very deep,
and she looked for the lighting controls. There were none.

She took another cautious step, toward the broken glass,
treading carefully since, although her feet were hard enough
to need no coverings, they could be pierced by sharp objects,
and she had no wish to lame herself.

Outside she heard the purr of the surf as it pushed and
pulled at the beach. She heard the cries of birds, too. She
didn't recall seeing any birds on her previous visit, but she
had been much preoccupied. Though the plague killed animals and even plants, it probably spared these birds because
most of its energies were spent in the sea. Perhaps the birds
had sensed instinctively that they needed to avoid the areas
where bodies were piled, though under most circumstances,

from what she knew of many species of seabirds, they would have relished carrion.

She stooped and looked more closely at the broken object. A filament, a socket, and much broken glass. A lamp. One with its own individual power source and control, as colonists sometimes used in places where the trappings of larger settlements had yet to be installed. Whatever the nature of the mysterious lights that Nanahomea had seen, this lamp was not responsible. Looking up she saw the empty wall sconce where it had been stationed. *How would the wind have knocked it down from there?*

Her eyes more accustomed to the light, Khorii saw that the desk, the chair, and the narrow bed that were the other furnishings of the room were also in pieces. Pictures and documents lay atop the rubble, more glass, more twisted metal and broken frames.

What could have caused all this? No puddles of water among the wreckage suggested a wave. A determined animal could do some of it—or a herd of determined animals. But the only amphibious animal she'd encountered here had been a turtle, and turtles were not only unlikely to be excitable, they also were low to the ground when on land and would never have been able to reach some of the objects, even by crashing into lower ones.

She shrugged to herself and stood. And whirled around when she heard something, or thought she did. Had there been a noise from just beside her, or was it some weird echo of the sound she made when she stood?

There.

Again.

This time from overhead. She looked up, but the shadows were even deeper at the top of the castle's towers, which rounded out the corners of the single room. The roof was flat. Perhaps it was coming from up there? There was no staircase, but peering into the tower enclosures more closely, she saw a ladder leaning against a far wall. She looked up and saw a thin rectangular thread of light above the highest rung of the ladder. She took it to be a trapdoor to the roof.

The round rungs of the ladder were not easy for her hard Linyaari hooves to manage. Ship's ladders had proper steps, narrow, of course, but flat enough that Linyaari were able to plant their feet on them. This ladder was more primitive. She propped it at an angle against the wall. She was small and light, but the ladder wobbled alarmingly.

Was that some sort of laughter or had her stomach gurgled? She really wished Elviiz were with her, or Neeva. Even Khiindi could have scampered up the ladder with his nimble paws, though she doubted he had the weight to open the trapdoor.

She tested her weight on the next rung and lifted herself, using her hands to bear most of her weight. As she took her foot off the lower rung, it rolled and slid loose, throwing her off-balance so that the other foot slipped from the ladder as well. For a moment she clung with her hands, then realized that was stupid. She wasn't that far off the ground, and if she clung to the ladder, she'd pull it down on top of her. So she let go and hopped down. The ladder tried to follow her but she caught it in time and propped it up. Well, it was a flat roof. She'd go outside and see what she could see. She hadn't heard any more noises that she was not generating herself because hers were so loud they would have drowned out anything softer.

She stepped out into the sunlight again and looked up at the roof, but the only sounds she heard were the wind and the sea, which were lost as the shuttle descended.

It set down on the beach, the roar of its landing drowning out the subtle sounds Khorii had been trying to trace.

Khiindi leaped from the hatch and landed protectively in front of her, growling up at the castle's flat roof.

She laughed. "Good show, cat, but I know you only came

here hoping that the LoiLoiKuan elders would be as generous with the fish as their children."

Khiindi cast a wounded glance in her direction, then let out a long ferocious hiss at the roof and with an unusually long spring placed himself on the rooftop where he made a great show of hissing, snarling, stalking, pouncing, then chasing something off the far edge. He jumped back to the beach and gave chase as far as the water's edge, then cast a reproachful look back at Khorii as if she should have prevented his imaginary quarry from escaping.

By that time, Elviiz was standing beside her. She was laughing so hard the tears were streaming, and she could scarcely draw breath.

"Oh, Khiindi Kaat, you were magnificent!" she said. "Whatever that was will think twice before returning while *you're* around."

Khiindi turned and stood up straight, head proud, chest puffed out, tail held like a standard with its fluffy hairs flagging in the wind, and pranced toward her, the conquering hero, or, if not conquering, at least undefeated.

And then, suddenly, her mind was full of frenzied thoughts, cascading over her so fast and so furiously that she couldn't separate them. The LoiLoiKuans were desperately agitated about something—fear, pain, more fear . . . Khorii waded back into the water and swam out in search of the emotional hornets' nest.

"What is it?" she called. *"Nanahomea, what's wrong?"*

"Korikori, come quick, the monster attacked Mokilau."

narhii is not going in that thing alone," Hruffli said.

"Don't be daft, old nag," Neicaair told him. "You can't use that machine."

"I can be with her," the old stallion said. "If we should land during the time of the monsters Grimalkin spoke of, I will defend her with hoof and horn, and she may escape while I fight them off."

"You don't know how to use it," Morniika said.

"I think I do," Narhii told her. "I've seen the Friends do it. I think I even know how to tell where to go. And Hruffli, if I chose a wrong time and we landed among monsters, I would never leave you to fight them. I appreciate your wanting to defend me, but you have family here and mine is there. I would not feel right if you come with me and then I'd never know if you safely returned to this time again."

"Couldn't be that much to it," the old stallion grumbled. But he nosed her neck, and she felt his relief in his touch. He was brave, he was willing, but he did not truly wish to leave.

She knew all about the timer, however. There was no need to involve him or the others. It looked very easy when she saw the Friends use it, but she had never had reason to try until now because she had not known before that she had family. All she had to do was find them.

There was another problem, she realized, once she left the Others and returned to her little cell off the laboratory. They could read her thoughts, but she couldn't read theirs. They would know what she was planning. Or would they?

They weren't ever interested in what she wanted to think about, only in what they wanted her to think about. Otherwise, they were preoccupied with their own much more important concerns. She didn't think she'd be able to hide the revelation the Others had given her, but unlike everyone else, she wasn't concerned about the mating aspects of finding her people. She only wanted to be among others like her, to belong. Still, it would be best if she could make her move before the next interrogation.

If only she could read their minds, too! Then she'd know exactly how to time travel and where to find her people. Why was it she could understand the thought-talk of the Others and not that of the Friends? Why couldn't the probing work two ways? It was so unfair!

Then, looking up at the ceiling, she saw something looking back. An eye. A viewer that had never been there before, in the one space that they had given her to be her own. She groaned. Why was she surprised? But inside her anger began to burn. The more they tried to see her, the more they erased her. And she did not want to be erased, especially when she felt for the first time that she might be somehow enlarged when others like her taught her more about what she was, *why* she was, other than an object of study for the curiosity of the Friends.

She leaped from her cot and charged to her closed door, which she could not lock from the inside. As she stormed into the empty laboratory, looking for someone to complain to, not that it would do any good, she was startled to hear voices.

Not hear with her ears, exactly, but hear in the way she heard the Friends. The voices were inside her head, muttering and murmuring, even counting sometimes. She walked through the lab to the outer chamber where the great skein of water and energy twisted upward through the ceiling. She had observed enough to know that this was the power generator of the time device, and that it pierced the entire building and spread outward to catch the rains and downward, thrusting out into all of the waterways of the world.

Why? she wondered, and received a distracted answer. *"Because time and water flow, of course."* Four technicians tended the timer, calibrating, tabulating, charting, and making adjustments she didn't understand.

The person who answered her seemed to think that her question came from one of his colleagues. *"Interesting,"* she thought, unconsciously mimicking the response she often received from Akasa or Odus.

That, too, was taken to be the comment of one of the time technicians.

When they did see her, they ignored her without thinking about it. She had been among them since she was a baby. Unaccustomed to children, for the Friends did not seem to have any, they assumed she was as stupid and harmless now as she had been as a baby. During her toddler period, when she was extremely exploratory, she had been penned in a special environment with playthings that taught her skills the Friends found it useful for her to have, though she had learned far more than that. She had learned quickly to watch and listen but not touch any of their devices or instruments without being invited. Someone told her once not to touch things, and that was all it required. She stopped exploring tactilely beyond her play environment, and soon she was released from it.

So the technicians paid her no heed, something much to her advantage.

She noted that on the wall where all time and events were laid out in a sparkling mural of coded light, there was one area devoid of light or movement. In fact, a large X had been painted over it. It looked broken and incongruous next to the rest of the sleek equipment.

"Pity," the nearest technician muttered aloud, then turned his body very slightly to bounce his remarks off the technician beside him, if not to open an actual dialogue. "Too bad we can't send someone in there to repair it, but the Khleevi monsters caused great damage. We cannot arrive after the damage is done using our apparatus because it is broken beyond that time and we can't arrive before it's broken or risk meeting the monsters ourselves. The only way to do it would be by using one of the personal timers the nobles wear, but they'd never entrust one to a lowly technician."

Narhii wondered why that was.

"They wouldn't be able to stand the inconvenience of not being able to flit about from now till then till once upon a time as they choose. We run this entire system and yet when the new model became available from the homeworld, were we given any, even to study in case it needed repairs?"

"Not on your life!" a fellow technician answered.

Narhii found all of this very interesting. These fellows seemed to resent the noble Friends almost as much as she did.

Technician number 2 continued. After all the years she'd spent among them, Narhii had no clear idea of which one was which or what any of their names might be, if they had mates or interests aside from maintaining the time mechanism. The nobles, the scientists, were very colorful, bursting into alternate forms frequently and dressing in vivid colors and sweeping robes when in humanoid form. The technicians could have been siblings, and although some bore female secondary sexual characteristics, all had short hair, wore uniforms, and were of similar size. She saw the time technicians most frequently, but sometimes around the city she would see others repairing or installing other devices.

One of the females spoke up, "It would have made sense, when Grimalkin fell and was stripped of his timer, to allow us to study it so that we might produce more, but no, into Milady Akasa's jewel box it went, and there it has remained, neglected and useless."

"How do you know she put it in her jewel box?" one of the others asked.

"One of my batch sibs services her suite," the female answered.

Batch sib? Here was another mystery and where she least expected it, among the dull technicians. A sib would be a brother or sister but why "batch"? Why not simply family or group, or even litter, as some of the smaller animals produced?

Who was this Grimalkin and why was he stripped of his timer?

As if she had asked aloud, the female continued. "Shame about Grimalkin, really. I always liked him."

"Females do!" one of the males said.

"No, not that way. But sometimes when he was in trouble, he would switch to his cat form and lie beside me while I worked or rested. I found it very soothing. And his antics were entertaining. He annoyed the other nobles even more than they sometimes annoy us."

"Hush! That's heresy. The nobles are not annoying. We are merely inadequate to understand the nuances of their needs at times."

"Oh please! You lot from the last batch are insufferable now, believing everything they coded into you. You'll learn as you age and are around your prototypes more. They are so arrogant I sometimes think they created us to hold any humility that may have been part of their original characters."

"Nobles have no need for humility. They are infallible,"

the new batch lackey replied with a sincerity that the others, Narhii could tell, found pitiable.

"That's what I liked best about Grimalkin. He was not infallible. And it was unfair, his disgrace. He brought back the mutant, even though he had to steal her egg from her mother, who had saved his life, you know, and was his friend, before the twin was born. But they were angry that he didn't take both twins!"

"How do you know that?"

"My sib overheard Lady Akasa complaining about it. She laughed about how, since he was so devoted to that family and had left the other poor twin to grow up among them, the nobles had stripped him of his timer. As if that wasn't bad enough, they froze him in his alter form, even regressing the form so that he was presented as a juvenile feline to grow up with the twin."

Narhii ducked back into the laboratory, stunned by this information and needing time to digest it. Not only did she have people, she had a twin! And she had been stolen from a brave mother before she could be born.

She had to return to her people—*had to.* But the timer was useless beyond a certain point, and she gathered from the chronology of the technician's thoughts that she had been born after the damage, in the distant future. If only she could lay hands on Grimalkin's timer and learn how to use it, she would be able to return to her family, to her twin, and expose the disgraced noble, now her sister's cat, for what he was.

"Mu, there you are!" Odus said. "It is time to continue yesterday's session. But today we must probe a bit deeper."

chapter 9

No, Khorii!" Elviiz said, holding her back when she would have dived into the water. "You will not swim." He dragged her back into the shuttle, Khiindi a jump ahead of them. "The *wii-Balakiire* has an amphibious mode. If there are monsters, the vessel will be much less vulnerable than you are."

And though she seethed at her android brother's assumption of command over her actions, she had to admit, as the *wii-Balakiire* sped into the sea and submerged, that he was correct.

"Aunt Neeva and the rest of our people, especially those on the rescue teams, would be displeased if you perished," Elviiz said.

"What if the monster can attack vessels more easily than people and kills us all?" Khorii asked, still sulking a little.

"Then at least I will not have to bear their reproach," Elviiz answered, quite seriously. Of course, he was seldom anything *but* serious.

Even so, the *wii-Balakiire*, with guidance from Khorii's psychic sense of the location of Nanahomea and the others, brought them there quickly and with an unexpected benefit.

Mokilau, though covered with strange sores and bruises

and clearly shaken, floated beside Nanahomea while the remaining elders supported him.

At Khorii's insistence, Elviiz opened the underwater airlock and she swam out to join the LoiLoiKuans.

"Your ship made the monster release Mokilau," Nanahomea said. Khorii swam to the old mer man and gently applied her horn to his wounds, which healed instantly.

All underwater healing did not deplete her—just the plague, so far. Unlike the last time she used her horn to heal while inside the ocean, the water was not disease-infested, nor were any of the other people, so her horn's power localized to where it was most needed and restored Mokilau's body to its uninjured state.

The old man's white lashes raised, his chest heaved, and he grinned, then flipped in the water, took a brief swim, and returned clutching something. "A trophy," he said, flourishing a long green object that looked half fin and half frond. "I took a piece of its tail." With a bow that turned into a somersault, he proffered the object to Khorii. "I thought to keep this for my regalia, but the victory is truly yours, Korikori. Wear this proudly."

She took it, though she couldn't imagine accessorizing her shipsuit with it. "We cannot chase the monster and slay it," she told them. "You understand, my people are not aggressive, and we do not kill."

She thought it was rather too bad Khiindi couldn't assume her size and command of the shuttle temporarily. She hated leaving these people unprotected and at the mercy of this mysterious monster after everything else they had endured. Khiindi would have had no reservations about dispatching the creature, as he had demonstrated on the beach.

Nanahomea brushed her cheek with webbed fingers. "Child, you have done enough for us already. You must not bear the weight of our world on your shoulders when you already have a universe to heal. We can take care of ourselves against tangible enemies." She opened her other hand to reveal a blade. "We know how to hunt creatures larger than ourselves with the weapons our reef gives us." Some of the others held blades in their hands or brandished long branches of coral with pointed ends as spears or harpoons.

Mokilau looked doubtful. "It is larger than the biggest whale, larger than a school of whales. And it has as many mouths and suckers like a squid or octopus—also it makes a cloud around it as they do so that you see nothing but cloudy water before it is upon you, stinging like a thousand jellyfish until one of its mouths can bite you in half."

"So it will take more than one knife," another male elder said. "Maybe a good harpoon."

"Can you hide from it, stay away from it until we can find people with the technology and know-how to help you?" Khorii asked.

"Did I mention that the suckers are attached to tentacles, each like a giant fire eel, long enough to penetrate deep into crevasses?"

Exasperated by her inability to help and by Mokilau's escalating description of the horrible features of the sea beast, Khorii resorted to one of Uncle Joh Becker's expressions. "Mokilau, work with me, will you?" But when she touched his mind, she saw that the beast was much as he had described. She recalled her dream. "If you can evade this beast a short while longer, perhaps we can find you a new place to live, a safe place, with a healthy and friendly land species. Would such a solution be acceptable to you? I understand that you sent your children to Maganos because this world is dying."

"Do what you can," Nanahomea said. "We will try to evade the creature, as you say."

"But it is very hungry," Mokilau said. "The disease killed most of the sea's creatures, and there is little left for it—or us—to eat. I do not think it will content itself with sea-weed."

When the shuttle returned to the *Balakiire,* the other crew members read her quickly and examined the piece of sea monster with scientific curiosity.

Neeva put it under the microscope while Khaari hailed one of the other rescue ships about relaying a message back to Vhiliinyar to ask if asylum for the LoiLoiKuans was possible, if the *sii*-Linyaari would accept another species and, if not, if there was some other world with a suitable environment and no sea monsters where the LoiLoiKuans could find a new home.

Liriili had apparently been monitoring the transmission, because she was the next to appear on the com unit. "We are organizing some appropriate dried food to drop into the sea on LoiLoiKua," she said. "It will rehydrate on contact and provide nourishment."

"Probably it will mostly nourish the sea monster," Khorii said ruefully.

"Sea monsters must eat as well as sea persons," Liriili said in the more-Linyaari-than-thou tone for which she was widely known and disliked insofar as one Linyaari could dislike another. She signed off.

Melireenya gave Khorii a close-mouthed grin. "Perhaps if the monster has enough to supplement its current diet, it will be less interested in your friends. Snacking among non-grazing species is said to spoil the appetite."

Khorii rolled her eyes. Elviiz said seriously, and with some enthusiasm, "That may well be true, Melireenya! Thus far we are uncertain of the monster's dietary preferences. Perhaps Mokilau's assumption was incorrect and the monster is a vegetarian like us."

Khorii was not certain that periodic battery charges, which were Elviiz's main source of nourishment, could be counted as vegetables, but it was true he was no meat eater, so she didn't comment.

"Hmmm!" Neeva said. She had taken a thin slice of Mokilau's trophy and was examining it under her portable electron microscope. "I have never seen a cellular structure quite like this before."

She stepped aside as Khorii attempted to peer over her shoulder. "What do you think?"

Khorii put her eyes to the goggles and viewed the strange arrangement of particles—long threads, amorphous green shapes around aqua centers. It didn't make any sense to her, though it made her feel uneasy. *"I would rather die than say it aloud, Aunt, but my education has been interrupted by the plague. Elviiz is the one to ask."*

"Of course he is!" Neeva agreed. *"I should have had him look at this to begin with. He's been rather quiet, and I forgot he was there, I'm afraid."*

Khorii thought the truth was that, much as Elviiz looked like a Linyaari and wished to be considered one, he was not telepathic precisely because he was not organic. This had the odd effect of causing Linyaari who were not members of their immediate family to forget about him unless he kept reminding them, which he usually did.

It was so not his fault and so unfair that it made her feel protective of her brother, and she said more gently and humbly than she usually did when addressing him, "I can't make anything of it, Elviiz. What do you think?"

With a nod he stepped past her and, after a noncommittal look in the microscope, asked, "May I examine the specimen with my own equipment?"

To Khorii's annoyance he was asking Neeva's permission. Mokilau had given the monster trophy to her, not Neeva. But she didn't want to look petty in front of the *Balakiire*'s crew, and, besides, there was something about that trophy, other than the fact that it came from a horrible monster, that made her feel she didn't exactly want to carry it around in her treasure pack with her beaded bracelet.

Retreating with the specimen to one of the *Balakiire*'s cabins, Elviiz "ahemed" and "ahahed" and made other professorial noises as he analyzed the specimen, but then, suddenly, he let out a long hiss like an accidentally disconnected oxygen tube.

Khorii and Neeva crowded into the cabin's open doorway. "What?" Khorii asked.

"I am amazed to tell you I cannot precisely say," Elviiz said, "but I think we must take this back to Jalonzo at the laboratory on Corazon. These are unlike any normal cells of any creature I have ever examined."

"A sea monster isn't exactly a normal creature," Khorii said. "And the one Mokilau described sounded like a whole zooful of horror."

"Precisely," Elviiz said. "And that may well be what it is. Some of the cells resemble those of ordinary sea creatures. But some of them look to me to be something nothing so large can possibly be."

"I know you're enjoying the suspense," Khorii said. "But we would appreciate enlightenment as soon as you can force yourself to stop being mysterious."

"But I'm not," he said. "And though I don't think it is possible, I could be wrong about this, but the cells appear to be not cells as we know them but similar in structure to those of a virus—but much, much larger."

chapter 10

For the first time, Narhii felt like kicking and scream-
ing, fighting Odus off before he could ask more stupid
questions or do anything else to invade the little she had
been left of who she really was. She was so close to—no,
better not think that.

But Odus said, tugging her into the lab's interrogation
cell, "Now, now, Mu, we'll have none of that. Our work is
becoming increasingly urgent as you learn your feelings as a
young female."

But inside the room, Akasa sat behind the table, an array
of colorful objects spread before her. "All the more reason,
Odus, why I should take over the—please pardon the expression—lion's share of the questioning. You may observe
from behind the mirror if you wish to learn more of females,
but Mu's reaction to your demonstration yesterday clearly
indicates she needs to begin her indoctrination into the mys-
teries of our mutual gender at a far less intense level than
you anticipated."

"But who better to teach a female the meaning of her gender than her opposite?" he argued.

"Obviously, someone more similar. And, pardon me,
with more finesse. Run along now."

Growling under his breath, Odus left. Akasa rose, exited the cell, and checked the observation chamber. She gave a sharp nod of satisfaction when she returned, then sat herself opposite her subject. "As you realize, dear, we have endeavored in our inquiries to elicit your natural and spontaneous responses, those instinctive to your species. However, I feel at this critical juncture in your development, it is time to provide a modicum of guidance and instruction, to answer questions that may puzzle you. The portion of your physical and psychological structure supplied by the Others may be instinctively and biologically guided; but you are also, according to your genetic coding, composed of the same stuff as we are, and therefore would have subtler, more sophisticated triggers for your primal functions. Do you understand?"

Narhii nodded, tentatively, "I think so, a little."

"Therefore, I thought we might start by showing you some of the feminine accoutrements I and other females of my species enjoy and see if you relate to them as well. Do you find that any of these objects attract you?"

The objects in question were a collection of long, bright scarves in colors of the sunset, delicate blossoms that looked real but had no scent and, when she touched them, after making sure she had permission, Narhii found were made instead of some soft fabric.

"Pick them up, hold them against your cheek," Akasa prompted. "See how transparent? Like an insect wing."

Narhii did as instructed and didn't have to feign enjoyment. The scarves and flowers were lovely to look at and to touch. Magnified wonder was at the forefront of her thoughts when she asked, "Is this the stuff you wear every day, ma'am?"

"Oh yes. My robes are of the finest and most gossamer materials."

She permitted Narhii to touch the skirt of her outer robe. "Will I ever wear anything like that—I mean, is it something I will do as I grow older?"

Akasa laughed triumphantly. How much better a female understood the feminine need for beauty, color, texture—and how these qualities aroused other needs. "Certainly, my dear, you may do so any time you're inclined. Your earlier developmental stages were too—active—for such opulence, but it is time for you to learn the refinement that will teach you the proper care and use of these embellishments."

Narhii had an idea, quickly concealed as she clapped her hands in delight. "Oh, may I wear some now? Robes like yours I mean—and those shiny things on your fingers, ears, and neck—what are those? May I have some of those, too?"

"Greedy little thing once you've awakened to the possibilities, aren't you?" Akasa said with a chuckle that was almost fond. She felt confirmed in her belief that females were much the same no matter the species—bipedal females at least, with a modicum of the proper genetic material. For the first time, she felt she was beginning to understand this curious and often sulky child. "I suggest we adjourn to my quarters. There you may see the array of my raiment and I will help you choose what might best suit you. You may also choose a bauble or two from among my jewels, if it isn't something too precious. If it is, perhaps we can have copies created for you or something even more suitable for your own age and coloring that we design together."

Narhii clapped again and hopped a little as she followed Akasa's sweeping skirts through the laboratory, the time chamber, the corridor, out the building, across the street, which today was paved with some golden substance, and down another lane. In a few strides Akasa stopped at the ornate entrance of a building whose every surface was decorated with what looked like more jewels, certainly some tiny bits and pieces of colored stuff that glittered in the sun.

There seemed to be many rooms within that had no purpose except to be cleaned by the technicians who were doing

so and to hold elegant furnishings. Narhii had difficulty de-
termining the purpose of many of those as well.

For that matter, though she saw several cleaning and serving technicians, she was unsure why Akasa or the others
needed them. They could change their own forms and those
of their homes and belongings at will. Could they not simply
change them from a disorderly or soiled version to one that
was not?

Picking up her thought, Akasa said, "My dear, we cannot
be expected to exhaust ourselves with trivialities. Besides, it
gives these other beings a purpose in life. Here we are."

A place on the wall looked exactly like Akasa's own
highly ornamented eyes without the nose between them. The
center of the pupil was an obsidian disk, the outer iris lavender, purple and aqua rays set in an alabaster oval surrounded
by a spiked trimming of cobalt with a long curl extending
from each side. The eyes grew larger, then swirled open to
reveal the room beyond.

Akasa, apparently fatigued by her unusual exertion, flung
open her wardrobe and flipped her fingers toward it. "Go
play, little one. Bring out your selections to show me, and I
will help you decide if they are suitable or not. The jewel
box is in there, too, and my cosmetics. We should do something with your hair. White is such a bore."

Narhii didn't have to feign the appreciative noises she
made at the display of colorful garments, dainty slippers,
veils, head wrappings, more scarves, and flowers. All swayed
from their display racks as if in a breeze.

"There's a draft?" Narhii asked.

"The ventilation circulates through here to keep my things
fresh and fluid," Akasa said. "Some of the fabrics are organic and require aeration."

"It looks wonderful," Narhii said, and it did.

Akasa led her to the cosmetic table, above which was a

huge mirror. As they approached it, the frame of the mirror glowed with flattering pinkish light.

Akasa sat on the padded bench in front of the table so that she faced Narhii. "Kneel," she commanded in an imperious tone. Then remembering she was assuming the role of Narhii's female mentor and hopeful confidante, she continued. "Please. I wish to prepare your face and hair to form a suitable background for the splendors I am about to share."

Twisting backward, she reached for several pots. With smooth strokes of soft fingers, she applied colors to Narhii's brows, eyes, cheeks, and mouth. Narhii still looked like herself, only, with darkened brows and eyes and dark pink on her mouth and cheeks, more vivid. Akasa inspected her, tilting her chin this way and that. "Still washed out," she pronounced. She twisted again and opened a drawer, revealing a number of other jeweled pots. Selecting one with a blue gemstone surrounded by golden butterflies, she opened it, flinging the lid unceremoniously onto the counter before turning back to Narhii. "Blue will bring out your eyes, I think," she said, dipping her fingers into the pot and smearing them with cobalt.

And without asking Narhii's opinion, Akasa then wiped her fingers on the side of Narhii's head, pulling them down the length of a side strand of hair. Critically she said, "Well, that's a little livelier though you still look as though you've snow for blood."

She used another of her ointments and a square of pristine white silken stuff to clean her fingers, then sighed heavily and said, "You look around and select what you like best and hang it by the door. I am going to rest while you play, but I'll be in the outer room to critique your choices when you're ready."

"Oh, thank you, ma'am," Narhii said, appearing at the door with several garments in her hands. "If I could change myself as you can, I'd change my colors and patterns all the time."

"How refreshing you can be, dear. This is an entirely new aspect of your personality development. I believe my innovative approach is helping us make tremendous progress toward our goal."

Fortunately, Narhii had already submerged herself amid the colors and prints, skirts, tunics, robes, and gowns. She picked the ones that most profoundly attracted her, collecting them as she approached the end of the room, where a large transparent chest with many compartments, lit from within, displayed Akasa's jewelry.

Narhii carried her garment selections back to the door and hung them, peering around the corner. Akasa was stretched out on her bed, snoring robustly for a creature who prided herself on her delicacy.

Narhii slipped on the closest of her selections, a light blue-violet gown, and then, looking into the mirror at the gown, which was too short for her since she was already taller than Akasa, made a show of studying herself, tilting her head to the side, and saying, "It needs something *more*." As she had sometimes overheard Akasa and other females do when assessing each other's costumes before or during some social event. Apparently it hadn't occurred to any of them *then* to introduce her to the realm of feminine finery.

But she had realized such a long time ago, when still quite small, that the Friends only gave her things or rewarded her when they wanted something from her in return. She rather took it for granted that was how it was supposed to be, except that the Others weren't like that. Of course, they had nothing to give but peace, healing, affection, comfort. No silks or jewels though. She sighed. Even the Others withheld knowledge from her that was hers by right and that they knew she had longed for her entire life.

Nobody really cared about her for her own sake, and she didn't care about them either.

Before Akasa could refresh herself enough to interfere, Narhii went to the huge jewelry chest and began searching for the time device. She expected it would look much like the one Akasa wore, though perhaps less gem-encrusted.

As she pawed through the box, she slipped on bangles, a necklace that caught in her mane, a tiara that teetered above her horn, to make it seem as if she were truly accessorizing instead of hunting. It was hard not to be distracted by the color and gleam, rippling ribbons of shining stones or metal links so fine the piece looked solid but infinitely fluid.

The jewels dazzled her to such an extent that, when she started to replace a fistful of bracelets in a drawer before closing it, she was startled to discover she had been holding the timer all along.

It was made for a wrist much larger than hers and flopped about even when she fastened it on the smallest setting. Now that she had it, what did she do with it? How would she get to that safe time when her parents lived in the world and somewhere she had a twin her own age?

How did one get past that broken time when the monsters destroyed the machine? The timers didn't depend on the machine, apparently, but she didn't want to end up among the monsters. Nor did she want to go back to her own birth so she could grow up with her loving parents and sister. She had been erased enough as it was, thanks very much. She wasn't about to erase further the life she already had lived. For better or worse, it was her life and what made it her own, and she wanted to know about it. She seemed to have learned some useful skills after all. Like finding things she wasn't supposed to find and finding out other things people didn't want her to know.

Hmmm. There was one person quite near who could tell

her how to use the timer. If Akasa would only start mumbling to herself the way the technicians had . . .

She stopped and listened, Akasa's jewels and silks draped all over her slight form. She listened hard. Akasa still slept, her breathy snores audible through the wardrobe door. But some knowledge of Narhii's activities remained in her dreams and thoughts. "*I should get up,*" she thought drowsily. "*Not that the mutant child will do any harm that can't be quickly mended, and she was enjoying herself so much. If only Odus and the other males realized that one pleasure is so conducive to seeking others, even if they are quite different, they would be heaping us females with little gifts and agreeable experiences so often we'd never get any work done.*"

Narhii was surprised that Akasa wasn't even concerned about the timer. Why not? Was it broken or disabled in some way?

"*Gracious me, and I am awfully gracious today, aren't I?*" Akasa's thoughts continued, the heaps of gifts and experiences and fine foods evaporating in her semi–dream state. "*I forgot all about Grimalkin's timer. But that's all right. I doubt the child would even recognize it for what it is and if she did, she wouldn't understand how to operate it. One does need to focus on something particular in the time when one wishes to be in the place where one wishes to be prior to activating it. And how would she do that? She's unfamiliar with anything other than what she has always known here. She'll be all right.*"

Narhii frowned at the timer. Yes, she would be all right indeed if only she could overcome the problem Akasa had just brought up. How *would* she find the right time. Maybe she could visualize people instead of a place—or, well, how much could a meadow change anyway? She'd visualize the meadow and the descendants of the Others who looked like them—and also males and females like herself only taller and—someone who looked like herself. Her twin. She pressed the area on the timer that Akasa's visualization of the device had shown.

For a long time nothing happened, then she saw a tiny red light. What did that mean?

Obligingly, Akasa's thought drifted back to her, *"All the child would see on the timer if she accidentally activated it is the red light that shows that one or more of the variables in her visualization is not viable. She won't know to eliminate them one at a time until the timer works."*

Narhii's smile to herself was an echo of the one Odus's face showed when he was feeling particularly pleased with himself. It didn't usually mean anyone else would be similarly pleased. She had what she wanted. She had somehow gone, with the dawning of her telepathic power, from being the manipulated to the manipulator.

Now, then. What would she eliminate?

The Others, the Meadow—that was safe, because if the Others were there, the monsters couldn't be and if the monsters were anywhere near, the Others would protect her until she could escape with the timer, she knew.

And she longed to meet her parents more than she could say. They must have missed her, somehow. Her mother must have realized she should have had two children instead of one. Narhii desperately wanted to reclaim her parents but in doing so—wouldn't a twin complicate things? Perhaps the twin had died or was somewhere else? That would be convenient, actually. It would give Narhii a chance to have her parents all to herself. After all, the other twin had had them for six *ghaanyi*.

It was Narhii's turn.

chapter 11

Every world between LoiLoiKua and Paloduro reported itself clear of plague. Plant species regenerated in the cleansed garden areas, and Liriili's teams were vigilant. After a consultation with the other rescue teams, they all agreed that the next emergency was to determine the exact nature of the sea monster and find a new safe harbor for the LoiLoiKuans.

The Linyaari Council, after consulting with the Ancestors and the *sii*-Linyaari, and with the cooperation of House Harakamian's resources, agreed to provide a provisional home in the sea of Vhiliinyar for Nanahomea's people, including the poopuus from Maganos Moonbase.

In the meantime, the *Balakiire* returned to Corazon. There Elviiz and Jalonzo could further analyze the sea monster specimen and its viral structure. They wished to learn if such abnormalities in the beast's basic composition might be, as they expected, mutations caused by the impact of the plague on the environment.

Khorii was looking forward to seeing her friends in Corazon as much as she had been to seeing the crew of the *Balakiire*. While it was good to be among her own kind and to be able to thought-talk at will, it was also good to be among others of a similar developmental stage to her own. She also enjoyed the comfort of the extended family atmosphere that Abuelita had helped impose on the city, becoming a surrogate grandmother for so many orphans.

As the *Balakiire* docked, the huge cargo hatch of the *Mana* opened and Jaya, a tiny figure in the opening, waved something in the air and jumped up and down to catch the attention of the other ship. Well, mostly, Khorii sensed, Jaya wanted to attract *her* attention. The girls met on the walkway outside the terminal.

"A message came from Lord Hafiz," Jaya told her excitedly. Uncle Hafiz was the founder of the parent corporation with which the Krishna-Murti Company, owners of the *Mana,* subcontracted. Since Jaya was only slightly older in human years than Khorii, Uncle Hafiz would have retired to the Moon of Opportunity around the time she was born, so Jaya could not have met him, but she would have heard of him. Uncle Hafiz's eccentricities and excesses, his somewhat piratical business style and his therefore amazing altruism (which came into play, some said, only after Hafiz met Mother), had made him legendary.

Khorii was curious as to what the message might be, but she was fairly certain that if it were bad news, she'd have known about it sooner. Corazon and the *Mana* were much farther removed from the relay than the *Balakiire* had been.

But if it was good news, why hadn't the *Balakiire* been contacted directly? Perhaps the specialized physician healers on Vhiliinyar had discovered a true cure for the plague strain infecting Mother and Father?

Jaya held up a printout. "Actually, the message is from Captain Becker, confidential to you, and was only forwarded by Lord Hafiz, but still . . . I'm sorry, I couldn't help seeing what it said, nor could Captain Bates. We didn't mean to look, but it's a bit hard when it comes over the com unless it's encrypted. I don't know what the *White Star* is anyway."

"It's a luxury liner from Dinero Grande with the Spandard name *Estrella Blanca*," Khorii said. "It was the first plague vessel we encountered, and we boarded it before we had any idea there was a plague. Captain Becker and the cats both almost died then. But my parents and I were able to heal them and cleanse the ship—at least, all the parts we came into contact with. Captain Becker claimed it as salvage and hauled it off to a private asteroid where he keeps some of his salvage." She shook her head, half-amused that Uncle Joh was still protecting his tainted merchandise after everything that had happened. He had to know that sooner or later the ship would need to be returned and its occupants, of whom Elviiz had downloaded a passenger and crew roster, officially declared dead and their bodies and belongings, once deemed safe, returned to what was left of their families. Her guess was that Uncle Joh wanted to keep his possession of the ship and its location quiet until he was out of quarantine and would have some negotiating room with the administrative remnants of the Federation. He had made himself and his ship quite useful during the plague until he was stricken with the mutant strain of the plague carried by her parents. To his way of thinking, he would be entitled to a certain leeway where the law was concerned once law was again enforceable.

She smiled when she read the message. Uncle Joh might be intent on protecting his interests, but he wanted to help her help others, too. "I think you got the message for a reason, Jaya," she said. "Uncle Joh knows I trust you, and he has decided to trust the *Mana* with a mission. I'll need to speak to Neeva and the others first, but if Uncle Joh is correct, this should help us decide once and for all if the plague has ended without me having to revisit every single infected planet in the galaxy."

Jaya nodded, "Yeah, I can see where something that would save that much time would be worth doing. Captain Bates and I will start the checklist for takeoff."

While they were talking, Khiindi and Elviiz had sped off toward the dormitory. Elviiz was anxious to consult with Jalonzo about the specimen. Khiindi no doubt was equally anxious to consult with Abuelita about cat treats.

"Where's Hap?" Khorii asked. The tall light-haired boy who looked like a Linyaari minus the horn usually came out to see what was happening when a vessel landed.

Jaya frowned. "Making some repairs. We've had some unusual damage to the ship since you've been gone and—other things, too. I'll tell you about it later."

Melireenya, Khorii, and Neeva passed them, and Mikaaye galloped out to meet his mother, who caught him up in a hug, as did her crewmates. As Khorii watched, he glanced her way and waved before returning his attention to his mother.

She had almost forgotten how wonderful the common room smelled. Even for a grazer, the smells of the spices Abuelita used were heady and luscious.

For Jaya's sake, Jalonzo's grandmother had learned Indian cooking as well as traditional dishes of her region, so there were chapattis and nan bread as well as tortillas and so-papillas, curries as well as dishes flavored with chilies, cheese, and mole sauce, and the air was filled with cinnamon and coriander, ginger, tumeric, curry, and chocolate.

Sesseli met her, carrying Khiindi, who was licking his whiskers, having already extorted tribute from the kitchen. "Elviiz went into the lab with Jalonzo," the little girl told her. "He wouldn't let Khiindi or me come in. He treats me like a baby."

"Don't be offended, Sess. He treats me like a baby, too, and has ever since *he* was a baby, or as babyish as he ever was. Any more incidents while we were gone?"

Sesseli nodded. "Yes, but we're getting kind of used to them now. Jalonzo and Mikaaye sleep in the lab, and when he leaves, Jalonzo backs up his work with copies of his notes and samples of his latest formulas. But Abuelita says that at night the square is busier than it was during the daytime before the plague. And people still think they see moms and dads and grown-up kids who died wandering around at night. Jaya and I sleep in your room, with Hap next door. Captain Bates and Abuelita are just across the hall. But you can have your room back now if you want."

"I don't think I'll be here that long. But the *Balakiire* crew is due for their rest, so they may join you. You'll feel safe with them around, won't you?"

For an answer, Sesseli gave her an appraising look. "Are you trying to tell me that wherever you and Khiindi are going, I can't go with you?"

"It wouldn't be a good idea, Sess," Khorii said, squatting so she wasn't *talking* down to the child. "It's going to be really gross. It's another graveyard, really, except there was nowhere to bury the bodies. There are all these dead people floating around. Only now they'll be decomposing, and it will stink—"

"You can purify the air," Sesseli pointed out.

"Yes, I can, but we're also going there to make sure the plague is all gone."

"But Khiindi is going?"

Khorii nodded.

"And Jaya and Hap?"

She nodded again.

"Elviiz?"

"I'm not sure. He may want to stay here and help Jalonzo. We found something weird on LoiLoiKua he thinks may be linked to the plague."

"How weird?"

"A sea monster," she said simply.

"I want to see it, too!" Sesseli said.

"No you don't. It almost ate someone while we were there. There are teams heading there now to evacuate the rest of the poopuus' relatives."

"You never want me to have any fun. You guys hog it all," Sesseli said. Khorii thought she was growing up. And her telekinetic talent could be very useful.

"That's not it, Sess. But there are so many scary things happening now, we don't know how to keep you safe."

"I'm as safe as you are," the little girl said."And Khorii, I lost everybody once when I was a baby. I don't want to be left alone again."

"Okay, then, if it's all right with Captain Bates and Jaya you can come."

Although Khorii knew Elviiz had very strong motivation for staying behind to help analyze the specimen, she hadn't really expected him to do so. He had always considered it his top priority to be with her their entire lives. He was always in her way, always lecturing and reprimanding her, always getting to learn and do things before she could.

So she was surprised when he said, "It is a dead asteroid and all of the people are dead. The mission requires your particular skills and perhaps those you possess as an organic Linyaari. You will have Jaya, Hap, Captain Bates, Khiindi Kaat and, if you need something heavy moved, Sesseli's telekinesis to assist you. My skills can be put to better use here. If you do not return within the time frame we have allotted for the mission, however, I will be with the *Balakiire* looking for you. However, Mikaaye will accompany you in my stead."

She snorted. "I'm sure that won't be necessary. I can look after myself." But she felt a little lost nevertheless. They both knew that while that was true under normal circumstances, Elviiz had pulled her out of many situations she couldn't handle alone. She didn't even know Mikaaye though he seemed nice enough. But if Melireenya was willing to part with her son for the length of the journey, Khorii could hardly object. Besides, he would give Hap another male to keep him company.

The only unsettling thing that happened before she left was when she and Khiindi climbed the stairs to her rooftop garden. It had been destroyed, the plants uprooted and the soil mounded in the middle of the roof. Khorii spent a rather soothing hour or two taking the soil back into place and re-planting what could be saved. Many of the mature plants had been broken or squashed, and traces of some sticky aqua material laced the area. She collected as much as she could and took it to Elviiz.

"A parting gift for your research," she said, explaining how she had discovered it. "Looks a bit like those viral cells in the monster slide, doesn't it?"

"Yes, and Khorii?"

"Yes?"

"I will do my best to make sure your garden is not destroyed again."

"Thank you, Brother," she said, and laid her horn against his forehead in parting.

chapter 12

Although an orphan, Marl Fidd was not without connections. He had learned early on that the way to get
what he wanted was to win friends and influence people,
even if he meant to lose the same friends after he influenced
them one way or another to part with something they had
that he wanted.

Then there were his other friends, the ones from whom he
would never dream of taking anything because they'd kill
him. These were friends who wanted something he had. His
skills were numerous, including expertise with demolitions,
weapons, and with disabling a wide variety of security devices and programs. What none of these more dangerous as-
sociates realized, however, was that Marl possessed more
than the standard array of qualifications for someone his
age.

His truest and best talent, and the one he figured would
take him to the top of the criminal heap in time to retire
while he was still young and pretty enough to enjoy the fruits
of his crimes, was his telepathy. Very few people knew about
it, and it wasn't something he advertised. Like the element of
surprise in warfare, it was far less useful when others knew
about it.

But the truth was, he could charm the birds from the trees if he wanted to, which he didn't most of the time since the kind of birds that sat in trees to begin with tended to be boringly short on cash, credits, negotiable bonds, or other liquid assets.

The criminal community of Corazon, like the general population, had been much diminished by the plague, to the extent that Marl had the jail all to himself. Marl found this disappointing to begin with as it gave him no chance to widen his galactic contacts with those in his chosen career field.

The food wasn't bad. However, after months of feeding himself into a butterball because there was nothing else to do, he decided to diet. Getting healthy food was no problem, since the old woman who cooked for the jail saved her goodies for the kiddies and didn't spoil inmates. She made what he did get tasty. Since nobody wasted any wine on him either, he had a chance to replace the expensive vintages that had been flowing through his veins for the last few months with regular blood cells instead. It wasn't fun, but he had no choice, and besides, all that funny business on the ship with the moving bits of things smacked a bit of the DTs. He exercised as much as possible in his cell.

However, the rest of the time was spent improving his interpersonal relationships with his guards. This was aided a bit by the much-diminished communications networks. Normally young people assigned boring tasks would have been on their mobcoms, called holas here, with their friends. But the channels that had been reestablished were fewer and weaker than they had been before, and without the same range. Casual use was no longer allowed, and all channels were monitored. So the kids were bored and in need of diversion, which Marl was all too willing to provide.

The younger guards, mostly husky boys except for the occasional sweet young thing who brought him meals, were secretly a bit impressed with a desperado such as he. When they found bossing him around or bullying him unsatisfying and realized they were outclassed, he would obligingly teach them a few moves. Two of the boys returned the favor by giving him Spandard lessons. His telepathy made him a quick study, then he could work on his older guards.

These geezers were less gullible than the younger guards but were also more comfortable around people of Marl's persuasion. Cops spent as much of their time with criminals as they did with other cops, after all.

Montoya, who had to be at least a hundred years old, started out answering every request or complaint from Marl with a story about who had lost how much in the plague and how it should have been Marl instead. He took it upon himself to scold Marl so fiercely about trying to rob the warehouse on Rio Boca that his dentures rattled.

Marl went through a routine that ended with his being tearfully remorseful but retaining an edge of defiance, not overdoing it for the skeptical old coot. He wanted to give an impression of himself as a potentially redeemable punk. As his own facility with Spandard increased, he asked the old man questions about his own losses, what was happening in the city, how it had been before and how it had changed since the plague. The more he and Montoya talked, the more he convinced his jailer that he truly wanted to change, to find a useful and valuable place in the new structure society was assuming.

The guard, as bored as the kids and, furthermore, lost without his fifth wife, his former wives, and all of the children and grandchildren who had succumbed to the plague, became increasingly willing to bring in new bits of news, even photos and films, to show Marl and discuss with him.

Jail was altogether a more educational experience than Maganos Moonbase had been.

Best of all, the nights were as peaceful as the days.

Nothing moved without an easily apparent reason for doing
so. All in all, Marl felt that Khorii and the *Mana*'s crew had
truly rescued him by bringing him to this nice, safe prison
where he could regroup and plan his next moves. That didn't
mean he forgave them, of course, or that they would be left
out of his plans for the future. Cozy as his cell was, he had
no intention of remaining there.

The day after Montoya told him that the *Mana* and her
crew had departed for a mission, leaving behind one ship
and three females from Khorii's pacifist race, Marl waited
for nightfall, then made his move.

Hafiz Harakamian now enjoyed complex acts of interspe-
cies philanthropy almost as much as he had once enjoyed the
challenge of cutthroat commerce. He consulted with the
Linyaari Council on the proposed project to help the endangered LoiLoiKuans. Since much of the Council was already
engaged in the plague-relief efforts, the conference was conducted by com relay. Finding his customary com screen a bit
restrictive for such conferences, Hafiz employed an enjoy-
able bauble he had customized for the purpose. It was a
globe two meters in diameter that hovered and spun in front
of his desk when needed and retreated into the purple, saffron, and aqua silk tented ceiling of his office when not in
use.

Its surface was split into cells, and at the top of each was
the name and location of the communicant. During the conference, the cell of each speaker enlarged so that the speaker
appeared life size on the surface of the globe. The other cells
scrolled past in succession above, below, and beside the dominant cell, so that Hafiz could see the effect of the current remarks on each conference member. If someone made an
audible aside or showed a strong reaction, their cell enlarged
beside that of the speaker. If two people were engaged in a
debate, their enlarged cells appeared side by side.

Hafiz was thrilled with his own ingenuity and had demanded regular teleconferences with his consultants, employees, and subcontractors since acquiring and modifying the globe. If only the intergalactic relay system could be made to function as smoothly, all would be perfect. Unfortunately at the present time, while it was reasonably reliable among planets and moons, it was far less satisfactory for communication with vessels in transit unless they were very near a stationary unit.

However, for the most part, it had been useful in keeping Aari and Acorna in touch with Khorii's progress in plague detection and the broader rescue effort. The *Condor*'s com unit served to connect the remote quarantined area with Hafiz's system.

At present Aari and Acorna, Captain Becker, and Maak peered out of one of the cells to interpret for the *sii*-Linyaari. These ugly multiple-horned creatures appeared in another cell. A com unit located on their favorite offshore basking place in a bay near where Acorna and the others were quarantined displayed their unfortunate and rather hostile-appearing visages.

"Would these LoiLoiKuans not prefer it if we eradicated the monster so they could remain in their own ocean?" Hafiz asked Neeva.

"Perhaps. However, the planet is in a moribund solar system as it is, and for that reason the adults have been separated from the children. Resettling them on a more vital world would allow what is left of the families to reunite."

"Ah, so terraforming is out of the question," Hafiz said.

"So is eradicating the sea beast," said Liriili sanctimoniously. "Do not forget, Lord Hafiz, that we Linyaari do not practice eradication of other species."

"Except for Khleevi?" Karina asked sweetly from her husband's side.

"We did not exactly eradicate the Khleevi," Liriili replied, "although we did permit the use of a defensive weapon, which does not violate our principles. However, as you know quite well, Lord Hafiz, we simply permitted the Khleevi to eradicate themselves."

"Ahh," Hafiz replied, pretending to study the fistful of rings on his right hand. "As you say, Madame." Although Liriili was his and almost everyone else's least-favorite Linyaari, she had demonstrated a talent for administering the nitpicking details of rebuilding the plague-decimated societies so he was inclined to accord her a measure of respect. "So, no terraforming, no eradication. Perhaps a dam or a seawall."

Neeva cleared her throat. "The beast is apparently large enough to destroy any such barrier between it and its prey. And then there would be the difficulty of installing such a barrier."

Hafiz nodded his understanding. "Even so," he said. "Therefore, relocation."

"Yes," she said. "Khorii thought perhaps the *sii*-Linyaari might host them in Vhiliinyar's sea. Of course, we also need permission from the Council and particularly from the more traditional members of our race, who wish to preserve Vhiliinyar as a sacred haven for our species alone—and the *sii*-Linyaari of course."

"Of course," Hafiz agreed.

An especially clever part of his device, a stroke of genius really, was that it could usually take visual clues in the form of the body language of telepathic beings such as the Linyaari (and, much more rarely than she liked to believe, his own Karina) to determine who was having intensive nonverbal discussions with whom. Aari and the *sii*-Linyaari were now engaged in such a discussion.

After a moment, Aari said aloud, "The *sii*-Linyaari wish me to say that their sea has not, as they had hoped, been returned to its original size, which would make it easier for them to entertain guests. They feel that the sea cannot accommodate another sentient species for an extended period of time. But of course, they are sympathetic to the plight of their fellow mer folk and feel they could manage to host them on an emergency basis, so long as the refugees bear in mind the ancient proverb that guests, like dead fish, begin to stink after three days."

"Colorfully expressed indeed," Hafiz said, inclining his turban in the direction of the ugly creatures.

Yiitir, the distinguished Linyaari historian, said, "I would just like to interject that although we ourselves are a pacifist people, the *sii*-Linyaari do not necessarily share our philosophy."

"Point taken," said Kiiri, the current administrator of Vhiliinyar. "I fear that the people who wish Vhiliinyar to remain totally Linyaari, with the exception of our esteemed guests from the *Condor,* of course, do object to another species among us, even if the *sii*-Linyaari do not."

"However," interjected Naaya, administrator of narhii-Vhiliinyar, "the people of narhii-Vhiliinyar have chosen to live here as a more outwardly focused culture, and our seas, not yet fully stocked with the plant and animal species that make them a viable habitat, have no *sii*-Linyaari. If Uncle Hafiz could give our seas priority in our ongoing terraforming process, we may be the ideal new home for the LoiLoiKuans. While they are not Linyaari and are more humanoid than we are, from what Khorii and Neeva say, they seem to be peacefully inclined."

Many heads bobbed in assent to this plan, and murmurs of approval swirled around the globe.

"An excellent notion," Hafiz said. "Now then, for the details of the transfers . . ."

But at that moment, the screen focusing on the *sii*-Linyaari suddenly frothed with foam and flashing tails until for a moment Hafiz feared it might have fallen into the water. But with eyes from all across the universe watching from their cells on his globe, the froth suddenly cleared, the tails were exchanged for heads, and two *sii*-Linyaari surfaced and hoisted something colorful and glittering but limp and sopping wet, onto the basking rock.

All cells ceased movement as, in the central one, the gaudy object sat up, revealing itself to be a girl clad in bright but dripping robes and a great deal of what appeared to Hafiz's shrewdly appraising eye to be quite precious jewelry. Her face was streaked with color and her white mane with a ribbon of blue dye.

She looked distressed at seeing the com camera, and said something in Linyaari that Aari automatically translated as, "Oh, no, I thought that in this time I'd be free at last of being spied upon!"

"Who are you, youngling, and how did you come to emerge from the sea?" Kiiri asked.

Karina reached out and squeezed Hafiz's hand. Her cheeks flushed with joy and triumph, her bountiful bosom heaving excitedly, she spoke. "Acorna, dear, and Aari, you will recall my prediction? I told you that you'd be seeing your daughter within the week and here she is, right on schedule!"

chapter 13

Khorii had imagined that without Elviiz or Marl aboard, life on the *Mana* would be more peaceful than it had been on the journey to Corazon. Mikaaye was quieter than either of them and seemed willing to do his part without objection or insisting on improving each and every procedure.

Their first shift out was so uneventful and pleasant that by the time Jaya replaced Captain Bates at the helm, Khorii felt rather restless. Sesseli played in the corridor with Khiindi, the ship's kittens, and a piece of Captain Bates's beading cord. Hap was still demonstrating the intricacies of the engine room to Mikaaye. Khorii felt rather superfluous.

Captain Bates, who relinquished the pilot's seat, lingered on the bridge.

"I've got it, Captain, really," Jaya said. "If I have any trouble, I'll be sure and wake you."

"I know, Jaya," their former teacher said. "It's just that I don't need a lot of sleep and with everything going so well—"

"You feel at loose ends, too, Captain?" Khorii asked.

Asha Bates's hazel eyes snapped open, then hooded as she drawled, "Yeaaah, loose ends. Exactly, Khorii. Come with me, please. I have an idea."

Khorii was surprised when the captain activated the lights in her quarters to reveal that Jaya's parents' quarters, which Jaya insisted the captain take since it placed her closest to the bridge, had been expanded by removing the bulkhead between it and the room formerly occupied by the first mate. Jaya remained in her old quarters across the corridor from the captain's. She had lived there while her parents were alive, and Khorii knew it helped her feel closer to the life she had shared with them.

A beaded curtain with the image of a many-armed dancer flowed like a waterfall between the captain's and first mate's spaces. Except for replacing the double berth, Captain Bates had left Jaya's parents' quarters much as they had been, but the first mate's quarters, beyond the curtain, were another story. The berth had been removed in favor of a table bolted to the bulkhead and deck. Cabinets with small transparent drawers were bolted to the bulkheads from the deck to overhead. Khorii recognized some of the cabinets from the bead store.

"The *Mana* is an older vessel, Khorii, built in the days when hard copy charts and maps were sometimes used to supplement the information provided by the ship's computers. Our space fleets are all modeled on the naval and merchant marine fleets of old Terra, with a similar command structure, similar language and nomenclature and also, on merchant vessels like this one, remnants in the architecture of what were once considered essential features on sailing ships. Like this map case." She patted the top of the case, which held a rack of pliers, scissors, and wire. "But we don't need paper maps these days, and manual navigation instruments are totally anachronistic when you're among the stars instead of looking up at them. The mate was using the case to store her jewelry, brass for her uniforms, that sort of thing. I added some smaller compartments and—"

She opened the top drawer to show stones and large beads

and other special components neatly arrayed by color. The storage tab on each drawer displayed the color contained by that drawer.

"I hope to collect more as we travel, Khorii. I had most of my stones in my kit already—Steve Reamer, who used to teach jewelry making to the children on Maganos, gifted me with some of them; others I've had even longer."

"You've really made yourself at home," Khorii said, meaning to compliment her on her adaptability. The gray floors had been covered with carpets from the *Mana*'s cargo, a bright coverlet was tucked securely into the berth, which was piled with silken pillows in many colors, many embroidered with golden threads.

"I had to do something. The bulkheads were in bad repair—the one between this room and the next was brittle and full of pockmarks. But I can easily repair it with a little spot welding and return it to the original layout," Captain Bates said hastily. "No, no, Uncle Hafiz would love this!" Khorii said. "Though it's possibly a bit understated for his taste."

Captain Bates grinned. With her hazel eyes, light complexion, and midlength wavy brown hair, dressed as she was in her utilitarian shipsuit, she didn't look like someone who would be the denizen of such an exotic den. "Have I ever told you anything about my background, Khorii?" Khorii shook her head. "Well, the short version is that I grew up among space nomads, pirates, gypsies, and traveling showmen. Our traditions were *not* based on Old Terran naval ones, so this is what home looks like to me, except I made this into a workroom for beading and other off-duty projects."

For the first time, Khorii saw the purpose of having five slender digits on each hand instead of three larger, single-knuckled ones, as her race did.

Captain Bates caught her look, and said, "That's no drawback. Come on, pick out some larger beads from here, and we'll do your hair."

A pleasant hour later, while Captain Bates's hands combed, tugged, and braided her mane like a particularly versatile wind, they spoke of their lives, friends, what had happened in Corazon while Khorii had been away on her rescue missions and what had happened on the missions.

When Captain Bates finally lowered her hands, she said, "Now shake your head." Khorii did so. Beads clacked and clinked together as she shook it. She rose and looked at herself in the polished metal portion of the bulkhead used to monitor grooming. Her entire head sparkled with the colors beaded and threaded into her star-clad mane, which also looked much longer, weighted as it was with the beads.

"Our star!" she exclaimed, clacking her braids again. "If it wasn't for my horn, I don't think I'd recognize myself."

"You're safe," Captain Bates said. "I haven't figured out how to bead a horn yet, though there are pigments and gilt . . ."

"Perhaps not," Khorii said.

"No, it might interfere with your abilities. I was going to put little bells on the ends of the braids but thought better of that, too. You might want to sneak up on someone, and bells would be counterproductive. Ask any cat."

As if on cue, Khiindi scratched at the hatch and Sesseli called apologetically, "I'm sorry, Captain, he keeps wanting to come in. He can be such a silly kitty."

But when she saw the quarters and Khorii's mane, Sesseli's eyes got wide. "Do mine!" she said. So she replaced Khorii in the chair in front of the table while Khorii found her new do was considered by Khiindi to make fine surrogate prey. She shook her head for him, and he batted her braids while Captain Bates twined and embellished Sesseli's baby-fine blond curls with smaller beads.

The child examined her reflection. "My beads aren't the same as Khorii's."

"No, because I didn't want them to pull and give you a

headache. But look here at this braid and at Khorii's in the same place." They came to stand by Khorii, and the teacher lifted a braided lock on the right side of each girl's head. "See this sequence? Hot pink, purple, saffron, and turquoise with the little gold spacers? Just alike. Among the nomadic crews they use beaded braids to identify their own and former crewmen. If you see a nomad with hair as full of beads as Khorii's, you know he or she has a long history with many crews and is probably highly experienced. What do you think about making this sequence our crew's uniform? This is our second voyage together, after all. We could have our own special insignia. Shall we see what Jaya thinks?"

"Yes," Khorii said, "but what about the males? I know Elviiz will feel left out if he doesn't get a braid, too."

"Males can wear them, too, although Hap may need to grow his hair a bit to hold the beads."

The intercom opened abruptly, and Jaya's voice, sounding shaky and tense, said, "Captain Bates? Are Khorii and Sesseli still with you?"

"Yes, Jaya. Is something wrong?"

"I'm not sure. Could you all please return to the bridge?"

"Certainly. Do you need Hap or Mikaaye?"

"I—I don't think so, but I'll buzz them to make sure they're okay," she replied.

Khorii, trailed by Sesseli and Khiindi, followed Captain Bates back across the corridor to the bridge.

Jaya's skin was naturally a deep honey color, but when she turned to them she looked almost as pale as Khorii.

"What is it?" Captain Bates asked.

But Khorii saw everything in an intense flash of memory.

"My parents," Jaya said, "and the rest of the crew. They were here."

*   *   *

Alone *on the bridge, Jaya had dutifully gone through her checklist and was playing a solitary game of 3-D chess with the computer when she happened to glance up to the wide viewport that stretched across the* Mana's *nose. She had been in space and aboard this ship most of her life, and though her role as pilot was relatively new, it was really no big deal. The ship's computer did most of the work. Even Sesseli could do this part, which was mostly minding the scanners and com set and watching the viewport to check on their position. That part was just a human thing for the most part. The computer and the scanners did the real "watching"—checking for all sorts of hazards, exploding heavenly bodies, other ships, asteroid fields, and adjusting the ship's course to avoid them.*

Nevertheless, computers, while less fallible than humans, were not entirely infallible, and besides, someone needed to be on the bridge to coordinate the activities of the rest of the crew.

Glancing up at the viewport, Jaya thought how like eyes the stars looked. And then she realized that they looked like eyes because there seemed to be the dim reflections of faces superimposed on them.

Which was weird because viewports were made of nonreflective material, which was very expensive precisely because it was nonreflective as well as heat-, cold-, impact-, shatter-, and pressure-resistant and, of course, transparent.

She twisted her chair around to see what was casting the reflection, and it followed her across the screen until the insubstantial faces, with equally insubstantial, and even transparent bodies, came away from it to float in front of her.

They almost looked like they belonged there. She had seen them, in a more solid form, so often throughout her life. But they'd never been grouped together like this, staring at her. Her mother's and father's faces and partially realized forms were the foremost, but she *could see others through them, behind them.*

She scanned them with feelings of eagerness, hopefulness, glad to see them again, even if they were only fragments of her dreams or some sort of ghostly memory left behind in the ship, as such memories were said to do in haunted houses.

But they looked down at her with empty eyes, their expressions uninterested, as if they didn't know her.

"Mom?" she asked, her voice almost inaudible even to herself. "Dad?"

The eyes didn't blink. Had she done something to rouse their spirits and make them angry at her? Did they disapprove of the way she was using the Mana? *Why?*

The empty eyes seemed to bore into her, so unlike the way her parents' eyes had been in life. They had been meltingly dark, and always expressing something, laughter, worry, anger, fear, approval, love . . . she would rather not have seen them at all than to see them like this, so distant, so . . . alien.

It wasn't until they receded, as if walking backward, footless, into the corridor, that she found the courage and the ability to move and speak. That was when she called for her friends.

no wonder all the children were crying!" Khorii said aloud when she had absorbed Jaya's impressions and feelings. "How awful for you. I wonder why this is happening."

By that time they had paged Hap and Mikaaye, and Mikaaye had arrived, saying Hap was on his way. The summons had not been an urgent one, as until Jaya explained aloud as best she could what had happened, they had no idea what sort of crisis had caused her to call for them.

Mikaaye's brow puckered around his horn. "Perhaps with so many dying so quickly, the spirits could not find their way to their transition points. I have never heard of such a thing occurring, but then, we know very little of what comes after."

Jaya was not crying, but she was very upset. Sesseli released Khiindi, who landed indignantly on the floor. Khorii thought it was a good thing the little girl had to let go of him sometimes, or her silly cat would forget why he had four legs.

He immediately jumped into Jaya's lap. Shortly after, Sesseli returned with Captain Bates's beading tray and handed it to the former teacher.

As they talked, Captain Bates and Jaya released her braids, and the captain combed her hair and slowly braided the beads into it as she had done with Khorii's. Jaya began relaxing with the gentle change of pressure on her scalp, feeling her hair lifted and released repetitively in that hypnotic soothing way.

Finally, she said, "I don't know why whatever that was looked like my family. I think maybe if it was them, they were so far away in whatever place people go when they die that they couldn't really come back enough to be them. Maybe it was just me wanting to see them again." She shuddered. "But not like that. Everything that made them themselves was gone."

"That's how it is," Captain Bates agreed. They all fell silent, thinking it over when Hap burst in.

"Jaya!"

She looked up. Hap was more agitated than she had been. Although he was extremely competent, he was also very excitable and imaginative and could not help showing his feelings.

"I'm sorry. I had to go to the head, but while I was there, all of a sudden I saw some—well, they were almost people, and they looked like your folks and the other crew members. I mean, they weren't real, couldn't have been because we'd have never all fit into the head if they had been but—"

"You saw them, too?" Jaya asked, looking up but not becoming overly excited again, still under the spell of the hair braiding. "And you recognized them?"

"Sure. I mean, I guessed it was them because what other older couple who looked like you and their friends would be hanging around here as ectoplasm or anything else?"

Hap was pretending that the idea of ectoplasmic forms was just one of those things people sometimes encountered, but Khorii could tell he was almost as shocked as Jaya had been.

When Hap walked into the room, Khiindi looked up. All the time the tall boy spoke, Khiindi had stared first at him, then up at Jaya, and finally, with a glance at Khorii, jumped down and ran to the hatch, which irised open automatically. Before it closed again, Khorii heard his paws thudding down the hall as if he had hooves like hers.

"You know what I think?" Hap said. "I think they want us to give them a proper burial, off the ship, somewhere dirt-side."

"Traditionally our people cremate the dead," Jaya said. "But the medical officials seemed to fear that might spread the disease."

"It won't with Mikaaye and me there to purify the smoke as it rises," Khorii said.

"There's only one planet on our course to Becker's worm-hole where we might be able to do that," Captain Bates said. "That would be Rushima."

"Then that's where we'll stop," Khorii said. "My people have friends there because we helped them repel the Khleevi invasion."

"Oh yes!" Mikaaye said. "That is a very good story. Both Khorii's mother and mine helped the settlers there and they were very grateful. They are certain to help us give proper ceremony to Jaya's family."

"Rushima it is then," Jaya said.

Khiindi pelted down the hall, knowing he would be able to see the specters that had disturbed Hap and Jaya. There was something extremely familiar about all of this. Perhaps in his former life he had seen the sort of thing Jaya's family had become in their next life?

Just when he thought he would need to search the entire ship, he heard a "RRRROWL!" and a hiss and saw four fe-lines bounding out of the cargo bay that contained the make-shift graveyard.

He might have known—had he not seen the other odd occurrence there himself? Except somehow, he thought at that time it was caused by the malign presence of that tail-breaking Marl creature.

Now the Vermin Eradication Squad stood hissing and spitting outside the hatch, even the half-grown kittens twice their size, every hair on their furry bodies standing at attention, backs arched, tails bristling, ears flat, and white fangs bared through peeled-back lips.

"I don't suppose I need to ask if you saw anything," Khiindi said.

"Wick-ed!" spat the queen.

"Nassss-ty," hissed the kits.

"Scared the crap out of *me,*" their father, now surgically celebate, like the rest of them, agreed.

"Did they look like your old humans?" Khiindi asked.

"Of course not!" the queen said, and Khiindi jumped back for fear she might give him a claws-out smack. "Didn't look like anything but a collection of evil dust motes."

"How can dust motes be evil?" Khiindi asked. He knew, of course, he just wanted to see if she could articulate what he felt better than he could.

"Well, they smell that way, don't they?" the unfortunate male responded. Of them all, he had calmed down the most quickly. Queens with kits, even when both were incapable of reproduction, could be excitable. "Worse stench than jellified mouse."

"Go see for yourself if you're so curious," the queen said, hissing the "curioussss." "But remember what they say about *that.*"

Khiindi may have been born on Makahomia, but prior to that birth he had been around enough to be familiar with that old saw. And in his experience, lack of curiosity at certain times could kill the investigatively impaired as quickly as the alternative.

Whatever it was couldn't be worse than it had been before, when Marl Fidd had been involved, too. Bravely, Khiindi strutted forward, into the cavernous cargo hold.

His gorgeous golden eyes—although he was of course behind them, he was well aware of how gorgeous they were, since others frequently remarked upon it, and he was not the sort of foolish cat who imagined that the magnificent creature in the mirror could be anyone but himself—quickly adjusted to the darkness. Fur erect, tail lashing, ears pricked and rotating to detect the slightest sound, he slunk forward, crouching and stalking toward the mound of soil held in place by banks of large containers.

He had spent a lot of lap time soaking up antique vids aboard the *Condor* and on Maganos Moonbase. He knew very well that hyperactive dead things tended to return to their places of not so eternal rest when they ran out of things to frighten or mischief to do.

Compared to himself, they were rank amateurs at mischief doing, and when he could switch shapes, he had sometimes been very frightening. The dead part was something else again. He had never been nor did he have any intention of becoming dead but he knew that dead things lay still. That was how it worked. They didn't roam around worrying their living offspring or interfering with the duties of working felines. Of course, there might have been time travel involved, but he didn't think so. In that case they would now look exactly as they had before. The VES denied recognizing them, and Jaya had said that though they resembled her family superficially, she felt that they were not the same.

Even the soft footfalls of his paws echoed in the emptied hold.

The distance from hatch to graves felt as if it could be measured in light-years. But hovering over the graveyard, he saw the same shimmering shapes he had seen before, except that now they seemed more solid and better defined. They did indeed seem to have coalesced into roughly bipedal forms.

He slunk closer, keeping his belly low to the deck, but they seemed unaware of him, or, if they were aware, not properly respectful of him as a potential predator.

The nearer he drew, the more his nostrils filled with their scent. He did not find it quite so thoroughly offensive as the ordinary cats did, but he did find it distinctly odd. A medley of rot, metal, and something like the smell of the cultures Jalonzo was growing in the laboratory was as close as Khiindi could come to describing it. It was also very much the same sort of odor he had detected around the sand castle on LoiLoiKua. Khorii had acted as if he were merely showing off, which hurt because he had definitely sensed this same sort of presence and had been trying to protect her from it.

But while the smell was strong to a cat's sensitive olfactory organs, he doubted that the blunted senses of the humans or even Linyaari could detect more than a whiff of it.

As he had thought they might, the forms began to pour themselves back into the soil, returning to their graves. Ooooooooooh. Khiindi was not going to let them get away with that spooky nonsense around *him*.

He put his paws into warp drive and raced for the mound, leaping the barriers with a single bound and landing stiff-legged, claws extended in the grave dirt.

Rats! The last few motes were sinking into the soil even as he stood there, escaping his wrath. Or almost.

A final trail of the dustlike specters spiraled before his eyes, sailed over his head and behind him, and curled itself around his tail, tugging it, tugging *him*, trying to pull him down after it. With a mighty yowl and a twist of his lithe body, Khiindi pounced on the thing holding his tail, dispersed it, and teleported across the cargo bay and through the hatch where he landed sprawling on the deck with the queen and a kit squashed beneath his prostrate form.

"They—they almost *got* me," he panted.

"Nasty *and* incompetent then!" the queen snarled. "Get off me, you, and unpaw my child or I'll finish what they left undone!"

Khiindi levitated and raced down the corridor toward the bridge and the protection of Khorii and Sesseli.

As he reached the hatch, it irised open and he leaped in, the queen half a body length behind him.

The two-leggeds watched stupidly, all except Sesseli, who snatched him up with her telekinesis and pulled him into her arms, while the queen braked, smacking her tail against the deck and glaring up at them.

Khiindi wriggled free of Sesseli and hopped onto Khorii's shoulders. Because it was expected of him, he laughed down at the angry queen, but his heart wasn't in it.

How was he going to find a way to warn Khorii that the plague was not dead after all but changing into another form?

chapter 15

"It is she, as I saw it would be!" An unusually round humanoid female pointed at Narhii. She was so covered in the feminine garb Akasa prized, and needed so very much of it to cover her, that she might well have used up half of Akasa's extensive wardrobe. Jewels hung from every part of her a jewel *could* hang from, covering her otherwise mostly bare upper chest, arms, fingers, and dangling from her ears and the draperies veiling her mane, which was a sort of roan color.

"Please, Karina, you're frightening the child," another female voice said, and a face much like Narhii's appeared on the screen. "Who are you, youngling, and how did you come to be in the sea?"

Narhii knew the female wanted to ask about her clothing as well. She also knew, just by looking at her over the com screen, that this female had been hoping to see her, though not perhaps in this fashion.

"I don't like talking into this thing, in front of so many others," she replied, feeling very daring. She hadn't heard all of the others, but she could feel them watching her even though the female like her was the only one she saw.

"It's really quite all right," the other female assured her.

"These are all friends and—well, I'm afraid that I cannot come and speak to you in person, nor can Aari, my mate."

"Why not?" Narhii asked.

"It's complicated, but we've been exposed to a disease that you might catch. It's a very bad one."

"You look fine to me," Narhii said. She didn't sense a trick, but neither did she see why the female wouldn't come to meet her. She had an idea about her, and as long as she was being very bold, she decided to go all the way. "I found out recently—they didn't mean for me to but I did—that I have a mother and father alive about now. Are you my mother?"

The female, confused, looked away from the screen as if to speak to someone else—the mate? Narhii's *father*?—and the first female appeared again. "Apparently so, dear, if my vision was correct, which naturally it was. Now then, tell us, from when came you and what are you called?"

Narhii didn't want them to see that she was just as confused as they were. They would think her stupid, or guess that she had run away from what the Friends had always told her was her destiny and her duty. They wouldn't want a stupid, lazy daughter.

"I came from—before," she said. "I thought I was the only one like me. There were people like them." She waved at the *sii*-Linyaari, who had left her the rock while they swam and dived around it. "And there were the Friends and the Others, who say they were saved by the Friends."

"Others?" the heavily bedecked and fleshed woman asked.

"Quadrupeds with horns like mine, white like me," Narhii explained. "And similar feet."

"She must mean the Ancestors," a male voice said. His face appeared on the screen, and Narhii guessed that this must be the mate of the female—her father? "I believe I have visited the time you speak of, *yaazi*, though I did not see you there. How *did* you come to be there and now—here?"

"Shouldn't someone be taking a boat out to fetch her to shore and dry her off?" the female like her asked.

Another female face appeared. "It is being done, Khornya. Thariinye and Maati have returned from their journey and will collect the youngling in a flitter."

Narhii felt some annoyance even though this exchange was in the interest of her comfort and welfare. She wanted to keep talking to the male and answer his questions. She was sure now that she had indeed found her parents, and, from what she could see, they were very agreeable. Nice. And not, she thought, because they wanted something from her.

"The Others tell me I was stolen while still in my mother— she was to have twins—and since the thief, someone named Grimalkin, left my sister and only took me, my parents didn't know. Are you them? Do you have a female child like me?"

"Yes," the male said, his voice odd, as if his throat had constricted.

"Is she there with you? Can I see her? Are we alike?"

The female—Khornya?—answered, the corners of her mouth lifting as she spoke, though her silvery eyes, much like Narhii's own, held sadness. "She didn't have your fashion sense when we saw her last, but that may have changed by now. I'm afraid she's not here."

"You sent *her* away, too?"

A gruff-looking humanoid with mane all over his face, especially between his nose and upper lip, said, "Don't worry, kiddo. She's okay. Khorii's just off saving the universe. It's what your family does. You'll catch on in no time."

"So am I? Part of your family, Khornya? You're truly my mother and your mate—"

"Aari," she supplied, her face replacing the humanoid male's.

"Is my father?"

"Yes, and the person who just spoke to you is Captain Becker, a dear family friend, quarantined with us."

"Can't you heal yourselves?" Narhii asked curiously. "I can, and the Others can, though the Friends aren't much good at it."

"We've always been able to before," Khornya said, "but this disease is much worse than any other one we've ever encountered. Little one—what do they call you where you—were?"

"The Friends just called me the Mutant. The Others called me Narhii."

"Mutant!" Aari exclaimed, his face bursting onto the screen with an anger that reminded her of Hruffli. "They would! Of all the arrogance! To treat this poor child that way. And if I ever get my hands on Grimalkin again I'll—well, I want everyone to look away because I mean to do something *ka*-Linyaari."

"Allow me instead, boy," furry-faced Captain Becker said. "It's the least I can do."

A flitter arrived—the Friends had such devices though not as pretty as this one, which was bright-colored and had golden designs on it. Another female opened the hatch and held out her arms to Narhii.

"Hop in, youngling. I'm Maati, and I understand I may be your aunt."

The spectral shapes didn't do any harm that anyone could see, but they upset Jaya and the cats. Neither Khorii nor Mikaaye ever saw them, which both Linyaari found disappointing.

Khorii was most troubled by Khiindi's increasingly odd behavior. He meowed and yowled at her constantly, ran back and forth and refused to be soothed or comforted. He also refused to let her rest, which she had been repeatedly warned could make her more susceptible to the disease. She tried to discuss his behavior with him because that often worked, but this time it did not. He was fixated on the cargo hold containing the graves, but although Khorii waited there for a full shift rotation, during which time Khiindi seemed calmer, though hyperalert, she saw nothing out of the ordinary aboard the ship.

As they docked on Rushima, however, things did not seem right to her at all. Rushima, an agricultural planet with a fairly uniform climate year-round, which made the crops abundant and several yearly harvests possible, looked remarkably barren from the air. As the ship descended, Khorii noted that all of the fields, regardless of the crop planted, seemed to be just beginning the growing cycle and were sparsely planted.

Jaya, sitting beside her, was looking, too. "At least it looks like they have lots of nice blue lakes."

"That's not water," Khorii said, for as they descended farther, she saw that what appeared to be wetlands were actually ruined fields overlaid with the aqua of the sticky stuff she had found in her own rooftop garden.

Nevertheless, she was glad when the ship docked, landing on Rushima's primitive airstrip, also pitted and in bad repair. The settlers seemed glad to see the *Mana,* too. A delegation of rather gaunt white-haired elders marched across the tarmac to meet them, followed by a gaggle of skinny children, including a young girl bearing flowers.

As on other planets, everyone was either a child or young teen or someone old enough to be at least a grandparent.

Khorii disembarked before her shipmates, looking for blue plague specks, but saw none. *"It's safe, Captain Bates. You can all come ashore."*

When all of the greetings had been exchanged, Jaya lost no time in pleading her case, saying to the elder who seemed to be in charge, "My parents and the crew of my ship died of the plague. Khorii purified their bodies and we gave them a temporary burial on shipboard. But we feel that it would be good now to give them a proper burial. I was hoping you would give us permission to bury my parents here." Her voice was remarkably calm and businesslike as she said this, though her eyes filled and her lower lip trembled.

"You just came to this decision all of a sudden, did you?" asked another elder sharply, a small pink-skinned man with scant hair on his head and a lot on his chin. Something about him reminded Khorii of Liriili. "Ever occur to you we might have problems of our own? Two crops ruined and stores contaminated so we'd little to eat, whole dang town falling to wrack and ruin, dead people roaming around like they still own the place . . ."

Then from the back of the crowd another man walked forward—the people parted for him as if it was his right. He was of medium height, with wavy silver-white hair and eyes whose green color was clear and startling in his deeply tanned face.

Ignoring the elder's litany of complaint, Hap rushed forward and embraced the newcomer like a child hugging a long-lost parent. The man enveloped the tall boy in a bear-like embrace and patted him gently on the back until Hap broke away to grin at him. "Scar! So this is where you ended up! I thought—I mean, you made it?"

The other man grinned, showing teeth a little lighter than his hair, and hooked his thumbs in the straps of his coveralls. "Of course I made it, Hap. Nice of you to worry about me, son, but I'm too old to interest the plague."

His face immediately clouded over with sadness, and he shook his head, his eyes filling with tears. "Lots of better folks, folks who were needed worse, weren't so lucky."

"No, Scar, that's not true!" the little girl who'd brought the flowers said.

The man ruffled the child's hair with a large hand.

"Don't get all upset now, Mabel Dean. You know what a

shortage of good water we've got here. You don't want to go wasting your share." He was teasing her, and coaxed a smile.

"Mr. MacDonald has been very useful indeed," the persnickety elder said. "He's used the machinery he had on board to help us clean our fields and replant and graciously put some of his inventory of diggers to use burying our dead. He'd be the fella to help you with yours."

Breaking in before the elder had finished his sentence, an excited Hap said, "Khorii, Captain Bates, Jaya, Sesseli, and Mikaaye, this is my old friend Scaradine MacDonald. He taught me as much as he could about taking care of ag equipment—that's what he does."

"Most popular grave digger in the history of the job," MacDonald said. Khorii saw reflected in his face all of the grief and pain around him. This was a warm-hearted man who felt much and gave what he could. Impulsively, she stepped forward and embraced him, laying her horn against his chest, hoping to heal a little of the sadness.

He patted her shoulder as if he were the one comforting her. "Thank you, honey. You're a real nice girl. You put me in mind of another girl I met one time on the way to Makahomia— Acorna they called her. Not just because she was a Linyaari, like you, but there's something else about you—"

"Khornya, her name in our tongue, is my mother," Khorii said. "She told me! She told me about meeting you! You helped her and RK and Uncle Joh get Nadhari Kando there in time to protect Miw-Sher and the sacred Temple Cats!"

"I didn't really do anything," he said modestly. "Drove a wagon, helped them through another plague. I've sure seen enough of that kind of thing. So, back to what you were asking, if Jaya's folks need burying and it's okay with Elder Bawb here, I'll be glad to help."

"We had hoped to cremate them," Khorii said to Elder Bawb. "That is the custom of her people."

"Out of the question," the elder who looked like Liriili protested.

Elder Bawb held up his hand to stop the other man, then said in an apologetic tone, "Much as we'd like to oblige you, it's been pretty dry around here lately. I don't reckon starting a big fire would be good, and well, there's no oven—"

"No, no, that's fine," Jaya assured him quickly so that she didn't have to hear anything more about ovens. She would do what was necessary but she didn't like to think about the details. "But if you will give their bodies a permanent resting place, I'd be very grateful."

The persnickety elder, whose name turned out to be Mr. Plimsoll, raised an objection about foreigners being buried among the native dead, but Elder Bawb overruled him, saying, "Good grief, Horace, what difference is a few bodies more or less going to make now?" He turned back to Khorii. "Can you stay the night? There was a terrible fire over at Bug Gulch last week. Took out an elder and three young'uns. But five others are injured and when we got your hail we told them you were coming. They're on their way now and will be here by morning."

Khorii turned to Captain Bates and Jaya, not because she thought they'd object but because until someone from Krishna-Murti Company said otherwise, the ship was Jaya's, and Captain Bates was the elder aboard. Since the plague, Linyaari had gone from being oddities who had to explain themselves to being treated as if they were in charge of the entire universe, a distinction they had neither asked for nor wanted.

Jaya shrugged. "Sure," she said.

Captain Bates asked, "Wouldn't it be faster if we went over there to them using one of the shuttles?"

"That's right kindly of you, ma'am, but they'll be here soon enough. And we have some healings we need here when you've finished your buryin'."

"The living come first, Elder," Captain Bates said before Khorii could.

"Sure they do. But if we can bring your folks out now, Scar can get them in the ground while the unicorn youngsters are doing the healing, then everybody can gather round to send them off proper."

"Will the injured coming from Bug Gulch be further damaged by the journey?" Khorii asked.

"No, ma'am. They have a team of geldings and a fine wagon that used to belong to the doctor. Ride will be smooth as a baby's bottom. These ben't life-threatening injuries, from what I hear. Everybody hurt that bad went to join their maker right after it happened."

A young girl, bright red pigtails flying, ran up to them, and said, panting, "Elder, there's been an accident over to the forge. Horse jack busted and the horse sat down on Grampa while he was shoein', and I think Grampa's back is broken."

"Show me," Khorii said.

The girl grabbed Khorii's hand and pulled her back through the crowd, which parted before them. Her feet were dirty and bare, and her simple shift dress was an extremely familiar saffron cotsyn, its humble origins as a shipping sack betrayed by the logo and title of the Krishna-Murti Company printed in purple curly letters down her back.

Behind them, Mikaaye's footsteps, as hard as Khorii's own, pounded the loose rocks of the street.

The smith, a wiry old man, was on the ground, groaning and sweating so profusely that the skin of his arms, shoulders, and upper chest visible above his coverall was shinier than if he'd just showered, except that dirt clung to the moisture, making dark patches against his cedar red skin and bald scalp. His eyes, when not squeezed shut with pain, showed a great deal of white. While his upper torso was tense with pain, his lower torso, hips, and legs were motionless and relaxed. A foul smell indicated that his bowels had also relaxed.

A large piece of equipment, a heavy metal frame with a hammock-wide sling of knitted plasteel attached, lay in pieces on the ground near him. Its metal seemed to have corroded and broken in midspan.

A horse, apparently the one that had injured him, stood to one side and regarded the man with a puzzled expression. Khorii caught a fleeting thought from it. *"Don't ask me. That thing almost broke my back when it gave out from under me. If it hadn't been for the smith beneath my belly, I might have been seriously injured."*

The beast looked startled when Khorii replied wryly, *"I am sure that will be of tremendous comfort to him."*

Two boys about the size of Jalonzo were bent over the injured man. When Khorii and the others arrived, the boys anxiously stood and stepped aside. One of them had big tears standing in the corners of his eyes, and one of them held a mug of water he'd been trying to give the injured man.

Khorii knelt beside the smith on one side, Mikaaye on the other.

The forge hearth had died down to nothing, tools gleamed dully against the metal sides of the building, but she saw these only peripherally, her attention focused on the man in front of her.

As she and Mikaaye bent their horns to him, the man's eyes focused, and his upper body relaxed from the contorted posture he'd assumed in his body's effort to protect its injury. She felt the spinal cord knit back together. Pieces of vertebrae found each other as if by magnetism and recombined their cells to a seamless whole. The damage to the tissue the shards of bone had invaded when displaced healed, and the bruised places lost their swelling as blood and other fluids were reabsorbed.

All of this took place in a moment, but she thought it must have seemed like an eternity to the man.

He sighed, a deep "aaahh," then stood up. "Thank you kindly. Be right back." His posture erect and his gait reasonably normal, he quickly entered an adjoining building.

"Thank you so much," the girl who'd fetched them said. "Gramps is all we got left. I'm Moonmay Marsden and this here is my brother Percy and our cousin Fleagle. I expect Grampa was off in search of clean britches."

"The air smells better anyhow," Fleagle said, his tears evaporated. He playfully punched his cousin in the arm. "Mercy, Percy, even *you* smell better."

The smith reemerged with a big grin. "I think you cured my sciatica while you were at it, young'uns. I retired about five year ago and let my son take over the business. Right away the aches and pains started, payin' me back for all the abuse I done myself in the past. But, shoot, now I feel like I could work another twenty years—or at least long enough to teach Fleagle and Percy here the trade."

"We were happy to help, but we need to return to our ship now, sir," Khorii told him.

"I don't suppose you could stay for supper? We'd be honored to have you, and Moonmay cooks as good as her mama. Fried chick—"

He started to say "chicken" but Moonmay, bearing in mind what most people now knew about the Linyaari and their vegetarian dietary needs, tugged at her grandfather's coverall. He tilted his head so she could say something into his ear.

"Fried chickpeas. Moonmay makes the best fried chickpeas on Rushima. Mashed tubers and of course, your pick of the garden."

"We'd love to, sir, but we have some friends to bury."

"Me and the boys will help, then, and pay our respects," the smith said, and all of them trooped back to the ship.

The smith and his grandsons followed Khorii and Mikaaye aboard the ship and into the cargo hold, where Hap and Jaya stood, shovels in hands, over the graves. Khorii introduced the blacksmith Marsden, Percy, and Fleagle, and, after a nod, Marsden took the shovel from Hap's hands and Percy the one from Jaya's, asking her if there was another for Fleagle. They wouldn't accept any help until it was time to pull the carton coffins from the graves. The coffins had deteriorated under the soil, which was to be expected. The black body bags containing the remains were not in much better shape, which was not surprising either. There seemed to be very little left of the dead, which was probably just as well.

"They sure don't stink much for dead folk," Fleagle said. "Don't weigh much neither."

"Hush, boy," his grandfather said. "Show some respect."

Khorii thought that any respect the boys might have had for the dead and the process of death had probably been eroded by so much close acquaintance with it in recent months. It was actually remarkable they were as sensitive as they were under the circumstances.

They loaded the remains into the trailer of the tractor Scar drove up to the dock. Moonmay had spent her time gathering flowers. Then people walked or rode out of town to the fields, where rows of stones, boards, and crosses marked graves newly green.

Scar stopped the tractor well outside the cemetery, apologizing. "Good thing I dug some extra graves earlier on. The ground has eroded something fierce—sinkholes big enough to lose a house in." The blacksmith's family served as assistant pallbearers, carrying the crumbling cartons cautiously to a tarp spread over the ground. Scar pulled it aside to reveal more holes for graves. "These ought to do the job," he said. "When there's been one death lately, there've been more with it so . . ." He waved an arm to indicate all the extra holes.

When the bodies had been lowered into the holes, Moonmay and several other girls stepped forward with fist-fuls of yellow-and-orange flowers. Moonmay handed some to Jaya, and said, "The marigolds came back real good, and Scar had seeds. They'll prettify the graves till the grass grows back. And we'll tend 'em with Mama's and Daddy's and Uncle John's and Aunt Mai Ling's."

Jaya hugged her, accepted the marigolds, and tossed some on top of the cartons before the tractor filled them in again. Jaya laid a handful of the bright saffron blossoms on each grave and led the others away.

She felt certain there would be no more spectral shapes keeping her mindful of happy memories turned sad by loss.

chapter 16

The brilliant thing about going straight to jail was that very few people knew Marl, or that he belonged there, if one accepted the authority of a handful of children, a one-horned alien, and a teacher pretending to be a lot better than she should be. Marl did not, of course. Once out of his cell he had no intention of returning. He had a clear idea from talking to his young jailers of where the com center was, and he headed straight for it. There was one closer to the docks as well, but that was mostly for ground-to-ship communication. The place he sought was conveniently situated on the same street as the police station. He wanted to speak with some friends on Kezdet.

He didn't spare a glance for the plaza/cemetery on the opposite side of the street. The dead didn't interest him, and, with his current grandiose plans, grave robbing for trinkets was far beneath him. He was not afraid of catching plague from the bodies. The Linyaari do-gooders would have made sure they were all nice and clean, according to his jailers. But it was hard, smelly work, and the population here had not been especially affluent.

The center was situated in a large dome-shaped building entered through a rotunda. It was very grand, with a mosaic ceiling in deep blue with a representation of the galaxy in gold, with the Solojo system at the center. The floor was, he presumed, an artistic topo-map of Paloduro's surface, with Corazon enclosed in a large heart. Touching, that.

The rotunda was entirely empty. Ah yes, the kiddies would all be in bed.

Good thing he'd brushed up on his Spandard while incarcerated. The lift had a detailed list of the contents of each floor in that language.

The transmissions center was on the top floor, of course. He hied himself there forthwith and entered a room whose entire ceiling was another model of the galaxy but a less Solojo-centered one. Various reception centers on planets, moons, stations, etc. and relay activity were represented. Laser beams of various colors streaked like comets from one to another or ricocheted around a bit showing, he presumed, where transmissions were headed. As he had expected, however, most of the room was operated by computer. A lone minder sat in a semireclining position for an optimum view of the ceiling, shifting around on invisible, presumably antigrav supports, so that the bit the operator was addressing was the one directly above.

Marl started forward, his footsteps making no sound on the rubberized flooring considerately designed to lessen ambient noise in the room. The operator, who appeared to be a girl, did not hear him. Good. But out of the corners of his eyes, both to the right and the left, something made a sudden movement. Then he almost dived for the floor when another operator's pallet sailed overhead. Where had that come from?

Standing stock-still, he darted quick glances to the right, the left, and up. No one. And the pallet was empty. Why had it moved then? Perhaps the other operator had called it or perhaps it anticipated his own need?

As to the other movements, they were probably nothing but reflections cast by the laser bolts flashing overhead.

No, truly, he and the other operator were quite alone. Good. She didn't look at all familiar, which meant he would not look familiar to her either. He stared up at the rogue pallet as it zoomed off again. Two others did the same thing, dodging around one another when a midair crash seemed likely. This time the girl sat up, moved her hand a bit, and her pallet sank to the nearest landing pad, a wedge-shaped space with a step leading to it located beside each computer station.

"Did you do that?" the girl demanded in Spandard. She looked to be eight or nine years old but could have been as old as twelve. Marl shook his head innocently and gave her his most ingratiating smile. He could be good with kiddies when it suited him. Girlies especially, though this one was not his type. Too pudgy and spotty, and her hair was thin and stuck out in wisps where it had been splayed out behind her pallet-cradled noggin.

"No! No," he said. That word at least worked in both languages. Fluency was not actually required though, he thought. The harmless, bewildered tourist with an emergency was more the ticket. In broken Spandard, he explained his plight. He had come to Corazon before the plague to visit relatives of his family on Kezdet. The little ones were orphaned now, but he was sure his own kindly parents, had they survived, would take them in. He had been sick himself and was barely saved by the Linyaari healers, then had dedicated himself to helping arrange things so others could manage. He hadn't imagined that his family on Kezdet were better off and frankly, until now, had been afraid to face the fact that he, too, might be an orphan. Then he had heard that the plague hadn't actually got a good toehold on Kezdet before the noble Linyaari came zooming to the rescue, so now he had hopes of a family reunion and could she help him at all?

He was a bit annoyed at how much longer and how many more strenuous charades it required to get his touching story across to her. You'd have thought they'd have put a brighter brat in charge of the com room at night. She kept losing track of what he was saying when another pallet lifted into the air to zoom around of its own accord, or more of those reflections darted past. Perhaps it was the dome shape that made them always seem to move at the periphery of one's vision. He didn't notice any of the beams reflecting directly down.

By the time he made the girl understand his request, however, she was whipping about at each little movement, totally spooked, despite what she surely must have seen as his reassuring presence. He found himself starting, too. If the child was this unnerved by the pallets and reflections, it could not be a normal occurrence. It could, however, play into his hands.

"Ought they to be doing that?" he asked in Spandard, as another pallet passed overhead. She shook her head, her eyes showing white all around the pupils.

Then, as he had hoped, she showed him, with gestures, demonstrations, and simple phrases, how the system was supposed to operate.

"A simple malfunction then?" he suggested. "¿Uh—*uno malfunctiamente tecnico? ¿Uno* glitch *electromagnetimente?*"

For a moment she looked at him like he was nuts, and he thought she didn't understand. Then she leaned closer to him, and whispered, presumably so that all of the hardware zipping about overhead wouldn't hear. "No," she told him, "*fantasma.*"

"Ghosts? Get serious, lovey. No such thing. No *fantasma,*" he said.

"*Sí,*" she said, gesturing rather hysterically at the flying pallets, "*Sí, sí, fantasma.*"

He sighed deeply. No reasoning with someone like this. "Tell you what then, you run along and I'll deal with them, *sí*? Uh, make *fantasma vamuso pronto.*"

She didn't even look skeptical. He was older, after all, and male, and obviously knew what he was doing, although he was very glad she didn't.

She jabbered something too fast for him to understand and was out of there before any dust that might have settled in her wake could do so.

Fine. Just him and the *fantasmas*. Uh *malfunctiamente tecnico*. He could deal with that. Picking up her control pad, he settled himself into the pallet and was carried toward the ceiling like a baby being delivered by a great bloody stork.

Brilliant. He homed in on Kezdet and microrouted the message to a code that landed him in the middle of a little-known area of the Nanobug Market. The shabby, slightly carnie atmosphere lent by the sights and smells of a plethora of merchandise that was secondhand at the newest actually concealed quite a sophisticated com system undetected by the Federation cops.

It would be midday on Kezdet now, and his friends would be touting their wares to the unwary or at least to those who didn't mind the wear and tear on some items, even if they knew to beware of the condition of others. Amused with his wordplay, he thought to repeat it to his contact, but the old man wasn't amused. "I was in the middle of a deal, boy. What the Demos do you want?"

Marl batted his lashes in a coy fashion, if not a koi fashion, since he, of course, had something fishy in mind. "Is that any way to speak to opportunity when it hails you?" he asked. "I've a much better deal that should interest you and your team. I have landed in a veritable pot of gold, my friend, and I wish to cut you in."

"You're too kind," the other man said gruffly. "Why?"

"I find myself in need of minions and transport."

"Sounds like a personal problem," the man said with a snort and seemed about to switch off the com and go back to peddling Linyaari bobble-headed dollies or whatever.

"You're right," Marl said. "It is. That's all right. Of course I wanted to cut my old pals in first, but if that's how you feel, there's plenty around here willing to retire young with a fortune, a mansion, and a harem of buxom teenaged cuties."

The man shook his head. "I know I'm going to hate myself for asking, but what is it you're on about?"

Marl told him. Some of it he knew of course, but it was necessary to the buildup to describe all of the properties, the drugs, the riches waiting for a clever operator and his gang to collect. The key, of course, was to do it without catching the plague, but he figured he had that angle covered.

"Here's the sweet part," he said, dangling the best bit of bait, "I happen to know one of them rather well." He made his relationship with Khorii sound much friendlier than it was.

"Who doesn't? Know some of them all too well indeed. One of them made me give away most of my best stock."

"*One* of them?"

"Her 'n' her family—some kinda Linyaari Mafiosi is my guess."

"Well, the one I know can not only clear the plague, she can tell if it's even still there or not. Besides which, she knows the location of a treasure ship from Dinero Grande and is on her way there even now. That's why I need the ship and the minions. Got to catch up with her."

"Cut you out, did she?"

"You could say, yeah. So how about it?"

"Just so happens we have agents on their way to Solojo for some of the reasons you mentioned in the first place. If they reckoned it was worth their while, they might agree to an alteration in their plans. Of course, if things is different than what you say, your life expectancy is going to diminish sharpish."

"Understood," Marl said. "I'm in the com room now. Give me their coordinates, and I'll patch us through."

By the time he'd finished his com-ferring with them all and was ready to descend and go wait for his lift, he was sweating profusely. The agents were unknown to him personally, but he had heard of this kind of person. They'd evidently weathered the plague in good shape because there were several adult males among them, swarthy, with colorful personal adornments both on and in their skins. They grinned at him a lot, which was not reassuring. Their teeth weren't all in the best shape, but there were quite a lot of teeth among them, and most of them had been filed to sharp points.

He had been so engrossed in conducting his own business that he hadn't paid much attention to the pallets still zipping around. But as he ended his transmission, he glanced over at one that hovered to the left and slightly lower than his own.

He had been wrong to assume that it was empty. It was not.

ut I want to see them—in person," Narhii argued. She didn't know what had gotten into her, really. She'd been meek and humble her entire life, but having taken the step of leaving the Friends with their laboratories and their mind probes and their need to control everything, she wasn't about to be thwarted now. The female sitting next to her in the flitter was a relative, but not the right one.

"You should take me," Narhii told her, pitching her thought to the same level she had used to convince the Friends to do as she wished. *"It will be all right. I can cure them."*

Her father's sister shook her head as if Narhii had spoken aloud. "I can't do that, you know. And if we can't heal them, and the ancestors can't, you can't either."

Narhii said nothing. So here she was among relatives and people like herself and that was good. But she was back to being as she had been before—a powerless youngling who must do as she was told and hope that sometimes what she wanted to do and what they wanted her to do would coincide. This hybrid people, this race to which she belonged, was less self-involved than the Friends and, therefore, harder to control. Maybe she should have stayed with the Friends a little longer and tested her new abilities? She would be just like everyone else here, but that meant she would have nothing special for herself. Not even, as it seemed, the parents she wanted to claim as her own.

Maati was glancing at her oddly. "Narhii, I'm sorry it's working out this way, but please be patient just a little longer. Khorii, Khornya's and Aari's daughter—other daughter," she corrected herself swiftly, but Narhii understood what she meant. Her own identity was still in question, ". . . is doing a last check, but we believe the plague may have died out elsewhere on its own. When she returns, she will be able to tell if the strain carried by her parents has also run its course. Meanwhile, our scientific teams, which include Mother and Father—mine and Aari's—your grandparents, in fact—and our brother Lariinye are working, as are human teams, on finding a cure."

"I guess I was a little early then," Narhii said, meaning to be apologetic but sounding bitter, even to her own ears. "I thought six *ghaanyi* was long enough but—"

"Narhii, this plague did not happen to inconvenience you!" Maati said, sounding almost as sharp as Akasa when she was between male companions. "Billions of people died throughout an entire quadrant of space. Societies and cultures were destroyed, the children of those people will never get a chance to see *their* parents again, and if they are to survive, they must become adults now, when many of them are even younger than you. Most of the law and order that kept worlds and worlds of people civilized and stable has disappeared. Aari and Khornya exhausted themselves into illness trying to help, and Khorii has been leading our teams in making their healing efforts less random and more effective. You have to understand that this has nothing to do with how anybody feels about you."

Narhii tried to grasp the images Maati was bombarding her with, but they were beyond her comprehension. Why didn't those people get up again? Why didn't they turn their color to its proper state, resume breathing, go about their business, and leave her family to go about theirs—which ought to have a lot to do about how they felt about her. They evidently felt extremely fond of one another, and they should feel the same way about her. She needed them to. It was as if she were terribly thirsty and water was just beyond her but nobody would let her drink any of it.

Maati heaved a deep sigh. "Come now. We're going to Kubiliikhan to meet other family members—the ones who are researching the plague. And your grandparents on your mother's side will be there. They will be so excited to meet you."

That was something, at least, she thought, but when she got there she saw that even these new relatives had agendas for her, too, more politely requested and executed than those of the Friends; but still, after a short introduction and what seemed a ceremonial grazing interval, plans that involved interrogating, testing, and poking her.

Although she tried not to balk, Maati sensed it quickly, and said, "Usually when one of us is born, we are given an identity disk with our DNA codes and those of our parents inscribed upon the surface and a sample of our DNA encapsulated within. Since you do not have one of these—"

"How could I?" Narhii protested. "I was never born here. I told you they took me while I was still an egg!"

"Exactly. That is why we are doing this now. Your birthing disk was not made for you when it should have been, so we are making one for you now. You may either keep it if you wish or give it to your mother."

"I could give it to her?"

"Not directly, of course, not yet."

"Then I'll keep it," she said. This, at least, would be hers and hers alone. But while she was being tested and questioned by these people she should have felt close to but didn't, she had come to a decision.

Having taken her sample, the female who was introduced to her as her father's mother smiled up at her. "Your information was correct, my dear," she said. "You are indeed the daughter of my daughter and of Aari, and the identical twin of Khorii." She rose and before Narhii knew how to respond, embraced her and touched horns with her. "Welcome, granddaughter. What an unexpected blossom you are in a meadow of what has been very bitter grass indeed of late."

Once more Narhii was bombarded by images of illness and death and also those of a very confused and tumultuous family history, all of which was much too much to comprehend.

But when her parents were again connected to her by com screen, something finally happened that she understood, and that pleased her.

"Aari, Khornya," her grandmother said to her parents by way of introduction. "This child is yours and the twin sister of your Khorii."

Her mother smiled at her, showing teeth for a moment, then closing her mouth suddenly but Narhii knew without being told that where her mother had grown up, showing teeth was a sign of pleasure, happiness, and goodwill, even humor, and it moved her that her mother had been so glad to see her as to temporarily revert to her early conditioning. Her father simply said, "We knew that already."

She wanted more than ever to embrace them both and feel the love they were trying to send to her from the screen. She touched her horn to the image of her father's, but, of course, it was a cold touch.

He gulped, then steadied his voice, and said, "Daughter, your mother and I have been talking it over. We do not think the name the Friends gave you was a good personal name, though if you wish to continue being called by it, we would understand."

"No," she said. "No, I do not like it. Have you—are you

going to—I mean, I would very much like to have a family name from you, like the one you gave Khorii, my sister."

"How would you feel about being called Ariinye, then?"

"It is a beautiful name!" she said.

"A little long, perhaps," her mother said. "Khorii's full name is Khoriilya. You might shorten yours, for your family and other friends to call you more simply, to Ariin."

"I like that even better!" she cried. A shortened name was so informal and yet, it seemed so personal, so affectionate. For the first time since she'd learned she could not be with her parents in person, Narhii—Ariin—was as happy as she had ever been.

Khorii and Mikaaye were each given a seat at a folding table at opposite ends of the rickety meeting hall, which was basically one long, empty room.

The people who came to the Linyaari for healing had mostly minor wounds and illnesses to cure. While Khorii and Mikaaye put their horns and powers to good use, Captain Bates, Hap, and Jaya searched the *Mana*'s cargo reserves for supplies the settlers needed, and specifically raided Khorii's 'ponics garden for healing and useful herbs and plants, the Rushiman counterparts of which had been blighted in the wake of the plague. Sesseli assisted them as best a small girl could. The child's telekinetic gift was difficult for her to use unless she was experiencing some profound emotion connected with the object to be moved.

A small seventy-year-old woman, her hair still black as a crow's wing, limped to Khorii with the aid of a cane. "My sciatica," she explained, gasping a little as she lowered herself onto the bench facing Khorii. "I haven't been able to think, much less run the mill, for nigh unto a week."

Khorii smiled, touched the sore place the woman indicated, and bent her head as if to examine it more closely. The Linyaari had hidden the power of their horns since her mother first made contact with them and discovered that some humans might seek to kill or enslave Linyaari for the benefit of the horns; but since the plague had killed and sickened so many and speed was of the essence, just now Khorii's people practiced only token discretion at the most.

Elder Plimsoll tried to be discreet about his digestive problems, which he called "sour stomach" but which Khorii felt originated in the organ known among humans as a gallbladder. He looked much friendlier and more relaxed once she had healed the inflamed organ and unblocked the duct, dissolving a large and painful stone.

Two boys, one almost her age, the other perhaps six years old, supported and corrected the course of a confused-looking woman whose face looked lopsided and whose left arm hung limply while she dragged her left leg. "Miz Alison said Gran had a stroke. Can you fix her up, miss?"

She did and cleared the cloud that whitened one iris and pupil of a cataract while she was at it.

As her sight cleared, her face straightened, and strength and sensation returned to the paralyzed side of her body, the woman looked as if she would faint with relief. "Young lady, you are an angel. All your people are angels from above," she said gratefully squeezing Khorii's hands between her own, which were quite strong now. Khorii had learned long ago from Elviiz's lectures in human folklore and theology what angels were and she knew she was not one; but it was true that, from the woman's perspective, she did come from above.

"Mind you, it's not that I'm opposed to meeting my maker when my time comes," the woman continued, "but I wasn't ready to go yet. Doctor Anne could have cured me easy if she'd lived, and Young Ali, even though she passed on, could have eased me with some of the herbs, but they all went in the blight. And someone has to look after these babies, even though it seems they spend too much time looking after us, they got no experience, and most haven't had enough schooling to take care of themselves. I want to get my boys raised up a little before I learn to play the harp."

Khorii found the last reference a bit baffling, but said, "My people understand the need to maintain your bodily systems perhaps longer than you would normally require in order that you may impart your experience and wisdom to your younglings."

"Not that they'll listen worth a plugged credit," a voice said as the grateful trio, who Khorii had imagined were her last patients, departed. Mikaaye still had three or four people lined up and she was going to go assist him. Somehow she had missed the arrival of this elderly female and the small boy accompanying her.

Perhaps the elder had tired of waiting in Mikaaye's line and, seeing Khorii idle, decided to take advantage of the opening. Khorii didn't sense any of the usual problems she'd been treating. In fact, she didn't sense anything at all.

The old lady, lowering herself to the bench with the help of the boy, said, "You're going to have to do something about 'em, you know. They ain't natural."

"Who?" Khorii asked. "The younglings?"

"No. They're all too natural. That's why I wonder how much experience or wisdom they're likely to pick up secondhand from any of these old fossils still hanging on. I mean the haants, of course, the new ones."

"Haants?" Khorii stumbled over the word, which certainly had never been entered in her LAANYE.

The old woman leaned forward, and whispered so loudly it seemed to Khorii she might as well have spoken in a normal voice. "You know, ghosts, girl, spooks. Boo!" Khorii recoiled briefly, and the old woman cackled. "Sorry, couldn't resist. I'm talkin' about spirits of the ones who died during the plague. Things that look like them are flittin' around everyplace like fruit flies at a picnic but it's only their looks that are like our dead"—she leaned forward and whispered again, stabbing a bony, wrinkled finger at Khorii for emphasis with each syllable—"only these ones got no spirit that's any kin to the last occupants of the forms they're takin'."

"They don't? How do you know?"

The woman didn't answer the question but gave her a withering look and sat back with an indignant expression on her face, as if she'd eaten something unpleasant. "It's disrespectful is what it is. And I am here to tell you that however much that bunch may look like our sons and daughters, nieces and nephews, they are up to no good."

"They? The haants, you mean?"

"Who else would I mean?" The old lady rapped the edge of the table with a cane that Khorii hadn't seen before. "Except, like I said, they ain't natural ghosts."

"I don't know a great deal of human folklore," Khorii said, "but my understanding is that ghosts are not natural in the first place. They're—" She started to say supernatural, but the old woman glared at her, clearly offended.

"Not too long ago I'd have said unicorn people weren't natural either, but here you are," she said.

Yes, I am, Khorii thought. *But are you?*

The boy and the old lady exchanged grins.

"Well, of course I am," the elder said aloud, as if Khorii had spoken, too, "in spirit, right, boy?"

Her grandson said, "Oh yes, folk always said my gran had more spirit than a still full of home brew. Dyin' didn't make a bit of difference in that with her, or me either."

Khorii tried to be matter-of-fact, but these people gave her a strange feeling that was neither dread nor fear, but more a sense of vertigo. She could see them, she could hear their words, and they could hear her thoughts, but she could not feel anyone *there* in the same way she felt a living person's presence. There was no *matter* to them, no substance. Though they were much more clear to her than any of the other specters had been thus far, they were communicating with her as if they were holos on a com, except that they didn't need technology, evidently, to manifest themselves.

"That's a good way to put it, honey," the old woman said. "My boy here and me passed over fifteen years ago, but it's close enough here on Rushima for us to come visit when we've a mind or there's a need. Bodies come and go, but spirits seem to stick around for a long time after the mortal shell turns into fertilizer. Something about the atmosphere, or the proximity of the string beans here, I reckon."

"String beans?" There were very tasty green vegetables by that name, but immediately Khorii knew she had misunderstood.

"That's what some non physicsy as well as physically disinclined among my kind call it. They don't believe in string theory, even though they've made the transition to the next strand themselves. They think we are in limbo or purgatory or some other place they heard about in one of their religions. I say call it whatever you will, it all amounts to the same thing. But what it amounts to is we have our own place but can come to visit, too. There's quite a few of us hangin' around, lots longer than me and my grandson, but mostly it's only their family members and friends can see them, usually just before that person is about to join us.

"Me, I've always been more sociable than that, so the boy and me get out a good bit. But my point is, we have a respectable society of haants that call in around here from time to time, and this new riffraff pretending to be our kinfolk is an offense and a disgrace to us."

"Because they're, as you said, unnatural?" Khorii asked.

"Because they're maniacs, that's why! They don't have the spirits of our families—they're mean and destructive and don't care about anybody."

She lowered her voice. "I happen to know they were responsible for that fire at Bug Gulch and for the horse jack breaking under Marsden."

"They can do that?" Jaya and the others had told her that the ghosts on the *Mana* moved things, but she naturally assumed it was just mischief. If Jaya's parents and other crew members were lingering aboard, however belatedly after their deaths, why would they want to do anyone harm? But other, malevolent spirits—

"Sure as I'm pushin' up daisies!" the old lady said with a snort. Khorii saw white hairs quiver on her chin when she did so. "But that's just a saying. Truth is, I can't move a thing. Most of us can't, not here leastways. But these fake haants—"

"This is really interesting, but why are you telling *me*?" Khorii asked.

"Because you got the healin' horn, girlie, and like it or not, that puts you in charge. Sooner or later, someone's gonna suggest you heal the heathen haants and send them to their rest, and we just want you to know who you are dealin' with. Me and my friends mind our own business, watch over our kinfolk, try to meet and greet them when it's their time to join us. We thought when that plague started up that we'd have a mighty big job to do and prepared to welcome and comfort our kin. But our sons and daughters and their wives and husbands never did join us, though we were right here waiting for them. I don't know what became of them, but I can tell you for sure that the haants that caused that fire may look familiar, but they are no kin of anyone I know."

Khorii thought that explained a lot, but it also left even more to be explained. "So who do you think they are? Other than unnatural, that is?"

"I don't know, but I can tell you that they are not human nor your kind neither and you can take that to the bank."

The old woman rose and started hobbling off with the boy's support, vanishing halfway across the room. Khorii rose and went to join Mikaaye, who was finishing up with his last patients, a man and a woman. As she approached, they rose, winked at her, and flicked from sight as if a holo had been switched off.

Mikaaye had had another "string bean" visit him as well. "I thought the old man standing beside me was a local doctor because he told me all about everybody I was seeing and who their families were and what had been wrong with everyone. I thought he wanted to coach me on the local customs. But when I told someone what he had advised, they said he'd been not practicing medicine for the last twenty years on account of being dead. This is a *very* unusual place, Khorii."

Hap, who had come up behind them in time to catch the end of the exchange, said, "No kidding! Listen, just now I almost got trampled by a horse galloping down the main street of town. Lucky for me I grew up around critters. I headed her off and calmed her down. Elder Bawb came out and said she was one of that team that was transporting the patients from Bug Gulch. Looks like something happened to them. Bawb tried hailing their mobile, but nobody answered."

"That doesn't sound good," Khorii agreed.

"So Jaya and Captain Bates think we'd better take a couple of the shuttles out there. Cap'n Bates said Mikey should probably come with."

"Mikey?" Khorii asked.

Mikaaye said, "It is my nickname. Hap says it is what my name is in Standard." He sounded very pleased. Khorii thought it likely that, since the human universe had become so familiar with the Linyaari recently, human boys named Mikey might soon be called Mikaaye as well.

They joined their shipmates in the shuttles, Jaya piloting the large shuttle cargo, Captain Bates flying her own personal craft. Hap came, because of his size and knowledge of animals, and Sesseli, because her telekinesis might come in handy. Khorii and Mikaaye both started to board Jaya's shuttle, but Captain Bates stopped them. "Khorii, I think since we don't know what's going on yet, or what the danger is, you should stay behind. That way there'll be one healer in reserve to help the rest of us if need be."

"I must be the one to go then," Khorii said. "If there is more plague among the injured, I will know, as Mikaaye would not."

"What does it matter if I can see the plague or not? I could cure it as well as you, Khorii, and I am larger and male," Mikaaye said, then added, "and you are unique among our people in that you can see the plague. You cannot be replaced."

"I'm sure your mother feels the same about you," Khorii said, and prepared to board, but Jaya and Hap blocked her.

"Mikey's right, Khorii," Jaya said. Khorii thought angrily that Jaya was just agreeing with Mikaaye because Hap was, and they were boys. Jaya was inclined to defer to boys, especially if it wasn't her they were disagreeing with. "You are unique. The entire universe needs you."

Captain Bates laid a hand on her shoulder. "You're right in that you're the senior Linyaari on this mission, Khorii, but that means Mikaaye needs a little experience soloing without another healer along. Also, if anything happens to the rest of us, you're better prepared to function independently to do whatever needs doing than Mikaaye is."

"Besides," Sesseli said from Khorii's elbow, "somebody has to keep Khiindi company. He's been acting like a real fraidy cat since we landed."

chapter 18

As more and more of her new family returned from the plagued worlds, Ariin met her uncle, Lariinye, her father's brother, as well as her grandparents on her mother's side of the family. She visited her parents often by com unit and also got to know "Uncle Joh" Becker and his odd-looking first mate Maak, who seemed to have a screw stuck in the center of his forehead where a horn would be. She also caught glimpses of the father of most Petaybean cats, the bushy-tailed RK.

She learned about the ways and customs of her people, stopping to wonder now and then that she not only had people but they had customs of their own, an advanced society, and a role in the broader universe much more important, it seemed to her, than the one the Friends played. *Her* people did a lot of good without kidnapping poor innocent eggs from their mothers' wombs. Even their scientific probing was done in a more kindly manner.

She was pleased to see that the Others had survived, unchanged, from her time as well, though people referred to them as the Ancestors. Her parents were quarantined in the midst of the grazing grounds preferred by these ancestors, who were apparently unaffected by the plague. Probably because it was gone, she thought.

Which made her all the more anxious to put her plan into action. She was able to do it more quickly and easily than she expected, and with less deception.

"Ariin," Mother said to her one day while they were chatting on the com unit, "do you remember the first day you met us speaking to Uncle Hafiz and Karina?"

"No," she said. "I remember you, and Maati, but I have not met these—"

"They were the colorfully dressed humans," she explained. "Karina was very excited because she had seen in one of her visions that you would be coming to us."

Ariin, who had had a lot to get used to over the past two weeks, still felt doubtful, though she began to recall some non-Linyaari biped—

"She wears a lot of purple, and an immense amount of jewelry," Mother added.

The woman's image swept into Ariin's memory at once. "Oh, yes, she reminded me of Akasa, only more"—she started to say fleshy, but Mother seemed to be fond of these people so she corrected herself, "purple."

"Yes, I can see the resemblance although I believe that Karina is a much more well-meaning person than Akasa, from what you've told me. At any rate, they would like to invite you to the Moon of Opportunity so they can meet you personally. Uncle Hafiz is one of my human family, and, as you have no doubt heard, has been a great benefactor to our people."

"So I have to do what he wants?" Ariin asked.

"No, dear, of course not. But you will enjoy MOO, and Hafiz and Karina grow lovely things in their gardens just for us and give entertaining parties. He is interested in you because he considers me a daughter, although I call him Uncle because he is the uncle of Rafik Nadazdek, one of my human foster fathers. He considers you part of his family as well."

"We have a very complicated family, don't we, Mother?"

She had heard many stories in many versions since she

had been there. Both sets of grandparents had been lost and considered dead at one time, as had her father and Uncle Lariinye. Grimalkin, the creature who had stolen her and given her to the Friends, had been responsible for reunions as well. She wondered if he thought that made what he'd done to her all right. If he did, she didn't agree.

"I suppose you could say that, yes. If you'd like to go, Maati and Thariinye will take you when they go to prepare for another foray into Federation space to relieve your great-aunt Neeva's team."

Reluctance and suspicion were banished from her tone as Ariin responded to her mother this time. "Oh, I'd love that, Avvi!" she said, beaming and using the Linyaari word for "mother." "When do we start?"

Three sleeps later she boarded a space vessel for the first time. Like the rest of the Linyaari fleet, this ship was egg-shaped and decorated with bright colors, aqua and yellow, and swags of gold with little floral flourishes.

Maati had been teaching her to speak Standard using the LAANYE, an interesting device that, once programmed, taught one a language while one slept. It didn't always ex-plain idiomatic expressions, however, or proper name refer-ences, so Maati expanded on the lessons the next day when Ariin asked her questions—or even thought them.

It was very hard to keep anything hidden from Maati.

The flight did not take long, and they didn't see a lot of space, which was rather disappointing, since MOO was fairly close, galactically speaking.

The entire surface was covered with large, rounded pavil-ions like the ones her people slept in. Though they were white on the outside, she quickly saw as soon as she entered the terminal that from the inside it looked as if she were on a planet with proper atmosphere, a sky, buildings, just like back on Vhiliinyar, only grander and more full of the sort of details Akasa would have liked.

In person, Karina Harakamian reminded Ariin of Akasa less than she had on the com unit. While Karina, like her husband, looked shrewd and as though she knew how to get what she wanted, she also looked as though one of the things she very much wanted was to be liked. In fact, she looked as if she wanted Ariin to like her, which was rather a new experience for the girl. Her Linyaari relatives could read her mind and judge her feelings and so were not unsure of how she felt about them, but although Karina could sometimes see things others could not, she couldn't read thoughts the way Linyaari could, though she believed otherwise, or pretended to.

Karina's conceit, however, could prove useful, Ariin noted.

The Harakamians received her, Maati, and Thariinye in a distractingly luscious surrounding—a garden layered with bursts of succulent grasses and blossoms among rows and ranks of other delicious greenery. Unlike the reception halls of the Friends, where guests approached through sterile and intimidatingly vast corridors, the Harakamians sat at the culmination of a meandering journey through outdoor rooms, roofed with boughs of graceful trees, and floored by mosses and blue, pink, and lilac ground-hugging flowers. Small waterfalls and splashing fountains tiled in colors that rivaled the flowers furnished these spaces, while streamlets bridged with filigreed arches laced the landscape together. The end of the pathway was paved with stones that emitted intricately intertwined melodies with each footfall.

Hafiz Harakamian himself was shorter than any Linyaari and much rounder in all respects. His cummerbund formed a band around his middle much like the stripe on a ball. His golden shoes had curling toes that would never have fit a Linyaari foot but would have pleased Akasa, Ariin knew. His trousers, of royal blue silk, billowed about his ankles before being concealed by the hem of a long vest striped with blue, rose, and lilac overlaid with a golden relief that resembled the stylized feathers of a peacock. Over this he wore a longer robe of fabric that shimmered from gold to red to purple with the same sort of figures as the vest, only larger. His head was wrapped with a magnificent twist of scarlet, bejeweled with a golden stone that looked very like a cat's eye, set in an elaborate structure of blue and red stones, into which a lilac plume had been placed so that it fluttered with the slightest movement.

His face was dark and the plump cheeks and chin somewhat masked by a dark, closely trimmed beard and flowing mustaches, both a startling black. His eyes were small and shrewd and slightly shifty, and when she touched his mind, she quickly withdrew, overwhelmed by a labyrinth of knowledge, contacts, power and resources, motives, reasons, plots, and schemes. He was the first human she had encountered in person. She hoped they were not all so complicated.

Karina, whose clothes and jewels were in the same style but different colors from those she had worn on previous occasions, felt almost as tricky.

One other characteristic of both that Ariin noted was that each had committed acts in the past that would hardly fit in with the Linyaari code of ethics. Hafiz's aura was not without undertones of violence. Karina had had no one to look after her as a child, and consequently had looked out for herself and no one else for a long time after. Perhaps the Linyaari had healed both of them so that they no longer required their less acceptable defenses, or perhaps it was that they had each other now. Ariin found them both extraordinary and didn't quite know what to make of it. These two could easily have been the same sort of beings as the Friends, though without the power to shapeshift.

Instead, they opened their perfumed arms and greeted her with affection and genuine relief that she had come to them apparently unharmed. She curtsied, as the Friends always wished her to do when they were wearing particularly grand aspects.

"Dear child, welcome to our humble Moon of Opportunity," Hafiz said, rising to meet her.

"Thaakew," she said, trying to speak Standard for the first time in public. It wasn't a good fit. She tried again, "Thaank yew."

She needed more practice. Her mouth and vocal cords were shaped awkwardly for this language. Her parents, Maati, and Thariinye managed well enough, so she should be able to as well. Her mother spoke Standard as well as the humans. However, the Harakamians were used to the Linyaari accent and found it charming, so Ariin didn't feel the need to try too hard to lose hers.

"Telepathy is so much more convenient, isn't it, my dear?" Karina sympathized. "However, my beloved husband is—telepathically challenged, shall we say—so we must speak aloud out of courtesy to him."

"Yezz," Ariin said, then, determinedly trying to force her tongue to mimic Karina's. "Yez-s."

It grew easier the more she practiced, and with the help of the LAANYE while she slept, Ariin found that her conversations the next day were almost effortless.

Finally, the time came for Maati and Thariinye to take their leave.

"Don't leave me!" Ariin cried, rising from the table they all had been dining at so quickly she knocked it sideways. Cutlery, dishes, and ornaments slid off onto the ground. Bowls of food overturned, and one dumped into Karina's lavender lap, making her squeal. A servant scuttled forward to sponge at the clothing, but Karina waved the woman aside.

"Zhorry," she apologized and bent to pick up the fallen objects, half-expecting a blow. The Friends had never beaten her, but they had occasionally cuffed her when irritated. As they seemed oblivious to their own strength compared to her size and relative fragility, she had quickly learned to duck.

Maati and Thariinye turned to her, but it was Hafiz who touched her and guided her to her feet. "There, there, child. We thought you might want to stay with us while your relatives are on their mission. You have yet to see all of the diversions and games we have to offer, all entertaining and educational, I assure you, with many young people of your own age, both Linyaari and human, to befriend you. Or, if you are not yet ready for so much novelty, a ship can return you to Vhiliinyar if you prefer."

"You really should stay here, Ariin," Maati encouraged, her. "It's a wonderful place. We have a mission to perform, and we must go. The sooner we all do our part, the sooner all of us can return home."

"Yezs," Ariin said, still in Standard and aloud, "but I need to go with you. I will find Khorii my twin and help her so that our parents can be healed."

Thariinye looked puzzled. "We did not know that was what you wished," he said. Of course he didn't. If he and Maati had known, they would never have brought her this far. They would have probed her thoughts and found what they would have considered questionable motives and forbidden her to come. In front of the powerful and more easily fooled humans, speaking aloud for their benefit, she had a better chance of getting what she needed.

"But it is very dangerous, my child," Uncle Hafiz said. "And you are very young and unused to the wider universe."

"I can learn," she said. "Khorii learned."

He was wavering. He was not actually averse to potentially putting innocents in harm's way if there was a point to it, or a profit to be made. But she needed something more compelling to convince him, something that would make him insist that Maati and Thariinye take her with them.

Karina, who had risen to see the damage to her gown, now swayed, a tidal wave of lavender veils rippling. Uncle

Hafiz was by her side at once, supporting her and attempting to lower her into a chair. Karina was having none of that.

"They walk!" she cried, her voice echoing and deep as if she were speaking from the bottom of a well. "The dead walk. They destroy all, enslave the living. Everyone, everyone in terrible danger. Khorii—oh no, must warn Khorii! Only her twin can save her!"

Staggering, she allowed herself to be lowered to her chair. Ariin tried not to look triumphant as she stole a peek at Maati and Thariinye. Compared to the friends, humans were so very easy to persuade. Karina suddenly straightened and, looking quite focused and alert, said, "That settles it. Ariin really must go with Maati and Thariinye. But do be careful, dears. What is lurking out there is something the likes of which none of you have ever encountered before." Despite the others' questions, Karina couldn't supply any more information.

Even though she had succeeded in continuing her mission to find Khorii, Ariin couldn't help shuddering at the human's words. *Enslave the living*—it sounded like what she had suffered at the hands of the Friends. And that was something she was determined never to go through again.

marl blinked hard, looked away, purposefully tracked the *Mana*'s progress out of the Solojo system, noted the coordinates and then, casually—nonchalantly he would have said—glanced back down at the form in the pallet. It grinned back up at him, a Jolly Roger grin under a translucent overlay of mud brown dust with rather sickening threads of red running through it. It would have been much easier to look at if the underlying skull had had dark empty sockets as it properly ought to have, but instead, jellied egg whites with rotted black centers swimming in the middle of them filled the holes. They stared at him with a thinly veiled malice that he had seldom seen outside the frame of a mirror.

He looked away again, hoping that somehow the thing was an aftereffect of staring at the laser lights too long. Other pallets swooped closer like buzzards, surrounding his perch until they were close enough for him to see their occupants as well. There was no beauty contest to be won here. Nobody reclining on any of the berths would qualify to become Miss Corazon, though some of the more solid figures did seem to be female. Not only did the corpselike figures on the pallets seem to be in various stages of decomposition—or were they indeed composing themselves?—but opacity also seemed to be optional. Coyly, a couple of the females turned into dust and dissipated as he watched, while the male beneath him grew more solid and human-looking.

No doubt this process would be of tremendous scientific fascination to someone with more curiosity and a less highly developed sense of self-preservation, but Marl was disinclined to stick around and see what other tricks these things could do. He tried dropping the pallet straight back to its dock, but the other pallets blocked him, much as if they were all in a large airborne game of soccer. Corpse hands reached for him.

Marl twisted on the pallet and leaped to the floor, landing lightly and thanking his jail-bound opportunities for fine-tuning his body. He sprinted for the door, the pallets zooming toward him, his head full of what sounded like canned laughter on a very old vid, full of crackle and buzz. He reached the opening seconds ahead of his pursuers, and as it irised shut behind him, a pallet slammed into the doorway and wedged there. The sound of other pallets crashing into the wall followed, or that was what he imagined it was anyway. He wasn't about to go back and investigate. Had he given the situation a little more reflection, he would have realized that while the perpetually solid pallets could not penetrate the portal, never mind the solid wall, there was no guarantee that the occupants of the pallets shared that limitation.

How will we know where Khorii is?" Ariin asked Thariinye as the *Nheifaarir,* the egg-shaped spacecraft assigned to Maati's family—Ariin's family, too, now—entered the area the ship's computer designated as Federation-controlled space.

"We already know where they are, little one," Thariinye said in a superior manner as annoying as that of the lordliest

Friend. "But that is not our main concern. Our mission is to assist in the rescue and relocation of the LoiLoiKuans." He could not say their name any better than Ariin could, and instead showed her the word on the LAANYE screen. "Your sister met the younger LoiLoiKuans at Maganos Moonbase, where they were brought by the Federation to spare them an earlier catastrophe their elders feared would overtake the planet before the plague came along."

"From what are we rescuing them?" Ariin asked.

"According to your sister's transmission, some sort of a mutant sea dragon."

"Is she going to help, too?"

"No, when last we heard, she was en route to Rushima for an undisclosed purpose."

"Why was it undisclosed?"

"That, too, was undisclosed."

"How are we going to assist? Or is that also undisclosed?"

"It was not disclosed because nobody is quite sure how to proceed. Let me check with your father-sister."

Thariinye seemed to be an intelligent male, but he could annoy her without the slightest effort. He acted as if she didn't know her own relationship to Maati.

"Dearest." He used thought-talk to address Ariin's aunt, who was monitoring the ship's controls and wore earbuds so that incoming communications did not disturb the peace of the off-duty crew members. *"Have we received any instructions regarding the rescue of the LoiLoiKuan?"*

Maati removed an earbud and swiveled in her seat to address them out loud. "No one is quite sure how to go about it. These LoiLoiKuans are aquatic and cannot survive outside of seawater."

"Are there many?"

"Not anymore. The plague eradicated a good portion of the population. Vessels that will hold enough water to sustain one or two individuals will not fit into the average Linyaari ship. Furthermore, our people and the survivors of the humanoid population have yet to locate enough tanks to rescue the entire population."

"How did the kids get from their planet to the school?" Ariin asked.

"As I explained," Thariinye said with exaggerated patience, "the Federation transported them."

"How? What did they use?"

"An excellent question!" Maati said as she toggled the comlink. "LaBoue Base, this is Maati on the *Nheifaarir* again. Has anyone asked the LoiLoiKuan students how they were transported to Maganos?"

The answer didn't come until Thariinye's shift at the helm. Ariin thought it a shame that thought-talk did not travel over the vast distances of space. Instead, the ship had to hail the nearest relay base or sister ship, and that ship or base then had to relay the next closest. Then, of course, as Maati pointed out, it would take even longer while someone on Maganos queried the LoiLoiKuan students. Finally, LaBoue Base transmitted the response. "They say they were brought in a Federation tanker filled with seawater."

"A tanker? They have ships large enough to hold great quantities of seawater?" Ariin asked.

She was immediately sorry she had. It gave Thariinye another opportunity to act superior even though he clearly hadn't known about tankers either.

"Naturally they would have that sort of vessel," he said. "It makes sense. They might have to transport all manner of liquid assets from place to place—drinking water, for instance, or liquid fuel for planet-bound vehicles."

"The next step is to have our people check each of the Federation bases and outposts for such a vessel," Maati said, and relayed the request via LaBoue. For three sleep periods as the *Nheifaarir* drove deeper into Federation space, they received a monotonous series of brief, negative responses. No tankers were located on any of the worlds or moons currently being visited by Linyaari, nor did any of their people recall seeing a vessel they could identify as a tanker.

"Do they look different than other Federation ships?" Ariin asked.

"Bigger," Thariinye said. "They'd have to be larger. After all, if you're transporting water, or the younger portion of an aquatic population, you could hardly dehydrate them, then just add water later." Ariin laughed a little at his joke in spite of herself, but Maati gave him a pained smile while he snorted and guffawed and chortled and chuckled until his eyes ran, he was so tickled by his own cleverness.

"LaBoue Base, please access Federation database for images of tanker-class vessels and transmit," Maati requested.

"We don't really need all that, dearest," Thariinye said. "We can extrapolate from what we've seen of their vessels and surmise that—"

"Perhaps you can extrapolate, Lifemate, or I can, but we need the image for those among our people who are less imaginatively gifted than ourselves. And don't call me dearest, please, dearest. You only use that sort of endearment because you used to court so many females it taxed your memory to call each by her proper name."

There followed a lengthy discussion of what he should call her, what she should call him, the impression of their relationship such endearments would evoke in outsiders, the impression *other* endearments would evoke in outsiders, the deeper psychological implications of addressing each other by such endearments and what each conveyed to the other and others about the person being addressed by such endearments.

Ariin found all of this only slightly less interesting than the questions the Friends had posed during their daily interrogation sessions. Her mind wandered, as did her gaze.

There was nothing new to look at, and she could hear the argument even when her aunt and Thariinye switched to thought-talk. The only thing that changed was the size of the blip on the sensor screen. It grew bigger and bigger, unheeded by her contentious fellow crew members. It occurred to her that the kind of discussion the two were having was a device they employed to relieve the boredom of space travel. Still, some times were less boring than others.

The blip in the screen approaching the central light hypnotized Ariin to the point that when she looked up and beheld a vessel in the viewport, she was quite startled to see it seemingly hanging there in front of them.

"Excuse me!" she said out loud. "Do you think a tanker-class vessel looks anything like that?" and pointed to the ship, which seemed to be on a collision course with them.

Maati let out an exclamation and took evasive action, which rolled the *Nheifaarir* out of the other ship's path. When they were clear, and all three of them could breathe again, Thariinye said, "Oh, I doubt it, dea—— Ariin. That would be a huge coincidence, and besides, that ship looks much too—"

The com screen lit up and an image of a ship very much like the one they had almost crashed into appeared on the screen, the image morphing into various views that continued to look very similar to the reckless vessel.

Maati said, "It looks the same to *me*," and, seeing a signal light indicating a waiting transmission, switched from remote relay to a local frequency.

A voice, mechanical-sounding in tone and yet with an underlying anxiety that was palpable to a telepath, even many months later, said, "Mayday, Mayday. This is niner two seven three zed Federation tanker-class vessel en route to Rushima with freshwater for plague survivors. Since our ship left base, sixteen crew members have died of plaguelike symptoms, including the entire command staff, our pilot, co-

pilot, navigator, and engineering crew. Six others are exhib-
iting similar distress. Mayday, Mayday."

Maati hailed them, but received no response except a rep-
etition of the distress signal.

"Sad, but convenient," Thariinye said.

"Yes," Maati said, casting a sideways assessing glance at
Ariin, "isn't it?"

"I didn't DO anything!" Ariin responded. *"I can't!"*

*"No, I suppose it is only luck that we encounter a ship we
need en route to where the sister that you so desperately
wish to see is."*

"YES!" Ariin said, but she didn't think Maati believed
her.

They boarded the ship, and that part was quite interesting, though Ariin was not allowed to board but was told to
stay on the bridge of the *Nheifaarir,* while Maati and
Thariinye checked for survivors. At least Ariin didn't have
to worry about the larger ship crashing into theirs, since
the Linyaari ship locked itself magnetically to the hull of
the tanker. Thariinye proved himself useful by detecting the
code necessary to open the hatch to the docking bay. A
bit of remote conversation between the ships' computers,
and the hatch irised open. Maati, having already attached
her helmet, gauntlets, and gravity boots to her shipsuit,
was out the Nheifaarir's hatch before Thariinye left the
bridge.

The helmets carried AV communication chips, so Ariin
didn't feel too left out as she watched while Maati and
Thariinye boarded, floating into the ship at first. When
Thariinye had closed the hatch, pointedly speaking the code
aloud as he punched the keypad so Ariin could clearly see
and hear everything he did, their boots touched the deck and
Ariin saw Maati's back and the brightly lit interior of the
bay ahead of her on half the screen, while the other half of the
screen transmitted the image from Maati's helmet showing

the bay, the room where the mechanics and other crew accessed it, and the corridors beyond.

"Someone must be alive!" Ariin said excitedly. "They turned on the lights for you."

"Sorry, youngling," Thariinye's voice answered. "The power cells on these Federation ships last for years and the interiors stay illuminated except in designated sleep areas."

They entered the room and found two bodies, both badly decomposed.

Maati removed her helmet. "Life support is still functioning, even though life seems to have ceased," she said.

"How do you know?" Ariin asked.

"For one thing, the suit's sensors tell us. And the bodies would not decompose without the presence of oxygen."

"They could have decomposed before the oxygen supply ran out," Thariinye said.

"Yes, but that's not the case, according to the sensors. However, I've purified the air here so you can safely remove your helmet without smelling the deceased."

"Please don't!" Ariin said. "I want to see, too."

"This is not pleasant, youngling," Thariinye said, "not a fit experience for one so sheltered—"

Maati, however, replaced her helmet on her head, and said, "Sorry, Ariin, I forgot. Of course you want to know what's going on, and it's safer if you do. We'll have to remove them if we need to purify something or if someone has survived, but otherwise you can monitor us throughout this phase of the mission."

"But corpses, Maati—" Thariinye protested.

"If she is to participate in this mission, then she will be seeing some, I imagine. Are you bothered by the state of these humans, Ariin?"

Ariin peered closely at the screen. The human bodies did seem altered from their normal living state, with parts of their interiors visible, parts of the exteriors sloughing off, and their colors somewhat unusual. "I am not familiar enough with the usual form these creatures take to be unsettled by the alterations," she said after thinking it over.

"True enough," Thariinye said. "Perhaps the smell is the worst of it. It will be easier to work here if we designate a certain area for the dead and take them there."

Maati's helmet view nodded in agreement. Thariinye looked at an instrument panel and pointed. "Here. There is a cold locker off the infirmary. Many of the bodies may have been taken there already."

"I doubt it," Maati said. "If the living suspected the dead died of the plague, they wouldn't have touched them. But I agree it is a good place. We are unlikely to need anything in the infirmary, since that is where humans keep their healing devices."

They collected more bodies, a process Ariin was happy to have no part in. Time and again Maati and Thariinye lifted a human in the unattractive state they attained after death and bore the body down the corridor to the infirmary. After the first six, the cold locker could hold no more, so they laid the other bodies on examining tables and the floor. On the bridge, four people had died at their duty stations. The latrines were where most of the dead had congregated. Ariin didn't see too much of this because Maati needed to remove her helmet to use her horn. The mess was only tolerable, she said, because their horns lessened the stench.

When the last of the remains were inside the infirmary, the internal temperature of the entire room reduced, and the hatch sealed behind Maati and Thariinye, the two located the sonic showers, cleansed themselves and their garments, and returned to the bridge of the tanker.

The com unit switched to full screen, and Maati spoke directly to Ariin. "According to the cargo manifest, the shipment of freshwater is still in the tank. If Rushima still needs it, the most practical course would be to deliver the water, then proceed with emptied tanks to LoiLoiKua. We'll delay as little as possible, but there seems no other logical course. Rushima is by far the closest inhabited world, and if we triangulate back to LoiLoiKua and have the others waiting for us there, we should be able to effect the rescue within the next week."

"How will the three of us fly two ships?" Ariin asked. "The tanker had a huge crew."

"Ah, but the *Nheifaarir* has a powerful tractor beam," Thariinye said. "We'll tow the tanker to Rushima."

chapter 20

Elviiz could not seem to power down. He should have gone with Khorii. His primary function was to instruct and protect her, and he had for the first time in their lives neglected that task.

It had seemed more urgent to assist Jalonzo in finding a cure for the plague, but the plague no longer manifested itself. The sea dragon specimen had proved disappointing, if somewhat puzzling. It contained not one strand of DNA but several, as if it were a collection of creatures instead of a single specimen. It was whale, fish, octopus, crab, coral, shrimp, krill and other fish, plankton and other seaweed, and LoiLoikuan.

Jalonzo had grunted disapprovingly. "Somebody's pulling somebody's leg. This isn't from a creature. It's a collection. A hoax."

"But I can assure you, it was real and the LoiLoiKuans feared it. It attacked one of them. Had Khorii not been there, he might have died."

Jalonzo shook his head.

"You can verify my account by cross-referencing it with testimony from Neeva and Khorii," Elviiz said. "I do not lie, Jalonzo."

"No, but anyone can be deceived. Perhaps these sea people just want a free ride off their dying planet to one where they can be with their grandchildren. Living among the Linyaari seems very safe at the moment."

Elviiz could not understand Jalonzo's reaction. While he found the sea creature's multiple nature confusing, even mysterious, Jalonzo found it suspicious and literally incredible. Perhaps he was disappointed at not being able to cure the plague, and it was making him cynical. Perhaps he was belatedly undergoing the grief experience that affected some peoples in profound and peculiar ways.

Whatever the reason, Jalonzo had now deserted the lab and was dedicating his energies to instructing himself and others on the proper care and maintenance of the city the adolescents and children had inherited. The older people provided some of the instruction, but many had been unable to function even before the plague, their bodies inadequate for the tasks they had once performed every day. Elviiz kept busy during the day accepting data from these elders and collating it, filling in places where their memories were faulty. But the best he could do was either perform the tasks himself or provide a tutorial. He was not a mentor with years of experience and anecdotes to illustrate his lessons, as he observed the elders doing.

So Elviiz had taken to watching the city square through the windows at night. He often thought he saw movement, though it had been indistinct and fleeting. Now that the rainy season was ending, the night before had been a period of high winds but clear skies. The moons, one of them full, the other a crescent, cast deep shadows of the buildings and trees. The howling wind gave the illusion that the shadows moved.

Tonight was another such night. He scanned the same cityscape as he stood at a second-floor window, while in the background he processed data he had collected from elders earlier that day.

There it was again. Definite movement, not a reflection or shadow. Someone was moving from the communications tower. Though the movement confined itself to shadows, Elviiz attuned his visual sensors to the discrepancy in the light and picked out the familiar face and form of Marl Fidd.

How had he escaped the jail? What had that scoundrel been doing in the com tower? Before Elviiz had made up his mind to go apprehend the fellow and question him, he detected a small vessel descending toward the docking bay. A shuttle? Marl was *leaving*? It was not authorized, surely, but neither was it necessarily a bad thing that the thug would no longer be in Corazon for them to worry about.

But who was that behind him? Had he acquired a gang?

Elviiz shut down his background function to add power to his kinetic faculties. He would have to be a posse of one, apprehending Corazon's foremost criminal and what appeared to be his gang.

But as Marl slunk from the shadows into the moonlight, the gang following him, members of which bore a resemblance to the pictures of some of the cemetery's inhabitants, seemed less solid. The buildings they passed by were clearly visible through them at times.

There were ten distinct forms besides Marl's. Elviiz knew he could be on the street and between Marl and his vehicle quickly enough to prevent escape, if that seemed the wisest course. However, interfering with Marl's departure would also interfere with collecting data on his companions. So Elviiz waited until Marl entered the deserted terminal at the docking bay, the others following him, passing straight through the door he closed behind him as if it didn't exist.

Only then did Elviiz run out of the administration building and over to the terminal, thinking that closer proximity would reveal the nature of the beings accompanying Marl.

However, the shuttle was waiting when Marl reached it,

and Elviiz was still some distance away when the teenager boarded it. The hatch sealed behind him, but, again, this did nothing to deter his companion from entering the shuttle by other means.

As the shuttle ascended with all of them, Elviiz tried to tabulate the data he had just collected. It refused to fall into place.

He returned to the street. From that level, undistracted by a specific goal, he sensed forms moving counter to the wind and a rustling noisier than the trees. His optical sensors sharpened their focus so that he saw several entities approaching him from three directions. At his back was the terminal.

The noises were not just noise, he realized, but some sort of communication. Spandard?

He sharpened his auditory focus as well and was able to increase the volume. Although he felt communication was transpiring, it was too indistinct for him to detect the meaning. But the movement, and the tone, both felt distinctly menacing.

"*Holá,*" he said in Spandard. "*Yo soy* Elviiz. Please speak clearly so that I may record and interpret your communications."

He was not afraid, although theoretically he was capable of fear. However, these entities could not harm him. They might try, not realizing that he was an android, and not a wholly organic being. They might inflict damage, but on the other hand, he might inflict damage on them. But such considerations were counterproductive. Attempting to understand them was the course that he alone was equipped to pursue.

They closed in, making no direct attempts to communicate that he could discern. "Attacking me is futile," he said confidently. But his optical sensors at that point informed him of a subtle distinction he had not detected previously.

The creatures to either side of him seemed transparent because he could see the walls of the building through them. But the walls had bands of ornate tile inlaid in them, and as one of the forms passed beyond the band of tile, the tile Elviiz had assumed was behind the creature moved *with* it. The creatures were not transparent with the wall showing through them. They had incorporated portions of the walls into themselves.

"Fascinating!" he said aloud. "Will you not please explain to me how you are absorbing portions of this structure without damaging it?"

Their expressions did not change, but as they drew nearer, Elviiz heard a distinct rattle and clatter from behind them. The upper portion of the walls was crumbling and showering unsupported fragments down onto the walkway.

That was his last observation before the roof, literally speaking, caved in.

Marl Fidd's ride, a geriatric shuttle of distant but uncertain origins, landed without notice. Marl boarded. Had the hatch been the sort of door he could slam behind him, he would have done so.

The shuttle pilot didn't turn around as Marl took his seat. "I thought you said you were coming alone," the pilot grunted.

"I am alone," Marl replied. He'd better be. But looking around, all he saw was the interior of the shuttle. There was no way this bloke could know about the ghosts or zombies or whatever those bloody bony buggers on the pallets had been. Marl's vision was still a bit dazzled from the laser bolts of the com tower, and sparkly dots seemed to glow like fairy dust all over the shuttle's interior, but he didn't see anything more alarming than that. "Something must be wrong with your instruments. You lot really should hijack a better class of vessel."

"Watch your mouth, or you can leave right now, mate," the pilot growled. "And your friends, too."

"What friends? Turn around and look at me, you silly git. I left my entourage back in my posh hotel suite. See here, I don't know what you've been shooting or sniffing, but you'd best get this bird off the ground unless you want to piss off some very influential people by bungling a juicy mission." Then, since he didn't actually know that the pilot himself was not an influential crewman, he added in a more conciliatory tone, "No offense, mate, but why fly a leaky bucket like this with entire abandoned space fleets to choose from?"

"Our buckets may leak, but we don't get plague from boarding them—*mate*," the man replied.

"Oh. Well, I know how to fix that problem," Marl said.

"How's that?"

"For me to know and you to find out," he said, then, seeing from the gleam of the pilot's eye that the man was considering ways of finding out that would violate Marl's personal privacy, not to mention his hide, added, "In good time."

Marl strapped into his seat and closed his eyes. He didn't want to engage in any more witty repartee with this bozo. He was afraid every time he opened his mouth he might shriek something that would tell the pilot of his adventures in the com tower. They didn't necessarily mind insanity on pirate vessels, but they mostly tolerated the violent kind aimed at potential marks or the law, not the kind that broke out in cold sweats and screamed like they were supposed to make other people scream.

Closing his eyes was a bad move, however. His sense of hearing took up the slack, and he heard what he was certain were nonstandard noises. By the time the shuttle hit the outer atmosphere, it sounded as if the entire damned ship was coming apart. Marl's eyes were wide-open by then.

"What by the fires of Krim did you do to this vessel?" the

pilot demanded, reaching frantically for toggles, buttons, and switches as he watched screens that shimmied with the vibrations of the craft as if they'd been jellied.

The pilot bawled a Mayday into his com unit.

The communication he received in return was in a language Marl did not understand, but it sounded reassuring. That was good, wasn't it?

His teeth threatened to shake from his head, and suddenly he was very cold, but perhaps that was fear. Then, too, judging from the frost forming on the instruments, perhaps not.

The shuttle gave a final jerk, and space whizzed past the frosted viewport. Marl thought that they were falling. What a nuisance, after all he'd done to escape Corazon, to end up crashing back into it again.

Had he known he was losing consciousness, he would have been glad. It wouldn't hurt so much that way, probably.

But the next thing he knew, he was looking into a bright, circular beam of light, and next to it was a pair of anthracite eyes topped by a single slick black wing of an eyebrow. The eyes did not look happy to see him.

"I'm alive, right?" he asked. First things first, after all. "On the ship?"

"Yes, thanks to our tractor beam," the single-browed pirate said in Standard thick with an accent that could have been Spandard, but wasn't quite. "Otherwise, we would not be having this little talk. What did you do to the shuttle?"

"Nothing!" Marl insisted. "Nothing. It's old. It's—"

"It was totally refurbished," a cold voice said from beyond the light. "And now, between the time it left our bay and returned with your sorry hide in it, the walls are falling down, the inner hull is corroded away, and it looks like it's been eaten from the inside out."

"Not guilty!" Marl said. "Your pilot can tell you."

"He could, except he didn't make it. The last thing he said

before he died was something about you bringing someone with you when you boarded."

"Did you find anyone else?"

"No one but you and him."

"Well, there you go. I don't like speaking ill of the dead, but had he been under any unusual stress lately? Frankly, I don't think the ship was the only thing that was cracking up."

The unibrow pirate grunted. "You stay where I can keep an eye on you at all times."

Marl followed him to the bridge, where the captain greeted him with cordiality appropriate from people who had every reason to think he was going to make them rich and powerful. "Our mutual friends say you can plot us a lucrative course, boy. Where's it to be, then?"

"Here it is," Marl said promptly. While contacting this ship, he had also scanned the files at the com tower for the *Mana*'s new course. "We're following this ship, see? They're the ones will lead us to the cargo."

"There are many rich cargoes not worth the lives of my people," the captain said. "We have steered clear of the plague this long, and I intend that we continue to do so."

"No problem there, mate. There's two horns aboard that ship. And they know me." Marl was very careful not to say how. "I'm sure that if they are not already inclined to decontaminate our cargo in the interest of public health, we can— talk them into it."

The captain nodded, and Marl programmed the course into the ship's computer.

He felt very nervous after that because he saw in the eyes of the captain and the unibrow, who turned out to be the first officer, that with the course plotted, there was no reason for them not to downsize the crew by one, namely him. He was so clearly the outsider, too, as the others all lacked his flair for grooming. Greasy snarled hair with lots of stuff in it he hesitated to try to identify, appalling teeth oddly gleaming with metal and sometimes gemstones, and a very random fashion sense, the unifying element of which seemed to be that the garment be torn, tattered, shredded, or with repairs proudly accentuated with wildly contrasting thread or fabric. No sleek shipsuits for these people. They also taxed the ventilation system with a peculiar bouquet of smells—sweat and more pungent body odors mingled with an overlay of musky, acrid perfume. He should have remained in the condition he'd been in during his stay in the mansion's kitchen. It would have been much more appropriate for this company.

The women and children among them did not give the ship a particularly homey air, nor did Marl find their presence reassuring. While the men looked like they'd think nothing of killing him, some of the women looked like they'd think about it very carefully, selecting the choicest cuts, seasoning him properly to bring out his flavor, and wondering whether he'd be better with a white wine or a red.

All in all, it didn't look to be a very comfortable trip out. But Marl consoled himself with the reward that waited for him at the end—and the chance to get back at that horned alien and her friends at the same time.

chapter 21

The truth was, as long as Khorii was busy in the thick of things, solving problems, healing, surrounded by her friends, she forgot about Vhiliinyar, and even forgot about missing her parents. Life felt like an ongoing adventure, like the ones she imagined her mother and father used to have, and she had a sense of purpose.

Alone, tired, all the necessary work accomplished for the time being, she finally had time to feel the gap between the self she had grown up with and who she was now. Even Elviiz was somewhere else, and the other Linyaari kid, an organic one, seemed to be an acceptable replacement for her as well as for Elviiz. She had wanted to like him and had tried to teach him things, but he seemed to prefer Hap's company, and both Hap and Jaya seemed to like him more than they did her. He didn't even look as alien among them, somehow, despite his horn. Not as alien as she had always felt anyway. But there was nothing special about him to another Linyaari. He was just another youngling, newly star-clad. He had more energy and strength than she did, she guessed, but then he hadn't been working like an adult for months and months the way she had. So he just butted in and took over, and everybody let him do so under the guise of her needing to "rest."

Horns, you'd think she was really old or something. Khorii decided that even if he was Melireenya's son, she didn't like Mikaaye very much. He was boring and shallow and didn't really know anything or how to do anything that *any* Linyaari couldn't do.

At least there was still Khiindi. She'd been told that Rushima had been full of animals before the plague and, although as with the humans, the adult animals had died, the babies just weaned had often survived. Or maybe those were cat and dog ghosts—or chicken, pig, or horse ghosts—she saw in yards and windowsills or peeking out from under porches or in alleyways. Maybe that was why Khiindi was choosing to spend so much time on the ship.

Khiindi was guarding the ship. Somebody had to. The VES were single-minded in their mission to exterminate rodents and other vermin but did not seem to have a clue how to deal with the real problem plaguing—his little kitty cat, double-crescent lips curled in a smile at the term—the *Mana*. Once the bodies were removed, he thought most of the threat would go with them, but one could never be too sure, so he was sleeping with one eye open. To remain vigilant, a guard needed his rest. The best napping place, other than Khorii's berth or Sesseli's, was the command chair on the bridge. It was usually warm and smelled like one of the humans or Khorii. His nap had been interrupted only once when some of the crew—but not Khorii—returned to take one of the shuttles out.

When Khiindi heard the first electronic noise, he thought it signaled the return of his crew and he opened an eye—the one not already at least metaphorically open—to keep watch on the ship. The beep and accompanying blinking light were not shuttles requesting the opening of the docking bay however—that was the toggle to the far left of the copilot's chair. No, it was the tiny red bulb of the com unit signaling that someone was trying to make contact. Khiindi sat up and put his front paws on the control panel to watch more closely.

Sesseli would have thought he was being cute, the typical curious kitty, but she didn't know about his past. Until the last few *ghaanyi*, he had been master of time and space and had flown many different sorts of spacecraft.

The inside of the cabin, which had been glowing softly with sleep cycle lighting, suddenly blazed with a harsh light that caused Khiindi's pupils to contract to narrow slits. The change of lighting was automatic when the com unit, ship's computer, or other salient functions engaged. The people who designed the ship didn't want the human guardians sleeping on watch either.

Instead of transmitting an image or a voice, the communicant sent a low electronic tone, or rather, a series of them, amounting to a muted electronic symphony. The ship's computer responded with its own harmonies. The navigation screen also activated, filling with numbers flashing past in rapid succession.

Khiindi hopped onto the panel and stood above the navigation screen, staring down at it. Someone was messing with the *Mana*'s course. That couldn't possibly be a good thing. Luckily, the faithful ship's cat was on the job!

Khiindi leaped up to add the force of gravity to his own meager weight and pounced on the appropriate switch. The screen died with a sigh. Victory! But the crew had to know about this. Now where in the stars was that hatch control?

The fartin' thing quit on me, Captain," complained the communications officer aboard the *Black Mariah,* the name of Marl's current ride. "You sure them was the right codes, mate?"

The pirate ship was approaching Rushiman atmo, having followed the *Mana* that far. The backwater agro colony would not be the *Mana*'s ultimate destination, though, of that Marl was sure. They'd be heading for that treasure ship Khorii and her little toy tin man had been talking about before lousing up his retirement plans on Dinero Grande. She and Elviiz had found a luxury liner full of rich stiffs in all their finest and an even richer cargo, according to research he'd done since Khorii had brought the *White Star*'s fate to his attention. All he needed to make it his were the coordinates to its hiding place. He had gathered that Khorii and her family had it stashed someplace. Then the only other thing he would need would be Khorii to ensure the safety of him and his mates, and they'd claim it for their own. After that, if the girl got tricky, he could dispose of her, or maybe sell the goody-goody little bitch to his buddy in the Nanobug Market, who could make good use of her talents on a retainer basis. If she didn't cooperate, he had also heard a rumor that Linyaari horns still worked fairly well without the Linyaari attached.

"'Course I'm sure," Marl replied. "I got us this far, didn't I?"

"Yeah you did, and a thrill it is to be here, too," the man said. Marl despised sarcasm and irony from beings he considered lesser creatures than himself.

"The ship is right there where I said it would be." He flipped his fingers up for the man to vacate his chair. "You probably entered the codes wrong."

"No I didn't. It started up okay, see them little numbers right there? But then it crapped out on me, like it switched itself off."

Marl tried the codes himself with the same result. "Somebody noticed then and shut us down."

"So now what, boy genius?" asked the captain, looking up from sharpening the short, curved blade he always wore for sentimental reasons, as he claimed. "We just keep following them?"

The captain's tone was bland, but Marl was not deceived.

The captain was not asking for suggestions from his least popular crew member. Marl knew that the rest of the crew and their families considered him a Jonah, not a genius. Ever since he came aboard, the ship had been falling apart. Though the engine room and features critical to the ship's function had remained unaffected, the bulkheads, decks, berths, and chairs crumbled as if attacked by termites. Marl knew why. He appreciated that the spooks had learned from their mistakes aboard the shuttle. However, he wasn't keen to share his insight with Coco, as the captain was known, and his crew. They were a superstitious lot already, and they really didn't need any encouragement to connect him with the damage and with the see-through stowaways they had glimpsed in corridors or darkened quarters.

As for him, Marl had already begun regretting including these unimaginative louts in his brilliant scheme. "We could," he answered the captain. "Or we could throw a boarding party."

"Why would we do that?"

"Because we're bigger than they are, and there's no one to stop us?" Marl replied. "Because that way we don't have to wait for them to make their milk run. Instead of just taking the codes, we can grab Khorii, add the ship to your fleet, and—since Rushima is a puny unprotected ag colony—stock up on fresh meat and eggs and wholesome veggies while we're at it?"

"Good plan," the captain said.

Marl swallowed his surprise. He had expected more of an argument, if for no other reason than that the idea was his. "Thanks," he said.

"So why don't you take the shuttle and do it."

"But, Captain, the shuttle is—"

"It's in a lot better shape than when you arrived. Good as new, the repair crew says. You can also let me know if they're right. Once you're dirtside and have the ship and the girl, you call and let us know it's safe to land and pick up the provisions as well as a crew."

It was a challenge of course. The captain gave his knife a final swish against the strop, sliced the air with it a time or two, and fixed Marl with a flinty glare that let him know—in case he had any doubt—what the consequences of failure would be.

Marl tried to look doubtful. "All by myself, sir? What if I'm killed or captured?"

"That would certainly save me a lot of trouble," the captain replied.

"But how about the rapin' and pillagin', Cap'n?" the com officer complained. "We haven't had shore leave in ever so long."

"Thoughtless of me, Pauli," the captain said. "I thought you'd appreciate missing out on the plague, but I can see I was neglecting your other needs. You can go with Fidd."

"With him? But, Cap'n, that's suicide!"

"So's mutiny, Pauli. So's mutiny."

"What if we're outnumbered?"

"Take Petit with you, then, but you three are all we can spare."

Petit was of course so named because he was huge. He would take up half the shuttle all by himself and, besides, he had an obvious fetish for his own body odors, which were as strong as the body to which they belonged. Certainly he never assaulted them with soap, water, or sonics in any sort of cleansing capacity.

Even Pauli stifled a groan, but Marl sighed. "Sorry to get you into this, Pauli, but orders are orders." The two would come in handy in any possible altercations between themselves and the kids and geezers who would be their only opposition. And, as they maybe shared one functioning brain between them, they'd be easily ditched when no longer needed.

"Aye," Pauli said.

"That's 'aye aye, Cap'n' to you, mate," Coco said.

Marl allowed his shoulders to slump and his feet to trudge as he turned toward the docking bay, but when he saw the shuttle he'd almost died in, he did not have to feign reluctance to board it.

moonmay Marsden approached Khorii, a basket hanging from the crook of her arm. "I heard you were still here, and I thought maybe you'd like to see our kittens. I bottle-fed Thomasina myself, and seems like no sooner she was off the bottle than she was out to do something personal about the cat shortage we've had here ever since the plague."

Khorii couldn't resist looking. There were four little kittens with gray stripes, and one orange one. She petted them very softly with a fingertip between each set of tiny ears, still kittenishly rounded and not standing up in proper cat-ear points. The orange one grabbed her finger in both front paws and tried to nurse from it.

"Khiindi was orange-ish when he was a baby," she said. "But I guess Makahomian Temple Cats can change colors as they get older."

"Not Rushima barn cats," Moonmay said proudly. "That there is Punkin. Looks to me like he would admire to have a career as a space cat if you were to take him on." She looked up at the sky, or what was visible of it through the fog. "Anybody would like that. I know I sure would. You must think Rushima is real backward compared to your planet, you being from a highly advanced civilization with notions and gadgets way beyond anything even the Federation thought of."

"No, not at all," Khorii said. She was just feeling a bit low. She didn't want to give Moonmay the impression she felt superior, though something inside her said, *You do. You think you're better than Mikaaye and all the others, too, or why would you be so angry*? Hushing that part, she said in a confidential tone, "Actually, where I live there are hardly any gadgets at all. Most of it is lush fields and tall mountains, rivers, and streams. My people have what you would consider tents, but we mostly only use them for shelter, and on fine nights, we often sleep in the open."

"All purely natural," Moonmay said. "Imagine that."

"Well, not exactly natural. It was originally, but when the Khleevi invaded, they completely destroyed and destabilized our world. If it weren't for my uncle Hafiz, who used some of his vast resources to restore it, we'd all be living on narhii-Vhiliinyar, the planet my people evacuated to when the Khleevi invaded."

"Isn't that a good place?" Moonmay asked.

"It was. Partially terraformed, too, by our people way back before I was born. All our plants and animals and things were brought over by our scientists. But then the Khleevi attacked us again, so Uncle Hafiz had to help out there, too."

"So lots of technology, like I thought."

"Mostly we use that of other peoples—we trade with them, and our techno-artisans learn to use what we acquire. But other than our space vessels and a few other things, those who stay planetside don't use a lot of what you would call 'gadgets.' "

"We just plain don't have all that many anymore," Moonmay said. "When the commodore and the first shipload of our ancestors arrived here, they had lots of technical things and lots of people had knowledge how to use things and invent more. But most of them wanted to live quiet, with animals and woods and such, kinda like your folks, I reckon. And I guess they just about had enough money to get here, and the Federation wasn't as big as it is now . . ." Her voice trailed off. Even on Rushima they knew how badly affected the Federation forces had been by the plague. "Anyway, lots of the surface here isn't very useful, but our patch was pretty easy to make like Old Earth. That's what the ancestors wanted. They made do with what they had, reused stuff, rebuilt it, or made new things in old ways."

"But you still have a place for ships to dock," Khorii said.

"That's Federation doing," Moonmay told her. "And we do trade for a few things, too, and buy or rent others. Weapons, some equipment, like what Scar brings."

"What do you trade?"

"Produce, animals, some handicrafts. But I wouldn't ask you to pay for a kitten, not after what you did for Grampa."

But Khorii shook her head, withdrawing her finger from Punkin, who gave a squeak and pounced into the middle of a sleeping gray sibling. "That's very sweet of you, Moonmay, but Khiindi wouldn't like it. He's been with me since we were both babies, and there's a litter of half-grown kittens on the *Mana* already."

"How about dogs?" Moonmay asked. "Maybe you could use a dog?"

Khorii shook her head again. "Khiindi would be even more upset if I brought a dog aboard."

"Too bad," Moonmay said. "We got a litter of the funniest-lookin' pups you ever did see. Mama was a little short herd dog and the daddy was a sled dog from way out on the cold fringe. His master moved here with twelve of them but old Dooley, we called him Drooly, is the only one left. Pups look like him in the face, but they got their mama's short legs."

Khorii forced herself to give the child, probably only a few years younger than she in Standard years, but much younger in other ways, a weary smile. "Hap might enjoy seeing the puppies when he returns," she said. Mikaaye probably wouldn't have thought about Hap's liking dogs if Moonmay had approached *him*. "He's very fond of dogs. Thanks again for showing me your kittens, Moonmay. Please have someone alert me when the others return. I'm going to go back to the ship to keep Khiindi company."

"You do that," she said. "Oh! Wait! Can you wait just a minute? I'll be right back! Uh, here, watch the kitties, will you?"

Thrusting the fur-filled basket at Khorii, she ran off with her bare feet flashing beneath the rolled-up cuffs of her blue trousers.

Khorii sat down and leaned against the nearest building, pulling the basket of kittens into her lap. She hadn't realized she was tired, but she closed her eyes for just a moment. It was then that she heard the thrum of a space shuttle and thought that the others had made short work of the crisis and were returning much more quickly than she thought.

However, the sound seemed to be coming from much higher than the shuttles would have gone for a surface jaunt. Khorii looked up but saw no lights, only a navy blue sky with patches of grayed clouds blocking out the cosmos. Mist steamed up from the ground, too, or maybe it was the local "natural" ghosts going about their nocturnal business. A kitten climbed her arm, and Khorii was distracted by trying to gently extricate the little beast with a minimum of damage to her skin.

Moonmay came running back again, another, smaller basket on her arm this time, filled with grasses.

"A snack? That's so nice of you, Moonmay!" Khorii said, but the girl shook her head.

"It's for your kitties. It's catnip. Although, well, maybe you'll like it, too. I forgot you folks like that kinda thing. I can go get more," she offered, but Khorii shook her head.

"I have catnip in the 'ponics garden, but not fresh, natural soil-grown nip like this. The flavor is much richer. I thank you, and I'm sure the cats will be crazy about it. I'll just take it back up to the ship and give it to them. Tell the others I'll be right back to help take care of the wounded."

"Okay, I *will* when they come back."

"I thought I heard a shuttle."

Moonmay shrugged. "Not so's I noticed. If you're lonesome, you could come to our house though."

"No, I think I'd better get back to Khiindi. He isn't used to being without me." *Especially,* she thought, *he isn't used to being without me when Sesseli isn't around to carry him everywhere.*

"I'll walk you over," Moonmay offered. "It's getting a mite foggy tonight, and you don't know the way as well as I do." It didn't take belonging to a psychic race to see that another being was emotionally unsettled and want to comfort her in whatever small way possible.

"I'll be fine," Khorii told Moonmay. "But thank you for your concern and your kindness—and for letting me see your kittens. Now we'd both better get some rest before the others return."

"Just don't seem right you goin' off like that all on your own," Moonmay said.

"I'll be fine," Khorii repeated. Moonmay looked unconvinced but ran off again.

The dock was a short walk from the center of the settlement. The mist Khorii had noticed before had indeed become a true fog now. It was odd to see it lying so thick and close along the ground and still be able to look up and see the sky in other places. There was no moon that night, though, and the way was dark. Fortunately, Khorii's olfactory and auditory senses made up for the diminished visibility under these conditions.

As she drew nearer, however, she smelled the hot scent of a shuttle's exhaust.

With it, she caught a faint mental call, followed immediately by a strong sense of something gone very wrong indeed.

chapter 23

"Congratulations, Elviiz, you're finally a *real boy*."
Elviiz looked up, and saw the dim outline of a large,
dark form above him, surrounded by bright, pale ones. The
voice was deep and sounded male, though Elviiz wasn't precisely sure how he knew that.

"What?" he asked. He hurt in many places, but the worst
part of this awakening was not mere physical pain. Unfamiliar
sensations flooded his being. For the first time ever he did
not know and could not instantly ascertain where he was,
who he was, why he was there.

"Oh, poor youngling!" one of the pale faces above him
cried.

"I'm sorry, buddy," a male voice said. "I wasn't trying to
be mean. It's from Pinocchio, remember, when the fairy
changes him so he becomes totally organic?"

Elviiz shook his head. It felt singularly light and empty.
"I don't know him. I don't know you. I am not certain I
know me."

"¡I'm Jalonzo, *mijo*! Your *compadre*."

The white-faced female was more informative. "You are
Elviiz, son of Maak, brother-friend-tutor of Khorii, foster
son of Khornya and Aari, and are culturally a Linyaari, like

your family," she said. "I, for instance, am Neeva, your sister's mother's mother's sister. In human terms, I am your great-aunt, or the great-aunt of your foster sister, which amounts to the same thing. You were attacked and injured. We healed you as best we could, but we could only heal your organic components. Your inorganic components, on which you have been used to relying for strength, much of your intellect and other functions, have been damaged or destroyed beyond our ability to heal."

"Am I going to die?" he asked. He did not know where that question came from either. It was not a matter he had previously considered.

"No, I do not believe so," Neeva said. "But you are changed profoundly and will remain that way until your maker is able to repair and reinstate your inorganic functions. We have one more mission to complete, then we return to our homeworld. By that time, if his disease follows the pattern we are seeing among others affected by the plague, your father/maker should be well enough to restore your missing functions."

"Why was I attacked?" he asked. "Who attacked me?"

"A very good question," Neeva replied. "Do you remember anything?"

He shook his head, pain ricocheting from the top of his skull to his ears, the nape of his neck and chin. Still, a few things were coming back to him, a few reminders of who he had been before he was diminished, if not demolished. "My memory chip must be damaged."

Jalonzo cleared his throat. "We are waiting on a relay from your papa on Vhiliinyar, *amigo,* but I have been researching android interfaces and from what I can tell, your chip was mostly used to store long-term memory—your education, your childhood memories, that kind of thing. Stuff that happens to you and emotional stuff ought to be in your organic brain—your mind."

Elviiz tried to remember, but another bolt of pain stopped him.

Neeva leaned toward him and touched his head with the tip of the horn that grew from the middle of her forehead. The pain vanished so suddenly he grunted with relief, and closed his eyes. Her horn still touching him lightly, she said, "If what Jalonzo says is correct, I should be able to retrieve that memory so we know who hurt you. Do I have your permission?"

"Yes," he said, barely breathing the word aloud. Peace and comfort he had never known he craved spread throughout his circulatory and nervous systems into his very flesh.

"Good," said a voice inside his head. Another new sensation! He had been robbed of his higher functions, and his brain no longer was crowded with data, with the virtual voices of every book or recording of any sort he had ever absorbed. It had become all but empty until now, when this new voice spoke to it so softly, so soothingly. He had company that had entered a part of him in a way he had never known possible. Thought-talk! Telepathy!

"Why, Elviiz, you seem to be able to receive now, just as all Linyaari young do at about your age. Your injury and loss have perhaps made way for your other abilities."

Elviiz did not want her to stop talking to his mind. It was a balm in itself, though the content of her remarks also had a positive effect on his . . . spirits. He had spirits. He had heard others speak of this vague and nebulous sensation, but had not known he possessed spirits himself. Fascinating. Besides which, it called up an associative thought, a connection. Spirits had something to do with his attack.

"Ah," Neeva's thought-voice said. *"Do they? Let us see if we can use the notion of spirits as a search indicator to find the images of your attack."*

In the next breath, he saw himself watching Marl and the seemingly transparent beings accompanying him. He saw those beings surrounding his own image and the tiles on the front of the building crumbling above and behind those seemingly insubstantial beings. He remembered thinking that he was not seeing the wall through them, that instead, they had made the walls part of their own substance.

"I believe that helps explain what happened to you," Neeva said. Aloud, she relayed Elviiz's memory to the others.

"So that is why Elviiz's inorganic parts were damaged," Jalonzo said. "They like chips. And bricks and tiles, too, apparently."

Another female shoved a plate of food under his nose—Jalonzo's grandmother, Abuelita! More memories were returning. "What *are* these things to attack innocent children?"

Elviiz scooted back. He was lying on a soft surface—a mattress with wrinkled fabric both below and above him. Behind him was a hard surface, and he sat up against it. Abuelita caught the plate of food before his sudden movement spilled it.

Jalonzo said, "They sound like the same ghosts that have been upsetting the *niños*—the ones that look like their families who died in the plague. Except for the part about eating buildings and android chips. That's new." His face contorted with an expression conveying that he did not like that idea one bit.

Elviiz was also puzzled by what had happened to him. "This was the first occasion that my current limited memory retains during which I viewed the creatures. I know what the children said they saw, of course, but I assumed this was an emotional reaction on their part, having something to do with resolving their feelings about their loss. I did not expect that I would perceive the same phenomena. However, I did, and as you see from my current state, they were substantial enough to damage me."

"And the buildings," Jalonzo said. "The com tower is in bad shape. Not just the outside either."

"Let's see if you're strong enough to rise and walk now, Elviiz," Neeva said.

He, who had always been the strongest of them all! What good would he be now?

Neeva, hearing his thought, comforted him with another horn touch. When he had to struggle to sit on the side of the bed, Jalonzo helped him. Once he was on his feet again, with Jalonzo on one side and Neeva on the other, he found he could walk, although a bit shakily.

"Luckily we caught you before your skeleton was damaged any worse than it was. You looked as if you had a metallic version of what is known among humanoids as osteoporosis, with your artificial bones all pitted and weakened."

He grew stronger after a few steps, but felt as if his inner structure were made of cables instead of rods and as if the fuel that flowed through him had been replaced with inert sand.

"He's exhausted already," Neeva said.

Water made Elviiz's already inadequate vision even worse, and coursed down his face. He was so inadequate this way! How did the others stand it?

There was a whirring sound from the hallway, and a contraption half Jalonzo's height stopped in front of him.

"Melireenya! You found it," Neeva said.

"Yes. It was where Abuelita said it would be, right inside the home of her deceased friend. I took it back to the *Balakiire* to charge its batteries, but it took a while to adapt the wiring to our power source. I believe I can also modify the batteries to last much longer than they do now." She stood up, and said, "Sit, Elviiz. You see? You no longer have to depend on feeble organic transport. What do you say to that?"

Elviiz would have fallen into the conveyance had it not

been for Jalonzo's support. He knew he should express gratitude to Melireenya and the others; but all he could say, whining like a vehicle trying to tow a load that was too heavy for it, was, "I want my father."

Khorii cocked her head to listen more closely. Yes, it was clearer now. She distinctly heard a shuttle landing near the *Mana*. At the same time, Captain Bates exercised her seldom-used psychic powers, and called to her. *"Khorii, where are you? I'm coming back for you now. There's been another accident."*

"What? Are so many injured that Mikaaye cannot heal them all?" Khorii asked, pretending to be shocked.

"Mikaaye is badly injured now, too. Sesseli moved the wagon, but we're afraid to move Mikaaye. I sure hope we get you to him on time."

Khorii felt shame for her sarcasm and jealousy. *"I am on my way back to the* Mana *to check on Khiindi. Shall I wait for you?"*

"I'll meet you there. We brought some supplies with us, but these people are in much worse shape than we thought. The wagon just fell to pieces as it rounded a sharp switch-back in the road and pitched the driver and passengers out and halfway down the hillside. Two people are dead. Two more were trapped under the wagon. Hap and Scar tried to hold it up while Mikaaye crawled underneath to heal the trapped people, but it broke again, falling on him, too, and dragging him off the road and halfway down the hill with it. He's not moving, but that may be from fear of finishing the fall."

"Understood," Khorii said. "I will meet you there."

Crossing the airstrip in the fog, she saw the glow from the landing shuttle through the veils of fog and smelled the heat of its retrorockets and the hot friction of the atmosphere against the hull. She could barely see the bulk of the *Mana* for the obscuring swirling gray mist. Perhaps some of this meant moisture, even rain, for the parched settlement? But if it did, she hoped it wouldn't be raining near the accident site, making the footing slippery.

She tripped in a hole in the tarmac then, a gaping hole, and fell full length into it. Things had certainly fallen to wrack and ruin in a hurry since the plague. A hand stretched toward her, to help her she thought, as she saw it from the corner of her eye, but when she reached up to grasp it, she looked up as well. There was the hand and a face but the rest seemed to be the matte black of the tarmac muted, though definitely not softened, by the fog.

Khorii rose under her own power, keeping one eye on the *Mana* and one on the ground, ignoring other faces and hands that sometimes seemed to reach toward her from the grayness, and continued forward.

She heard a hatch opening, the shuttle, though no further call from Captain Bates. No doubt she and whoever was with her would be hurrying to the *Mana* to find the supplies they needed. But why not use the docking bay hatch? Khorii slowed her pace, then quickened it.

"Captain Bates?" she directed her thought to the shuttle, but no answer came from that direction.

Instead, behind her, and distinctly farther away came an answer. *"On my way, Khorii."*

She was about to ask if they'd sent the other shuttle back as well, when suddenly something streaked toward her through the fog, barreled into her chest, and pierced her over and over again through her suit and on her unprotected face and head. Grabbing her horn, it clung, covering her mouth and nose with a thick smothering coat.

"Khiindi!" Khorii's shout was mental as well as the mutter she could produce through the cat's body before she carefully reached up and dislodged him, one claw at a time.

chapter 24

Hhorii didn't have to ask Khiindi what his problem was, not that the cat would have given her a direct answer. She had only seen Khiindi so frightened of one thing in his entire life, and that was Marl Fidd, who had once swung the poor cat by his tail into the pool where the poopuus lived. If Sesseli had not been there to break his fall with her telekinesis, if the poopuus hadn't been there to rescue the disabled cat from drowning, and if Khorii herself hadn't arrived almost at once, she might have lost her feline friend forever. Of all of the horrible things Marl had done, this was by far the most heinous crime, the one she could not forgive, especially since both she and Khiindi knew Marl would do it again or worse. But they had left Fidd in the jail in Corazon. Either he escaped, or someone else just as bad had frightened her cat.

She petted Khiindi until his small heart thumped less violently, then set him down so she could creep closer to see what was happening with the *Mana*. "Captain Bates, approach with caution. A shuttle landed next to the *Mana* and from Khiindi's reaction, the boarding party seems to be hostile."

"We'll be there as soon as we can, Khorii. We seem to be

*experiencing some problem with the fuel pump, and just now
a tile fell off the hull. Stay clear meanwhile."*

"*I will,*" she said, trying not to let the captain see how
close she already was to the *Mana,* despite Khiindi's batting
at her ankles and sending images of Marl Fidd with fangs,
horns, and accompanied by two large friends. He made it
clear that the *Mana* was off-limits, but it wasn't as if she
were going to go inside. Khiindi pretended not to be telepathic most of the time, but he was unusually emphatic now.
To reassure Captain Bates, Khorii told her, "*Every time I try
to step closer I get an image of the* Mana's *outer hatch with
a 'Danger! Keep Out!' sign on it. Khiindi is herding me
away from there even now.*"

"*Good. If they hijack the ship, we'll probably get it back
at some point and if not, there are other ships. You, on the
other hand, are one of a kind.*"

That was fine with Khorii. Her parents might have han-
dled the situation more heroically, but Linyaari were *supposed* to be healers, not fighters. She wasn't about to tackle
Fidd by herself, especially if she was needed elsewhere.

Khiindi suddenly bristled and swelled while hissing as if
he'd sprung a bad leak.

Before she could scoop him up again, her upper arm was
clasped in a painful grip, and Marl Fidd's voice said, "Gotcha!"

How could you save him?" Maak asked Neeva when the
relay was patched through. "An android is not merely an in-
organically enhanced human—the organic and inorganic
functions are thoroughly integrated."

"We almost failed to do so," she told him. "But the creatures who attacked him did not entirely destroy his inorganic
parts, and with the help of Jalonzo, a young scientist here in
Corazon, we were able to visualize the humanoid physiol-
ogy on which you based his form and augment it to some degree with our own structures."

"You brought him back to life!" Captain Becker said, uncharacteristically awestruck.

"No, he still had life when we found him, but he had lost some of its conduits. We repaired and extended existing organic tissue to make the required connections."

"Thank you, Neeva!" Maak said.

Khornya and Aari also crowded into the com screen. The reception was faulty—they flickered so badly and seemed so insubstantial they almost resembled Elviiz's attackers, except, of course, that no bits of ship showed through them.

"We thank you as well," Aari said. "Elviiz is our son as well as Maak's. Now he will live to meet his other sister."

"*Other* sister?" Neeva asked.

"Yes, it is quite wonderful, but now Maak would like to speak with Elviiz."

"Of course," Neeva said.

"I suppose direct connection is out of the question now?" Maak said.

"It is," Neeva affirmed, but stepped aside. The *Balakiire* remained docked at Corazon, since planet-to-planet relay was stronger than when the ship was in transit, even when the transmission bypassed the city's com tower.

Jalonzo helped wedge Elviiz's autocart between the command chairs on the *Balakiire*'s bridge.

"Hello, Father," he said. "I seem to be broken. Can you fix me?"

Maak assured his son and creation that he would not only fix him, but had some new and improved modifications to make which he had been saving for Elviiz's seventh *ghaanyi* anniversary. "It will be close to that time, if not past it, when you arrive here. We shall have to set up a remote repair theater so that I can repair your remaining injuries without breaking quarantine."

"You think maybe the universe as we know it could spare Khorii long enough for her to come home and test us?"

Captain Becker asked. "I feel great myself, never felt better, and the only thing being hurt by our presence here are the little mousie-ratty varmints the *aagroni* recently introduced to the grasslands. RK is having a—you should pardon the expression—field day with them. My guess is if the rest of the universe is over the plague, so are we. It would make it way easier for Maak to operate, and that way we could help."

"She is on a mission with the *Mana* at the moment and unaware of Elviiz's injuries; but as soon as we can contact her, we will suggest it."

Captain Becker suddenly took on an expression that Neeva found difficult to describe. When she consulted the LAANYE later she found that the word she was looking for was "shifty." He seemed to be experiencing some sort of inner conflict. Finally, he gave a resigned sigh, and said, "I can give you the coordinates of the place where they'll be heading. It's on your way home."

"Thank you, Captain. However, I am sure the *Mana* filed a flight plan with us before departure—"

She looked at Khaari, who looked up from the ship's computer and shook her head.

"Perhaps not."

"Okay, but it's a secret—sort of. It belongs to me, and while I know you and your crew will be cool about it, Neeva, I don't want it to become general knowledge. It's a sort of storage depot for my cargo, and if every yahoo in the universe can find it well—it wouldn't be real convenient."

"We will not divulge your secret, Captain Becker," she promised, and he gave them the coordinates.

"We do have one other mission first, but I think given Elviiz's state and the need to return to Vhiliinyar—"

Elviiz, reassured by his brief exchange with Maak, had fallen asleep with a childlike trust that was at odds with his usual inquisitive and challenging manner.

After disengaging from the relay to Vhiliinyar, the

Balakiire contacted the *Huhuraani,* which had landed on LoiLoiKua in an attempt to protect or at least heal the indigenous population and to expedite their transport.

Neeva explained the situation to Yiitir, the Linyaari historian who was on duty as communications officer.

While she was explaining, he received another hail. "Wouldn't you know it? We've been here for days and heard from no one and all of a sudden there are two hails at once. Hmm. The *Nheifaarir.* It has the urgency code embedded in the signal, *Visedhaanye* Neeva."

"If there is some difficulty, perhaps we can help as long as it doesn't take us too far out of the way," Neeva said.

He nodded and blinked out of sight for a few moments. "Hmm," he said when he reappeared on the com screen. "I'll just patch you two together and let you sort out the details then, shall I?"

Ariin was amazed to see how the small, gaudily colored and gilt-encrusted egg-shaped *Nheifaarir* could tow the lumbering gray tanker. Of course, without gravity, the size difference wasn't a significant factor with one ship dead in space and the other under full power.

The large ship followed the smaller like a pet far more docile than the Makahomian Temple Cats that lived with some Linyaari. Once she got used to the sight, the subjugation of the tanker somehow seemed disappointingly easy. Maati, who had returned to the *Nheifaarir* with Ariin while Thariinye stayed aboard the tanker, caught the thought.

"Don't worry, Ariin, this operation will not be boring. Tedious but not boring. Once we get to Rushima's atmosphere we will need help maneuvering the tanker in for a landing. Let's hail LoiLoiKua now, shall we, and ask them to send a relay to another ship to join us?"

But this time there were no visuals and Ariin heard only Maati's side of the brief conversation. Maati was so absorbed she forgot to turn on the speaker. "Neeva! Yes, we need your help with this tanker. No, it will be on your way home. I am so sorry to hear that. Yes, Khorii is on Rushima, and I'm sure she'll want to be with him. We have a passenger who came with us seeking adventure, too, but I rather think she might change her mind and return with you as well. It shouldn't delay you for very long, then you can be on your way. I know Maak must be anxious. Here are our coordinates."

"You're not sending me home again?" Ariin asked. The journey, long and dull as it had been, was just beginning. Nothing much had happened yet except finding the tanker. She hadn't had a chance to show how heroic she could be, or that she was just as talented and praiseworthy as her wonderful twin.

"Not sending you, but I thought you'd want to go since your sister and foster brother will both be returning home, at least for a little while. Elviiz has been injured, and only his father/creator can help him at this point."

"If she can't help him, why is she going home, too?"

"First of all, because they have been together since she was a baby and he a very small child."

"Yes, I was told that but—" Maati's expression said that Ariin was either very dense or somehow lacking the proper concern for the injured Elviiz. That was so unfair! How was she to know? She hadn't even known another Linyaari until a short time ago.

Maati, reading her correctly, relented, "I'm sorry, Ariin. I forget your unusual upbringing. If it's any comfort to you, your mother's unusual upbringing among humans caused her to be misunderstood often, too. It's just that in our society, and even in human society, if you are as close to someone as Khorii and Elviiz have been to each other for as long as they have been, when one of you is hurt, the other tries to be nearby for emotional support."

"*What is that? How can you support an emotion? Emotions have no mass.*"

"*Yes, well, perhaps when you've been among us longer you will understand better,*" Maati said. Underlying her words, Ariin heard her exasperated thought that those Friends had certainly confused her brother's long-lost daughter. "*The other reason we would like Khorii to return with Elviiz is to see if the plague strain carried by her parents and the others is still active. If it is not, it will be much easier for Maak to help Elviiz. I rather thought you'd like to be there, too, if Khorii discovers that quarantine can be lifted.*"

"*Oh, yes! Yes, I would. I am sorry to have questioned you, father-sister. You are wise as always.*"

Maati snorted, but was pleased. And Ariin, while also pleased and more hopeful than she had been in some time, wondered what it would be like to have the kind of power Khorii had to determine the fates of the people she loved. If the plague had vanished from the human universe, as people had been saying, then surely Khorii would not see the plague indicators on their parents, and the quarantine would be lifted. They would be very grateful to her sister. They would probably forget all about Ariin in their joy to see her twin home safely.

If so, Ariin would deal with that when it happened. Meanwhile, she could hardly wait for the *Balakiire* to arrive with her illustrious great-aunt *visedhaanye* Neeva, and her sister's (she couldn't think of him as her own) android foster brother Elviiz. And that other. The trickster who, according to the Friends' technicians, had been responsible for dooming Ariin to life without her people and family. She was very interested indeed in meeting Grimalkin at last.

Meanwhile, Maati was on the com with Thariinye, giving him the news about the *Balakiire*.

When she signed off, she said, "Now to let Khorii know

what's happening. Can't have the *Mana* taking off before we arrive."

Maati hailed the *Mana*. Ariin could see her laying out the logistics for Khorii—first the *Balakiire* would arrive, with the injured Elviiz on board, and assist the *Nheifaarir* in guiding the damaged tanker to the surface of Rushima, where its tank could be emptied and any nonessential personnel would help pilot the tanker back to LoiLoiKua to pick up the locals and transport them to Vhiliinyar. Meanwhile, Khorii, Elviiz, Ariin, and Maati would return in the *Nheifaarir* to Vhiliinyar, where Elviiz could, they hoped, be healed.

When that was done, Khorii could return to the *Mana* if she liked, to complete the original mission. The crew of the *Mana* was invited to wait for her on the Moon of Opportunity.

But Maati did not get to explain any of that, because her hail went unanswered. She switched on a visual that should have shown her the bridge of the *Mana,* but instead displayed the startled faces of two extremely rough-looking characters who appeared almost monstrous to Ariin, all greasy, long, matted hair, scars, pointed teeth, and—of course—no horns. It did not take a telepath to tell that they were not local mechanics performing free maintenance on her sister's ship, or that good intentions of any sort were as foreign to their natures as their appearance was to Ariin.

Neither did it require a telepath to understand that Khorii was probably in danger from these toughs and that, therefore, Ariin's chances of finally making physical contact with her parents was also endangered.

"Who are they? What are they doing on Khorii's ship? Where is she? Maati, we have to help her!" Such an outburst would have caused the Friends to administer a sedative to her, but Ariin had apparently responded appropriately in Maati's estimation. Ariin's aunt looked up and took her hand consolingly.

"We will, youngling. Don't worry, we will."

But how? Ariin wondered. She and Maati were alone on the *Nheifaarir* while Thariinye, the only male, was elsewhere. Furthermore these strange people of whom she was a part had somehow or other, after they had supposedly (though so far no one knew how) descended from a combination of the Friends and the Others, decided that no one of their race did war or violence. Ariin had never seen bad men before but she recognized that, had circumstances been different, had he not been able to get anything he wanted without force, Odus was perfectly capable of using it. Even the Others, good as they had been to her, were ready to fight. Hruffli would have protected her, she knew. And Neicaair and Nrihiiye were definitely feisty.

Maati was on the com again. "Rushima base come in. This is Linyaari expeditionary vessel *Nheifaarir,* towing a water transport tanker for the relief effort. Come in, Rushima base. Over."

For the longest time there was no answer at all, then a young hornless head with red hair tied into two plaits and brown dapples on its nose appeared on the screen. Before it could speak, a smaller furred face popped up in front of it. "Get down, kittencat. Commin' is for people, not kitties," the youngling said, removing the offending creature. "Hi, Linyaari ship. This is Rushima base, Moonmay Marsden, comoff for right now, speaking. Can I help you?"

Maati said, "The cargo vessel *Mana,* docked at your landing facility, appears to have been boarded by unauthorized personnel. Please alert the *Mana*'s crew to return to their ship, but proceed with caution."

"Khorii is headed back that way. Everybody else is off rescuin' the folks from Bug Gulch."

"Khorii should not face those men by herself. We do not know how many of them there are."

"I'll go tell her, then," the girl said, rising.

"Don't go alone!" Maati said. "The men look dangerous."

"Okeydoke," the girl said. "There's nobody else to call this minute, ma'am, but don't you worry about it none. I'll tend to it."

Maati leaned back in her chair, the expression on her face not one that Ariin liked at all. And the words she spoke were not soothing either. "Two girls against those men? How is she possibly going to 'tend' to it?"

chapter 25

What are you doing here, Marl?" Khorii demanded, trying to sound calm, although she could feel her heart thudding against her chest wall.

"Jail got boring, and I missed you, pet," he said, maintaining his grip on her shoulder. "I made some new friends, and I told them all about you. They've been very anxious to meet you." He smiled, baring his teeth without the slightest degree of warmth. "And you and I have some unfinished business to take care of."

Khorii searched the underskirts of the fog for Khiindi, but didn't see her faithful feline companion anywhere. She was glad. Marl had been cruel to Khiindi before and, after all, there wasn't much a helpless little cat could do to defend her, was there? Of course, he was supposed to be a Makahomian Temple Cat, and they were supposed to defend their temples and their human followers, but Khiindi was a runt as Temple Cats went. Even full-grown he was smaller than his sire, and was not inclined to be aggressive except toward fish.

"I see no other ships here, Marl. Only that shuttle." Meanwhile she was sending a mental message to Captain Bates. *"Fidd is one of the boarding party, Captain, and he has me now. Please approach with caution."*

"Tell Fidd to be cautious himself," Captain Bates replied tersely. *"I'll mow his candy ass down if I see him. Uh—can you get away from him?"*

Marl spun Khorii around and shook a finger in her face. "Don't you know it's rude to use telepathy in front of others? So who's that? Bates, Hellstrom, and Jaya coming to save you, are they?" He gave a jerk and pulled her after him toward the hatch.

She backed up to him enough to get her balance, then aimed a backward kick at his knee. It did not land solidly, however. He let go of her arm, but before she could escape him entirely, grabbed hold of her mane with the hand that wasn't cradling his injured leg. He jerked down viciously, pulling her to the ground.

"What's the matter with you? Why'd you do that? Aren't you people supposed to be pacifists?" He yelled toward the hatch, "Pauli, Petit, come and help me, you useless louts!"

Khorii, watching the fog for signs of Khiindi or the *Mana*'s shuttle, saw that although the fog had receded from the *Mana*, it had enveloped the shuttle, which shuddered convulsively as the tendrils of mist climbed higher on its hull, seeming to pull itself up by what looked like partially defined human fingers. Khorii thought she saw a face grinning at her, and gleaming, translucent teeth, then heard a metallic noise as—what? The fog? Something took a bite out of the shuttle.

"Drop it, varmints!" a girlish voice with a slight lisp snarled. "You're surrounded, so you two blocking the hatch put your weapons down, and you there take your hands off Khorii."

"Pull the other one, kid!" Marl called back, laughing, but there was an explosion and something zipped past close to Khorii and closer, she guessed from his exclamation, to Marl.

Behind her she heard the clatter of plasteel on the tarmac.

Marl jerked her around toward the sound as he bellowed at his companions, two unwashed and poorly groomed individuals, both hirsute and gaudily attired. One of them was still armed, though the other's hands were raised tentatively to shoulder height.

"Petit, you idiot, it's just some kid," growled the third man, who raised his weapon and shot into the fog in the direction of the first shot's origin. "Put it down and go home to your mama, girly. That twelve-gauge is too big for someone as little as you."

Moonmay zinged another shot past. It bounced off the hull. "My mama is dead, hairball face. And my gramps reengineered this here weapon so even a baby could use it."

The fog that had been climbing the shuttle receded and swirled toward them in coils, like some great drifting serpent.

Marl pulled Khorii in front of him and backed up. "Lay off, kid. You wouldn't want to hit your friend here, would you?"

"Weren't aimin' at *her*," Moonmay said. The fog carried sound strangely. Moonmay's voice seemed to be coming from several directions at once and something rustled and crunched from elsewhere.

Khorii saw one of Marl's accomplices point his sidearm into the fog. The fog pointed back. The man fired, but the shot suddenly became muffled as if wrapped in heavy fabric. Then the weapon began disappearing. The man let go and stepped back but not before he was enveloped by the fog.

"Petit, come back here!" Marl bellowed after the man.

"We got what we come for, Fidd. We can take her with us," the other miscreant advised.

"No you won't!" Moonmay cried, but as if that had been what he was waiting for, the man fired directly into the fog and guessed right this time. There was a shriek and another shot, this one going wild.

"We may as well take their ship, too," Marl argued, oblivious to the muffled sobs of the child in the distance.

"Let me heal her, Marl, and I'll go with you without a fuss," Khorii said. "She's only a child."

"In case you haven't noticed, most people are these days," Marl said.

He shoved her toward the hatch, and another shot rang out. Khorii whirled to see Marl dropping to the ground behind her, his mouth opened in a silent moan of pain, blood seeping between his fingers where they clutched his right knee.

"Not all of us, Fidd," Captain Asha Bates said, stepping through the coils of fog with the modified twelve-gauge trained on him. The remaining man, who had grabbed for Khorii when she turned, released her and stepped back with his hands in the air.

Khorii dodged past Captain Bates and found Moonmay crumpled on the ground, her left shoulder shattered. Tenderly, Khorii lay beside the little girl and pressed her horn to the wound, knitting vessels, nerve endings, bone to bone, muscle fiber to muscle fiber, and, finally, flesh to flesh.

She supported Moonmay as the little girl sat up. Water dripped onto her face and blood ran from her clothing. "Hey, it's raining," Moonmay said.

So it was. The two of them stood and walked to where Captain Bates held the pirate at bay while Marl writhed on the ground.

Something odd was happening between Captain Bates and the uninjured intruder.

"You're Asha, aren't you?" the pirate asked.

"Hello, Pauli," she said. "I guess that would be Coco's ship orbiting waiting to pick us off, right?"

"Aye. The brat yours?" he asked, nodding to Moonmay.

"No, though if I had one, I'd hope she'd be as brave as this one. What are you and Coco doing with this punk?" she asked, but before he could answer, said, "Khorii, no. Don't heal him before you tie him up. Moonmay, there's tape in the utility drawer under the console on the bridge. That'd be to starboard as you enter the hatch and forward down the corridor, last hatch on the starboard side.

Moonmay looked confused.

"Right," Khorii said. "Starboard is right."

"How do ya know?" the child asked.

Without breaking eye contact with Pauli, Captain Bates said, "The phrase to remember is 'There's no red port left,' Moonmay. Port is left, so starboard's the other one."

"Right—I mean starboard," Moonmay said, and entered the ship, returning after what must have seemed a very long time to Marl Fidd with a roll of duct tape.

Moonmay didn't surrender the tape to Khorii, but bound Fidd's wrists and ankles together with a few quick twists of her wrist and a little wrestling of the boy, which caused him to scream.

"Go ahead and heal him now, Khorii," Captain Bates said. "Moonmay, you can tape Pauli up, too."

"Now, Asha, we're more trouble than we're worth. Let us return to the ship, and we'll be out of your space for good. We'll only be a burden to you as prisoners."

"Not to me you won't. And these folks will most likely hang you."

"You can't let them do that! I'm your father!"

Khorii had knelt to heal Marl's knee but looked up before she touched it. The tarmac shook with a terrible rumble and roar. Cleared of fog, the pirate shuttle shuddered and shook like a wet dog, showering hull tiles to the ground. A hatch opened and the other large, fat pirate raced toward them, making very good time for someone of his size. Out the hatch behind him came a chair, trailing its bolt, and a sputtering com screen. The viewport burst, showering the retreating pirate with fragments.

Just when it seemed about to explode, the shuttle collapsed instead, leaving a fractured superstructure of metal that looked like wood gnawed by beavers.

Captain Bates smiled sweetly at Pauli. "You're not my father, just my clan father. But you're free to go now, as far as you can fly in that thing you rode in on."

Khorii smiled herself as she applied her horn to Marl's knee, taking the same care she had with Moonmay's shoulder, even though the task was a distasteful one.

Moonmay busied herself tying up the other two pirates in the same fashion as she had Marl. "They won't go nowhere now, ma'am," she told Captain Bates.

"Fine, but we have to get back to the accident. Khorii has injured to attend to."

"I didn't hear the shuttle land," Khorii told her. "But with all of the shooting . . ."

"I didn't exactly land. It crashed. Well, belly-flopped in a field not far from here. When I knew I wasn't going to make it in one piece, I looked for a softer place to set it down." She nodded to the wreck of the pirate's shuttle. "It wasn't as bad as that one, but pretty much the same thing happened, to a lesser degree. Let's see if we've got anything left sound enough to make a round-trip."

She didn't add that, if they didn't, Mikaaye and others might die before Khorii could reach them.

chapter 26

"*If that ain't just like an offsider,*" a rough-edged voice complained. "*Come to poor little Rushima to save the world and ends up gettin' himself hurt so bad it takes us locals to save them instead.*"

"Hush, Hector," answered a female voice familiar from the earlier healing sessions. Mikaaye hurt too badly to be able to recall much about her except—oh yes, she was dead. "*This boy already cured bushels of arthritis, rheumatism, sciatica, cataracts, heart ailments, pleurisy, and pneumonia today as well as earaches, hives, colic, bad teeth, hardening of the arteries, ringworm, shingles, and hives. I'd say that was a pretty good start on saving the world, or at least our people. Even Doc never had a day like that, did you, son?*"

"Ali, I never had a *month* like that. Stay with us, son, there's help comin'."

Mikaaye groaned. He was cold, and it made the pain worse, but at least he was not alone. Although, recalling the salient feature of the female visitor, perhaps that was not entirely a positive thing. "*Live help?*" he asked. "*I am still alive?*"

"*You'd be the best judge of that,*" the female said. "*You look solid enough to me, though.*"

"Except that horn of his." Hector, his whine unmistakable, spoke up again. *"It looks a might see-throughish to me."*

"That's how they get when they've been working too hard," Doc told him. *"I remember that happening to Acorna when she was helping with the wounded after the Battle with the Bugs. You'll be fine, boy. Everybody get back from him. You know how the living are always complaining about us making cold spots."*

"I say we just go and let the living look after each other," Hector said. *"What have they done for us lately?"*

"Don't go," Mikaaye said. The doctor and Alison were comforting; some of the other figures crowded into his unconsciousness were peculiar and might have been frightening had he been better able to tell what they were or what they were doing. Hector was obviously a sad spirit with a poor view of himself and everyone around him. But Mikaaye wanted them near simply because he didn't want to be alone. Until he'd begun his duties on the Moon of Opportunity, he had always been surrounded by his own kind. Even on MOO, there were lots of other people around. Dead company was better than being by himself. *"I have done what I could for your living people,"* he said. *"But I do not understand what I or other living people could do for you. Tell me."*

Hector began to do so, and Mikaaye learned how dead company could actually be. Old Alison and the doctor receded as Hector told Mikaaye the story of his life and death and all the injustices that had been done to him and of the ingratitude and indignity he had suffered. Mikaaye thought he might have been bored to death, except for the probability that if he died on Rushima, he would have Hector as an eternal companion.

Hector was reiterating how his stupid daughter-in-law, who was not good enough for his son and had probably been responsible for his falling off his horse and being a cripple, had stolen his grandchildren from him and when he died had had him buried facedown. "Trash," Hector said. *"Hey, what in tarnation is going on here? Don't you young people know it's rude to interrupt a conversation? You, girl, get out of my face! What are you doin' hangin' around here anyway?"*

Mikaaye felt a brief, light pressure, and the cool of a horn against his chest. The pain fled, along with Hector, replaced by a comfort as sweet as clover. The horn traveled to his neck and head. He opened his eyes and saw Khorii. It could hardly have been anyone else, since they were the only people with horns in the vicinity.

He sighed and smiled at her. Not only was she his own kind, and had made the pain go away, but he had never known before how gentle she could be. She'd always seemed pretty bossy on the ship. But now she was the most sublime being he could possibly imagine, and, best of all, she had driven Hector away.

"Who is Hector?" she asked. *"Here, hold on to me. Sesseli will pull us both up."*

"You heard that?" he asked.

"You're not shielding very well at the moment. I'm surprised I didn't hear you all the way back on the landing field. You must have been having nightmares at one point."

"I was. I had a very bad one about a spirit who drove all the others away. He could not be satisfied in life or in death and never tired of complaining."

Khorii giggled. *"He drove you away from death, then. I suppose if we only knew it, everyone and everything has a use, and that must be his. But I was not referring to him. There were other things."*

"I remember very little. Even Hector is fading, which is a relief." What he did remember was the touch of her horn and her hands soothing his nerves, washing away his pain and filling him with the pleasure of her touch instead. It was something all of his people could do, of course. He could do

it himself. But not like she did. They were almost up to the road, and the injured and their friends would demand their attention, so he had only this moment to reassure himself. *"Khorii? Are you still angry with me for going on the mission and not you?"*

"I wasn't angry!" she replied. *"I just—it doesn't matter, Mikaaye. As long as the injured are healed and what needs purifying gets purified and the plague is truly destroyed so we can go home again, what does it matter if you do it or I do?"*

"None at all," he said. *"I just was wondering. I did not intend to cause you emotional distress."*

"You did nothing wrong," she said, although the feeling he got from her was that he had. However, he knew that her words were truer than her feelings, and therefore her feelings were unreasonable, and that annoyed him.

But by that time Hap, Scar, and the others were hauling them over the edge and onto what was left of the road.

The road was destroyed in so many places that in the end they healed the injured then ferried everyone back to town. Scar, Hap, Captain Bates, and Mikaaye returned to her damaged shuttle and spent hours repairing it with spare parts from the *Mana*—many of which were inexplicably damaged as well.

Khorii thought wistfully of her uncle Joh, who could have had the entire shuttle and the *Mana* besides completely refurbished in less time. Thinking of him made her think of his asteroid and the *Estrella* Blanca, the *White Star*. This thought was less fond. He was the one who had sent them—what was the phrase?—to pursue wild geese? His flaw of lusting for riches had attracted Marl and the other men of mercenary motivation.

By the time the *Mana*'s crew was ready to depart, two days and nights had passed.

Elder Plimsoll declined to take charge of the prisoners. "We've been held up by pirates for less in the past," he said. "We don't want them messin' with us again because we have what they think is theirs."

The cargo nets that had formed Marl's shipboard prison weeks before were still in place. "That's fine," Captain Bates said. "We may find a use for them yet."

Khorii couldn't read her former teacher, who used telepathy rarely and was expert at shielding her thoughts. She had a connection to the pirates, that much was clear from her conversation with Pauli, who had claimed to be her father. Whether that connection was warm enough to keep the captain's clan from trying to kill her shipmates was not clear. Khorii didn't think Captain Bates knew herself yet, but it would bear discussion once they were under way.

Jaya started the countdown.

The com unit beeped and Maati, Thariinye, and Khorii appeared on the screen.

No one was more startled than Khorii herself. To the others, most star-clad Linyaari looked alike but to Linyaari, there were many variations in appearance that distinguished them—the shape, length, and color of the horn, the color of the eyes, texture of the mane, conformation of the skull and body. The girl standing beside Maati looked to Khorii like her own reflection.

"Where have you been?" Maati asked. "We've been trying to hail you since yesterday."

"There were emergencies," Jaya said.

"We've had a few of those, too," Maati said. "If you can delay your departure until we arrive, we can explain more fully."

"How soon can you be here?" Jaya asked.

"We're unsure. We await the arrival of the *Balakiire*."

"Maati, what is the situation? Who is your companion and why must you wait for the Balakiire*?"*

"I thought you would never ask. It is so awkward at times to have humans, however competent and friendly, in the middle of our communications. I wanted you to know this news ahead of the others. My companion is your twin sister Ariin, who will be accompanying you and the Balakiire *back to Vhiliinyar so Elviiz's father can finish healing him."*

"Wait! Why does Elviiz need healing, and when did I get a twin sister?"

Maati sent her a series of images of how they found Ariin, or rather, how Ariin found them, followed by other, less-distinct images of the horrific way Elviiz had been injured.

While Khorii digested this, her twin watched her face carefully. So did Jaya. "I know I'm missing something here, Khorii. What's going on?"

"Family issues," Khorii said. Jaya's lids came down to shutter her eyes, and she pretended to be very interested in the instrument console. She no longer had family to cause problems or to give her joy or support. Khorii did not know what she should do first, but finally said to her look-alike, "I am very surprised to learn that I have a sister, Ariin."

"I was surprised, too, Khorii, but very glad. I have heard so many wonderful things about you. I will try to live up to your example and be of some small assistance in your great work." She inclined her head in what almost amounted to a bow.

"This is my friend Jaya," Khorii told her quickly. Hearing praise about herself from someone who looked so similar was extremely unsettling, and she wanted to get away from the subject of her "great work" as quickly as possible.

Captain Bates, Hap, and Mikaaye entered and prepared to strap themselves in for takeoff. "These are my other friends, our teacher Captain Asha Bates and Hap Hellstrom. You probably know Mikaaye already?"

Both Mikaaye and Ariin shook their heads, their manes ruffling slightly as they did so.

Sesseli entered last, clutching Khiindi. The cat looked at the com screen as if he had seen a larger carnivore and bolted, scratching a track across Sesseli's forearm as he ran to hide beneath a storage bench. *Leave it to a cat to capture all of the attention in the room,* Khorii thought. Ariin barely acknowledged Sesseli, but had watched Khiindi's flight intently. Surely she had seen cats before? Since Nadhari Kando became regent on Makahomia, litters of temple kittens had become ceremonial gifts between her world and Vhiliinyar. Quite a number of Linyaari pavilions hosted Temple Cats these days.

Sesseli, holding her bleeding arm, came to Khorii and held her injured limb up to the Linyaari's horn. Khorii absently rubbed her horn against the wound as a *good* cat might rub his head against a beloved friend.

"And this is Sesseli," Khorii concluded.

Sesseli scrutinized the screen, then looked back at Khorii.

"Maati says that Ariin and I are twins," Khorii told Sesseli.

"Hi, Ariin," the little girl said with a giggle. "Now I don't know how I'll tell you apart."

Jaya asked, "Why are you waiting for the *Balakiire*? When is it due?"

"Soon," Maati told her. "We need help towing a Federation tanker with a cargo of freshwater safely to the surface of Rushima. Then we need an extra crew to fly the ship to LoiLoiKua, where we can fill it with water from there to evacuate the sea people."

"Perhaps we can help you with that," Jaya said. "The *Mana* is larger and more suited to towing than the *Balakiire*. In the past we sometimes hauled strings of cargo barges for outlying ports."

"We still need to rendezvous with the *Balakiire*, because of Elviiz," Maati said. *"Oops, forgot she could not hear us before, Khorii."*

"The ghost-beings attacked Elviiz shortly after we left, destroying many of his inorganic parts," Khorii told her shipmates.

"I knew we shouldn't have left him," Hap said. "Shoot, I liked him, too. I thought it was safe making friends with a droid, but now he's bought it, too."

"Oh no, Elviiz is alive," Maati told him. "Simply . . . somewhat diminished. The *Balakiire* is returning with him to Vhiliinyar, but they wish to pick up Khorii to accompany him. If she can determine that the strain of the plague affecting her parents and the *Condor*'s crew has vanished like the rest of it, then Elviiz's father/creator Maak will be able to repair him more easily."

"And I can finally meet the rest of my family in person," Ariin said. "So I am coming, too."

"So we're going to have a basic switcheroo, is that it?" Captain Bates asked. "We'll help you off-load the water and rescue the LoiLoiKuans with the tanker, and sometime in the course of all that, Khorii and Ariin will transfer to the *Balakiire* to return to their homeworld. Right?"

"But we also have another mission," Jaya said. "Captain Becker in particular asked us to perform it."

Khorii said, "Even Uncle Joh would not value his cargo above Elviiz's and my family's well-being. Besides, we do not have a specific function, simply to check on the status of his cargo, and the *Balakiire* can do that as well as the *Mana*. The *Balakiire* is also programmed with Uncle Joh's universal shortcuts, so locating the cargo will pose no particular difficulty."

"Brilliant," Jaya said, "but whatever we're going to do, we should do it quickly. Doesn't the attack on Elviiz give anyone else a clue as to what has been causing all of the accidents and deterioration here?"

"Do you mean that these ghosts are absorbing—perhaps even feeding on—inorganic matter?" Khorii asked. That much was obvious. What was less evident was any other motive or methodology the entities might use in selecting their targets, or how they came to exist in the first place.

"We should do a final check, then lift off before they decide to chow down on *us*," said Hap.

he settlers of Rushima were delighted to receive their overdue shipment of freshwater. Jaya used the tractor beam aboard the *Mana* effortlessly to take control of the tanker and guide it to the landing field, where it occupied almost all of the space provided.

Everyone from Elder Plimsoll to Moonmay was waiting with hoses, pumps, wrenches, and buckets.

"Buckets?" Hap asked. "That tank holds the capacity of a small sea. That's a lot of bailing you're looking at, people."

"Marsden is working as hard as he can repairing the pumps and pipes of the irrigation system, but it's taking longer than we thought," Elder Bawb said.

"There may be similar items aboard the tanker," Khorii suggested. She strode back toward the larger ship in time to see Thariinye emerge and the *Nheifaarir* settling in to land in a nearby field since the docking bay was full.

"Never fear, youngling, I read the problem in your thoughts and investigated the ship's resources. It appears that all the people will need is a reservoir to hold the water. There are pumps and tubing attached to the tank, no doubt ready for the transfer," Thariinye said to Khorii.

Khorii beckoned the elders over, and they entered the

ship with Thariinye. Meanwhile, she trotted over to meet her new sister.

Maati waved at her and hastened, Ariin trailing her, to meet Khorii. Khorii hugged her aunt, then turned to her own mirror image.

Up close, she saw that although Ariin's features, form, and, of course, her coloring were identical to hers, she had an air of reserve about her. She met Khorii's embrace a bit hesitantly, though Khorii felt the other girl relax as they separated.

"Please don't let me keep you from your work," Ariin said aloud.

"There are many others who can do the same work better," Khorii told her. *"They understand that I wish to get to know my sister! Are you thought-talking yet? It is so much easier than verbal speech, especially with all that noise."*

On the landing pad, people swarmed over the tanker like busy ants. A new hatch had been opened in the tanker's hull. A very loud mechanism extruded compressed coils of flexible pipe, thick as the torso of an adult male. Thariinye and the others pulled coil after coil away from the ship, stretching it as it was released. In pairs stationed every few feet, people supported the hose, hauling it off the landing strip, across an adjacent field, and up the hill that cupped their reservoir in its center. Because the volume of water carried by the tanker was expected to be so great and the weather had been unusually dry, the irrigation ditches had been opened to accommodate the runoff.

As soon as the grinding noise of the hose ended, a rattle and wheeze heralded the start of the pumps. Almost immediately, they stopped again with a shudder and an alarming bang. Scar, Marsden, Hap, and Thariinye hastened to repair the damaged equipment. With a flare of welding torches and other mysterious mechanical rites, along with the two men, one boy, and one Linyaari all working on it, the pump was soon mended. With a quite loud hiss-clump, hiss-clump noise, it began pushing water in rationed portions at a steady rate through the pipe, which fattened like a huge snake gorging after a long fast.

The twin girls sat on the banked soil and stones rimming the landing field. The air was clear today, the sky bright, and the sunshine warm, bringing out a sweet scent from the grasses and wildflowers. Khorii and Mikaaye hadn't rid all of the land of its aqua overgrowth, but they had done so to the fields near the landing strip so that they could graze.

Once the pumps started, the noise was less distracting, and Ariin waited until then to reply. *"Yes, I can send and read thoughts, but it is very new to me, and I do not always like to do it. Where, or perhaps I should say when, I lived before, people were always trying to learn everything about me. They could read thoughts, too, although for a long time I could not. So I felt that nothing of myself was only mine."*

"I think a lot of us feel that way when we're young, before our own telepathy develops. I suppose it is for our own protection. It lets our elders know if we are planning to get into danger or trouble, or to find us if we are. And it keeps us from reading their thoughts, which contain what my friend Jaya would say is 'too much information.'"

Her sister stiffened and stood up. *"I'm hungry. Shall we graze?"*

Khorii looked up in alarm. *"I offended you. I'm sorry. I just thought . . ."*

"I know what you thought, sister, but unlike you, I did not grow up with loving parents who cared if I got into trouble or danger. I grew up in a laboratory with beings that considered themselves not only older and wiser but more sentient than I was, who monitored my every move, word and, yes, thought. The only time I escaped their scrutiny was when I visited the Others."

"Others?" Khorii asked and received an image of Ancestors—in fact, these creatures were not the same ones she knew, so they must have been ancestors of the Ancestors. *"I see. What I do not understand is how you came to be there. If we are twins, we should have been born at the same time in the same place and of course, to the same mother. No one ever told me I had a sister, much less a twin, though I always wanted one."*

"Why? You had your parents and all of your relatives who love you around you and everything else you wanted."

"Parents aren't the same thing, sometimes especially ours. I had Elviiz, of course, but he is not exactly a peer. He seems to be my age, but with his android attributes and vast intelligence and data banks, he is too much my teacher and guardian to be a real friend."

"If he teaches you and protects you, is that not friendship?" Ariin asked. Khorii had put her foot in it again complaining about Elviiz, because behind Ariin's question was real puzzlement. She did not even know what a friend was.

"Yes, of course he is my friend, but it is usually more in the same way that the Others were your friends. Friends who are more similar can do things for each other. I cannot do anything for Elviiz very often because he does everything so well himself."

"I see. Well, we are sisters so we must be friends, too. I do not know what I can do for you, but I do have a gift." She stopped grazing long enough to reach into the pocket of her shipsuit. She pulled out something that sparkled in the sunlight and tossed it to Khorii, who caught it in midair.

"Oooh, pretty!" she said, holding up the small piece of jewelry so that prisms of light shot out of the little stones and danced across her face and the grass around her. *"This is as beautiful as some of the things in the mansion on Dinero Grande. I really wanted to take some of them with me, but, of course, they belonged to others."*

Ariin was quiet. *"You wear it on your ear,"* she said finally. *"People wear that sort of thing a lot where I was."*

"Thank you very much. I'm afraid I do not have a gift for you." She wondered if Captain Bates might make a beaded bracelet for Ariin similar to Khorii's. Since the bracelet was a gift from a friend, she did not feel it was right to give hers to her sister, but one like it would be nice—then they'd have something to mark their kinship—other than the striking physical resemblance, of course.

"It will be gift enough for me if you are able to lift the quarantine on our parents so I may greet them in person. Also, I would like to see the human ships and meet more of the human people. I have seen Captain Becker on the com screen, and I met Uncle Hafiz and Karina and their household, but I would like to meet your friends, too."

"Of course!"

That night, with the ships in dock, Khorii suggested that people light fires around the perimeter to keep the fog at bay.

"What good is a fire going to do against a ship-eating ghost?" Elder Plimsoll asked. "If lighting fires would help, we should be guarding our own homes and businesses."

"Never mind what happens to the ships that bring you water and people to heal your sick and clean your cropland?" Captain Bates demanded.

"What good will that do us if everything turns into ghost food?" the elder demanded.

"What have we done for you lately? Huh?" Hap demanded angrily.

Elder Bawb and Marsden had disappeared and now reappeared with armloads of kindling. They were followed by a dozen children, each carrying all of the kindling they could. Moonmay trudged behind them, pushing a wooden wheelbarrow full of wood.

"You got any special places in mind we should light these fires, Khorii?" Marsden asked.

"All around the ships," she said. "Close enough together that a person sitting by one campfire can feel the warmth of the adjacent ones and visit with the neighboring tender."

"That's a lot of campfires. Going to get pretty hot," Marsden said.

"Are you trying to protect your ships or burn them up yourself?" Plimsoll asked derisively.

"Elder, if you have any constructive suggestions, we would be happy to entertain them," Khorii told him. "We have determined that the ghosts or whatever they are absorb inorganic material, and last night they traveled under cover of fog. If we keep the real fog at bay, at least we will be able to see our adversaries."

"And do what? You gonna shoot 'em with your ray guns, Missy?"

"What is a ray gun?" Ariin asked Mikaaye, who shrugged.

"My people are peaceful and do not employ offensive weapons, Elder," Khorii said. "But we will defend ourselves and so should you. It seems to me that if the ghostly beings absorb inorganic materials, they should be warded off with organic weapons—perhaps a burning brand from the fire, as wood is organic?"

"But you don't know that, do you, young lady?" Elder Plimsoll demanded.

"No, sir. I have only a partial theory constructed from what I've observed. Many of you have also encountered the ghost-beings, and if anyone has more promising theories, I'd ask that you please share them."

Even that plan was nearly foiled when the wind picked up, roaring across the flat field, scattering the kindling and making it too dangerous and difficult to maintain open camp-fires. Moonmay's braids lashed her face and shoulders like whips. Everyone who wasn't wearing shipsuits had their clothing belling and bannering around them like sails. The beaded braid in Khorii's mane beat against her face and neck, and the rest of her mane felt as if the wind were tearing it out by the roots.

"Now what?" Plimsoll demanded, his fists on his hips like a scolding mother.

Marsden and his grandchildren disappeared as the wind came up, returning a little while later with another convoy of wooden wheelbarrows, each of which contained a fuel barrel cut in half.

Words were blown away as soon as they were spoken, but the smith and his kids set the barrels on the runway, filled them with sticks of stray kindling, and placed them a safe distance from the ship, but within range of each other. Then Scar arrived on his tractor, hauling a wooden trailer full of more barrel halves. When all of the fire pits were in place, Scar parked his tractor, digger, and the trailer under the fin of the tanker, between it and the campfires. "I've had a fair amount of repairs to make on my equipment, thanks to the not-so-dear and not-so-departed," he said. "I checked on my ship this morning, and it looks like I'll be needing to hitch a ride off-world with one of you."

Each barrel was tended by four people. Two sat by the fire, huddling against the wind, keeping the flames from being extinguished. Meanwhile, two other tenders camped inside the ships, sleeping, eating, or visiting away from the whistling swoosh and rattle of the air currents whipping around the landing field.

Captain Bates fixed pot after pot of hot soup and Kava, and some of the girls and women from the town brought bread and more vegetables for the soup and for the Linyaari, who welcomed the change from what they could grow in their 'ponics gardens, though the vegetables, preserved from previous harvests, were dried and old.

It was a good party, but a bit anticlimactic, since the wind kept both fog and ghosts away.

"Maybe they're just full from last night," Moonmay said.

But the next morning, on the far side of the fires where the darkness eclipsed their light but their heat still warmed the tarmac, the departing guards saw that footprints, whole and partial, were indented in the heat-softened landing field, round and round and back and forth, as if patrolling the fire line, looking for a way inside. Oddly enough, the only place where no footprints appeared was in the field around the *Nheifaarir.*

Hap was elated. "Hah! They can't get in. You did it, Khorii. You thought of a way to fool them,"

But Khorii shook her head grimly. "It only shows they've mutated from mist to mass enough to leave prints." Indeed, this development worried her even more, for the ghosts had been dangerous enough when they were incorporeal, but who knew what destruction they might wreak if they ever got physical bodies of their own?

That day the ships and equipment were checked and re-checked for damage. Scar, Hap, Captain Bates, and Marsden repaired and recalibrated the tanker, pronouncing it space-worthy under its own power. Scar and a burial detail also hauled the remains of the crew members to the graveyard. No sooner had they set off than the com units on both the *Nheifaarir* and the *Mana* beeped on to announce the *Balakiire's* arrival.

"It would be best if you sent only a shuttle," Maati advised the *Balakiire.* "We have ship-eating entities aboard down here. Though they didn't seem to bother the *Nheifaarir,* so perhaps they don't care for the taste of Linyaari ships."

"If you've room for one more shuttle, open your hatch and we'll dock inside the *Nheifaarir,*" Neeva said.

After some discussion, they decided that Elviiz would go

with Ariin and Khorii aboard the *Mana,* which would continue on its original mission, but Hap and Jalonzo would
augment the crew of the tanker with Thariinye. Scar was
going, too. His own ship had been lodged in a local barn during the aftermath of the plague, and had suffered damage he
needed more equipment to repair. The Marsden men were
traveling with the tanker as well, to hold it together as much
as possible. Of them all, only Thariinye, Hap, and Scar had
any navigation experience, but with the *Nheifaarir* and the
Balakiire "riding shotgun" as Scar put it, they would be fine.
Mikaaye stayed with the *Mana.* And everyone agreed it
would be better to transfer the prisoners to the brig of the
Federation tanker than to take them anywhere near the
Linyaari homeworld.

Moonmay was there to see her brother, cousin, and grandfather off. In the crook of her arm was a basket of kittens,
while trailing behind her was a low-slung, furry-faced dog.

"What in tarnation did you haul the livestock out here
for?" her grandfather asked.

She carried the kittens over to her grandfather, and he
leaned down while she whispered into his ear. "Okay then,
you talk to them, but make it snappy. Khorii, honey, my
granddaughter needs to jaw at you."

Khorii looked up from Elviiz's cart. He was using his
legs somewhat better than he had before, but still tired easily, even with the help of the horns. There was no substitute
for building his own muscles and endurance so he could get
around without the help of his bionic extras.

It was sad to see him like this, weaker than she had ever
thought possible, and often bewildered by what was happening around him. He seemed baffled by Ariin, but she was
very sweet to him and already he seemed to like her a lot.

Moonmay said, pointing to the dog, "This dog here is the
one I was telling you about that you thought that big boy
might like." When she turned to show Khorii the dog in

question, the animal was no longer there, having trotted straight to Hap, who was rubbing her ears. "I reckon he likes him okay."

"It's up to Hap, of course, but it looks like he wouldn't mind having her. And there will certainly be room aboard the tanker."

Moonmay held up her basket and looked around Khorii to where Ariin was patting Elviiz's hand. "And I thought your new sissy might want a kitty cat for herself, bein' as you've got Khiindi and all. I reckon he won't care if the kitty belongs to your sis."

To Khorii's surprise, Ariin looked at the kittens in much the way RK might have done, or Khiindi himself. Then she smiled, and said, "Thank you, youngling, but I prefer to lavish my attention on my two new siblings."

Moonmay's face fell, but Sesseli said, "Can I have a kitty for my own? A little baby one?"

Jaya and Captain Bates joined them, and Jaya picked up a little black fellow with a white chest, and said, "Ooh, he's cute. I never got to play with the ship's cats. Papa said spoiling them would distract them from their pest control job."

Captain Bates scratched another kitten's chin, and asked, "How much do either of you know about caring for animals?"

Jaya rolled her eyes. "Who do you think changes the pan and feeds the ship's cats? Or the other animal cargo we used to carry, for that matter."

Khorii remembered Moonmay saying how she thought her kittens would like to travel on a spaceship and how Khorii had known that the little girl was investing her pets with her own dreams. "I don't know, Jaya. It seems a shame to separate the kittens from each other, and that is adding a lot of new creatures to our crew. Elviiz was never programmed for cat care, Khiindi will not take kindly to them, Ariin is evidently not fond of cats, and we will all be busy with our missions. I think if we are to take extra feline crew members on this mission, they should have their own specialist. I wonder if Mr. Marsden would allow Moonmay to go with us if she wishes. While she couldn't go to Vhiliinyar, I think she'd like MOO, and I might be able to convince the Council to let her visit narhii-Vhiliinyar. What do you think?"

Moonmay was dancing up and down, almost jostling kittens out of the basket. Jaya and Captain Bates looked at each other and shrugged.

Mr. Marsden had been watching the conversation with a proprietary eye on his granddaughter, and now, as the females all turned to him, he said, "If you all think you can put up with her and will see that she gets home safe, I see no harm in it. We were all a damn sight safer with you than we were before you got here, and I expect that Moonmay will be safe with you, no matter where you go."

chapter 28

The *Mana* was a much more interesting ship than the *Nheifaarir,* Ariin thought. It was bigger, and the only two people who thought-talked with her were Khorii and Mikaaye, who were usually both too busy to bother. Everyone was pleasant to her, from the child offering one of her mewling feline younglings to the adult human female who offered to braid and bead her mane as she had done everyone else's. Ariin thought about refusing, just because she was pretty sure she could and nobody would do anything to her. Then she thought that if her mane looked exactly like Khorii's, maybe nobody would be able to tell them apart. The idea intrigued Ariin, who had up until recently been so completely different from everybody else around her. It was a way to hide and also a good way to find out the things that were happening that nobody bothered explaining to a stranger.

Even Captain Bates remarked when she was done that now she wouldn't be able to tell the twins apart. Ariin knew she couldn't fool Khorii, of course, or probably Mikaaye, but she thought perhaps she could fool Elviiz. Unfortunately, he and Mikaaye were always together so Mikaaye could help him with male-specific functions.

Khorii caught on to that part of what was on her mind and looked up from her duties long enough to close and open one eye rapidly while smiling. *"I just winked at you, Ariin. It is a human gesture of complicity, although it sometimes has something to do with their mating habits, though I'm not certain about that. But I think you and I will have great fun on MOO fooling everyone into thinking I am you and the other way around."*

"Yes," Ariin answered with what she hoped seemed to be similar enthusiasm. *"It will be fun."*

While others were busy, the younglings Moonmay and Sesseli tried to interest Ariin in the antics of the young felines, but there was only one feline that interested Ariin. Khiindi. According to the technicians, the Friend who had stolen her from her family before she was born had been punished for not bringing Khorii as well. His punishment had been to be frozen into the shape of a regular domestic feline to be Khorii's companion.

He probably thought that was a terrible punishment, and so did the Friends, but Ariin could see that her kidnapper had enjoyed the love of her family while she was being used as an experimental specimen by his people.

She tried to guard these thoughts carefully, but she knew that somehow he knew. No one said that he was no longer sentient, just that his form had been frozen. He pretended to be no more intelligent or capable of understanding words or thoughts than the kittens or the ship's cats, but she was pretty sure that he understood exactly who she was and how she felt about him. If she surprised him as he lounged across the back of Khorii's chair or purred in her lap or sometimes in Sesseli's if she wasn't cuddling kittens instead, the animal was a furry gray streak out the hatch or, if that was closed, under the nearest object as far out of reach as he could get.

Sesseli and Moonmay were sitting in the cargo hold where the cats lived most of the time, watching the kittens trying to play with the older cat's tail. It amused Ariin as much as it did the younglings to see how aggravated Khiindi got when the kittens would not stop playing with him no matter how he growled or postured. They probably knew he would not dare lift a paw to them while their young protectors were near. But she had only watched for a moment before he looked up, saw her, and shot off into the shadows of the cargo hold, the kittens looking puzzled for a moment as to where he might have gone, then turning to wrestle with each other in a tangled ball of fur.

"Hi, Ariin," Sesseli said.

She had just had her braid done and decided to see if she could fool them. "Sesseli, I'm Khorii!"

"You're not either!" Moonmay said.

"Why do you say that? Is it my voice? My accent?"

"It's cause Khiindi runs away from you, and the other kitties don't come to you for pettin' nor play," Moonmay said. "They know you don't like them, Sissy."

Ariin preferred her new name to the one Moonmay had assigned her, but understood from the girl's thoughts that it was almost an endearment in her culture, often used for one's own siblings, so she did not object.

"So they don't like you," Sesseli said, looking at her in exactly the way Hruffli might have when she was being difficult. Her brow was wrinkled and her jaw had a stubborn set to it.

Ariin sat down beside them and scooped up the kittens. "That is not so." She petted the soft small life-forms as she had seen the others do. They made agreeable sounds that caused their entire bodies to vibrate and rubbed against her fingers before wriggling to get down. "You see? I am larger than you, and I startle them with my size and movement. I am not used to such small creatures. Where I lived before, there were not very many of them around, and none were kept as companions."

"City girl, were you, Sissy?" Moonmay asked.

"In a manner of speaking. As for Khiindi, I have tried to befriend him, but he always runs away. Do you suppose he does not like it that Khorii has someone of her own race who might become closer to her than he is? He has been her companion for many years, she said."

"That makes sense," Moonmay said, after considering it. "Cats are mighty jealous, and they do take against even nice cat-lovin' people, even their own people, if they take up with somebody else or especially another cat."

"Maybe," Sesseli said, "but Khiindi's used to Elviiz, and he likes everybody else."

Ariin sighed, suddenly sad, not because her enemy disliked her, but because it seemed that even he had forged closer relationships among the people who should be her friends than she had been able to do. *But of course he has,* she thought dejectedly, *he's had years to ingratiate himself, while I've only been here a short while.*

"Now don't take on, Sissy," Moonmay said, patting her. "He'll come around likely as not when he sees you're here to stay. He's accepted the baby cats already, you saw. Just give him time, and pretend you don't care about him one way or the other and he'll be wantin' you to pet him before long. In fact, if you really *hated* cats, he'd probably be all over you. They're ornery like that."

Ariin nodded as if consoled, but she knew that Khiindi, the former Grimalkin, was far too canny to try that brand of orneriness with her.

"I'll try that and see if I can win him over," she said. "After all, he is part of my family now." Besides, if she could gain the cat's trust and lead him to believe she had forgiven him or did not fully realize his part in her involuntary exile, she could more easily lay hands on him when she finally figured out the form his punishment should take.

Khiindi stared at Ariin's feet as she walked past his hiding place in the shadows of the cargo bay. An old trickster himself, he was not deceived by her vow to "be kind to Khiindi." If his own people had been angry with him for bringing them only one of Acorna's children, the child herself, somehow, he was sure, had found out his part in her upbringing and was far more furious than they had been.

He had to admit that his people had taught her well. She was good at shielding her feelings and intentions from other Linyaari and the humans, even the sensitive ones, but Khiindi wasn't fooled. He smelled her anger every time she came near him, and the heat of it singed his whiskers. It was totally unfair, of course. He couldn't defend himself, and if he started thought-talking enough to explain his side of the story, to be winsome and charming enough, even pitiable enough to dissuade Ariin from her bad feelings about him, then Khorii would realize he had been fooling her all along, and she'd despise him, too. And he had been a good friend to her, her good little kitty-cat. If he didn't exactly keep her out of trouble, at least he ferreted it out first so that he got into it before she did, thereby alerting her to its presence.

How could his people have treated this child so badly that, even after she escaped them to the collective bosom of her own people, she still harbored such an unhealthy (for him particularly, but of course he was far more concerned about the toxic effect of such negative feelings on one so young) grudge against him? How could his people have let her escape, period, for that matter? They were in a different time, the machine was broken and had not been repaired in present-day Vhiliinyar, and they would never have allowed a child as valuable to them as Ariin to touch a crono.

Not if they could help it. Not if they knew about it. Not if they realized what a sneaky little creature she really was. Apparently they hadn't realized it, of course, or she would not be here, and since, from what he could pick up from Maati's and Thariinye's thoughts about the girl, she had arrived alone, the only way she could have done it was with the help of a crono.

He would have to be very brave if he wanted to save himself. He would have to remember that he was not merely a small and weak domesticated feline, albeit one carrying a reasonable facsimile of the DNA of fierce Makahomian Temple Cats. He had to remember what it had been like to be Grimalkin, the father of half the universe, the maker of cultures, the shaper of societies, lord of time and space. So from that point on, although his claws dug into the back of Khorii's chair or Sesseli's shipsuit when Ariin approached, he did not allow himself to run. As long as one of his other people was there, he stayed put when she drew near and even allowed her to touch him, commanding his fur not to bristle, although the purr he offered was the Purr of Tension, not the Purr of Pleasure. No one who was not a cat seemed to be able to tell the difference anyway.

When she did touch him, rubbing his fur the wrong way quite as if she didn't realize that cats hated that, he quelled his qualms and opened his mouth and rubbed his cheek against her hand. And he smelled it. Or rather, he smelled himself as he had been, long ago. She had something of his, and although she was not wearing it on her wrist, he knew what it was and he knew he had to get it away from her before any more trouble could happen.

"See there, Sess," Moonmay said as the younger girls and the insufferable bullets of feline energy trooped onto the bridge. "Khiindi knows he's hurt Sissy's feelings by running away from her. He knows she wants to be his friend. Look how he's rubbing against her."

"That's good," Sesseli said, but Khiindi thought—and certainly hoped—that the child, who was unusually sensitive and had saved his tail at least once, was not entirely deceived.

chapter 29

Captain Becker's storage asteroid was on the outermost fringe of Federation space, in an unpatrolled loophole in the cosmos reached by navigating through a section of what Becker called "pleated space" and a wormhole. As the *Mana* drew close to the coordinates that would require it to warp out of space as most navigators knew it, they received a relay from the tanker that all three of the vessels had arrived safely on LoiLoiKua.

"I hope the monster took no more lives before you arrived," Khorii said.

"No," Neeva told her. "Not a single one. The people were going to hide in the reef, but the monster was more interested in it than it was in them. Then it transferred its attention to diving to the sea bottom and attacking the shores of the islands. It hasn't been seen for several days, but the odd thing is, the reef seems to be growing. We scanned it to see if we could determine what was happening and found that the new section is stone, not coral. I do not suppose the LoiLoiKuans are in any actual peril at this time, but since their world is endangered in other ways already, and in the new sea on narhii-Vhiliinyar they will be reunited with their grandchildren from Maganos, we all agreed to continue the evacuation as planned."

The tanker, the *Balakiire,* and the *Nheifaarir* were about to leave LoiLoiKua in a convoy that would soon be joined by another Federation tanker found by other Linyaari on Kezdet. This tanker had already transferred the poopuus from their watery classroom along with their educational equipment, which had been graciously donated by the school under the direction of Khorii's human grandparents. Then all of the vessels would meet on MOO, where the Linyaari crews would transfer the aquatic people and their grandchildren to the seas of Vhiliinyar and, when the terraforming of a new sea was complete, to narhii-Vhiliinyar.

The transmission ended when the *Mana* entered the first of the "pleats" that took it out of range of the normal relay channels.

Captain Bates had used the same techniques as the Beckers long ago, she said, but she was rather tense through the first few pleats.

On her previous voyage aboard the *Condor,* Khorii had gone through a route that was similarly endowed with the physical anomalies, but these were different.

The entire crew, except for Mikaaye and Elviiz, were on the bridge for these maneuvers. Moonmay and Sesseli squealed at the swift shifts in starscape, when individual stars blurred past like comets in the night skies of their home-worlds. The abruptness of each shift gave the illusion of the ship diving down and climbing up, and of one's stomach and heart doing the same.

"How are we doing, Mikey, Elviiz?" Jaya asked through the intercom. "Holding together?"

"We seem to be," Elviiz replied. "Great holes are conspicuously not gaping in any critical equipment, and there are no untoward rattles, bangs, pops, or vibrations that we can detect."

"Thanks, guys," Jaya said, and let out a long sigh. She looked to Captain Becker, who nodded and turned to Khorii.

"I'd feel much better if we had Elviiz the android in the engine room instead of Elviiz the invalid, but it sounds like it's all good so far."

Then the smooth sailing was over, and they started spinning through the wormhole.

"Can the ship take it?" Jaya asked Captain Bates, whirling one finger in the air.

"Relax," the captain said. "The hole is spinning, not the *Mana*."

By the time they were through it, the novelty had worn off for the younger girls. Moonmay had stopped squealing and threw up in the cat basket at some point during the transition. "Don't anybody tell my cousins," she begged after she had cleaned herself and the basket. "They never would let me live it down."

"Good thing those kittens weren't in their basket," Captain Bates said, grinning.

"No, they think Khiindi is their ma now," Moonmay said, pointing to a motley pile of furry lumps sprawled and curled around a larger one. "They slept through the whole thing. They're gonna make good ship's cats, Khorii."

"It's too bad they are using Khiindi as their example then instead of the mother ship's cat," Khorii said. "She and her offspring and male colleague are far more aggressive at hunting counterproductive life-forms than Khiindi."

Khiindi opened an eye, and one ear poked up above a tiny paw as if he'd heard and resented his girl's lack of loyalty.

Khorii laughed and unstrapped herself to go give him an apologetic stroke. "It is not your fault, Khiindi. You were raised on Vhiliinyar, and have adopted our peaceful Linyaari customs."

The cat snagged the cuff of her shipsuit with a lightning paw.

"Khiindi!" she scolded. He let his paw go limp and closed his eye as if the threat of claws had been unintentional.

Moonmay and Sesseli giggled, but when Khorii looked up, she found Ariin watching her and Khiindi with an unreadable expression—and an unreadable mind.

Where's the sign?" Khorii asked when their course finally brought them to the asteroid that should have been the one where Captain Becker had stowed the *Estrella Blanca.*

Captain Bates cocked a questioning eyebrow at her. "Captain Becker made a sign all across the face of the asteroid warning trespassers away," Khorii said. "You could see it from space."

"You were approaching from the other direction," Captain Bates told her. "It's probably on the far side."

But although they circled the asteroid, they didn't see the sign, though there was indeed a lot of other, well, stuff, on the surface.

None of it looked like the *Estrella Blanca,* however, or anything else Khorii found familiar.

"What in the zodiac is that stuff?" Captain Bates asked.

Khorii was puzzled. The material on the surface of the asteroid looked nothing like the collection of parts and wrecked ships and other "good stuff" Uncle Joh had collected. It almost looked like there was a network of connected dwellings down there. One thing for certain was that, however the salvage had been altered, Uncle Joh had not done it. He'd been in quarantine with her parents and had not had time to return here, she was sure.

She noticed as they drew nearer the surface that one especially large rounded hump still bore the letters "anca" on its side. Why was there something wrong about that? She pointed at the area, and Captain Bates used the ship's computer to enhance and enlarge it. Had Elviiz been himself, he could have given them a detailed analysis, but of course, he wasn't.

Then she remembered. "We camouflaged the ship completely by covering it with other salvage," she told them. "We should not be able to see any of the hull, much less read its name."

"Maybe a meteor or something knocked part of the camouflage off?" Captain Bates speculated uneasily. "But I have a feeling that something even weirder than usual is going on down there. Jaya, I believe it's time to change course and head straight to the Moon of Opportunity. I don't know why Joh Becker wanted us to come here to begin with, but if Khorii pronounces him and her family plague-free, he can come here himself and check his own darn cargo. I don't like the looks of this, and I don't want to take any unnecessary chances with you kids. From what Khorii says, the ship was cleansed the first time and . . ."

"That was just the parts we saw, and the air, Captain," Khorii told her. She caught her breath and suddenly felt the roots of her mane all the way down her spine bristle like Khiindi's. Even the feathers on her calves pushed against the legs of her shipsuit. Why did it put her on alert, even frighten her, to look at the asteroid's altered surface? "We did not realize at that time that there was a plague. It was the first place I saw the plague indicators, however. If there are still some there, we will know—well, something. That it can live when there are no living organic hosts, if nothing else. In which case, other humans could still catch it and our people cannot return home as we hope."

Jaya, her dark eyes blazing with indignation, said, "With all due respect, ma'am, it is my ship and Khorii's mission and you are here in an advisory capacity only. While your advice is duly noted and your concern appreciated, we're not babies! Whatever is down there can't possibly be any weirder or more dangerous than what we've been through lots of times already."

"There's Sesseli and Moonmay. They're babies where I come from," Captain Bates replied stubbornly.

"They've had to grow up like the rest of us," Jaya argued. "Sesseli can protect herself better than most of us and Moonmay brought her grandpa's twelve-gauge shotgun as well as the kittens."

Mikaaye's thought voice spoke from the engine room, *"Khorii, Ariin, what reading are you getting? Who is on that asteroid and what is it that they fear?"*

"You may be picking up remnants of the last moments of the passengers," Khorii suggested, *"There's nobody living down there—I've seen for myself."* But the thought had barely formed, her mind's eye once more seeing the over-dressed corpses floating in zero G amid the sparkling blue motes of contamination, when she knew that was not what concerned Mikaaye. Perhaps because there were fewer people in the engine room, the psychic static was less, and he was reading the signals more quickly and strongly than she was.

"No, sister, there are extant life-forms there. I feel them. Do you not?"

By then, Khorii knew that the fear she had been feeling earlier, perhaps the same fear that was making their telepathic teacher try to turn them from their mission, was not her own. It was her heart that beat faster and louder, her eyes that constantly scanned the surface looking for the source of the danger, but it was someone else's fear.

"Jaya is right, Captain. We have to land. Someone seems to be trapped down there, and they are in some kind of trouble."

"I don't suppose you could be more specific?" Captain Bates asked.

"Perhaps I should take the shuttle and go down alone to scout the area," Khorii suggested.

"No way!" Jaya said. "We land and do this together, or we don't do it at all."

"We'll be okay, Khorii," Sesseli said, reaching around

Khiindi and patting her on the shoulder. "Even if those ship-eating things are there, from what you said, Captain Becker has plenty of spare parts we could use to repair it."

"Hap is not with us," Khorii reminded her.

"Hap isn't the only one who knows how to repair a ship," Captain Bates growled. Their normally cheerful mentor was not a bit happy about this sudden mutiny, and didn't mind letting everyone know it.

They landed on what looked like a clear patch as close as they could find to the buried ship's logo of the *Estrella Blanca*.

"Okay," Captain Bates said, standing up and stretching. "Khorii and I will go take a look around."

"Sesseli and me are a-comin', too, ma'am. Like Jaya said, we can look after our own selves. She's got her moves, and I got Grampa's twelve-gauge."

"I'm afraid not, girls. Someone has to guard the ship." She knelt and looked them both in the eyes. "Who will look after the cats if something happens to you? Khorii just has to see if the plague is still active, then we'll all leave for the good part of the trip. And Jaya, you need to stay here so there'll be someone left on board who can fly this bucket or pilot a shuttle if we need you in a hurry."

"Aye, aye, Captain," Jaya said, only a little sarcastically.

"Well, as you keep pointing out, it *is* your ship."

"I'm coming, too," Ariin said. "If things need cleansing, two horns will be better than one."

"Three is even better," Mikaaye said, appearing in the hatch as they were about to leave. "And you need a male along for protection."

Elviiz expertly zoomed his cart onto the bridge, narrowly missing two scampering kittens, and parked. "I will protect our remaining shipmates here," he announced.

"And I'll protect Elviiz with Grampa's gun," Moonmay

said, brightening. "On account of he's mostly Linyaari and not s'posed to shoot folks, even when they need it."

Khorii, her hackles still vibrating with tension, very much hoped the altered landscape would contain no folks or anything else who needed shooting by anybody.

inyaari environmental suits were less bulky than those the humans had to wear. Since they could endlessly purify and recycle the air already inside their helmets, they didn't need fresh oxygen supplies. Their shipsuits could be sealed to gauntlets, gravity boots and hoods with faceplates and a vacuum seal through which the horn could be freed. Oxygen and temperature gauges in the gauntlets kept them apprised of the need for their protective clothing.

Almost at once it became clear to Khorii that the difficult part of this mission would be getting back inside the *Blanca*.

"Do you not remember the way in?" Mikaaye asked, hopping over the back of a discarded tank of some sort and landing with a clang of gravity boots on a metal plate. Towering above them like cliffs were mounds of weathered metal, plasglass and plasteel, hull plates and stair grids, broken cables and torn cargo nets, bits that looked like they came from engine rooms and old berths, toilets, shuttles, some wrecked and in pieces and some that seemed undamaged, storage containers, old lockers, and a vast majority of other objects, the use of which Khorii could not begin to guess. Everything was covered with a thick coating of gray-brown dust.

Captain Bates tapped Khorii on the shoulder, pointed down, then bent over and adjusted her boots to put more bounce in her step on the low-gravity asteroid. Khorii passed along the suggestion, and she and the others followed the captain's example.

"When we came here before, although things appeared chaotic, there was actually an order to them. Uncle Joh had parts of each sort of ship piled in one place. Miscellaneous fittings were in other places according to their use, furnishings in still another. There was a large sign on the asteroid's surface warning trespassers to keep away. And although we camouflaged the Blanca with salvage, it did not spread over so great an area as this."

Mikaaye picked up the first large object in his path and flung it aside, watching it fly with the force of his throw. His face held the joy of a child with a new ball until the pile shifted and other debris slumped toward him.

He jumped clear and landed on Khorii, who fell back with the impact but easily righted herself. Ariin and the captain fell back, too, then everyone grabbed debris and began flinging it to the sides to make a passage.

Captain Bates planted herself in front of them and pointed back to the ship. "It's too damned dangerous, kids." Her voice came through Khorii's earbud. "We can't just bull our way through. This stuff could avalanche and kill us all."

"Maybe that's what happened to the people who are trapped here," Mikaaye said. "We are the only chance of rescue they may have."

"Try to get a better idea of their location then, you psychics. We could kill them by piling more junk on top of them if we don't know where they are."

Khorii felt the fear, now stronger and fresher than before, which told her that whoever it was still lived. *"I'm getting nothing specific,"* she told the others. *"Perhaps they're unconscious or sleeping or so low on oxygen, they . . ."*

"Yes, it would be nice if they'd give us some way to locate them," Ariin agreed.

"If Elviiz still had his android bits . . ." Mikaaye began, but then stopped as they all felt it, at some distance but directly ahead of them, not fear alone but a complex stew of human emotion. Khorii identified terror, anger, hostility, pain, and even love, some fragmented images of faces, flashes of color and music, but she thought these might be dreams instead of communication. Still, it provided the direction they needed.

"Ahead, Captain Bates, and not dead," Khorii said. "Whoever it is might even be aboard the *Blanca.*"

"Survivors?" Captain Bates asked incredulously.

"Not from the time we were there," Khorii said. "My mother and father were there, too, and even if I missed it, they would have known. Elviiz was with us as well, and Uncle Joh had an infrared scope. But obviously this place has been disturbed since our previous visit."

Captain Bates made a huge shrug, magnifying the gesture with her puffy, oxygen-holding suit, and turned to begin digging through the debris more carefully as the rest of them stepped up to join her.

They cleared only another foot or two, however, when Ariin pulled aside a large hull plate and revealed a long open tunnel, tall enough and wide enough for them to walk into it four abreast.

"That's luck," Captain Bates said. "This must be some old ship's hold—a central corridor maybe, that will take us through the trash without our having to move all of it manually. Now if it's not collapsed at the other end . . ."

She switched on the lanterns mounted in her helmet and gauntlets. Each Linyaari suit also carried a small glow tube in an outer pocket as part of its standard equipment.

If it was a ship, it was unlike any she had been on before, though in some ways the interior of the tube reminded her more of the egg-shaped smoothness of the Linyaari ships than the more clumsily constructed human vessels.

The deck, walls, and ceiling were a single piece, without joints or division. Khorii ran a glove along one bulkhead—or was it a wall?

Although the texture of the walls seemed smooth for the most part, there were odd indentations and shadows every few meters in the corridor.

Captain Bates ran her glove over one set. "This is like the handprints you see in some cave painting on elder worlds."

"Yes!" Khorii said, though she'd never seen the paintings in question. "Except more like a reverse sculpture. Here, you see, this looks like the profile of a human face."

As they progressed down the hall, they saw other prints, backs of torsos, a leg, a face, more hands, all imprinted in the smooth walls.

"Ugh," Captain Bates said, as they went farther. "This is creeping me out. It looks like people just stepped out of these walls."

Although the tubular corridor did not resemble any ship Khorii had ever been aboard, as they continued, it ended in a hatch the size of the entire administration building in Corazon.

All four of them stopped in front of it.

"Look familiar?" Captain Bates asked Khorii.

"Yes, this looks like the hatch to the docking bay on the *Blanca.*"

"It can't be," Mikaaye said. He held his glow tube aloft. "It's part of this corridor—see how the ceiling swoops up to encompass it, then it's all part of the same structure."

"At least there aren't any bits of people imprinted on the hatch," Ariin said.

"How do we get this son of a gun open now without a ship's computer telling it to?" Captain Bates wondered.

Mikaaye examined the opening. "We could try pushing,"

he said, and before anyone could stop him, did. To their surprise, the gigantic hatch slid open at his touch.

The proportion of the inner space was familiar to Khorii, but that was all. Where she expected to see the docking bay with the silent ships sitting waiting for owners who would never return, instead there was what could have been a small city or a very large and extremely abstract and rather ugly sculpture.

Although Khorii and her parents had cleansed the air of the poisons the *Blanca*'s captain had released to kill the passengers and crew, the suits' gauges showed that the oxygen level remaining inside the docking bay was so low as to be negligible. Of course, without a functioning airlock, the oxygen in this section would have dissipated once the hatch opened to the outside. Someone would have to restore power before the area could be examined without portable oxygen. That was also assuming they could find any intact and functioning equipment.

What had once been a docking bay had now been morphed into something far more changed than mere indentations in the walls. As far as the explorers could tell from their limited light sources, instead of ships and ramps, the cavernous room was now filled with hillocks and hollows that lumped and humped out into each other. Where the decks had once been, there were steep ramps or perhaps slanted roofs that descended into what seemed to be more of the same forms. Also, although they could see a vast unbroken space overhead, in front of them the hillocks formed walls that loomed up and twisted and turned, making their progress through the area very slow. Once in a while, Khorii thought she recognized another piece of salvage off to the side somewhere, but most of the surrounding structures bore little resemblance to the ship's interior she remembered. Also, while they watched, the structures seemed to shift slightly, glacially, as if they were expanding even as they sat there.

"Probably a trick of the light," Captain Bates guessed, turning her head so that her helmet lantern danced across the undulations. The structures seemed to shift again, giving Khorii the feeling that her brain had vacated her head for a moment, then reentered her skull turned the wrong way round. Her vision blurred for a moment, as she got the sudden, maddening impression that the entire room was somehow, impossibly alive, moving around them as they walked.

When the sensation lessened but did not pass, she wanted nothing so much as to return to the ship and fly far far away.

Ariin and Mikaaye felt the same, she read, and Captain Bates's glove rose to her face mask as if to steady her head so it didn't fall off her shoulders.

Khorii said, trying to lighten everyone's mood, "At least I'm not seeing any blue particles in the air here."

"We should check those bodies you said were in the corridor," Captain Bates said.

"It wasn't too far when we were here before," Khorii said. "But the distance seems much greater because of these impediments."

"Right. I've had enough of this," the captain said, and adjusted her boots again. "Let's skip over this part, kids, shall we?"

The gravity within the former hold seemed no greater than on the rest of the asteroid, and the four of them bounced to the top of the nearest wall, then jumped from one to another.

Captain Bates's lantern made their leaping shadows fly, swoop, and undulate grotesquely up onto the overheads and down into the hollows between the humplike structures. The sense of vertigo was still disturbing, but it lessened a little as they kept moving. Twice, when they jumped for the next prominence, it wasn't there when they landed, and they found themselves halfway down its distant side.

On her last hop, Khorii's boot went through the top of the structure she landed on and stuck fast. Ariin steadied her while Mikaaye helped her extricate her foot. It came out streaked with what seemed to be a muddy mixture of the gray-brown dust of the asteroid's surface, melted sand, and taffylike, yellowed plasglass.

"It looks wet," Ariin said.

"It's certainly gooier than it was on the other humps," Mikaaye added.

"Maybe it's fresher," Ariin said.

"That explains how the imprints could be there, but not *why* they are," Captain Bates said. "But I'm starting to form a theory."

"It's the ghosts, isn't it?" Khorii asked. She could think of no other explanation, but suddenly all that she had seen, heard, felt, theorized, or heard others theorize about the plague and its aftermath was starting to meld into a shape or shapes like those into which she'd just inserted her foot. Ariin and Mikaaye had come to the same conclusion, she could tell from the posture of their bodies even before she read their minds. Captain Bates would not be far behind.

"How did ghosts do all this?" Captain Bates asked.

"Digestion," Mikaaye said.

"Exactly," Khorii agreed. "I think what we're seeing is a stage in an alien life cycle. First, these organisms came as the plague virus and killed people and other organic life of certain types. Then they used some of what was left in the bodies of those they'd killed to start to form themselves, except there wasn't enough useful matter, or perhaps their molecular structure is too loose for them to have manifested themselves as solid individuals. But I think they never intended to become entirely like their victims, although they may have randomly acquired some of their appearance or even memories. I think that's why even though some of the shuttle was destroyed, neither the *Mana* nor the Federation ship, both of which held plague survivors who were also seasoned spacefarers, was seriously harmed. At some point they entered a stage when the wraithlike organisms needed to ingest inorganic material to achieve solidity. And once they do"—she looked ruefully at her foot—"they keep eating. Maybe the solid form is transitory, so it needs to keep eating to maintain mass. Once it's overeaten, the excess may be excreted into—er—" She looked meaningfully at the goo which still held her footprint.

"Ewww," Captain Bates said.

"That theory would also explain the sea monster on LoaLoaKui," Mikaaye said. "Once the organism had evolved, it also began absorbing matter from the sea, including, of course, the poopuus it might have found. This also coincided with the seeming elimination of the plague carriers as well."

"But that is good!" Ariin said. "It means they are in the post-plague portion of their life cycle and are no longer a danger to humans or Linyaari. If that is so, there will be no plague indicators here, and our parents can be released from quarantine."

"Provided there are no new organisms starting the life cycle all over again," Captain Bates agreed. "Based on what we know so far, this theory of yours sounds plausible enough, Khorii, and explains a lot of what has happened, but I don't think we're safe in predicting what will happen next based on it." She stuck out her arm, pointed forward.

The diagram of the ship near the airlock was gone, as was the airlock, for that matter; but the corridor where Khorii had first found the bodies was just beyond.

It had become another tube like the one through which they had entered, round and smooth but with many indentations giving the appearance that people had just stepped out of them. They saw no other signs of the hundreds of bodies that had floated amid the plague particles when Khorii and her family first boarded the *Blanca*.

The miasma of death had been replaced by one of fear, and it was as thick as the matter that had trapped Khorii's foot.

"Whoever it is, they woke up," Mikaaye said. "I think it's coming from a little way down and to the left."

"Port," Captain Bates corrected automatically, her word bracketed by loud huffs of breath in their earbuds. She gestured forward with her arm, and they bounced forward while their shadows capered ahead of them.

chapter 31

They must have saved the ballroom for dessert," Captain Bates said, when the tube cave segued somewhat abruptly into a portion of clearly identifiable ship's corridor, complete with separate deck, bulkheads, and ceilings. The carpet and wall coverings were even intact as were the ornate sandblasted-glass double doors leading to the opulent room beyond.

Khorii checked her gauges. The temperature was barely warm enough to sustain life, as was the oxygen level. "There was supposed to be a big dance," she mused. "But when the plague broke out, people decided to board their private ships and leave. The captain killed them rather than let them spread the epidemic. So the ballroom may have been deserted."

"There would have been serving staff and musicians, maybe," Captain Bates said. "Anyhow, that's how it is on vids I've seen advertising the posh liners."

"They were still people," Khorii said. "They probably ran out to see what all the fuss was about and got killed, too."

The ballroom was completely empty, however, and the vast walls, covered in what looked like blue and white marble tiles, was bare of bodies or alien structures of any kind.

Captain Bates tried to activate the light panel on the wall

inside the door, but nothing happened, which was not surprising. The power had probably been drained long ago by whatever was transforming the ship into an alien cityscape.

They crossed the ballroom, their boots echoing against the stone. Linyaari helmets permitted the wearer to hear external sounds, though the helmet worn by Captain Bates did not. Their steps on the "digested" material had made no noticeable sound, Khorii realized. If the shifting of the stuff made any kind of noise, they had been too preoccupied by its strangeness and by the psychic alarms drawing them onward to notice.

As they crossed the room, those alarms grew louder, until Khorii realized the distress was no longer merely in her mind, but audible.

"Someone is crying," she said.

Captain Bates turned deliberately and looked into her face, her eyes widening in alarm.

"Someone else is shushing," Mikaaye said.

"It's coming from behind that wall," Ariin said. "There, do you see the doorway?"

"It probably leads to the kitchens," Captain Bates said, her breath puffing in shallow counterpoint to her words. "This would have been the large dining room when there was no party."

They wasted no more time in reaching the door and pushing through it. At the last moment, Captain Bates placed herself in front and held out her arms to restrain the others as she ventured into the room. At the same time, someone screamed.

The three Linyaari trained their glow tubes on the screamer, who was huddled beneath some open counters along with several other people, two women and a dozen or so children.

Khorii knelt and peered at them. "Do not be afraid. We will help you," she said.

A knife flashed in the hand of one of the women, but

Captain Bates seemed to anticipate it and knocked Khorii back through the hatch with a blow of her inflated arm.

The knife tried to cut the captain's suit, but her boots bounced her out of range, and the knife wielder, as if exhausted by her effort, sank back against the two children tucked into the thermal blanket she clutched like a shawl and clinging to her skirts.

"You can't trust these people any farther than you can throw them, kids. Any farther than you can throw them under normal gravity conditions," Captain Bates said.

"But they are in trouble and afraid!" Mikaaye said.

"They are pirates, and you are prey," the captain said. "I should know. I was raised with them."

The woman who attacked them was coughing, and her skin had a bluish tinge.

Khorii poked her horn through its hatch. There had to be oxygen, or these people would not be alive, but there were perhaps a dozen of them and there could not, after all of this time, be very much oxygen left anywhere aboard the *Blanca*. Her horn could convert the carbon monoxide back to oxygen for them as it did for her. She was amazed that there had been enough to sustain these people, but perhaps the rooms were sealed from each other, and each kept its own supply. She recalled that the *Blanca*'s captain had reversed the airflow in the corridors to kill her mutinous passengers and crew, but Khorii's party had restored the oxygen when they first investigated the derelict vessel.

Ariin and Mikaaye poked their horns out, too, and in a very short time they saw that the humans were breathing more easily.

Captain Bates took off her helmet and looked down at the women. "So, Nisa, long time no see. Funny isn't it, how you don't see or even think of people in years and here in just the last week or two I've seen Pauli and Petit and now you and Cleda. You've picked a strange place to bring the kids."

"Asha?" Nisa rolled her eyes. "Why didn't you say these aliens were with you? How were we supposed to know with you in that suit? How's your mama?"

"I dunno. You've probably seen her more recently than I have."

"You saw Pauli?"

"Yes, he was going to shoot me, but I talked him out of it."

"Sure you did. Did you shoot him?"

"No, Nisa, I didn't. A friend of mine almost did, though. He and Petit are on another ship."

"Going to jail?"

Captain Bates shrugged a big-suited shrug. "Jail doesn't mean a lot with no Federation to enforce things. He and Petit will probably find their way home one of these days."

"Yeah, well, you know how Coco feels about widows and orphans," Nisa said, and made an ugly noise while running her long and very dirty red fingernail across her neck. "I wasn't looking for it, you know? My man's been his first mate for twenty years. So I believed him when he told me the ghosts had damaged the ship, and he was loading us women and children into the shuttles. Only the only families he loaded were Cleda's and mine, and the only place the shuttle had to go was this creation-forsaken rock."

"How did you get in here?" Captain Bates asked.

"We were running out of fuel and oxygen—the extra canisters and our suits had somehow disappeared from the shuttle. I spotted what looked like a hatch in all that junk out there. Turned out to be the servo-hatch for the galley, and we were able to dock the shuttle. Our instruments showed that there was still some oxygen in here and that if we bundled up, we could withstand the temperature for a little while and conserve what little remained on the shuttle, so we got out. I hoped there might be some food, but if there is, none of us have found it."

While Captain Bates was questioning the woman, who seemed to be an old friend, about how and why she and the others had come into the *Blanca*'s galley, Khorii knelt to try to comfort some of the children. They ranged in age from an infant in Cleda's arms to two kids, one in each family, Khorii guessed, close to her age or Jaya's. Khorii wondered if the mothers, who looked close to Captain Bates's age, had older children, had started their families late, or had been bearing young yearly. She was too unfamiliar with human family structure to know, but the children were small, and though most of them tried to look tough and even mean, they were frightened and had to have been damaged by the lack of oxygen.

Sitting down beside them, she took one of the younger ones who had been crowded away from the mother by its siblings and pulled it into her lap, laying her horn against the child's head and saying silly things that the child seemed to find comforting. It was very dirty and had been quite cold, so Khorii wrapped her arms around it—him, she learned when she investigated a certain squishiness in its nether regions that indicated it—he—was eliminating properly, and so must not be starving. Her horn was not quite prepared to do that sort of cleansing. Other children, seeing that she was not eating their brother, crowded closer. One started rifling her pockets. Others besieged Ariin, who protected her pockets with one hand while trying to pat heads awkwardly with the other. Mikaaye was engaged in a mock—at least on his side—battle with one of the older boys, a child of about seven.

"Nice horsie," said a small girl, stroking Khorii's mane.

In the course of all of this activity, she lost track of the conversation between Captain Bates and Nisa until the captain said, "Okay, gang, we're going to have to get these folks back to the *Mana,* back through the area with no oxygen. Khorii, why don't you and I go back for the shuttle while Ariin and Mikaaye keep the air sweet here?"

Khorii looked up. "Either that or perhaps Jaya could bring the shuttle to us."

"She doesn't know what it's like," Captain Bates said. "The docking bay and tubes have plenty of clearance above those whatever they ares, but I'd rather go back and make sure everything is still navigable and bring it back ourselves."

Khorii started to rise, and the child she had been cuddling bellowed and grabbed her horn.

"I'll come with you," Ariin said, batting little hands away from her pockets and the hands of an older boy away from other areas of her shipsuit. "Khorii is busy with her little friends."

But as Captain Bates and Ariin headed back for the door, they heard footsteps clomping unmistakably across the marble floor toward them.

The door flung wide and four men in shipsuits and helmets entered, then closed the door behind them. "Hah! Thought you'd take the bait!" a male voice rasped through the helmet's speaker. "Now tell me, where is all the treasure the punk was blathering about?"

nisa started to stand. *You're a right bastard, Coco,* she was thinking, but dared not say. Khorii sensed that the woman had not completely believed the captain would abandon the women and their children, whatever she said; but until that moment, he had not given any reason for her to think otherwise.

Captain Bates was less circumspect in her reaction to him. "You almost suffocated the wife and kids of two of your loyal followers just to see me again, Papa Coco? I'd be touched if I weren't so revolted."

Khorii looked from one to the other. She detected no family resemblance, despite Captain Bates's addressing the man as "Papa."

His appearance was presentable, even attractive, Khorii supposed, if one were human. But the only similarity he shared with her was that his dark hair and beard, worn long, were braided and beaded in the same manner that she had braided and beaded Jaya's, Sesseli's, and Moonmay's hair and Mikaaye's, Elviiz's, and Khorii's manes. Petit and Pauli had also worn the same style, Khorii realized belatedly, but because their hair was so dirty and matted, she had overlooked that detail.

"Asha! You do turn up in the strangest places, wench. Good of you to lead me to the treasure as well as bringing along a passport to more and a couple of spares." He nodded toward the three Linyaari. "I'd no idea *you* were shipping with this lot or, of course, I would not have had to alarm Nisa, Cleda, and the kiddies by having them pose as families in distress. Mako, pass them the packet."

One of the men had been pulling a large package behind him on a tether and he reeled it in and handed it to Nisa. She opened it and two adult enviro suits and several smaller ones with collapsible plas helmets tumbled out.

"You girls forgot those when you left," Coco told her. "The oxygen tubes in those are full enough to get you and your broods back to the ship."

Ignoring the seething women, he returned his attention to Captain Bates. "If I'd known our exalted Linyaari ambassadors were being chauffeured around the galaxy by my own clan daughter, I'd simply have asked nicely if you would pretty please send us one of your new playmates, along with our absent crewmen. I see by their dos you've already initiated these three into our clan. I'm sure they—especially Khorii, is it, who has been here before?—won't mind showing us to the treasure."

Khorii stood, handing the child to its mother, much to the displeasure of the siblings who had previously claimed her. "How did you get here, sir?" she asked politely. She saw no reason to respect the man, but she did respect the fact that he could probably kill them all or have them killed.

"Through the door. You saw me," he said, as if she were developmentally challenged as well as freakish, which was what he was clearly thinking.

"Before that," she said. "How did you get to the ballroom?"

"From my ship, the *Black Mariah*. Which is, I'm sure you'll be happy to know, docked right next to the *Mana*, where my people can keep an eye on both ships for us."

"If you have harmed those kids, Coco . . ." Captain Bates began.

"Kids? Of course, the crew would be children these days, wouldn't it? I am so out of touch with the tragedies that have befallen the universe outside the clans. I must be losing my touch. If it had occurred to me that only children remained on board, we'd have boarded the ship already. Ah well, I had other things on my mind. The treasure? You were saying something about that, Khorii?"

"Yes, Captain Coco. What I was saying was that I doubt that anything you would find valuable here remains, at least where you can access it."

"Ah, it would not be accessible, of course, because of the plague, but you are going to protect us—"

"That's not what I mean, sir. Didn't you find those hills in the docking bay odd?"

"That was a docking bay? I assumed that was the result of the deck having been destroyed when the ship was wrecked and that was the asteroid's surface . . ."

Khorii shook her head. "And the corridor you came through to get here? When we arrived, there were the bodies of richly dressed and jeweled people floating around. We have a theory about what happened to them and to the other inorganic bits of the ship that seem to have disappeared. Most of your treasure would have been included in that, I think."

"Maybe so, but we're not giving up that easy." He turned to one of his henchmen, "You, Bunco, put the extra fuel cartridge in the shuttle and take the women and kids back to the ship. Take Asha with you. You"—he pointed to Khorii—"come with me and Fori."

"I'm coming with Khorii," Mikaaye said.

"I am, too," Ariin agreed.

Coco looked like he was going to say no, then changed his mind and brandished his weapon at them. "Okay, Khorii, you've been here before. You lead. If you get tricky, though, one of your friends could get hurt. Any sign of the plague there, you fix it before we get there, right?"

Khorii sighed and rolled her eyes. "That's why *I'm* here in the first place. To see if there's any more plague. I don't care about your stupid treasure, and neither does anyone else."

"Fine," Coco said. "Because if you did, you'd be disappointed. I intend to keep it all."

Khorii strode out the hatch to the ballroom, Mikaaye and Ariin behind her, followed by Coco and Fori.

Once back inside the tubelike corridor, she followed it as far as she could, until it sloped steeply upward. Since the Linyaari suits and Coco's weren't programmed for intercommunication, she pointed to where the bridge had been.

If not for the low gravity and the magnetic settings on their boots that allowed them to cling to the sides of the well-like passage, they would not have made it to the top. Once there, however, they found that although the bridge was damaged and the hatch open, it was still recognizable and some of the equipment seemed to be intact.

None of the crew members Khorii had seen on her first trip remained, not even the captain. Nor did she see any of the plague indicators. She pointed at the ship's computer and looked questioningly at Coco. He waved his weapon toward it, indicating she should try it.

She did not expect that with the structural damage to the ship the computer would function, but it turned on at once. Coco shoved her aside and began pushing buttons with his heavy gloves on. Khorii remembered the location of the switch that the brave copilot had tried to flip to cause oxygen to flow back into the ventilation system. If they could breathe, parts of this search might be easier and quicker. The plague as a disease had vanished from the *Blanca* as it had from so many other places once the second stage of the alien life cycle began.

The pirate punched and punched, and Khorii felt murderous rage coming off of him in waves at his frustration. He wanted the location of the safe. All three Linyaari looked on anxiously as he met with failure after failure.

Then Khorii felt, rather than heard or actually saw, her sister shift her thinking slightly, and the security system welcomed Coco with open menus. He searched for the safe. It was located in the purser's office.

Khorii had been there before and she was about to tap him on the shoulder and suggest that she lead the way again, but he had lathered himself into such a state that she didn't want to startle him into using his weapon. Instead, as she watched, he found the security cameras.

The huge com screen lit up with a many-celled diagram of the ship. Many of the cells carried live feeds from the areas they represented. Many more, including the docking bay, did not.

The purser's office had been empty the last time Khorii saw it. It was no more. From the diagram, Coco could see that it was just down the corridor off the bridge, clearly labeled as such. He turned to go, but Khorii caught a movement within the picture of the office and leaned over and clicked. Suddenly the screen was filled with a scene that caused Coco and his accomplice to stand back and watch with wide eyes.

Creatures that were roughly human-shaped, many still bearing a faded version of human coloring, crowded the room, which seemed to be missing a wall, the same wall where the safe had once been.

These forms, in addition to their human coloring, were metal gray, plasteel black or white, the brilliant orange of safety-painted equipment. There were perhaps forty of them, the remnants of former crew members, Khorii guessed.

They sank into the walls, deck, furniture, and equipment of the room, and that crumbled around them as she had seen the ships do. But, perhaps because they did not know they were observed, they speeded up the process. As they moved through the crumbling material, they left other matter behind, smoothing it as they passed it through and the next figure came after them. The furnishings and walls of the purser's officer began to merge with a smooth tunnel like the others, growing forward as the wraithlike beings gradually lost their human form in the walls until, in their wake, there remained only the impressions where they had last stepped inside to feed and meld.

Without waiting for Khorii, Ariin, or Mikaaye, Coco and Fori bolted out of the hatch and jumped down the long well to the tunnel deck below, then bounded down it toward the docking bay.

Guess *it's still a work in progress,"* Khorii told Ariin and Mikaaye when they had finally escaped through the tunnels and bounded over the hills and valleys that were probably the remains of the ships once docked in the *Blanca*'s bay. The most disturbing part of their escape was when they found that the tunnel connecting with the hatch had extended itself and now reached well beyond where the pile of debris had once been, as if stretching out like a long, hungry straw to suck up the two space vessels docked away from the bulk of what had been Captain Becker's salvage cache.

Coco and a complete complement of henchmen were waiting for them, along with Captain Bates, whom Coco held on to awkwardly, one puffy space suit holding on to another. "He's going to use us as human shields to take the *Mana*," Captain Bates told her friends. "They tried while we were gone, but Moonmay and her grandpappy's twelve-gauge persuaded them to wait until we were here to host them."

Each of the Linyaari was grabbed by one of Coco's men as they pushed their way through the *Mana*'s hatch.

Once aboard, Coco hustled everyone to the bridge, where the rest of the *Mana*'s crew met them.

Coco unsealed his helmet. Weapon at Captain Bates's back, he pulled the awkward thing off his face, and said, "Lay down your gun, little girl, or I'll shoot her dead."

Captain Bates nodded. Moonmay put her weapon on the floor, then backed away. Coco kicked it back into the corridor, then he and his henchmen removed their helmets and allowed the Linyaari to remove theirs.

"Everybody on the deck, now!" Coco ordered. Reluctantly, the *Mana*'s crew obeyed. Elviiz wore a miserable look as Jaya helped him from his chair to the floor, afraid that the intruders would injure him. Khorii knew that her brother, who would have ordinarily been talking fast and full of ideas, was thoroughly demoralized at being unable to defend his friends with his former strength and intellect.

"You, too, Asha," Coco ordered, nudging Captain Bates forward.

"Coco, you've become even harder than you used to be," Captain Bates said, making herself comfortable with her legs crossed in front of her and drawing Moonmay under one arm and Sesseli under the other. "You never used to hold up kids."

"Nobody else is left!" Coco said, running his free hand through his helmet-matted hair in exasperation. "With Petit and Pauli gone, I don't have crew enough for the *Black Mariah,* much less to take this one in tow, but it seems a shame to waste a perfectly good hijacking opportunity, and with these handy horned kiddies on board, too. There's a lot of wealth lying around loose in the universe right now, and not all of it has got alien tunnels running through it, but some of it might still have plague."

"This is a lousy time to be greedy, Coco," Captain Bates said. "There's plenty of opportunity out there for able-bodied adults who aren't in their dotage. Plenty of money to be made rebuilding things—maybe rebuilding them your way with you in charge. Let us go."

Coco cocked his head to the side, and for a moment Khorii actually thought he might be considering the idea. Then he shook his head with an abrupt jerk. "Naw, my way's easier."

"Captain?" Ariin spoke up.

"What?" he demanded angrily.

"Captain, my sister and I are on our way home to see our parents. I've never met them before, and if Khorii can see that they are as free of the plague as everywhere else seems to be here, they can come out of quarantine."

"Wouldn't that be dandy!" Coco replied, clearly unmoved.

"But the thing is, she would also be reporting to our Council that the plague is gone and our people can come home. As I understand it, our people have been the ones maintaining order since the plague. With no more plague and with our people out of your systems, would you not have more freedom to ply your trade? Whereas if you take my sister, well, the thing is, sir, our people are nonviolent, but they are highly intelligent, extremely advanced, and very persistent. You may have heard of the Khleevi? Our people, led by mine and Khorii's parents, were their downfall."

"Yeah, well, your sister doesn't know the plague is gone everywhere yet, does she? We need her to—"

Mikaaye interrupted. "All you need is someone to cleanse the place if there is plague, sir, and we do that automatically if one of us is along. You don't need Khorii in particular."

Coco started growling, but Mikaaye continued. "And well, the truth is, ever since I saw the vids on MOO, I have wanted to be a pirate. Not a violent one, of course. I would just like to have adventures with you. And I could keep your families safe and heal your men's wounds, too."

"Mikaaye, what would your mother say!" Captain Bates demanded.

Mikaaye, who had already seemed to have become a pirate in his own imagination, stared levelly back at her. "My mother would say that as long as this is my decision to join Captain Coco's crew, she would let me choose my own path and not interfere, nor would she or any of our other people pursue me or my new friends."

And privately he added, *"And she would know that one of us among these people could possibly help turn them to being useful rather than destructive to others. It seems to me, from what we've seen here, that these worlds are in for much more trouble. I want to go, really. I want to see what it's like."*

"And you know that my sister and I very badly want to see our parents again, don't you?" Khorii asked.

This time she heard Ariin's little suggestion to Coco. *"It's the perfect solution, and you want to take it."*

Coco and the others looked at each other as if trying to and failing to find anything wrong with the scheme. He looked out the viewport and his eyes opened wider in alarm. The others rose to their knees and turned to look, too. Below, the metallic junk heap was shifting and stirring as a tunnel advanced like a beckoning finger.

Coco jerked his head back toward the hatch, and his men began filing out. He nodded to Mikaaye to go ahead of him, saying, "Come along then, boy, and shake a leg before both our ships get taken."

chapter 33

H e's not really a brutal captain, as the breed goes," Captain Bates said, trying to reassure Melireenya. "I think Mikaaye picked that up from him. And he's right, you know. A Linyaari could have a very good influence on that lot, especially the kids."

The *Balakiire,* the *Neizayir,* and the tanker had arrived on MOO days before the *Mana.* The *Balakiire* had remained, hearing that the *Mana*'s crew had an important message it preferred to deliver in person to members of the *Balakiire*'s crew. The tankers, with Linyaari crews, were already on Vhiliinyar, off-loading the LoiLoiKuans.

"But he endangered the families of his crewmen!" Kharii protested. She and Neeva both were fiercely protective of Melireenya's maternal feelings and rather miffed that the *Mana*'s crew had not relayed their message earlier and in more detail. Khorii knew they would have sent a search party after the pirate ship, but what would unarmed Linyaari have been able to do against such ruffians?

"I have a feeling Coco was monitoring them all the time," Captain Bates replied. "They could not have been in any real danger. In fact, when Nisa intimated to me that I knew what Coco does to widows and children, what I really knew was that he'd be showing up soon. My mother and I were once a widow and child at his mercy, and although he was hardly the soul of altruism, and in many ways, pardon me, a total bastard, I survived the experience with fewer traumas than experienced by the average child slave my age. Besides, if he hadn't had them under surveillance, he wouldn't have known where they were on the *Blanca,* or more important to him, where we were when we went to save them. He probably didn't expect them to leave the shuttle, and being on the planet's surface would have been enough to lure us."

Melireenya, somewhat to Khorii's surprise, nodded. Her eyes warmed, and she smiled, "I have a brave youngling, worthy of his lineage. He will do well. Your clan cannot change his Linyaari nature, nor his gallant spirit in speaking up to spare Khorii and Ariin for the needs of their families and the humans coping with this new phase of the—I suppose we must think of it as an invasion now, rather than an epidemic? It is entirely probable that my son will change those around him for the better, which is good. The humans will need the strengths and skills of all the survivors if they are to fend off this new threat."

She held out her arms, and first Khorii, then more hesitantly Ariin, embraced her.

"Now then, young ones, come. The *Balakiire* has the honor of transporting you to the quarantine area, where you will surely be reunited with your beloved parents, and Elviiz may be healed by his father."

Khorii and Ariin had very little time to spend bonding, or even commiserating with Elviiz. The girls spent most of the trip to Vhiliinyar making a detailed report of their findings on Becker's asteroid and the development of the alien beings. Captain Bates was making a similar report to Uncle Hafiz and Grandsire Rafik. With so little of the Federation force remaining, the Linyaari healers and House Harakamian had assumed many of its administrative functions.

The journey from MOO to Vhiliinyar by ship was a short one, and instead of landing in Kubiilikhan and taking a shuttle, the *Balakiire* took them straight to the edge of the quarantine meadows. The Ancestors, so like Ariin's beloved Others, formed a protective ring between the newcomers and their family. In the center of the area sat the *Condor*, looking as dilapidated and unspaceworthy as ever.

Mother, Father, Uncle Joh, Maak, and RK were lined up to meet them, tension in every line of their bodies.

The girls, Elviiz, and the entire crew of the *Balakiire* disembarked. It was midday, the sky was a gorgeous periwinkle blue, the grasses lush and waving in a sweetly scented breeze. Beyond the meadow, the sea shone, and from the air the passengers of the *Balakiire* had seen the tankers on the shoreline along with other equipment necessary for the transfer.

A large delegation of *sii*-Linyaari frothed the water just offshore, waiting for their sea's newest tenants. Already many other Linyaari lined the shore to watch and welcome the newcomers.

Ariin saw her sister staring in that direction. *"What's the matter with you, Khorii? You haven't seen our parents since before I did. Pay attention!"*

"I'm afraid of what I'll see. What if they're not cured? What if the plague is still there? Could you bear it? Won't you hate me for seeing it? I—"

"Do not be so negative and silly. The plague has disappeared and mutated everywhere else we've looked. It won't have lasted any longer here, not on Vhiliinyar, with all of this wholesomeness and healing energy surrounding it."

Khorii grabbed her twin's hand as they stepped away from the hatch, toward the ring of Ancestors. Everyone was waving. Khorii and Ariin took two steps forward. Sending everything she saw to her twin, Khorii narrowed her focus and looked first at Maak. Her android uncle looked exactly the same as he had the last time she saw him except—no blue dots surrounded him. She felt almost faint with relief. Elviiz could be treated and returned to his old self. He would be so happy. Captain Becker and RK were also surrounded by nothing but periwinkle sky and fragrant delicious grasses. No blue dots.

Ariin squeezed her hand and forced her to look at Father and Mother, who stood with their arms around each other.

The sunlight sparkled almost prettily on the halo of blue dots surrounding them. Ariin dropped Khorii's hand. "No! It can't be. It's your imagination. The plague is gone!"

But she knew as well as Khorii that it was not.

Everyone knew almost as quickly as they did. Their parents did.

"Khorii, by now you have more experience than we do with this disease," their father said. *"Why do you suppose we remain infected when everyone else can be cured?"*

It wasn't just a family conversation. Practically the entire planet was reading the images and words passing among them. Wanting to weep or scream or rant as much as Ariin did, Khorii instead methodically explained what had happened on Becker's asteroid and what she thought it meant. *"I believe that you are not so much infected as infested at this point,"* she told them. *"Because you and everyone around you survived, the organisms that mutated into your strain of the disease did not further progress into the next phase of their development. It had no dead organic tissue from which to morph into its inorganic-matter-absorbing form, so it's simply stayed the same with you. Perhaps—perhaps it will die of its own accord, without being able to change."*

"Or maybe not," Father said glumly. *"Maybe somehow or other we keep it thriving because we are Linyaari. Perhaps that is why Joh and Maak and RK have become free of contamination, yet we are still carriers."*

Mother said, *"There has to be a way to beat it. Once*

Maak has all the data—perhaps he'll find even more clues when he works at restoring Elviiz's inorganic modifications—he may help us formulate a cure. Or perhaps one of our own scientists, having studied the disease and its aftermath, will be able to cure us. You girls have both done your best, and we're very proud of you."

"But I miss you," Khorii said.

"And I want so badly to be with you," Ariin said.

They could see Mother's smile from where they stood. *"We are Linyaari, children, and we will always be close no matter what. While we cannot physically touch without endangering you and others, we've asked that pavilions be erected for you and for Elviiz. Maak will bring the instruments, tools, and materials he needs to work with Elviiz out there. We can talk as often as we want. Meanwhile, we will have some time together."*

But under Mother's soothing words, Khorii and Ariin were both aware that the description of the new forms that the alien invasion were assuming had alarmed and disturbed their parents. Time seemed to be eternal on this pleasant plain, with the sun sparkling on the distant sea and the grass just waiting to be grazed; but elsewhere, in Corazon and on Rushima, time was running out.

They felt the same consciousness among the other Linyaari who had been to the human worlds trying to help and returned thinking they'd cured a plague, only to learn it had become something even more sinister.

Still, it was almost like home for Khorii as she and Ariin settled into their tent and helped Elviiz and Maak with theirs. Uncle Joh chose to remain aboard the *Condor* and near Mother and Father. He had evidently gained true immunity after his acute attack of the disease, cure from the symptoms, and prolonged contact with the strain Mother and Father carried. Maak had already begun work on a vaccine from his blood, but so far they'd had no one to try it on. RK was also plague-free and chased poor Khiindi around the field as if he were a mouse until Khiindi, no doubt hardened by his own spacefaring experiences, turned on his sire and began chasing him instead.

When the sun went down, all concerned were very tired and much sadder than they expected to be.

Long after they should have been asleep, Ariin lay on her back, her thoughts racing. Though she was trying to shield her thoughts, Khiindi had picked up on her agitation and was pacing with clicking claws back and forth on the floor of the tent, over Khorii's body and back and forth again before walking over Ariin again.

Finally, Khorii sat up, flinging her blanket aside. *"What?"* she demanded of her sister.

Ariin turned to her with a troubled expression. *"Something,"* she said. *"Look, can I trust you? Do you trust me?"*

"You have to ask that after all we've been through? We're twin sisters, of course you can trust me! And yes, I trust you, too."

"I have a sort of a secret. I didn't mean to keep it as a secret—everyone should know about it, but they seem to have forgotten, what with everything else that's happening."

"Please stop being so mysterious. And Khiindi Kaat, will you please stop that!" she said, forgetting that she did not normally try to thought-talk to her cat. To her surprise, though, he did stop, and came to crouch on top of her, glaring at Ariin.

Ariin glared back, but said, *"The thing is, everyone thinks we may be running out of time but that is not true. I have plenty of time, right here."* She pulled a metallic object from her pocket and clasped it on her wrist. Khiindi made a sound that was half growl and half plaintive mew. Ariin smirked at him. *"And here's something else. I've been thinking and thinking about the way that alien thing moved in the bay of the Blanca. There was something familiar about its shifting, and I think some people where I lived before I came here may know something about it."*

Khiindi gave a startled meow and hopped off Khorii to bat at Ariin's wrist. She caught him by the scruff of the neck and clutched him in her arms. *"Khiindi knows, too. Where I was happened a long time before now, back before our people were created."*

"You're talking in riddles!" Khorii complained.

"Maybe so. But we could go there and find out what we need to know and be back without anyone ever knowing we had gone. We could find the answer to everything, how to get rid of the aliens and save the humans, how to cure Mother and Father." She squeezed Khiindi and placed a kiss that was strangely unaffectionate on the top of his head. *"What do you say?"*

Khorii didn't have to think about it long. *"When shall we leave?"* she asked.

Ariin smiled. *"Soon."*

"How soon is soon?" Khoril asked.

"Soon enough," Ariin replied enigmatically.

Glossary of Terms and Proper Names in the Acorna Universe

aagroni—Linyaari name for a vocation that is a combination of ecologist, agriculturalist, botanist, and biologist. *Aagroni* are responsible for terraforming new planets for settlement as well as maintaining the well-being of populated planets.

Aari—a Linyaari of the Nyaarya clan, captured by the Khleevi during the invasion of Vhiliinyar, tortured, and left for dead on the abandoned planet. He's Maati's older brother. Aari survived and was rescued and restored to his people by Jonas Becker and Roadkill. But Aari's differences, the physical and psychological scars left behind by his adventures, make it difficult for him to fit in among the Linyaari.

Aarkiiyi—member of the Linyaari survey team on Vhiliinyar.

Aarlii—a Linyaari survey team member, firstborn daughter of Captain Yaniriin.

abaanye—a Linyaari sleeping potion that can be fatal in large doses.

Abuelita—grandmother to Jalonzo Allende.

Acorna—a unicornlike humanoid discovered as an infant by three human miners—Calum, Gill, and Rafik. She has the power to heal and purify with her horn. Her uniqueness has already shaken up the human galaxy, especially the planet Kezdet. She's now fully grown and changing the lives of her own people, as well. Among her own people, she is known as Kornya.

Akasa—one of the Ancestral Friends who raised and experimented on "Narhii," better known as Ariin, Khorii's twin.

Al y Cassidro, Dr. Phador—headmaster and dean of the mining engineering school at Maganos Moonbase.

Ali Baba—Aziza's ship.

Allende, Jalonzo—a young genius from the planet Paloduro.

Ancestors—unicorn-like sentient species, precursor race to the Linyaari. Also known as *ki-lin*.

Ancestral Friends—an ancient shape-changing and spacefaring race responsible for saving the unicorns (or Ancestors) from Old Terra, and using them to create the Linyaari race on Vhiliinyar.

Ancestral Hosts—*see* Ancestral Friends.

Andina—owner of the cleaning concession on MOO, and sometimes lady companion to Captain Becker.

Annunciata—a victim of the space plague on the planet Paloduro, whose form was appropriated by the Ghosts.

Aridimi Desert—a vast, barren desert on the Makahomian planet, site of a hidden Temple and a sacred lake.

Aridimis—people from the Makahomian Aridimi desert.

Arkansas Traveler—freight-hauling spaceship piloted by Scaradine MacDonald.

Arrinye—Ariin for short, Khorii's twin sister, stolen from Acorna while still a tiny embryo, and raised by the Ancestral Friends in a different time and place under the name Narhii.

Attendant—Linyaari who have been selected for the task of caring for the Ancestors.

avvi—Linyaari word for "daddy."

Aziza Amunpul—head of a troupe of dancers and thieves, who, after being re-formed, becomes Hafiz's chief security officer on MOO.

Balakiire—the Linyaari spaceship commanded by Acorna's aunt Neeva.

Basic—shorthand for Standard Galactic, the language used throughout human-settled space.

Bates, Asha—teacher on the Maganos Moonbase.

Becker—*see* Jonas Becker.

Bulaybub Felidar sach Pilau ardo Agorah—a Makahomian Temple priest, better known by his real name—Tagoth. A priest who supports modernizing the Makahomian way of life, he was a favorite of Nadhari Kando, before her departure from the planet. He has a close relationship in his young relative, Miw-Sher.

Calum Baird—one of three miners who discovered Acorna and raised her.

chrysoberyl—a precious catseye gemstone available in large supply and great size on the planet of Makahomia, but also, very rarely and in smaller sizes, throughout the known universe. The stones are considered sacred on Makahomia, and are guarded by the priest class and the Temples. Throughout the rest of the universe, they are used in the mining and terraforming industries across the universe.

Coco-leader of the pirates that Marl Fidd tries to enlist in his efforts to kidnap Khorii and use her to purify the riches on other deserted worlds.

Commodore Crezhale—an officer in the Federation Health Service.

Condor—Jonas Becker's salvage ship, heavily modified to incorporate various "found" items Becker has come across in his space voyages.

Crow—Becker's shuttle, used to go between the *Condor* and places in which the *Condor* is unable to land.

Declan "Gill" Giloglie—one of three human miners who discovered Acorna and raised her.

Delszaki Li—once the richest man on Kezdet, opposed to child exploitation, made many political enemies. He lived his life paralyzed, floating in an antigravity chair. Clever and devious, he both hijacked and rescued Acorna and gave her a cause—saving the children of Kezdet. He became her adopted father. Li's death was a source of tremendous sadness to all but his enemies.

Dinan—Temple priest and doctor in Hissim.

Dinero Grande—a world in the Solojo star system.

Domestic Goddess—Andina's spaceship.

Dsu Macostut—Federation officer, Lieutenant Commander of the Federation base on Makahomia.

Edacki Ganoosh—corrupt Kezdet count, uncle of Kisla Manjari.

Egstynkeraht—A planet supporting several forms of sulfur-based sentient life.

Elena—a youngster who survived the space plague on the planet Paloduro.

Elviiz—Mac's son, a Linyaari childlike android, given as a wedding/birth gift to Acorna and Aari. According to Mac, the android is named for an ancient Terran king, and is often called Viiz for short.

enye-ghanyii—Linyaari time unit, small portion of *ghaanye*.

Estrella Blanca—also known as the *White Star*, a pleasure spacecraft that was where Acorna, Aari, Khorii, Jonas Becker, and Khiindi first encountered the plague. It was a ghost ship after Captain Delores Grimwald killed the crew and passengers to prevent the plague from spreading.

Fagad—Temple priest in the Aridimi desert, who spied for Mulzar Edu Kando.

Felihari—one of the Makavitian Rain Forest tribes on Makahomia.

Feriila—Acorna's mother.

Fidd, Marl—a student on Maganos Moonbase, later a committed criminal and pirate. A true cad.

Fiicki—Linyaari communications officer on Vhiliinyar expedition.

Fiirki Miilkar—a Linyaari animal specialist.

Fiiryi—a Linyaari.

fraaki—Linyaari word for fish.

Friends—also known as Ancestral Friends. A shape-changing and spacefaring race responsible for saving the unicorns from Old Terra and using them to create the Linyaari race on Vhiliinyar.

Gaali—highest peak on Vhiliinyar, never scaled by the Linyaari people. The official marker for Vhiliinyar's date line, anchoring the meridian line that sets the end of the old day and the beginning of the new day across the planet as it rotates Our Star at the center of the solar system. With nearby peaks Zaami and Kaahi, the high mountains are a mystical place for most Linyaari.

ghaanye (pl. *ghaanyi*)—a Linyaari year.

gheraalye malivii—Linyaari for navigation officer.

gheraalye ve-khanyii—Linyaari for senior communications officer.

Ghost—a deadly alien life-form with the ability to take on the forms of the dead of other species and cultures, which feed on the higher forms of inorganic matter produced by those other cultures.

giirange—office of toastmaster in a Linyaari social organization.

Grimalkin—an Ancestral Friend who became entangled with Aari and Acorna in their voyages through time. He even impersonated Aari for a while. He was punished for his impudence by his people, who trapped him in the body of a cat and took away his machinery for time travel and time control. He has become Khorii's boon companion—she calls him Khiindi. He is the key to a number of secrets that none of the humans or Linyaari are privy to, including the fate of Khorii's formerly lost twin, Ariin.

Grimwald, Dolores M.—captain of the ship *La Estrella Blanca,* deceased. She sacrificed herself and everyone on her ship to avoid spreading the space plague.

GSS—Gravitation Stabilization System.

haarha liirni—Linyaari term for advanced education, usually pursued during adulthood while on sabbatical from a previous calling.

Hafiz Harakamian—Rafik's uncle, head of the interstellar financial empire of House Harakamian, a passionate collector of rarities from throughout the galaxy and a devotee of the old-fashioned sport of horseracing. Although basically crooked enough to hide behind a spiral staircase, he is genuinely fond of Rafik and Acorna.

Hellstrom, Hap—a student on Maganos Moonbase, and one of Khorii's best friends. He crewed on the *Mana.*

Heloise—Andina's spaceship.

Highmagister HaGurdy—the Ancestral Friend in charge of the Hosts on old Vhiliinyar.

Hissim—the biggest city on Makahomia, home of the largest Temple.

Hraaya—an Ancestor.

Hrronye—Melireenya's lifemate.

Hruffli—an Ancestor stallion, mate of Nrihiiye.

Hrunvrun—the first Linyaari Ancestral attendant.

Iiiliira—a Linyaari ship.

Iirtye—chief *aagroni* for narhii-Vhiliinyar.

Ikwaskwan—self-styled leader of the Kilumbembese Red Bracelets. Depending on circumstances and who he is trying to impress, he is known as either "General Ikwaskwan" or "Admiral Ikwaskwan," though both ranks are self-assigned. Entered into devious dealings with Edacki Ganoosh that led to his downfall.

Jaya—captain-in-training on the *Mana*.

Johnny Greene—an old friend of Calum, Rafik, and Gill; joined the Starfarers when he was fired after Amalgamated Mining's takeover of MME.

Jonas Becker—interplanetary salvage artist; alias space junkman. Captain of the *Condor*. CEO of Becker Interplanetary Recycling and Salvage Enterprises Ltd.—a one-man, one-cat salvage firm Jonas inherited from his adopted father. Jonas spent his early youth on a labor farm on the planet Kezdet before he was adopted.

Judit Kendoro—assistant to psychiatrist Alton Forelle at Amalgamated Mining, saved Acorna from certain death. Later fell in love with Gill and joined with him to help care for the children employed in Delszaki Li's Maganos mining operation.

Kaahi—a high mountain peak on Vhiliinyar.

Kaalmi Vroniiyi—leader of the Linyaari Council, which made the decision to restore the ruined planet Vhiliinyar, with Hafiz's help and support, to a state that would once again support the Linyaari and all the life-forms native to the planet.

Kaarlye—the father of Aari, Maati, and Laarye. A member of the Nyaarya clan, and life-bonded to Miiri.

Kaczmarek, Calla—the psychologist and psychology/sociology instructor on Maganos Moonbase.

ka-Linyaari—something against all Linyaari beliefs, something not Linyaari.

Karina—a plumply beautiful wannabe psychic with a small shred of actual talent and a large fondness for profit. Married to Hafiz Harakamian. This is her first marriage, his second.

Kashirian Steppes—Makahomian region that produces the best fighters.

Kashirians—Makahomians from the Kashirian Steppes.

kava—a coffeelike hot drink produced from roasted ground beans.

KEN—a line of general-purpose male androids, some with customized specializations, differentiated among their owners by number, for example—KEN637.

Kezdet—a backwoods planet with a labor system based on child exploitation. Currently in economic turmoil because that system was broken by Delszaki Li and Acorna.

Khaari—senior Linyaari navigator on the *Balakiire*.

Khiindi—he is supposedly Khorii's cat, one of RK's offspring. He is, however, much more than that. He is actually Grimalkin, an Ancestral Friend who got into more mischief than his shape-shifting people approved of. They trapped him in the body of a cat and gave him to Khorii, as penance for his harm to her family and also to allow Grimalkin time to work out his destiny.

Khleevi—name given by Acorna's people to the space-borne enemies who have attacked them without mercy.

Khoriilya—Acorna and Aari's oldest child, a daughter, known as Khorii for short.

kii—a Linyaari time measurement roughly equivalent to an hour of Standard Time.

ki-lin—Oriental term for unicorn, also a name sometimes associated with Acorna.

Kilumbemba Empire—an entire society that raises and exports mercenaries for hire—the Red Bracelets.

Kisla Manjari—anorexic and snobbish young woman, raised as daughter of Baron Manjari; shattered when through Acorna's efforts to help the children of Kezdet her father is ruined and the truth of her lowly birth is revealed.

Kubiilikaan, the legendary first city on Vhiliinyar, founded by the Ancestral Hosts.

Kubiilikhan—capital city of narhii-Vhiliinyar, named after Kubiilikaan, the legendary first city on Vhiliinyar, founded by the Ancestral Hosts.

LAANYE—sleep learning device invented by the Linyaari that can, from a small sample of any foreign language, teach the wearer the new language overnight.

Laarye—Maati and Aari's brother. He died on Vhiliinyar during the Khleevi invasion. He was trapped in an accident in a cave far distant from the spaceport during the evacuation, and was badly injured. Aari stayed behind to rescue and heal him, but was captured by the Khleevi and tortured before he could accomplish his mission. Laarye died before Aari could escape and return. Time travel has brought him back to life.

Laboue—the planet where Hafiz Harakamian makes his headquarters.

lalli—Linyaari word for "mother."

Likilekakua—one of Khorii's poopuu friends on Maganos Moonbase.

lilaala—a flowering vine native to Vhiliinyar used by early Linyaari to make paper.

Linyaari—Acorna's people.

Liriili—former *viizaar* of narhii-Vhiliinyar, member of the clan Riivye.

LoiLoiKua—a water planet in the human Federation, with human-descended inhabitants that have become fully water-dwelling. Khorii first met people from LoiLoiKua at the school at Maganos, where they were known as pool pupils, or poo-puus.

Lukia of the Lights—a protective saint, identified by some children of Kezdet with Acorna.

Ma'aowri 3—a planet populated by catlike beings.

Maarni—a Linyaari folklorist, mate to Yiitir.

Maati—a young Linyaari girl of the Nyaarya clan who lost most of her family during the Khleevi invasion. Aari's younger sister.

MacKenZ—also known as Mac or Maak, a very useful and adaptable unit of the KEN line of androids, now in the service of Captain Becker. The android was formerly owned by Kisla Manjari, and came into the captain's service after it tried to kill him on Kisla's orders. Becker's knack for dealing with salvage enabled him to reprogram the android to make the KEN unit both loyal to him and eager to please. The reprogramming had interesting side effects on the android's personality, though, leaving Mac much quirkier than is usually the case for androids.

madigadi—a berrylike fruit whose juice is a popular beverage.

Maganos—one of the three moons of Kezdet, base for Delszaki Li's mining operation and child rehabilitation project.

Makahomia—war-torn home planet of RK and Nadhari Kendo.

Makahomian Temple Cat—cats on the planet Makahomia, bred from ancient Cat God stock to protect and defend the Cat God's Temples. They are—for cats—large, fiercely loyal, remarkably intelligent, and dangerous when crossed.

Makavitian Rain Forest—a tropical area of the planet Makahomia, populated by various warring jungle tribes.

Mana—a supply ship whose crew and former owners died in the plague with the exception of Jaya, the captain-in-training, now captained by Asha Bates and a crew of young survivors.

Manjari—a baron in the Kezdet aristocracy, and a key person in the organization and protection of Kezdet's child-labor racket, in which he was known by the code name "Piper." He murdered his wife and then committed suicide when his identity was revealed and his organization destroyed.

Marsden, Moonmay—a plucky Rushima settler child, very accurate with her shotgun. With her brother Percy and their cousin Fleagle, the Marsden family help Khorii and the company from the *Mana* bury their dead.

Martin Dehoney—famous astro-architect who designed Maganos Moonbase; the coveted Dehoney Prize was named after him.

Melireenya—Linyaari communications specialist on the *Balakiire*, bonded to Hrronye. Their son is Mikaaye.

Mendez, Concepcion—a grandmother on the planet Paloduro, mother to Annunciata, who died in the plague, and grandmother to Elena, who survived it.

Mercy Kendoro—younger sister of Pal and Judit Kendoro, saved from a life of bonded labor by Judit's efforts, she worked as a spy for the Child Liberation League in offices of Kezdet Guardians of the Peace until the child-labor system was destroyed.

Miiri—mother of Aari, Laarye, and Maati. A member of the Nyaarya clan, life-bonded to Kaarlye.

Mikaaye—Melireenya's and Hrronya's son. He worked on narhii-Vhiliinyar with his father helping shape a new and less exclusive Linyaari society, then joined Khorii, along with other Linyaari, as they all worked together to eradicate the galactic plague. He almost lost his life on Rushima as he and Khorii fought the Ghosts.

mitanyaakhi—generic Linyaari term meaning a very large number.

Miw-Sher—a Makahomian Keeper of the sacred Temple Cats. Her name means "Kitten" in Makahomian.

MME—Gill, Calum, and Rafik's original mining company. Swallowed by the ruthless, conscienceless, and bureaucratic Amalgamated Mining.

Mog-Gim Plateau—an arid area on the planet Makahomia near the Federation spaceport.

Mokilau—a LoiLoiKuan elder.

MOO, or Moon of Opportunity—Hafiz's artificial planet, and home base for the Vhiliinyar terraforming operation.

Morniika—Linyaari Ancestor mare and Neicaair's mate.

Mulzar (feminine form: Mulzarah)—the Mog-Gimin title taken by the high priest who is also the warlord of the Plateau.

Mulzar Edu Kando sach Pilau dom Mog-Gim—High Priest of Hissim and the Aridimi Plateau, on the planet Makahomia.

Naadiina—also known as Grandam, one of the oldest Linyaari, host to both Maati and Acorna on narhii-Vhiliinyar, died to give her people the opportunity to save both of their planets.

Naarye—Linyaari techno-artisan in charge of final fit-out of spaceships.

naazhoni—the Linyaari word for someone who is a bit unstable.

Nadhari Kando—formerly Delszaki Li's personal bodyguard, rumored to have been an officer in the Red Bracelets earlier in her career, then a security officer in charge of MOO, then the guard for the leader on her home planet of Makahomia.

Nanahomea—a LoiLoiKuan elder, grandmother to Likilekakua, one of Khorii's poopuu friends.

narhii—Linyaari word for new.

Narhii—the name given by the Ancestral Friends to Khorhii's twin sister, later renamed Ariinye, who was stolen from Acorna's womb while still an embryo.

narhii-Vhiliinyar—the planet settled by the Linyaari after Vhiliinyar, their original homeworld, was destroyed by the Khleevi.

Neeva—Acorna's aunt and Linyaari envoy on the *Balakiire*, bonded to Virii.

Neicaair—a Linyaari Ancestor stallion.

Neo-Hadithian—an ultraconservative, fanatical religious sect.

Ngaen Xong Hoa—a Kieaanese scientist who invented a planetary weather control system. He sought asylum on the *Haven* because he feared the warring governments on his planet would misuse his research. A mutineer faction on the *Haven* used the system to reduce the planet Rushima to ruins. The mutineers were tossed into space. Dr. Hoa has since restored Rushima and now works for Hafiz.

Nheifaarir—the egg-shaped spacecraft assigned to Maati's family, often used by Maati and Thariinye.

Niciirye—Grandam Naadiina's husband, dead and buried on Vhiliinyar.

Niikaavri—Acorna's grandmother, a member of the clan Geeyiinah, and a spaceship designer by trade. Also, as *Niikaavre,* the name of the spaceship used by Maati and Thariinye.

Nirii—a planetary trading partner of the Linyaari, populated by bovinelike two-horned sentients, known as Niriians, technologically advanced, able to communicate telepathically, and phlegmatic in temperament.

Nisa—one of Coco's pirate band, a friend of Captain Bates's.

Nrihiiye—an Ancestor mare, mate of Hruffli.

nyiiri—the Linyaari word for unmitigated gall, sheer effrontery, or other form of misplaced bravado.

Odus—one of the Ancestral Friends who raised and experimented on "Narhii." When Khorii's twin was reunited with her parents, Narhii became better known as Ariin.

Our Star—Linyaari name for the star that centers their solar system.

Paazo River—a major geographical feature on the Linyaari homeworld, Vhiliinyar.

pahaantiyir—a large catlike animal once found on Vhiliinyar.

Paloduro—a planet in the Solojo star system, infested by the space plague.

Pandora—Count Edacki Ganoosh's personal spaceship, used to track and pursue Hafiz's ship *Shahrazad* as it speeds after

Acorna on her journey to narhii-Vhiliinyar. Later confiscated and used by Hafiz for his own purposes.

Pauli—one of Coco's pirate band.

Petit—one of Coco's pirate band.

Phador—*see* Al y Cassidro, Dr. Phador.

piiro—Linyaari word for a rowboatlike water vessel.

piiyi—a Niriian biotechnology-based information storage and retrieval system. The biological component resembles a very rancid cheese.

Poopuus—a term for water-dwelling students from LoiLoiKua used on Maganos Moonbase, an abbreviation from the words "pool pupils."

Praxos—a swampy planet near Makahomia used by the Federation to train Makahomian recruits.

PU#10—human name for the vine planet, with its sentient plant inhabitants, where the Khleevi-killing sap was found.

Raealacaldae—the corrupt Federation head of LoiLoiKua, who died after poisoning the waters of the planet. His palace on the dry land of the planet remains, and has been inhabited by the Ghosts.

Rafik Nadezda—one of three miners who discovered Acorna and raised her.

Red Bracelets—Kilumbembese mercenaries; arguably the toughest and nastiest fighting force in known space.

Rio Boca—a planet in the Solojo star system.

Roadkill—otherwise known as RK. A Makahomian Temple Cat, the only survivor of a space wreck, he was rescued and adopted by Jonas Becker, and is honorary first mate of the *Condor*.

Roc—Rafik's shuttle ship.

Rushima—a planet with an agriculturally based economy invaded by the Khleevi, and saved by Acorna. After the galactic plague and the Ghosts made things miserable there again, it was saved by Khorii and Mikaaye.

Scaradine MacDonald—captain of the *Arkansas Traveler* spaceship, and galactic freight hauler.

Sesseli—a curly-headed blond student on Maganos Moonbase with very strong telepathy, she is the first person to spot the Ghosts.

Shahrazad—Hafiz's personal spaceship, a luxury cruiser.

Shoshisha—a student on the Maganos Moonbase.

sii-**Linyaari**—a legendary race of aquatic Linyaari-like beings developed by the Ancestral Friends.

Siiaaryi Maartri—a Linyaari Survey ship.

Sinbad—Rafik's spaceship.

Sita Ram—a protective goddess, identified with Acorna by the mining children on Kezdet.

Smythe-Wesson—a former Red Bracelet officer, Win Smythe-Wesson briefly served as Hafiz's head of security on MOO before his larcenous urges overcame him.

Solojo—a star system in the human galaxy, one of the first infected with the space plague.

Spandard—a varient dialect of Standard Galactic Basic, once known as Spanish.

Standard Galactic Basic—the language used throughout the human settled galaxy, also known simply as "Basic."

stiil—Linyaari word for a pencil-like writing implement.

Taankaril—*visedhaanye ferilii* of the Gamma sector of Linyaari space.

Tagoth—*see* Bulaybub.

techno-artisan—Linyaari specialist who designs, engineers, or manufactures goods.

Thariinye—a handsome and conceited young spacefaring Linyaari from clan Renyilaaghe.

Theophilus Becker—Jonas Becker's father, a salvage man and astrophysicist with a fondness for exploring uncharted wormholes.

thiilir (pl. *thilirii*)—small arboreal mammals of Linyaari homeworld.

thiilsis—grass species native to Vhiliinyar.

Toruna—a Niriian female, who sought help from Acorna and the Linyaari when her home planet was invaded by the Khleevi.

Twi Osiam—planetary site of a major financial and trade center.

twilit—small, pestiferous insect on Linyaari home planet.

Uhuru—one of the various names of the ship owned jointly by Gill, Calum, and Rafik.

Vaanye—Acorna's father.

Vhiliinyar—original home planet of the Linyaari, destroyed by Khleevi.

viizaar—a high political office in the Linyaari system, roughly equivalent to president or prime minister.

Virii—Neeva's spouse.

visedhaanye ferilii—Linyaari term corresponding roughly to "Envoy Extraordinary."

Vriiniia Watiir—sacred healing lake on Vhiliinyar, defiled by the Khleevi.

Wahanamoian Blossom of Sleep—poppylike flowers whose pollens, when ground, are a very powerful sedative.

White Star—see *Estrella Blanca*.

wii—a Linyaari prefix meaning small.

yaazi—Linyaari term for beloved.

Yaniriin—a Linyaari Survey Ship captain.

Yiitir—history teacher at the Linyaari academy, and Chief Keeper of the Linyaari Stories. Lifemate to Maarni.

Yukata Batsu—Uncle Hafiz's chief competitor on Laboue.

Zaami—a high mountain peak on the Linyaari homeworld.

Zanegar—second generation Starfarer.

Brief Notes on the Linyaari Language

By Margaret Ball

As Anne McCaffrey's collaborator in transcribing the first two tales of Acorna, I was delighted to find that the second of these books provided an opportunity to sharpen my long-unused skills in linguistic fieldwork. Many years ago, when the government gave out scholarships with gay abandon and the cost of living (and attending graduate school) was virtually nil, I got a Ph.D. in linguistics for no better reason than that (a) the government was willing to pay, (b) it gave me an excuse to spend a couple of years doing fieldwork in Africa, and (c) there weren't any real jobs going for eighteen-year-old girls with a B.A. in math and a minor in Germanic languages. (This was back during the Upper Pleistocene era, when the Help Wanted ads were still divided into Male and Female.)

So there were all those years spent doing things like transcribing tonal Oriental languages on staff paper (the Field Methods instructor was Not Amused) and tape-recording Swahili women at weddings, and then I got the degree and wandered off to play with computers and never had any use for the stuff again . . . until Acorna's people appeared on the scene. It required a sharp ear and some facility for linguistic analysis to make sense of the subtle sound-changes with which their language signaled syntactic changes; I quite enjoyed the challenge.

The notes appended here represent my first and necessarily tentative analysis of certain patterns in Linyaari phonemics and morphophonemics. If there is any inconsistency between this analysis and the Linyaari speech patterns recorded in the later adventures of Acorna, please remember that I was working from a very limited database and, what is perhaps worse, attempting to analyze a decidedly nonhuman language with the aid of the only paradigms I had, twentieth-century linguistic models developed exclusively from human language. The result is very likely as inaccurate as were the first attempts to describe English syntax by forcing it into the mold of Latin, if not worse. My colleague, Elizabeth Ann Scarborough, has by now added her own notes to the small corpus of Linyaari names and utterances, and it may well be that in the next decade there will be enough data available to publish a truly definitive dictionary and grammar of Linyaari; an undertaking which will surely be of inestimable value, not only to those members of our race who are involved in diplomatic and trade relations with this people, but also to everyone interested in the study of language.

Notes on the Linyaari Language

1. A doubled vowel indicates stress: **aavi, abaanye, khleevi.**

2. Stress is used as an indicator of syntactic function: in nouns stress is on the penultimate syllable, in adjectives on the last syllable, in verbs on the first.

3. Intervocalic *n* is always palatalized.

4. Noun plurals are formed by adding a final vowel, usually **i**: one **Liinyar,** two **Linyaari.** Note that this causes a change in the stressed syllable (from **LI-nyar** to **Li-NYA-ri***)* and hence a change in the pattern of doubled vowels.

For nouns whose singular form ends in a vowel, the plural is formed by dropping the original vowel and adding **i**: **ghaanye, ghaanyi.** Here the number of syllables remains the same, therefore no stress/spelling change is required.

5. Adjectives can be formed from nouns by adding a final **ii** (again, dropping the original final vowel if one exists): maalive, malivii; Liinyar, Linyarii. Again, the change in stress means that the doubled vowels in the penultimate syllable of the noun disappear.

6. For nouns denoting a class or species, such as Liinyar, the noun itself can be used as an adjective when the meaning is simply to denote a member of the class, rather than the usual adjective meaning of "having the qualities of this class"— thus, of the characters in ACORNA, only Acorna herself could be described as "a **Liinyar** girl" but Judit, although human, would certainly be described as "a **linyarii** girl," or "a just-as-civilized-as-a-real-member-of-the-People" girl.

7. Verbs can be formed from nouns by adding a prefix constructed by [first consonant of noun] + **ii** + **nye***:* **faalar**— grief; **fiinyefalar**—to grieve.

8. The participle is formed from the verb by adding a suffix **an** or **en: thiinyethilel**—to destroy, **thiinyethilelen**—destroyed. No stress change is involved because the participle is perceived as a verb form and, therefore, stress remains on the first syllable:

enye-ghanyii—time unit, small portion of a year (**ghaanye**)

fiinyefalaran—mourning, mourned

ghaanye—a Linyaari year, equivalent to about 1⅓ earth years

gheraalye malivii—Navigation Officer

gheraalye ve-khanyii—Senior Communications Specialist

Khleevi—originally, a small vicious carrion-feeding animal with a poisonous bite; now used by the Linyaari to denote the invaders who destroyed their homeworld

khleevi—barbarous, uncivilized, vicious without reason

Liinyar—member of the People

linyaari—civilized; like a Liinyar

mitanyaakhi—large number (slang—like our "zillions")

narhii—new

thiilel—destruction

thiilir, thiliiri—small arboreal mammals of Linyaari homeworld

visedhaanye ferilii—Envoy Extraordinary

If you enjoyed the fantastic adventures
and perils in

Second Wave,

turn the page for a sneak peek at the
final book in the series,

Third Watch:
Acorna's Children,

available soon in hardcover from Eos.

Then

One moment they were in the water, the next they were inside a room bursting with fancy flowing robes framing a huge mirror and a chest brimming with jewels and cosmetics. Ariin looked around and nodded.

(Where are we?) Khorii asked.

(Akasa's wardrobe. That's where I found this) Ariin said, holding up her wrist to show off the crono, which dangled loosely on her small arm. *(No more questions now. It's complicated. I need to get us back to an earlier time, before we were born.)*

(This is *before I was born)* Khorii said.

(Right. This thing seems to default to the time and place it was before starting the next time sequence, but we're not ready to be here yet. I have something to show you a little further back.)

She gave Khiindi a look that was, in one so young, remarkable for its wickedness. He knew what she intended then, but it fit in well with his own wishes so he sent her the desired information. He could, of course, still converse without resorting to Linyaari, Standard, Makahomian, or even Cat. Nor did he require the cruder forms of thought-talk. He simply formed a picture of the time they needed to go. Back before he had brought Ariin's egg to his people. Back before he had first befriended her father, Aari. Back when he could walk on two legs. Ariin recklessly tapped the crono without even looking at it, allowing his image to flow from her to the device. He picked the time, but she picked the place.

They stepped out of the water again, onto the grassy banks. Behind them the sii-Linyaari dived and fished, or sunned on the island just offshore. Before them, a meadow full of wildflowers, insects, and small animals stretched up to the mountains. Over the mountain peaks shone Vhiliinyar's two moons, one of which was to become the Moon of Opportunity. It glowed with the fullness and benevolence of Hafiz Harakamian's face gazing fondly at the profit balance on his ledger. The other moon was a mere crescent-shaped sliver of light.

Reflecting the light of both moons were the white and shining coats of the creatures hunted on their home world for the healing, purifying, and supposedly aphrodisiacal properties of their spiraling, golden, opalescent horns. There they were called unicorns, for obvious reasons. Here they were simply the Others, who were not the same as the Friends, although their kind varied. The Others were beautiful, useful, and innocent beings that the habitually self-centered Friends had become uncharacteristically enchanted with. Usually the Friends were the ones who did the enchanting, chiefly of themselves, when they beheld their own reflections. If they didn't like what they saw, they simply changed it to something more suitable.

Most had a bipedal and humanoid form that generally alternated with a dominant alter form. Khiindi's own dominant alter form had always been feline, though not always or even usually a mere moggy.

"We must hide Khiindi here until we need him," Ariin told Khorii. "He has enemies in this time, and even more enemies later on, when we're going. We'll have a use for him soon, but we have to lay some groundwork first."

Khorii bent and picked him up, his head against her neck, his front paws on her shoulder, his magnificent, fluffy tail curled around her forearm. "Khiindi-cat, you know the Ancestors in our time. These are their ancestors. They are very good creatures and as you know, they like cats. You'll be safe here. There are fish in the sea and other creatures for you to eat in the meadows. We'll return for you before you know it, if I understand this timing thing correctly."

Khiindi clung to her with every available claw. He knew Khorii would not abandon him willingly, but he had no idea what Ariin was up to. That one had a positively *ka*-Linyaari ability to conceal her thoughts. He also knew she meant to repay him for bringing her to be studied by his kind as their experiments in creating the Linyaari race continued. They knew they had created the Linyaari. They just didn't know how or when. Of all of them, Grimalkin was, if not the only empath, certainly the one in whom the quality was best developed. He had imagined he would be around during Ariin's youth to see that she was well treated and reasonably happy. Instead, his people, who were angry because he had brought only one of Acorna's embryonic twins instead of both, took away his crono and froze him in little cat form for all time, the first part of which he was to serve as Khorii's guardian and friend. Which had left Ariin out in the cold, an object of pity and even scorn.

She hadn't taken it at all well.

DON'T MISS A SINGLE
REMARKABLE ADVENTURE OF
ACORNA, THE UNICORN GIRL

"Entertaining fare indeed."
Booklist

ACORNA
by Anne McCaffrey and Margaret Ball
978-0-06-105789-2/$7.99 US/$10.99 Can

ACORNA'S QUEST
by Anne McCaffrey and Margaret Ball
978-0-06-105790-8/$7.99 US/$10.99 Can

ACORNA'S PEOPLE
by Anne McCaffrey and Elizabeth Ann Scarborough
978-0-06-105983-4/$7.99 US/$10.99 Can

ACORNA'S WORLD
by Anne McCaffrey and Elizabeth Ann Scarborough
978-0-06-105984-1/$7.99 US/$10.99 Can

ACORNA'S SEARCH
by Anne McCaffrey and Elizabeth Ann Scarborough
978-0-380-81846-4/$7.50 US/$9.99 Can

ACORNA'S REBELS
by Anne McCaffrey and Elizabeth Ann Scarborough
978-0-380-81844-1/$7.50 US/$9.99 Can

ACORNA'S TRIUMPH
by Anne McCaffrey and Elizabeth Ann Scarborough
978-0-380-81848-8/$7.50 US/$9.99 Can

Visit www.AuthorTracker.com for exclusive
information on your favorite HarperCollins authors.

Available wherever books are sold or please call 1-800-331-3761 to order.

ACO 0407

NEED SOMETHING NEW TO READ?

Download it Now!

Visit www.harpercollinsebooks.com
to choose from thousands of titles
you can easily download to your
computer or PDA.

Save 20% off the printed book price.
Ordering is easy and secure.

HarperCollins e-books

Download to your laptop, PDA, or phone for
convenient, immediate, or on-the-go reading. Visit
www.harpercollinsebooks.com or other online
e-book retailers.

Visit www.AuthorTracker.com for exclusive
information on your favorite HarperCollins authors.

Available wherever books are sold or please call 1-800-331-3761 to order.

HRE 0307

SAME GREAT STORIES, GREAT NEW FORMAT . . .
EOS TRADE PAPERBACKS

THE DIAMOND ISLE
by Stan Nicholls
978-0-06-073893-8/$14.95 US/$18.95 Can

TIME'S CHILD
by Rebecca Ore
978-0-380-79252-8/$14.95 US/$18.95 Can

ODALISQUE
by Fiona McIntosh
978-0-06-089905-9/$14.95 US/$18.95 Can

THE AWAKENED CITY
by Victoria Strauss
978-0-06-124283-0/$14.95 US/$18.95 Can

THE NEW SPACE OPERA
by Gardner Dozois
978-0-06-084675-6/$15.95 US/$19.95 Can

ILARIO: THE LION'S EYE
by Mary Gentle
978-0-06-082183-8/$14.95 US

DANGEROUS OFFSPRING
by Steph Swainston
978-0-06-075389-4/$13.95 US

Visit www.AuthorTracker.com for exclusive
information on your favorite HarperCollins authors.

EOT 0407

Available wherever books are sold or please call 1-800-331-3761 to order.

HARPER (LUXE)

THE NEW LUXURY IN READING

**Introducing a Clearer
Perspective on Larger Print**

With a 14-point type size for comfort reading
and published exclusively in paperback format,
HarperLuxe is light to carry and easy to read.

SEEING IS BELIEVING!

To view our great selection of titles in a
comfortable print and to sign up for the
HarperLuxe newsletter please visit:
www.harperluxe.com

*This ad has been set in the
14-point font for comfortable reading.

HRL 0307